the
Devil's Bed

Also by William Kent Krueger

Iron Lake
Boundary Waters
Purgatory Ridge

WILLIAM KENT KRUEGER

the
Devil's Bed

ATRIA BOOKS

New York   London   Toronto   Sydney   Singapore

ATRIA BOOKS
1230 Avenue of the Americas
New York, NY 10020

ISBN: 0-7434-4584-8

First Atria Books hardcover printing February 2003

10 9 8 7 6 5 4 3 2 1

ATRIA BOOKS is a trademark of Simon & Schuster, Inc.

For information regarding special discounts for bulk purchases,
please contact Simon & Schuster Special Sales at 1-800-456-6798
or business@simonandschuster.com

Printed in the U.S.A.

For my brothers, David and Mark, and my sister, Margaret,
playmates still;
and for Gary Peterson, a brother in all respects except birth.

Acknowledgments

It has been my experience that people are generous beyond measure. This is especially true when it comes to sharing knowledge. Those who have it tend to give it freely to those who do not. In my writing, and the writing of this book particularly, I have often been on the receiving end of that tremendous generosity.

Thank you: To Dr. Jordan Hart, who helped shape my thinking about the early development of the human mind and the resilience of the human spirit; to Tom Kremer, who squired me safely about the grounds of the Minnesota State Security Hospital and suggested unorthodox solutions; to Megan McCarthy, who taught me about trauma, hospitals, and ICUs; and to Sergeant Major Clif Evans, who trains men and women in how to disappear and be deadly, and who offered me the same.

I owe a tremendous debt to Jane Jordan Browne, Scott Mendel, and all those at Multimedia Product Development, Inc. for their insight, suggestions, patience, and above all their perseverance.

God smiled on me and gave me a great editor in George Lucas. George, I will justify your faith.

A special thank-you to the United States Secret Service. Although I've taken some liberties in the writing of this story, I have tried to be true to the nature of the organization and to the spirit of the men and women who, as agents, risk their lives in service to their country.

To the Crème de la Crime—Carl Brookins, Julie Fasciana, Scott Haartman, Michael Kac, Joan Loshek, Jean Miriam Paul, Charlie Rethwisch, Susan Runholt, Tim Springfield, and Anne B. Webb—the best friends a mystery writer ever had, thank you.

Always last in my acknowledgment but first in my heart, Jim and Elena Theros and the staff of the St. Clair Broiler. Thanks, guys. How anyone could write a book anywhere else is beyond me.

the
Devil's Bed

La Cama del Diablo

andall Coates turned off the Virginia highway and one last
time took the narrow drive that curled through the dogwood
trees toward his house. Halfway up the hill, he killed the
headlights and navigated by the glow of the moon. Before he broke
from the trees, he stopped the car, grabbed the night-vision binoculars from the seat beside him, and got out. For several minutes, he
studied his house. From a distance, everything looked the same as it
had that morning when he'd left.

But Randall Coates knew that appearances could no longer be
trusted.

Keeping to the trees, he circled, reconnoitering the whole of his
property. With the moon at his back, he approached the house from
the east and slipped along the rear wall, peering in at the windows.
He leaned against his shadow on the siding and listened. Finally he
slid the key into the back lock and let himself in. He left the lights off
and reset the alarm. Laying the binoculars on the kitchen table, he
pulled the Glock from his shoulder holster and moved through the
house, securing it room by room.

When he stood again at the back door, he turned the lights on and let himself relax. "Fuck this," he said. "Tomorrow I get motion sensors."

He retrieved his car, then strolled the lazy curve of flagstones toward his front door. One last time he paused on the porch steps to study the night sky. The pale yellow eye that was the moon, one last time, studied him right back.

Inside, he shrugged off his jacket, but he continued to wear the shoulder holster and the nine millimeter that were underneath. The jacket he hung in the hallway closet.

At the bar, he poured enough Johnnie Walker Black for four or five long swallows. He carried the glass to the kitchen and opened the refrigerator to see what he might have on hand for dinner. It didn't matter. Although Randall Coates was unaware of it, he'd already eaten his last meal.

He was thinking at that moment about fear, something he knew well. He'd seen fear destroy men, turn them into blubbering idiots. He believed that if you had half a spine and kept your head, you'd be fine. If you truly had *cojones*, you used the fear, turned it to your advantage. Fear sharpened you. Fear made you ready.

As he reached for a plate of cold cuts covered in Saran Wrap he said to himself, The hell with Moses. The asshole wants me, let him try something.

In the next moment, when the kitchen lights died and he heard behind him the voice of Moses speak his name, he wet his pants. The reaction was as involuntary as the quick suck of his breath or his desperate turning.

He spun. The whole house was dark, and his brain stumbled over the details that he'd noted in the light but had inexplicably failed to register as significant. The countertop, for example, on which that morning the electric toaster had sat was now empty. Or the faint, out-of-place odor in the kitchen, an oily smell that reminded him of a garage.

He'd come around less than ninety degrees when Moses pulverized the cartilage in his nose. For a while, Coates went into a black nowhere.

He came to lying on his back on the hard oak rectangle of the kitchen tabletop. He was naked and spread-eagled. The middle of his face hurt like hell, but when he tried to lift his hands to assess the damage there, he discovered that each wrist had been bound with duct tape and secured to a table leg. Ankles, too. A strip of tape sealed his mouth. His shattered nose was plugged with coagulated blood, and he breathed through a straw that had been inserted through the tape and wedged between his lips.

"Comfortable?" Moses said.

Coates rolled his head to the left, where the voice spoke out of the dark. He didn't see Moses, only the LED time readout on the microwave. 10:15 P.M. He'd been out nearly two hours.

"How does it feel? Your own little *Cama del Diablo?*"

Moses tapped the wood next to Coates's head. Coates looked there quickly, but Moses had already moved.

Cama del Diablo. Coates didn't need to translate. He understood exactly what Moses meant.

"Of course it lacks the defining finish, that unrivaled lacquer, equal parts puke and shit and blood. And you're missing the ineffable stink of course. But we'll do something about that in a bit."

Coates tried to speak, to reason, but the duct tape over his mouth prevented it. All that came out was a whining mumble, pathetic even to him.

"Remember what you said to me in Agua Negra? You said, 'David, when you die you'll think hell is a vacation.' Christ, where did you get that line? A Bruce Willis movie?"

In the dark, sparks suddenly exploded between Coates's widespread legs. The flash illuminated Moses for an instant and also the countertop behind him. In the place where the toaster had been an old car battery now sat, covered with a film of grime and oil. Coates recognized that it had come from his own garage. In his gloved hands, Moses held two cables that were connected to the battery terminals. He brought the cable ends together once again, and their kiss produced another explosion of sparks.

"You always enjoyed this," Moses said. "But then, you were never on that side of the experience."

Coates heard water running in the sink, then the filling of a glass tumbler.

"I've been thinking," Moses said. "Jesus had it easy. He had only one Judas to contend with. After you I still have two more."

Although he knew it was coming, Coates still winced when he felt the cold water splash over his testicles. He tensed when he heard the cables snaking toward him across the tiles of the kitchen floor.

"Let's get started," Moses said.

Coates screamed, a sound that died in the sealed hollow of his mouth.

The last of almost everything in his life was behind him.

But the worst was just about to begin.

chapter

one

Nightmare used a combat knife, a Busse Steel Heart E with a seven-and-a-half-inch blade. He made two cuts, a long arc that half-circled his nipple, then another arc beneath the first, smaller but carved with equal care. The effect was a rainbow with only two bands and a single color. When he lifted the blade, he could feel the blood on his chest, black worms crawling down his skin in the dark of his motel room.

From the warehouse across the old highway came the long hiss of air brakes and the rattle of heavy suspension as a rig and trailer pulled out onto the potholed asphalt and geared away into the evening. There was an air-conditioning unit under the window, but Nightmare never used it. Even in the worst heat, he preferred to keep the drapes pulled and the windows open in order to track the sounds outside his room.

In the dark, he reached to a wooden bowl on the stand beside the bed. He filled his hand with ash from the bowl, and he rubbed the ash into the wounds to raise and set them. It was painful, this ritual, but pain was part of who he was, part of being Nightmare. He performed the ritual in the dark because that was also elemental to his being. He loved the dark, as a man will love anything that has taken him into itself and made him a part of it.

It was past time, he knew, but there was no hurry. He put on his sunglasses, then took the remote from beside the bowl on the stand and turned on the television. The set was old, and the signal flowed through a faulty connection. The picture bloomed, vibrated, then settled down.

Barbara Walters was on the screen. She sat in a wing chair upholstered in a red floral design. She wore a blue dress, a gold scarf draped over her left shoulder, pinned with a sapphire brooch. From a portrait above the mantel beyond her right shoulder, George Washington seemed to look down on her sternly. The broadcast was live from the Library of the White House. Barbara leaned forward, her face a study of deep concentration as she listened. She nodded, then she spoke, but soundlessly because Nightmare had muted the volume to nothing. Finally she smiled, totally unaware that on the television screen, dead center on her forehead, was a red dot from the laser sight on Nightmare's Beretta.

A different camera angle. The eyes of the man whose face now filled the screen were like two copper pennies, solid and dependable. Every hair of his reddish brown mane was under perfect control. He wore a beautifully tailored blue suit, a crisp white shirt, a red tie knotted in a tight Windsor and dimpled in a way that mirrored the dimple in his chin. Daniel Clay Dixon, president of the United States, faced the camera and the nation. When his lips moved, Nightmare could imagine that voice, the soft accent that whispered from the western plains, not so pronounced that it might prejudice a listener into thinking of an ignorant cowpoke, but enough to suggest a common man, a man of the people, the kind of man whose example encouraged children to believe they could grow up to be anything they wanted, that nothing in this great land of opportunity was beyond anyone's reach.

Nightmare had no interest in the words the silent voice spoke.

They would be lies, he knew. Anyone who rose to the top in a government always rose on a bubble inflated by lies. He concentrated on keeping the red laser dot steady on the black pupil of the president's left eye.

After Clay Dixon talked awhile, he glanced at something to his right, off-camera at the moment, but obviously of tremendous importance to him.

And then it happened. What Nightmare had been patiently waiting for all week, had been considering in almost every moment of his thinking.

The First Lady appeared.

In the soft dark, Nightmare wrapped himself around a hard vengeance.

Kathleen Jorgenson Dixon's eyes were pale gray-blue. Although she looked composed, there was something immeasurably sad about those eyes. To Nightmare they seemed like two unhealed wounds. She'd been hurt, he could tell. But that didn't matter. Her suffering was nothing compared to the suffering she'd caused. He was glad for the ritual of the blood and the ash and the pain, because it kept him strong.

"For the murder of David Moses," Nightmare pronounced, "your sentence is death."

He sighted the Beretta. The laser dot settled in the dark at the back of the First Lady's throat. Slowly he squeezed the trigger, and grimly he whispered, *"Bang."*

chapter

two

As Daniel Clay Dixon strode into the Oval Office, the members of his senior staff who waited there stood up.

"Great job, Mr. President." Communications Director Edward McGill stepped forward and shook Dixon's hand.

"You think so, Ed?" Clay Dixon grinned back at him. "Did we play well in Peoria?"

"Peoria, Poughkeepsie, Patagonia. That was a telecast for the world."

"They can't vote for me in Patagonia, Ed."

"I'd guess the polls will continue their swing this week," Patricia Gomez, Dixon's press secretary, said.

"Let's not guess. Do what you can, okay? Work that hoodoo you do so well." Dixon looked to his chief of staff, John Llewellyn. "What do you think?"

Llewellyn was a tall, gray-haired man in a gray suit. He had a long face where deep lines like empty gullies ran. The irises of his eyes were so dark they ate his pupils. "I remember a game you played against Tampa Bay a couple of years before you retired. At halftime you were down twenty-four points."

"Twenty-seven," Dixon said.

"Second half you engineered four unanswered touchdowns. Went into the locker room on top. Mr. President, you're going into the locker room tonight a winner." Although he smiled, nothing but that hard darkness showed in his eyes.

"Thanks, John."

"You want me to contact Wayne White? See if he's ready to concede?" McGill asked, grinning.

"That poor son of a bitch," Dixon said. "You know, I feel genuinely sorry for him."

Wayne White was a third-term congressman from Ohio. A war hero and a widower. He was well respected in Washington and had been his party's choice to run for the presidency. No sooner was he out of the starting blocks, however, than a scandal sheet got hold of the record of a domestic abuse charge that had been lodged against him twenty years earlier. Before the information became public, Wayne White had held a significant lead in the polls. Clay Dixon resolutely declined to use the opportunity against his opponent, and Americans seemed to appreciate that kind of decency. The polls had begun to reflect it.

"Your father sends his congratulations."

"I guess that's the icing on the cake, isn't it?" Dixon laughed. "Has Lorna finished her report yet?"

"Any minute now," Llewellyn said. "We'll all have copies first thing in the morning."

"Will you have her call me when it's ready. I want to see it as soon as possible."

"We won't be meeting with the legislative staff until Wednesday."

"I want Kate to have a look at it." Dixon glanced at his watch. "Well, folks, it's been a long day. I don't know about you, but I intend to relax with a glass of sherry. I'll see you in the morning."

As his staff began to leave, Dixon said, "Bobby, would you stay for a minute."

Robert Lee held back.

"Close the door," Dixon said. When they were alone, he asked, "So, Bobby, what's on your mind?"

Officially, Robert Lee was the White House chief counsel. More than that, he was Clay Dixon's oldest friend. He had a face the press perennially and unimaginatively characterized as boyish, and a smile the cameras loved, all dimples. Because he had a relaxed feel about him and because his eyes were soft brown and a little lazy-looking, people sometimes thought the mind behind them was simple. That was a mistake, for Bobby Lee was a man of immense intelligence and could be a formidable opponent when he had to be. But he was also a careful man, a considerate man, a gentleman.

"Kate," Lee said.

The president sat in one of the armchairs, crossed his legs, and looked up at Lee. "She's fine, Bobby."

Lee sat down, too. "She doesn't look fine."

"She's tired, that's all. Under a lot of strain. She's facing a long political campaign. That's enough to make anyone want to cry."

Lee didn't look convinced, but he didn't push the issue. He folded his hands on his lap. "I got an early look at Lorna's report. Llewellyn's not going to like it."

"I didn't ask for the report in order to please him."

"Will you go ahead with a legislative proposal?"

"Not until after the election."

"I think delaying would be a mistake. In this campaign, you need to take the initiative."

"We all discussed this at length. You were the only one who disagreed."

"That doesn't mean I was wrong."

There was truth in that, and there was a gentle barb in the way the truth was spoken.

"I still think the advice is sound, Bobby. I don't want to launch anything controversial at this juncture." The president loosened his tie and undid his shirt collar. "I can tell there's more on your mind. Spit it out."

"I'm wondering more and more what I'm doing here. There was a time I thought you relied on me, for more than just legal counsel. Lately I'm feeling like I'm moving my lips but not much is getting through to you."

"That's not true."

"Ever since Carpathian died, it's Llewellyn who has your ear, Clay. And more often than not Llewellyn is just an echo of your old man."

"John Llewellyn knows politics better than anyone on Capitol Hill. I'm heading into a tough battle to hold on to this presidency, and goddamn it, I want to win. Llewellyn's the man who knows how to make that happen."

"I don't like his tactics."

"What do you mean?"

"Come on, Clay. I can see his hand all over the Wayne White thing."

"That's politics, Bobby."

"Alan Carpathian wouldn't call it politics. He'd call it character assassination."

"Carpathian's dead," Dixon snapped. He took a moment, then forced a grin. "Remember the Michigan game?" He was talking about their days together at Stanford, when they'd both played on the team that won the Rose Bowl in their senior year. "I called a post pattern. You argued for a hook."

"I know. That pass won the game."

"The post pattern." Dixon stood up, walked to his old friend, and put a hand on his shoulder. "I know what I'm doing, Bobby. I can handle Llewellyn and my father. And don't worry about Kate. She'll be fine. Look, it's been a long day. How about we call it quits for this evening?"

"Sure, Clay." Lee got to his feet and headed for the door.

After Robert Lee left, Dixon wandered to the window behind his desk and looked out. It was a hot, humid August night. He knew if he were able to slide open the pane, the air would hit him like warm water. Even after nearly four years in the White House, he wasn't used to summer on the eastern seaboard. He thought about August along the high plains near the Rockies in his home state of Colorado. He missed the clear, dry air, the smell of sage. He missed the million stars that were the gift of the night. In D.C., the ever-present haze and the city lights generally made the night sky a murky, impenetrable darkness.

He glanced at his watch and realized it was his daughter's bedtime.

Dixon left the West Wing, accompanied by two Secret Service agents on POTUS detail. At the private stairs to the Executive Residence, he bid the agents a cordial good night. Unless called upon by the First Family, or summoned by an alarm, the Secret Service kept away from the second and third floors of the White House. As much as possible, the Residence was maintained as a sanctuary of normal life. At the top of the stairs, Dixon turned left down the center hall toward the west bedroom, where Willie Lincoln and John-John Kennedy had slept and Amy Carter had played with her dolls. He found his daughter Stephanie already under the covers. Kate sat in a chair next to the bed, reading from a Harry Potter book. Stephanie was so engrossed in listening to the story that she didn't notice her father come into the room. He stood inside the doorway, watching silently.

Stephanie was seven, and Dixon loved her deeply. She had her mother's long, blonde hair and pale complexion. She was smart and funny and loved to laugh, all very like her mother. From her father, she'd inherited athletic ability, a willful way, and a love of football. They often spent a Sunday afternoon together watching the Broncos or the Redskins on television.

Stephanie's eyes drifted down from the ceiling and found him. She smiled and said happily, "Hi, Daddy."

Kathleen Jorgenson Dixon looked up from the book she held. She didn't smile.

Dixon came to the bed, leaned down, and kissed his daughter's forehead. Her skin smelled faintly of Noxema. "What did you think of Ms. Walters?"

"I thought she was nice."

"Me, too."

"I got her autograph."

"You can add it to your collection." His daughter had practically grown up in the White House, surrounded by celebrities and the great people of the day. She collected autographs that she kept in an album. Her favorite was J. K Rowling, creator of Harry Potter, whom she'd met at a charity reading her mother had sponsored.

"I think that's enough about Hogwarts for us Muggles tonight," her mother said. She closed the book, set it on the stand, and rose from her chair. She kissed her daughter's cheek. "Sleep tight."

"Can I read a little more? I'm not very sleepy."

"A little more," her mother agreed.

"Night, Pumpkin," Dixon said.

As they left the room, Kate closed the door behind them.

"I was going to have a glass of sherry," Dixon said. "Care to join me?"

"I don't think so." She walked past him.

"You were great this evening," he said behind her. "I know it wasn't easy."

"I did what I had to do."

He accompanied her down the hall to the master bedroom of the presidential suite. Inside, she continued toward the dressing room. Dixon followed but hung back at the doorway, watching as she opened a bureau drawer and began to gather a few things.

"Do we need to talk some more?" he asked.

"I don't know what else there is to say."

"That you understand would be good. You haven't said that yet."

She bowed her head, thought, then turned to him. "Do you remember the night Alan Carpathian came down to the ranch and asked you to run for governor?"

"Of course."

"We sat on the porch until midnight, the three of us, drinking scotch."

"We talked until sunup. You were on Alan's side. You encouraged me to run, Kate."

"I couldn't stand watching you mope. When you retired from football you were lost."

"That night on the porch you said I could do great things."

"And you said *we* could do great things. That you wouldn't do anything unless we did it together, remember?"

"I remember."

"Four years ago when Alan finally convinced you to run for the White House, I thought we made the same deal."

"Things have changed. Alan's gone. I have other advisers now. Rooms full of them."

"Your father's people."

"They know what they're doing."

"Do they? It was on their advice you ambushed Wayne White."

"It wasn't an ambush. It was a political maneuver."

"Dredging up an allegation twenty years old? Anybody who knows Wayne White's history knows that his wife was an alcoholic then. What the truth of the incident really was, God only knows. The woman has passed away and can't help her husband refute the sordid aspects of the story. And Wayne White, God bless him, is too fine a man to defend himself by sullying her memory. All very convenient for you. And I love how the information just happened into the hands of a tabloid. And that awful picture of her with the bruises. My God, where did that come from?"

"Nothing that came out wasn't the truth. And it's not as if Wayne White isn't above a little slander himself. I quote, 'It's hard to believe this nation has chosen as its leader a gridiron gorilla who barely made it through college.'"

"There was a time when you thought 'gridiron gorilla' was a compliment. And it's true that you were no scholar. Besides, Wayne White said those things long before he put his hat in the ring. He's been quite civil since." She turned back to the bureau. Her hands moved quickly, selecting then discarding with an angry motion.

"Your father was the architect of all this duplicity. But you, you're worse because you pretend you're not like him. I think you even believe it."

Dixon quit the dressing room and walked to a small rosewood table near the window where he kept a decanter of sherry. He poured himself a glass.

"Tell me something," she said, her voice coming disembodied from the dressing room.

"Anything."

"During the primaries, when opponents in his own party questioned Wayne White's war record, did the senator have a hand in that? Did he feed the information?"

"That's a crazy question."

"Is it? After what's happened, I don't think so. The senator seems to know anything bad about anybody. Was he already at work trying to torpedo the man's campaign, even then?"

"There was good reason to doubt the congressman's claims about his military service."

She stepped into the bedroom, looking stunned. "You knew."

"The questions that were raised were reasonable questions."

"They were inflammatory. My God, Clay."

"What would you have me do?"

"A public confession would be good for starters."

"Don't be ridiculous."

"Maybe I'll leave you instead." She vanished into the dressing room again.

"Walk out on me? Because we disagree on tactics?"

"Because I don't like who you've become. And because I hate being used."

"Used?"

She came back out, clutching a handful of clothing. "Do you have any idea how hard it was for me sitting there tonight, keeping my mouth shut while you postured and looked so full of integrity. The perfect First Family."

He sipped his sherry. "Why didn't you say something? You certainly had the chance."

"Because despite everything, I still love you. I keep hoping there's a way to salvage something of who you used to be."

"I am who I've always been."

She stared at him, her face pallid and disappointed. "This is just another game to you, isn't it? You have to win no matter what. You know, I'm beginning to wonder if you've sold your soul, maybe the soul of this nation, just because you never got a Super Bowl ring." She looked at the clothing crumpled in her hand and shook her head. "I'm tired. I'm going to bed."

"Lorna Channing's finishing her report. Would you like to see it?"

She hesitated, almost taking the bait. Then she said, "I don't care anymore."

Dixon moved to the bedroom doorway and stood, barring her way for a moment. "Sleeping in the Lincoln Bedroom again?"

"I used to sleep in a great man's bed. I want to remember what that was like." She glared at him until he stepped aside. Then she walked down the center hall and never looked back.

Dixon went into the bathroom. He splashed water on his face and looked at himself in the mirror. He was forty-eight years old, a handsome man. And big at six foot four inches, 238 pounds. He worked out almost every morning to keep the flab at bay. There were two scars on his face from his years on the football field, one across the bridge of his nose, from high school when he played for St. Regis, and the other a long gash above his right eye opened by a collision with a Chiefs linebacker in a division playoff game. He bore them proudly.

What Kate had said was, in part, true. Politics was a kind of game to him, one he played to win. If a man gave his best and still lost, that was no failure. Failure was going into a fight with half a heart. Failure was giving in before you'd given all. And Clay Dixon was damned if he was giving in.

The phone rang.

"Mr. President, this is Lorna. You wanted to know as soon as the report was ready. It is. Shall I bring it to you first thing in the morning?"

"No. No, I'd rather see it tonight. Where are you?"

"My office at OEOB."

"Could you bring a copy up to the Residence?"

"Certainly."

"I'll be in my study."

Dixon checked on Stephanie. She was asleep. The Harry Potter book lay on her chest. He crept in, put the book on the nightstand, kissed his daughter gently. He turned off the lamp, and slipped out of the room. In the center hall, he paused in front of a painting by Mary Cassatt, *Young Mother and Two Children.* In it, a woman sat with her arms protectively about her children. The painting was one of Kate's favorite things in the Residence. She said the woman was portrayed as strong and caring and there was nothing sentimental about the depiction. Dixon didn't know art, but he liked the painting, too, because the woman in it reminded him of Kate.

He entered the Treaty Room, which served as his private study. It had been called the Treaty Room since the Kennedy era and had been used for a variety of purposes under various administrations. Dixon had decorated it with mementos of his football days, gold and silver trophies, photographs, the football with which he'd thrown the winning pass in the Rose Bowl game. He was just finishing his sherry when Lorna Channing knocked on the opened door.

When he'd first entered the White House, the president had chosen most of his advisers in consultation with Alan Carpathian, his chief of staff. But Lorna Channing and Bobby Lee were entirely Clay Dixon's choices. Lorna Channing, who served as his domestic affairs adviser, he'd known all his life. Her father's spread bordered the Dixon ranch on the Purgatoire River in Colorado. Their families had expected them to marry someday, and until he went to Stanford, Clay Dixon had expected it, too. Lorna, when she graduated from high school the following year, chose to attend Yale.

Eventually and inevitably, more than just a continent separated them. After college, Lorna had worked as a reporter for the *Baltimore Sun*, then the *Washington Post*, and finally the *New York Times*. She became a regular on the syndicated news journal *The American Chronicle*, where her articulate and astute observations on the condition of the nation (and the fact that the camera loved her) won her a large following. Somehow, she'd also found time to teach at Columbia University, to marry twice, and to divorce both times. At forty, she'd been offered the opportunity to create and then head the School of Contemporary American Studies at the University of Colorado, and she'd finally gone home. She was one of Clay Dixon's closest advisers when he was governor. When he won the presidency and asked for her continued help, she'd agreed.

"I hope I'm not disturbing you and Kate," Channing said as she entered.

"Kate's gone to bed."

Lorna Channing had long chestnut hair and eyes the color of steamy green tea. She wore a green dress that matched her eyes and dark stockings that made her legs look like two slender shadows. She handed him the report. It was a hefty document. Dixon held it with both hands.

"What do you think?" he asked.

"Bottom line? It'll be a tough sell to Congress, but it's good. Bold, different. Kate's right on the money. It's the kind of initiative that would mark a great presidency."

The report was an analysis of a program that for years Kate had advocated establishing—compulsory youth service, a requirement that all young women and men in the United States give a year of service to the nation upon graduation from high school. It wasn't at all a new idea, and Clay Dixon knew it had never enjoyed great popularity in the United States. However, Kate had grown up with the concept of service to the nation as a basic tenet of her life, and she'd lived her belief. She'd helped to organize a number of international conferences on youth service, had spoken across the country, written dozens of articles. She argued that too many Americans grew up without any sense of national responsibility or even a sense of belonging. They grew up separated by economic status, by religion, by race, by creed, by color. Only in times of war did Americans seem to unite, to feel the sense of oneness that came with common sacrifice. America *was* at war, she insisted. The enemy was poverty, ignorance, neglect. America needed its young women and men to bolster the ranks of understaffed hospitals, nursing homes, day care centers. They were needed in the fields and in the inner city, in the parks and in the streets, in programs of national importance where the money was too little and the personnel too few. And they were needed abroad in the same way. She saw it not only as a pragmatic way of dealing with labor shortages in areas of social need, but also as a way of instilling a sense of stewardship in youth and an allegiance to the nation and its people. She'd stumped for the idea long before she married Clay Dixon.

Upon entering the White House, however, she'd been strongly advised by Alan Carpathian to discontinue her public crusade. It was, he pointed out, an issue without popular support, and it risked putting the president in a politically awkward position. She'd acquiesced, but only after extracting a promise from her husband and the chief of staff that they would undertake a study of the feasibility of such a program. After Carpathian's death, John Llewellyn advocated scrapping the whole project, but Lorna Channing had championed the idea, and Dixon had listened. Although it had taken nearly four years to keep his promise to Kate, he now held the study in his hand.

"What will you do with it?" Lorna asked.

"Sit on it for a while."

She looked unhappy. "A lot of effort just to have it end up buried."

"Just until the election is over."

"Don't rock the boat, huh? That's your father talking."

"Llewellyn, too."

"If you're not careful, Clay, they'll keep it buried. I think that would be a mistake. Besides, Kate would shoot you."

"She's already got her finger on the trigger," he said.

She crossed her arms and relaxed against the door. "I watched your interview this evening. You were stellar."

"Thank you."

"Kate seemed a little . . . reserved."

"You're a great diplomat, Lorna."

"Anything you want to talk about?"

"No. But thanks."

He was standing very near her. "Nice perfume. What is it?"

She laughed, a brief but enticing utterance. If chocolate had a sound, Dixon thought, that would be it.

"You don't recognize it? Chanel. You gave it to me for Christmas. I was impressed that you remembered my favorite scent."

Dixon decided not to tell her that it was Kate who'd chosen the gifts, who'd noticed her preference for the perfume.

"You know," he said, "just before you came I was thinking about that night on the Purgatoire the summer before Stanford."

"That was a long time ago."

"But you remember?"

"Of course."

"Christ, everything seemed so simple then."

"It wasn't. We just didn't realize it."

He saw her face change, saw something sad creep into her expression.

"What is it?" he asked.

"Talking about the Purgatoire. I got a call from my father yesterday. He had to put Sultan down."

"Oh, Lorna, I'm so sorry."

Tears glistened suddenly in her green eyes, and he put his arms around her.

"I knew it would happen," she said. "He was so old. But it still feels awful."

"He was a magnificent horse," Dixon said.

"Thanks." She wiped her eyes with her hand. "I should be going.

It's late." She started to leave, but seemed to think better of it, and turned back to him. "Listen, Clay, if you need someone to talk to, about anything, think of me, okay?"

"Of course."

After she left, he thumbed the thick report, but he made no move to read it. For a long time, he simply stared at the open door where Lorna Channing had been, and he savored the ghost of her presence.

Ghosts. There were too many of them in his life now. He lifted his glass, and with the last swallow of his sherry, he toasted the dead.

"To Alan Carpathian, and all the dreams that died with him."

chapter

three

Tom Jorgenson left his house and headed to the barn. Although the night air was warm, he took with him a Thermos of hot coffee laced with Bushmills Irish Whiskey. He paused a moment in the yard and looked west where he could see the waning moon descending in the sky above his apple trees. To Tom Jorgenson, there was nothing quite so lovely. Myrna had believed there was special power in the moon. As she lay dying in the room at Bethesda Naval Hospital, the last request she ever made of her husband was that he open the curtains so she could see the moon.

All his life, Jorgenson had been a man up at first light and about his business until well after dark. "Slow down, Tom," Myrna had always advised at the end of the day when he tottered near exhaustion. "Come and look at the moon with me." He hadn't accepted her offer often enough. After she died, he created a ritual of watching the moon. New, crescent, gibbous, full, he'd learned to observe and appreciate the phases and, in doing so, had learned to better observe and appreciate himself. That, of course, had been Myrna's purpose all along. How a man could be offered such wisdom and so consistently ignore it was a question that, in the twenty-three years since his wife's death, he asked himself a thousand times. It had been easy to believe that the political concerns that occupied his life were so vastly important. But Myrna only smiled patiently at his too-full agenda, and whenever he'd felt so pressed he could barely breathe, she would take his hand and say, "Time to look at the moon."

She died near the end of his second term as vice president. When his obligation to the electorate was complete, he retired from politics and returned to Minnesota, intending to spend his time finishing the raising of his teenage children, caring for his apple trees, and practicing the nightly ritual that was part of his wife's legacy.

The apple trees were the glory of the Jorgenson estate, a large tract of land called Wildwood that crowned a quarter mile of bluff along the St. Croix River. The orchards had been a Jorgenson hobby since the last part of the nineteenth century, when the family fortune was secured in the granite halls of the Minneapolis Grain Exchange. During Tom Jorgenson's absence in Washington, D.C., while he served the people of Minnesota as their senator and then the nation as vice president, care of the orchards had been in the hands of his sister, Annie, and his brother, Roland, neither of whom had married. Annie had helped raise the children, and Roland—well, Roland had been himself and there hadn't been much Tom Jorgenson could do to change that.

As he opened the barn door and switched on the light, Jorgenson thought about how fortunate he had been in the person he'd chosen to love and to marry. Kate, it seemed, had not been so lucky. That evening, he'd watched his daughter sit with her husband under the scrutiny of the entire nation. To those who didn't know her well, she appeared to be in a good relationship, to have made a good match. But Tom Jorgenson, who spoke with her regularly, knew there was a mask over the true face of the marriage, knew the rumblings that lay below. He'd hoped his children would be as happy in their marriages as he had been, but he understood the odds were against it.

When his son-in-law entered the White House, Jorgenson had actually been hopeful. Alan Carpathian was Clay Dixon's mentor and his chief of staff, and Carpathian was as good as they came. Unfortunately, Carpathian had died in a skiing accident less than a year after Dixon took office. The focus of the presidency seemed to die with him. Although Jorgenson didn't dislike Clay Dixon, he understood that men often became their fathers. The more he'd observed of the president's politics recently the more he saw the specter of Senator William Dixon. Tom Jorgenson knew the president's father well, knew him to be a man charming on the surface but ruthless underneath, and the shadow he cast over the White House was a chilling one.

At Wildwood, Jorgenson always observed the moon from the same place, a bluff at the end of his orchards that overlooked the river. He would have preferred to walk, but he'd twisted his knee a week before and was still hobbling gingerly. He'd been driving his new Kubota tractor the quarter mile instead. He tucked his Thermos under the tractor seat, kicked the engine over, and pulled out of the barn. Annie was in the house, filling a teakettle at the kitchen sink, and she waved to him through the window as he passed.

Early in the season, maneuvering among the rows was easy. Now, as August wore on, the fruit grew heavy and the boughs began to sag. Jorgenson picked his way carefully between the low-hanging branches illuminated in his headlights. Near the end of the orchard, he turned back to glance at the western sky. The moon was already nestled in the tops of his trees. He didn't have much time, and he gunned the engine. As he turned his attention again to guiding the Kubota, he thought he saw, caught in the glare of the headlights, a solid black shape crouched among the leaves of an overhanging branch directly ahead. It reminded him of a black panther poised and ready to spring. He had only a second to consider this vision before he was under the branch and a powerful blow caught him on the left side of his forehead, sending him tumbling from his tractor seat.

chapter

four

An hour after first light, Special Agent Bo Thorsen was sculling in his Maas Aero, cutting swiftly south over the glassy surface of the Mississippi River. He'd started at the rowing club just above Lake Street, and he was now a few hundred yards above the bridge at Ford Parkway. At first, the air was dead still, the water gray and flat. As the sun rose, the river became a perfect mirror of the wooded bluffs that edged the Mississippi on both the St. Paul and the Minneapolis sides. Bo loved rowing at that time of day. The river was clear of noisy speedboats and barge traffic. He often spotted large waterfowl—egrets, herons, sometimes even cranes. Occasionally he was lucky enough to catch sight of a bald eagle. He couldn't see the big houses that stood back from the bluffs, so it was easy to imagine he had the river and the land it flowed through all to himself.

Long before he reached the bridge, he dragged his port oar as a rudder, dug in on the starboard side, brought the shell around, and pointed the bow north. He started back upriver against a wind that rose with the sun, working his arms and legs hard, keeping his heart rate well elevated, sweat flying off his face. Although he exercised in many other ways, the morning workout on the river was his favorite. He was always disappointed when he reached the rowing club. It meant that he had to climb out of the beautiful chasm carved by the Father of Waters and rejoin a world of people in which he'd been trained to see mostly menace.

He stowed the Aero at the club and headed back toward his apartment, the rented upper of a duplex in a fine old section of St. Paul called Tangletown. It was an area that derived its name from the chaotic weave of narrow streets nestled among the city's east-west grid of traffic. The homes were old, several-storied, and beautifully maintained. As he stepped from the garage where he'd parked his Contour, he saw a man sitting on the back steps of the house, a tall man with a long, graying ponytail and a hollowed, haunted face. He wore dirty jeans, ragged running shoes, and a T-shirt with an image across the chest so old and faded Bo couldn't tell what it had been.

"Hello, Otter," he said.

The man called Otter stood up. "Hey, Spider-Man. Working out, huh?"

"Rowing," Bo replied. "Come on in."

Otter followed him around to the front of the duplex, inside, and up the stairs. Bo unlocked and opened the door. "Make yourself at home. I'm going to shower."

When he was clean and dressed in the dark blue suit and tie that were his normal working attire, Bo stepped into the kitchen and found Otter sitting at the table, eating toast.

"Mind?" Otter asked.

"No. How about some eggs with that?"

"I'd eat some eggs," Otter said.

Bo took off his suit coat and hung it over the back of a chair. He started some coffee brewing, then went to work at the stove. "What happened this time?"

"Somebody's been dipping from the cash register. Of course, they blamed the guy who goes to AA. They didn't even give me a chance to defend myself."

"Where are you staying?"

"Last couple of nights at the Union Gospel Mission."

Bo added cheese to the scrambled eggs, then cut a grapefruit in half. He put the food on two plates and gave one to Otter. He poured coffee for them both and joined Otter at the table.

"I saw Freak again," Otter said, chewing fast, his mouth full.

"Freak's dead." Bo ate his own food slowly.

"I saw him. He was standing in the mouth of a culvert down on the river near the High Bridge. He was saying something, but I couldn't hear it. What do you think it means, Spider-Man?"

"Nothing, Otter. It doesn't mean a thing."

"It does. It all means something. It all connects."

"Not in any way I've ever been able to see," Bo responded.

Otter aimed his empty fork at Bo. "You know, that's always been your trouble. You only see what's in front of you. But the important stuff, it's never where your eyes are looking, Spider-Man. You think I saw Freak with my eyes? I've been seeing a lot lately, but none of it with my eyes."

"Don't get spooky on me, Otter."

"I'm telling you, Spider-Man. It means something."

"Eat," Bo said.

When they'd finished the food and their coffee, Bo wrote something on a piece of paper and gave it to Otter.

"What's this?"

"Job and a room, if you want it."

Otter read the note. "Church janitor?"

"Only if you want it."

"Thanks, Spider-Man."

"I've got to go," Bo said.

They stepped out, and Bo locked the door. They went downstairs and outside into the morning sunlight.

"Need a lift?" Bo asked.

Otter shook his head. He reached out and hugged Bo.

"Great," Bo said. "Now I'm going to smell like you for the rest of the day. Are you going to check that out?" He nodded at the piece of paper in Otter's hand.

"I don't know."

"Whatever," Bo said. "Next time you see Freak, tell him hello for me."

Otter didn't smile. He looked at Bo as if he were disappointed, turned, and walked away down the winding streets of Tangletown.

As Bo headed toward the garage in the alley where he parked his car, the cell phone he'd picked up in his bedroom gave a jingle. He saw from the number that it was Stu Coyote calling from the field office.

"This is Thorsen."

"You dead?" Coyote said. "Or just your pager? We've been paging you for two hours. And trying your cell phone every half hour."

Bo glanced at the pager clipped to his belt. "Pager's showing nothing. Must've broken in the scuffle yesterday when we took down Holtz."

"We've got a situation."

"What?"

"Tom Jorgenson had an accident last night."

"How bad?"

"Bad. The First Lady's flying out."

"Shit."

"I know."

"I'm on my way."

Bo took Snelling Avenue, merged with the morning rush on I-94, and laid on the gas pedal, heading into downtown Minneapolis.

The field office of the U.S. Secret Service was located in the United States Court building on South Fourth Street. Bo parked his Contour in the ramp underground, passed through security on the main level, and took the elevator to the seventh floor. He tapped in the code on the key lock and entered the suite of offices.

Citations of merit and photographs of agents standing post as they protected various presidents decorated the hallway walls. Presidential protection was the most visible of the responsibilities entrusted to the Secret Service, but it was not, in fact, the department's raison d'être. The Secret Service had been established at the close of the Civil War in order to combat the proliferation of counterfeit paper currency. Not until 1901, following the assassination of President William McKinley, did Congress direct the Secret Service to provide protection for the nation's commander in chief. In 1917, the directive was expanded to include the entire First Family. Shielding the vice president didn't come about until 1962, and in 1971, Congress voted to provide Secret Service protection to visiting foreign heads of state. Although it was with these protective responsibilities that most Americans associated the Secret Service, the vast majority of special agents continued to be assigned to investigation of counterfeiting and other federally punishable fraud. Most often Bo dealt with currency crimes. Unless the Twin Cities was expecting an important visitor.

He could feel the timbre, the tense energy that preceded all high level visits. Coyote was already seated in the office of Special Agent-in-Charge Diana Ishimaru.

Stuart Coyote was a block of granite chiseled into a man. He had a broad face that broke easily into a smile, coal black hair, and skin that was a soft-toned earth color, the genetic legacy of the coupling of his Kiowa father and his French mother.

As Bo stepped in, his boss glanced up from a document she was scanning.

"Get yourself a new pager," Ishimaru greeted him. "Today, if not sooner."

"How's Tom?" Bo asked.

"Unconscious but alive. Sit down."

Bo pulled up a chair beside Coyote. "What happened?"

"He was on his tractor in the orchard last night," Coyote said. "Hit a branch and got knocked off. The flatbed he was hauling ran over him, crushed his pelvis. He hit his head, too. In a coma now."

Ishimaru took it from there. "The First Lady's been notified. She's flying in this afternoon. ETA is twelve-fifteen. She wants to head immediately to the hospital, of course. After that, she'll be driven to Wildwood. Stu will be liaison with local law enforcement and public service. Bo, you're on rotation to be in charge of the Operations Center this time. Jake Russell's signing out the ordinance and perimeter equipment. He'll join you at Wildwood. Additional agents are coming from Fargo and Sioux Falls to help. They'll be in this afternoon." Ishimaru looked down at the top document on her desk. "Tom Jorgenson was admitted to the St. Croix Regional Medical Center. I'm sure the First Lady will want to visit regularly. I have the contingency plans for routes and hospital security. Here." She handed both agents a copy of the document. "I'll be in touch. Any questions?"

"Just one," Bo said. "Is Chris Manning still in charge of the FLOTUS detail?" He used the common acronym for the First Lady of the United States.

"Yes. Do you have a problem with that?"

"No. But he might have a problem with me."

"Special Agent Manning's primary concern is the protection of the First Lady. I'm sure that consideration will override any uncomfortable history between you two. And I'm sure he appreciates that I'm putting my best agents at his disposal. He'd better, by God, appreciate it." She stood up. "Gentlemen, I have four thousand things to see to."

Stuart Coyote and Bo left her office.

"Promise me one thing," Stu said as he headed to his own office.

"What?"

"Don't hit Manning this time, okay?"

chapter

five

Bo always kept a suitcase packed and ready. He spent less than ten minutes in his apartment in Tangletown, then took I-94 east out of St. Paul, eighteen miles to the St. Croix Trail exit, where he headed south through the little river town of Afton. A couple of miles beyond, he turned east onto a private drive. He passed beneath a stone arch with the name WILDWOOD set in big tile letters. The drive threaded between tall cedars for a quarter mile, then approached the gate of a seven-foot-high stone wall. The gate was open at the moment and the gatehouse deserted. That would change as soon as the rest of the protective detail arrived. Beyond the wall lay the orchards of Wildwood.

After his wife passed away, Tom Jorgenson had come home to the estate to retire, but he didn't retire long. Within two years of his return, he'd established, in conjunction with the University of Minnesota, the Myrna Jorgenson Institute for Global Understanding, a think tank for world peace and prosperity. An invitation to his annual Symposium on World Unity was a highly sought-after prize, and his home had become a destination for leaders of nations all over the world. A full decade after abandoning the politics of Washington, D.C., he'd proved instrumental in negotiating the Abu Dhabi Accord, which clearly enunciated the guidelines for humane treatment of international refugees. Because of his efforts he'd been short-listed for the Nobel Peace Prize.

Bo had been in charge of security at Wildwood on numerous occasions. Although former vice presidents were not accorded Secret Service protection (a benefit enjoyed only by former presidents), the Secret Service did have the responsibility of protecting visiting heads of state. Jorgenson was famous for putting his guests to work in the orchards, regardless of their rank. Prime ministers, premiers, presidents, and sultans propped and pruned and picked the fruit. While they sweated at a labor as old as mankind, they talked with Tom Jorgenson and with one another. And while they talked, Bo and his fellow agents kept them safe.

The house, nestled in the orchards, was a big place, three stories, white frame, half a dozen gables, and a wraparound front porch. Forty yards south stood the guesthouse. There were two outbuildings, one a sturdy red barn and the other an equipment shed, and near the main house a small swimming pool.

Bo parked on the gravel drive in front of the house, under a sycamore. Annie Jorgenson must have been expecting him, because she opened the door as he stepped onto the porch.

"Hello, Bo." She gave him a hug and kissed his cheek.

"How is he, Annie?"

"Not conscious. They tell me it could go either way."

Annie Jorgenson was in her early sixties. A slender woman, she stood nearly as tall as Bo, and when she spoke to him, her crystal blue eyes were level with his own. Bo had always admired the intelligence and beauty in those eyes. Now he saw tears there.

"Ruth's with him," she said, speaking of Jorgenson's youngest daughter.

Someone called from inside, "Annie?" Bo had been on detail at Wildwood often enough to recognize that the voice belonged to Sue

Lynott, who prepared the meals for the Jorgensons and their guests, and also for the Secret Service agents while they were on protective duty at Wildwood. Her food was considered one of the true perks of the job. "Shall I fix you and Bo some tea?"

"Thank you, Sue," Annie called back. "That would be nice."

They sat in the porch swing.

"How did it happen?" he asked.

She shook her head. "He was going down to the river bluff to look at the moon. You know his ritual. He's been taking the tractor lately because he twisted his knee a couple of weeks ago. When I finished the dinner dishes, I went out to join him and there he was. A branch had knocked him off his seat and the flatbed had run over him. He must have been careless." Her voice, by the end, had broken.

"Did you get any sleep last night?"

"Not much."

"The team will be here soon to set up. I'll keep things quiet if you'd like to try to get some rest."

"I'm fine, Bo."

Sue brought them tea, said hello to Bo, then went back into the house. From the orchards came the sound of a meadowlark. Annie's eyes seemed to try to track the source of the song, and for a while she simply stared at the apple trees and drank her tea.

"If there's anything I can do," Bo finally said, "let me know."

She smiled. "You're doing it."

When Special Agent Jake Russell arrived with the rest of the operations detail, Bo left Annie and headed out to prepare the guest-house.

Originally a carriage house, the structure had at one time served as the home and the studio for Roland Jorgenson, who'd been a famous metal sculptor. After Roland's death, the structure was remodeled to accommodate the visitors who journeyed to Wildwood seeking Tom Jorgenson's counsel. The frequent presence of foreign heads of state necessitated installation of permanent security equipment. Behind the kitchen was an area originally designed as a sunroom, but that had become the Operations Center. Although Tom Jorgenson understood the need for security measures during these high-level visits, he never allowed the devices to be operable at any other time. Part of Bo's responsibility was to run a check of the system and ensure that every piece of apparatus was functioning properly. He directed some of the agents to check the monitors that were connected to cameras mounted around the building. Jake Russell took part of the team into the orchard to calibrate the sensors of the motion detectors and infrared cameras on the stone wall around the orchards of Wildwood. Bo secured the weapons and the additional equipment in the Op Center lockers. Once the perimeter security system was functioning, he had his team run a test to make sure the signals were firm and all the equipment was transmitting properly.

Near the end of the setup, he received word that the First Lady's plane had arrived and she was en route to the hospital. Shortly after, a Washington County sheriff's deputy dropped by to say two officers had been posted at the entrance to Wildwood to control traffic and access from the main road. Media vans were already gathering along the St. Croix Trail. Bo thanked him and did a final check of everything.

He spent another hour preparing before he was satisfied that all was in order. Finally, he stepped out into the yard and stood looking down the orchard lane that Tom Jorgenson always took when he went to watch the moon. At the far end, Bo could see the tractor.

He walked slowly between the rows of trees. The apples were a nice size but still green. The branches sagged, in need of propping. Bo had to walk a crooked line and bend occasionally to make his way. When he reached the idle machine, he circled it, then stood looking back for the branch that had thrown Tom Jorgenson into harm's way. The most likely candidate was a thick limb a few feet back of the flatbed. It hung low, but not so low, Bo thought, that it couldn't easily have been avoided. Bo climbed onto the tractor seat, looked back, and confirmed his assessment that if Jorgenson had made the slightest effort, he'd have missed the limb. Bo had known Tom Jorgenson long enough to believe that he was a man with great presence of mind. What could have distracted him? The moon? As he dismounted, he spotted a silver Thermos wedged under the seat. He unscrewed the cap and sniffed. Coffee and—maybe this explained a lot—whiskey.

Bo walked to the edge of the bluff thirty yards in front of the tractor. A sheer sandstone cliff fell fifty feet to a rocky, tree-covered slope that ran down to the St. Croix River. The river was a silver sparkle of sunlight a half-mile wide, edged on both sides by tall, wooded bluffs. Sailboats and power launches skimmed over the water. Bo turned back, stared at the tractor, and wondered about something. He returned to the Kubota and checked the ignition. The key was still there, but the ignition was in the off position. He was pretty sure Tom Jorgenson didn't have time to kill the engine before he fell to the ground. So probably the ignition had been switched off by someone in the aftermath of the accident. Still, the elements of the situation felt odd to him.

He puzzled only a brief moment before he heard his name called over the walkie-talkie he carried, and the cryptic message, "Dreamcatcher is en route to Mount Olympus."

Communicating over the airwaves, even when using a scrambled signal, Secret Service always employed code names to designate protectees. Dreamcatcher was the First Lady. Mount Olympus was Wildwood.

chapter

six

The First Lady arrived in a dark blue Lincoln Town Car escorted by two state patrol cars and by two Regals from the field office, each carrying several of the agents on permanent FLOTUS duty. Bo stood just behind Annie Jorgenson as the limousine stopped in front of the house.

Special Agent Christopher Manning emerged first. He wasn't tall, just under six feet, nor remarkably broad in chest and shoulders, yet in his compactness there was something powerful. He'd always reminded Bo of a jack-in-the-box, tense and ready to spring. He wore his red-blond hair in a neat crew cut. To Bo, the most remarkable feature of Manning's face was that it usually displayed all the emotion of a bowling ball.

The woman who stepped out after Manning, Bo had met only once in person, when she was seventeen. During all the operations Bo had overseen at Wildwood, Kathleen Jorgenson Dixon had been absent, either in Colorado as the state's First Lady or in Washington, D.C., bearing the same title for the nation. He'd seen the family pictures, of course, framed inside the Jorgenson house, and along with most other Americans, he'd been treated to more than enough television, magazine, and newspaper coverage to know the basics of her life story. It was of a vivacious young woman, always smiling, eyes bright, raised in an international arena. There were pictures of the Jorgensons in Paris, Rome, London, Amsterdam, many posed with leaders of great renown. In them, Kate Jorgenson, the oldest of the children, usually stood holding hands with her sister, Ruth, and her brother, Earl.

Kate had grown into a Nordic beauty, tall, large-boned, blonde, with striking gray eyes. Although Bo had always been impressed with her composure and with the strength of her character, when he saw her emerge from the limousine, it was, much to his own chagrin, her long and slender legs that he noted. He considered wryly whether this might somehow be a breach of his patriotic duty.

"Aunt Annie." The First Lady sounded near tears.

"It's all right, Katie," Annie Jorgenson said as they hugged. "We're all together now. It will be okay."

"He looks so broken."

"Come on in, sweetheart, and we'll get you settled. Then, if you'd like, we'll go back and see him together."

Two more agents stepped from the Town Car, along with a woman whom Bo knew from report and reputation, Nicole Greene, who functioned as the First Lady's communications director.

"Agent Aguilera," Manning instructed one of his team, a tall woman, "you're with the First Lady. Gooden, give a hand with the luggage." He turned, finally, to Bo. "I've been in communication with Diana Ishimaru in the Minneapolis office. She indicated you have the Operations Center ready."

"The guesthouse," Bo replied, pointing toward the maples. "We've checked the security cameras and radio equipment. We still need a frequency cleared for emergency communication, but we should have that momentarily."

"Good," Manning replied with a nod.

Stu Coyote, who'd driven one of the Regals, joined them. "County deputies are stationed at the entrance to Wildwood. State patrol's assigned us these two units for the duration of the First Lady's visit." He indicated the burgundy-and-tan patrol cars. "Anywhere she goes, they clear the way."

Manning said, "We're going to try to limit her traveling to between Wildwood and the hospital. According to the contingency report I have, there's only one main road to Stillwater."

"The St. Croix Trail. The road we just traveled," Coyote said. "That's it."

"I don't like the idea of keeping to a single route." Although his words betrayed concern, Manning's face didn't show it. "Show me the Op Center. Carter, Searson, Jones," he called to the other agents. "Get your things."

Bo led him to the guest house. On the lawn in front, secured to a concrete slab as if it were being held captive, stood a huge, twisted sculpture of stainless steel. As they passed the polished metal, a blast of reflected sunlight blinded Manning, and he lifted his hands to block the glare.

"Jesus, what the hell is that?"

"Don't you recognize great art when you see it, Chris?" Bo said. "That's a bona fide masterpiece, or so I've been told. The guesthouse used to be the studio for Tom Jorgenson's infamous brother, Roland. A true eccentric, from what I understand. Died twenty years ago in a car accident. Drove his Porsche into a tree. Created his final sculpture, a heap of metal with him at the heart. *Goddess* here is the only piece left at Wildwood. Everything else is in museums."

"*Goddess?*" Manning said. "My ass."

Bo shared the lack of enthusiasm. The sculpture was a wild thing that gave the feel of monstrous forces barely contained. The polished steel itself was beautiful, but to Bo it had always seemed like a dream that had been warped by a dark subconscious into a nightmare.

"You learn to ignore it," Bo said and led Manning inside.

Bo briefed him on the layout and the bedrooms. Manning made assignments for his team. Then they went down to the Op Center, where Bo's people were already at work. Manning checked the sweep of the cameras. "Nothing that looks beyond the buildings," he said. "At night, you could hide an army in those orchards."

"We have motion detectors and motion-activated cameras on the wall around the orchard," Bo told him. "During periods of heightened security, I have agents patrolling the perimeter around the clock."

"What about the river bluff?" Manning said. "No wall there."

"Tom Jorgenson won't let anything ruin the view of the river. We've had to settle for mobile tripods that we set up each time we come out."

"How about duty shifts?"

"Eight hours for everyone but me. Until the First Lady's visit is over, I'm here twenty-four, seven. The only thing we haven't done yet is run an electronic sweep. We had such short notice."

Manning shook his head. "Forget the sweep. We're not holding a summit meeting. It would be too disruptive for the First Lady at this point."

"A sweep is standard protocol at Wildwood," Bo said.

"When heads of state meet here, of course. But no state secrets are going to be discussed this visit. Let's keep it simple and focus on the First Lady's safety." Manning took a last look around. "Everything seems in order, Thorsen."

"I have a print of the hospital layout if you want to go over it."

Manning dismissed Bo's offer with a wave. "I had it faxed to me on the plane. Everything's already under control."

"Anything you need for covering the First Lady, just let me know."

"All I need is for you to do your job."

Later in the day, the Jorgenson family made another visit to the hospital. It was nearly dark when Annie and the First Lady returned to Wildwood. A while later, Tom Jorgenson's other children, Ruth and Earl, arrived. Half an hour after that, as Bo stood near the sculpture outside the guesthouse, he saw the front door open, and all the

Jorgensons stepped out. When the door closed behind them, they were lost in the dark on the front porch. A moment later, Bo heard the creak of the swing that hung there. When Wildwood had distinguished visitors, Tom and Annie often would sit with the guests in the evening, rocking in the porch swing and talking. Bo always waited until the guests had retired for the night, before turning on the porch light and activating the sensors that protected the house.

He gave them a few minutes, then he headed their way. Although he was reluctant to disturb them, he had a question that was begging for an answer.

"Evening, Annie. Ruth. Earl. Mrs. Dixon," he said from the walk.

"It's Bo," Earl shouted. He leaped from the swing and bounded down the porch stairs, where he pumped Bo's hand with great pleasure.

Earl was thirty-three, but his mind was still somewhere in childhood. Usually he lived in a group home in St. Paul, but his father's accident had brought him back to Wildwood.

"How you doing, Earl?"

"I'm real good, Bo. Real good. I got a girlfriend."

"Good for you. What's her name?"

"It's Joanie, Bo. Joanie Bones."

"Bonds," Annie said gently from the railing against which she and Ruth leaned. "Joanie Bonds, Earl."

"I like Joanie Bones better. She thinks it's funny."

"Hello, Bo," Annie said.

"Hi, Bo." Ruth gave him a familiar little wave.

Annie said, "Kate, I don't think you met Special Agent Thorsen this afternoon. He's local Secret Service."

"How do you do, Agent Thorsen?"

He couldn't see her well. She was a light shade moving toward him and back with the slow rock of the swing.

"Fine, thanks," he said. "I'm sorry about your father."

Earl returned to the porch swing and sat beside his sister.

"Bo's been our guardian angel out here many times in the last few years," Annie said. "But Bo and I have known each other a lot longer than that. Twenty-five years, I believe."

"Come September," Bo said.

"Oh?" the First Lady said. "How's that?"

Annie laughed quietly. "I made Bo's acquaintance when he came before me in juvenile court."

"You were in trouble?"

Bo smiled. "I didn't see it that way."

"He was living on the streets," Annie said.

"Your parents?" the First Lady asked.

"By then I had none," Bo replied.

"I'm sorry." She sounded as if she were. Sincerely.

"I was lucky. I found my way into Annie's courtroom."

"He was arrested for theft," Annie explained. "The police found him living with four other children in an abandoned school bus in a grove of trees on the Mississippi River. They were surviving mostly off Bo's ability to steal."

"What can I say?" Bo shrugged. "It was a gift."

"Why have we never met before?" the First Lady asked.

"Actually, we have," Bo said, "a long time ago. Just before I headed off to college, I stopped by Wildwood to thank Annie for all she'd done. I watched the moon rise with you and your father that night."

"I'm sorry. I ought to remember."

Bo laughed easily. "You were memorable. I was not. I didn't come back to Wildwood again until after I was posted to the field office in Minneapolis. That was three years ago."

"And you haven't visited Wildwood since you moved into the White House," Annie said to her niece with a note of mild criticism. "If we want to see you, we have to go to Washington. Bo, on the other hand, visits regularly. He and Tom have become good friends."

Ruth held out her hand, indicating a tray on the table next to the swing. "Would you care for some iced tea, Bo?"

"I don't want to intrude."

"It's no intrusion," Annie assured him.

"I'll skip the tea, but I'd like to ask you something, Annie. About Tom's accident."

"What do you want to know?"

Bo mounted the steps but kept a discreet distance. "Was the tractor still running when you found Tom?"

"I don't really remember. The lights were on, I do recall. I could see them when I stood out there in the yard. I think . . ." She closed her eyes and put a hand to her forehead as she concentrated. "It seems to me that it was very quiet when I got to him. So I guess the tractor was turned off. But I couldn't really say for sure. Everything was so rushed and confused."

"I understand, Annie."

"Agent Thorsen." Chris Manning's voice brought Bo around. Manning materialized from a shadow and stood at the bottom of the porch steps. "I'm sure the First Lady and her family appreciate their privacy."

Annie said, "That's quite all right . . . Chris, isn't it?"

"Special Agent Christopher Manning, ma'am."

"Yes. Chris. Bo and I are old friends. He's no intrusion."

"Actually, Ms. Jorgenson, I need to take him from you. There are a few security issues we need to discuss."

"Very well. 'Night, Bo."

"Good night, ladies," Bo said. " 'Night, Earl. Say hi to Joanie Bones for me."

"Joanie Bones," Earl said, laughing.

Manning walked briskly toward the guesthouse. When he believed, apparently, that they were out of hearing range of the porch, he turned angrily to Bo. "What the hell do you think you're doing?"

"What do you mean?"

"As much as possible, Agent Thorsen, we become the woodwork. We remain unobtrusive. In carrying on conversations with our protectees, we not only intrude in their affairs, but we lose our vigilance and risk their lives."

"Look, Chris, I was just—"

"I don't care, Thorsen. The First Lady's safety is my responsibility. I won't have that responsibility compromised by your incompetence. I'm noting this in my report."

"Do what you feel you have to, Chris. You always have."

Manning left him and went into the guesthouse.

From the dark of the porch, Annie's voice carried to him. "Sorry, Bo."

"No problem, Annie."

The guesthouse door opened again, and Coyote came out. "Whoa, is he steamed. What did you do? Hit him again?"

"Let's go to the barn, Stu," Bo suggested. "I want to run something by you."

They stepped into the opened doorway. The yard light cast their shadows inside where they merged with the dark of the barn.

"That Manning is some piece of work," Coyote said.

"Forget about him. He's just doing his job. Listen, Stu, something about Tom Jorgenson's accident has been bugging me all day."

"Yeah? What?"

"When the limb knocked Jorgenson from his seat, the tractor should have kept on going, but it didn't. When Annie found him, she thinks the tractor was turned off, although she's not absolutely certain. But suppose she's right."

Coyote said, "Then the question would be, if Jorgenson didn't turn the tractor off, who did?"

"Right."

"Does this have anything to do with the First Lady's safety?" Coyote asked.

"Not directly. Not in any way that I can see."

"Then forget it. Look, it's been a long day. I'm heading home." Coyote put a friendly hand on Bo's shoulder. "Do me a favor, will you? Manning's gunning for you. Don't give him any ammunition."

After Coyote left, Bo stood in the yard and looked toward the west. The setting moon, only a couple of days past full, cast a brilliant glow over the apple trees. He knew that Tom Jorgenson would see beauty in that bright light. Bo saw mostly advantage. It always meant that anyone moving among the orchard rows could be more easily seen.

chapter

seven

W hen he saw the two agents head toward the barn, Nightmare switched to the camera he'd concealed in a hay bale in the loft two days earlier.

In the weeks before, access to Wildwood had been easy. The grounds were large, and unsecured. Tom Jorgenson liked to think of himself as a man of the people, and unless a dignitary was visiting, he didn't believe in extensive security measures. Nightmare had scaled the stone wall dozens of times, coming and going in the night as he studied the layout of the buildings and the equipment the Secret Service would eventually use to create the illusion of safety. While the Jorgensons slept, or while they were absent, Nightmare had walked their rooms undetected. He felt like a ghost, and he liked the feeling. He would show them what the dead could do.

The two agents stood in the open doorway of the barn. On Nightmare's monitor and seen through the sunglasses that he wore even in the dark, they were black shapes against the glare of the yard light. He turned up the microphone and listened as they discussed the concern of the one called Thorsen.

The tractor. It was a small detail. Why hadn't he let it run off the cliff? The answer was simple. Too much noise. Too great an announcement of the event. Nightmare had always been an operative who appreciated the quiet and the dark. Execute and evaporate. Gone before anyone knew he'd ever been there.

But this Thorsen was observant and smart. Nightmare knew he would have to watch the man, and eliminate him if necessary. Not difficult. Nightmare had dealt with dozens like him, men who thought they were too smart to get killed.

When the two agents split up, Nightmare switched cameras again, this time to a view of the house from a unit he'd secreted in the sycamore tree. The three women had quit the porch. Nightmare checked the kitchen camera hidden in a false fire extinguisher with which he'd replaced the real one, then he flipped to the camera hidden in a book on a shelf in the living room where the agent on duty was playing a game of solitaire on a coffee table. Finally he checked the camera he'd placed in the bedroom that had once been Kate's. He found, as he'd hoped, that the room was still hers. She sat on her bed, staring at a bare wall.

What do you see there, Kate? The future? The past? You don't see me, I'll bet. But you will.

He remembered the first night twenty years ago that he'd watched her like this, unseen. He'd climbed the sycamore, climbed as easily as a snake up a vine. In those days, there'd been curtains over the windows, gauzy things not dense enough in their weave to block his vision of her undressing. He remembered her breasts especially, tumbling from the bra that had held them captive. For weeks in that summer of his seventeenth year, he'd made a ritual of the sycamore tree. On those nights when she was gone, when they were all gone and the house was deserted, he climbed the porch supports, swung himself easily over the eaves to the roof, and crept to her window. He was already a genius at picking locks, at easing through the smallest breach in someone's privacy. Her screen presented him no challenge at all. He wandered her room, fingering everything she'd touched. He lay on her bed, breathing the scent off her pillow.

He loved her, of course. How could he not love that which had possessed him?

In the present, he watched the First Lady drift left, just beyond camera range. She reappeared a minute later. Her yellow dress was gone, and she'd removed her bra. Her breasts were fuller now, heavier-looking, and there was a roundness to her belly and hips that was the signature of time, of the two decades that separated this intimate view from the last. She stood a moment, as if lost. Then she turned her back to the camera and bent her head. Nightmare could tell from the way her shoulders quivered that she wept.

Until that moment, he'd been hard in his thinking, brutal, in the way that time and circumstance had shaped him to be. But when he saw her cry, a different feeling nudged him, one that he had not expected. He remembered how his own mother used to cry, from confusion and loneliness.

He fingered the festering wound above his heart, full of ash and old blood. He put his sunglasses back on and closed himself like a fist around an understanding: It didn't matter if what he did was done out of anger or out of pity. The end was the same.

Kate put on a nightgown, lay down, reached for a book on the nightstand, and began to read.

The sun will rise for you tomorrow, Nightmare thought as he watched her. *But soon there will be nothing for you except the night, the unending night. And I will be the one who takes you there.*

chapter

eight

Midmorning the next day, Annie Jorgenson, the First Lady, and Earl headed to the hospital. The word on Tom Jorgenson was that his condition had stabilized, but he still had not regained consciousness.

Protective detail was among the most important of a Secret Service agent's duties, and also among the most tedious. Usually it entailed hours of doing nothing while trying to maintain a level of readiness to deal with the worst-case scenario. Bo thought the electronic sweep of Wildwood that hadn't yet been done would be a good way to break the routine. At the briefing that morning, he discussed the possibility with Chris Manning. Manning vetoed the idea, pointing out once again that the purpose of the First Lady's visit was personal, and that no state secrets were in jeopardy. Bo decided not to argue.

Shortly after the motorcade left, Bo put Jake Russell, the shift supervisor, in charge of the Op Center and left Wildwood. He checked in with the deputies posted at the entrance, Morgan and Braun, men he'd worked with before. Except for seeing the First Lady in person, it was dull duty. The news journalists in the cars and media vans that sat parked along the highway knew the drill. Cameras rolling when the First Lady appeared, but no access to Wildwood itself. Bo saw that there were more vehicles parked than he'd anticipated and heavier traffic on the usually quiet highway. Gawkers, hoping for a glimpse of Kathleen Jorgenson Dixon.

Bo drove toward Stillwater and headed to the office of the Washington County sheriff. He flashed his ID at the desk officer and waited a minute before he was buzzed through the security door.

Sheriff Douglas Quinn-Gruber was a big man with a wry smile and sharp, discerning eyes behind wire-rimmed glasses. He had a quick wit and an understanding of local politics that had kept him in office for three terms. He also had a taste for exotic beer. He brewed his own. Each Christmas for the last three years, Bo had received an assortment of home brews that tasted of raspberry or hazelnut or honey, and occasionally like beer. Bo's own tastes were simple. He usually drank Pig's Eye, brewed in St. Paul on the banks of the Mississippi River, but he appreciated the sheriff's gesture.

"Hey, Bo," Quinn-Gruber said, coming out of his chair. He reached out with a strong handshake. "I'm surprised to see you. I figured you'd be swamped at Wildwood."

"Everything's under control, Doug. We have a small army out there. How's Mary Lou?" Bo always asked after the sheriff's wife. He liked hearing what she was up to, always something interesting.

The sheriff laughed. "In two weeks, she turns fifty. Know what she's planning on doing to mark the occasion? She's going to canoe—by herself—the entire length of the St. Croix River."

"You worried?"

"Naw. I called the counties up north and in Wisconsin, talked to a few fellow officers. They're going to keep an eye on her progress. Discreetly. Have a seat." He indicated a chair and sat back down at his desk. "So, what brings you here? I'm in touch pretty regularly with Stu Coyote. Everything seems fine."

"It is, as far as the First Lady's concerned. I wanted to ask about Tom Jorgenson's accident."

"A shame, that."

"Doug, did any of your people investigate?"

"Investigate? An incident report was filed, but I don't think anybody saw any reason to investigate. Why?"

"Something bothers me." Bo explained his concern about the mystery of the stopped tractor.

"What are you saying? Tom wasn't alone out there?"

"I'm not sure. But it kind of looks that way."

"Are you thinking maybe it wasn't an accident?"

"On occasion, Tom's received hate mail because of the work he does with the Institute for Global Understanding. I've always been afraid he might end up a target someday. And you know how lax he's always been about his own security at Wildwood."

The sheriff removed his wire-rims and squinted through them. He drew a handkerchief from his pocket and wiped the lenses. "That tractor was hauling a trailer. Maybe the extra drag on the engine made it stall."

"I thought of that," Bo said.

"I don't want to take a chance where Tom Jorgenson is involved," the sheriff said. "I'll have one of my investigators look into it. Think we'd get anywhere dusting the tractor for prints?"

"Couldn't hurt."

"Consider it done."

"Thanks." Bo stood up. "I appreciate your help, Doug."

"No problem. Hey, I'm trying a new recipe. Rhubarb beer."

Bo grinned. "Can't wait till Christmas."

Less than two hours later, an investigator named Timmons showed up at Wildwood. He spoke with Annie. Just a routine follow-up, he told her. Then he checked in with Bo. Tom Jorgenson, Timmons reported, had had no threats in almost two years. One of the sheriff's deputies admitted to moving the tractor ahead a bit so that the paramedics could work more easily on Jorgenson but couldn't remember if the ignition had been in the "off" position, so there was no way of telling whether the engine had died on its own or had been turned off. Bo accompanied Detective Timmons to the tractor. While Timmons dusted for prints, he pointed out to Bo that in the last two months, Tom Jorgenson had suffered several minor accidents, due entirely to carelessness. "Everyone gets old," he said with a shrug. "And sometimes forgetful."

After the investigator had gone, Bo stood in the shade of the limb that had apparently knocked Tom Jorgenson into harm's way, and he studied the line of the flatbed and the track of the wheels. Finally, he went to the Kubota and climbed into the seat. It was comfortably padded, with a soft, cushioned back. Bo sat and imagined the limb catching him in the forehead, knocking him backward. The seat back would probably have prevented him from toppling off. He thought awhile, then let himself tumble sideways into the soft orchard grass where he lay, looking back at the flatbed.

"Comfortable, Bo?"

The First Lady came around the tractor and stood gazing down at him. She wore a white T-shirt, jeans, and a dark blue ball cap with *Twins* printed across the crown. She carried her sandals, leaving her feet bare. She looked more like a country girl than the wife of the nation's commander in chief. She was smiling. Not a large smile, but the first Bo had seen since she'd arrived. Two of Manning's people trailed at a reasonable distance.

Bo stood up. "I was just admiring the machinery."

"From every angle, I see. Do you know about tractors?"

"After I was arrested, Annie arranged for me to live with a foster family down in Blue Earth," Bo said. "Farmers. I did my time on the seat of an old John Deere Model B."

Her smile grew. "We had a Model B when I used to help my dad in these orchards. That was a monster. Not like this Kubota." She put a hand on the tractor, but she pulled it back quickly from the sting of the metal that had turned hot in the afternoon sun.

"You know about the Kubota?"

"An M-series narrow. Specially built for orchard work. Hydrostatic power steering. Synchronized main and shuttle transmission. Three Vortex Combustion System diesel engine. Eighty PTO horse-power."

Bo let the fact that he was impressed show. She laughed, and he liked the sound.

"I'm not as smart as I seem," she confessed. "Dad and I talk on the phone almost weekly. He told me everything. He was so proud of his new toy. What interests you so much about the tractor?"

Manning had been explicit in his directive. The First Lady wasn't to be worried.

Bo said, "On the farm, I fell in love with machines. The smell of grease and gasoline and field dust. I appreciate their purpose and their power."

"But you didn't become a farmer."

"Wrong temperament," Bo replied.

"Katie! Katie!"

The First Lady turned back as Earl galloped toward her down the orchard row. He was a big, ungainly man who ran without any grace but a lot of joy. He smacked into a low-hanging branch, spun around, and came on as if nothing had happened. When he reached them, he was breathing hard and smiling big.

"Hi, Bo."

"Morning, Earl."

"Beautiful, huh?"

Bo looked at the First Lady, and thought, *Yes*. Then Earl touched the tractor, and Bo understood what he'd meant.

"I get to drive it sometimes," Earl said.

"But not now," Kate told him.

Earl looked disappointed and climbed onto the seat anyway. He began to pretend to drive the machine, making engine sounds. *"Vrrooom! Vrrooom!"*

The First Lady moved to the flatbed and sat in the shade of an apple limb. She put her sandals beside her and crossed her long, brown legs. "I used to come here with my father almost every night.

He'd bring his telescope and we'd look at the moon and the stars for hours."

"It's easy to see why he loves it."

"Am I keeping you from your work?" she asked.

"You are my work."

"My aunt thinks the world of you, you know."

"I'm pretty fond of Annie. I owe her my life. What I've made of it, anyway."

"What about the others?" she asked. "The children who lived with you in the bus."

"Otter, Egg, Pearl, and Freak."

"Those were their names?"

"Street names. We all went by them."

"What was yours?"

"Spider-Man."

"So, what happened to the others?"

Earl was pretending to shift through gears and bouncing on the seat as if he were driving over rough road.

Bo leaned against the ridges of the Kubota's big rear tire. The limb that shaded the First Lady also shaded him.

"They still had homes somewhere. Social Services sent them back to their parents."

"And they all lived happily ever after?"

"Pearl got pregnant at sixteen. The first time. She has five children now by three different men. Her oldest daughter ran away this summer. Pearl still hasn't heard from her. Otter's an alcoholic, been in and out of treatment for years. Those are the success stories," Bo said.

"The other two? Egg and Freak?"

"Egg's doing time in Eddyville, Kentucky, for armed robbery. Freak died of AIDS, two years ago. He was a heroin addict."

"I'm sorry, Bo."

"Me, too."

"What about you? Are you happy with the life you've put together?"

"Happier some days than others. Isn't it like that for everyone?"

Instead of answering, she rose and said, "I should be getting back. Earl, are you coming?"

"Yeah. Do you want to go swimming?" He climbed down from the tractor and took his sister's hand.

Before she started away, the First Lady said, "Shouldn't that tractor be moved?"

"Your safety is our priority right now," Bo said. "Eventually I'll have one of my people put it in the barn."

"Or put it there yourself. Why give someone else the thrill?" She laughed, turned away, and headed toward the house with Earl, following the orchard lane Tom Jorgenson had taken a couple of days before. The two FLOTUS agents trailed her.

When they'd gone, Bo walked to the apple tree behind the flatbed and climbed the trunk. He eased out onto the limb that seemed to have been the culprit in Tom Jorgenson's accident. He crouched and examined the bark. Some of the very small sucker branches were bent or broken. It looked to Bo as if someone might well have climbed out onto that limb not long before him.

chapter

nine

The St. Croix Regional Medical Center stood on a hill overlooking Stillwater and the St. Croix River. The wing that housed the trauma intensive care unit faced east, with a good view of the historic old town and of the broad, beautiful river that had been designated a national scenic riverway. The rooms in trauma ICU were all single patient rooms situated around the central nurses' station like spokes around the hub of a wheel. The lovely view from the windows was lost on Tom Jorgenson. He lay unconscious in his bed, living through tubes and wires. His head was wrapped in a thick gauze turban. His eyes were black as a raccoon's, as if he'd been beaten. A tube from a ventilator snaked down his throat. Another tube had been inserted into the side of his chest. Lacerations and bruises covered his arms. Even to Bo, who didn't love him nearly as much as did Annie and his daughters, he looked like death already.

Bo didn't enter the room, just stood in the doorway. Keeping vigil at that hour were Ruth and Earl. Ruth Jorgenson, who'd kept her maiden name after marriage, had a successful law practice in St.

Paul and was the attorney for her father's Institute for Global Understanding. Like most attorneys with whom Bo was acquainted, she always seemed to be long on responsibilities and short on time. However, sitting at her father's bedside, reading aloud from *Wind in the Willows*, one of Earl's favorite books, she appeared to be in no hurry at all. Bo knew from his own experience that tragedy had this effect. It slowed the world so that every second of life counted. Earl sat near her, listening with a big smile on his face as she read.

Bo returned to the nurses' station where he'd previously flashed his ID. The nurse there, a stout woman with silvering hair and a name tag that identified her as Maria Rivera, R.N., asked, "What can I do for you, Agent Thorsen?" She spoke with a slight Hispanic accent.

"Can you tell me who treated Tom Jorgenson last night?"

"Dr. Mason was in charge in the E.R. I believe she oversaw the treatment of Mr. Jorgenson herself. Let me just check the chart." She started to reach toward a rack of charts filed by room number but stopped abruptly and snapped sternly, "Mr. Cooper, stop that."

Bo followed her eyes. A large aquarium tank sat on a stand against one wall of the Trauma ICU. The bottom of the tank was covered with colorful marbles. An old man in a white robe had his arm in the tank, almost up to his shoulder.

"You put those marbles back."

The old man opened his fist, and an array of marbles sank back to the bottom.

Nurse Rivera shook her finger at him. "You wait right there. Don't move." She dialed a number and spoke with exasperation, "Mr. Cooper is up here again. You'd better bring a dry bathrobe."

The old man looked duly chastised. He waited until an orderly arrived, and he let himself be led away.

Nurse Rivera shook her head. "He means no harm. He comes up from the geriatric unit on the floor below. The marbles have some significance with his childhood, I think. If we don't watch carefully, he takes a handful and disappears. He ought to be restrained, I suppose, but he's really no danger to himself. Just a nuisance to us. Now then." She pulled Tom Jorgenson's chart. "Yes, it was Dr. Maggie Mason."

"Is she on duty now?"

"I'm not sure. I'd be glad to check."

"Thank you."

Bo waited while she made the call. Waited uncomfortably. He hated the smell of hospitals, a smell that took him back to the days when Freak was dying and the doctors could do nothing but try to make him comfortable. Bo had never felt so helpless. He and Otter had sat at the bedside, taking turns holding their friend's hand while the life slipped away little by little until Freak was gone and no one but Bo and Otter seemed to have noted his passing.

"Agent Thorsen?"

He came back mentally. "Yes?"

"Dr. Mason's in the E.R."

Bo headed to the elevator and pushed the signal button. When the car arrived and the doors opened, a man stepped out. He was a hard man to miss. The first thing that caught Bo's attention was the scar tissue. It was thick and agate colored and bubbled up from beneath his shirt collar to spread over his neck and right cheek. His right ear didn't look natural, and Bo was certain it had been reconstructed. Bo stepped back to let the man pass, then got on the elevator himself.

He caught the doctor between patients, a fisherman with a hook imbedded deep in his thumb and a seven-year-old boy who'd fallen from a garage roof and was being prepped for an X ray.

"I'm interested in the blow to Mr. Jorgenson's head," Bo explained.

Dr. Mason, a woman in her late forties and with long dark hair just beginning to streak gray, glanced up from the intake form she was scanning. She didn't seem pleased at the interruption. "Which one?"

"What do you mean?"

"There were two blows. One to his forehead." She indicated a place above her right eye. "And one to the back of his head."

"The blow to his forehead. Was that consistent, do you think, with hitting the limb of an apple tree?"

"We cleaned a bit of barklike material from the skin before we dressed the area, so I would say it probably was consistent with hitting a tree limb."

"What about the one to the back of his head?"

"I assume when he fell from the tractor he hit his head on something."

"What about his black eyes?"

"Battle signs, we call them. They often accompany trauma to the back of the head."

"And his other injuries?"

"Crushed pelvis, hemothorax—"

"What's that?"

"Bleeding in the lung space. We checked for pulmonary contusion and found nothing. It's all pretty consistent with the kind of accident that was reported. But I explained all this to a policeman earlier today. A Detective Timmons, I think. And not more than fifteen minutes ago to one of your people. I'd appreciate it if you could all share information with one another."

"One of my people? Secret Service?"

"A federal agent of some kind."

"Do you recall his name?"

"I don't. But he's an obvious burn victim."

"Thanks," Bo said.

The doctor returned her attention to the form in her hands.

Bo didn't know the agent he'd passed in the elevator and was sure he wasn't Secret Service. It was possible Dr. Mason had made a mistake about him being an agent at all. Considering Tom Jorgenson's stature, however, it was very probable that law enforcement agencies at several levels were taking a look at things, and Bo knew only too well how bad the communication among them all could be.

His next stop was the main lobby, where the security officer on duty was posted. Bo found C. J. Burke reading a newspaper.

"Yeah?" Burke looked up from the sports page. He was a thin man with a ratty black mustache that curled around the corners of his lips. Bo guessed him to be thirty. Bo flashed his ID, which didn't seem to impress Burke in the least. Mostly, the guard appeared unhappy at the interruption.

"I'm interested in the security here at night."

"You're looking at the security here at night. Half of it, anyway."

Bo already knew from the contingency reports that two security officers in the hospital after hours was SOP. "Do you patrol?"

"We rotate. Here two hours, patrol two hours."

"You lock the front doors at ten-thirty?"

"Yeah. Then the only public access is through the E.R. We move to a desk down there."

"Your shift ends at eleven-thirty?"

"Graveyard comes on then."

"Contact your partner and bring him down here. I'd like to talk to you both about security while the First Lady's here."

"They already talked to us about that. Plenty."

"I'd like to go over a couple more items."

With an obvious effort, C. J. Burke closed the newspaper on his desk and reached to the walkie-talkie lying there. He raised his partner and passed along Bo's request. In less than three minutes, Randy O'Meara strode briskly out of the elevator and approached them. Bo was relieved to see that at least one of the men took the job seriously. O'Meara was big and broad shouldered, midtwenties. He had brown hair, neatly trimmed. His uniform was pressed, and his shoes were polished.

"This is Agent Thorsen, Randy. More Secret Service," Burke said.

O'Meara brought out a nice smile and offered Bo a firm hand-shake. "How do you do?"

"Good, thanks."

"What can I do for you?"

"He wants to talk about security for the First Lady," Burke said without enthusiasm.

"Not really," Bo told him.

"I thought you just said—"

"It's not the First Lady I'm concerned about here. It's Tom Jorgenson. I'd like to make a few suggestions."

"Go ahead," O'Meara said.

"First, I'd like to suggest you do the rounds tonight without rotating with Burke."

O'Meara glanced at his partner. "Why?"

"Someone needs to be able to make a consistent assessment of the security of the hospital, particularly the floor where Jorgenson's room is located. Rotating might cause you to lose that perspective."

O'Meara shifted on his feet and hooked his thumbs into his belt. "What exactly are you worried about?"

"I'm concerned about Tom Jorgenson's vulnerability. Some people don't feel about him the way most of us Minnesotans do."

"You think somebody might try to hurt him?"

"I'd just like to make sure that security in the hospital is as good as it can be."

"We'll do whatever we can," O'Meara promised.

"I'd also like to suggest varying your rounds. Don't keep to the same routine."

"Because that would make it easier to plan something?"

"Exactly."

"Sure, no problem."

Bo looked at Burke, who hadn't bothered to rise from his seat. "Are you okay with this?"

He shrugged. "Randy's the one whose feet are going to get tired."

Bo turned again to O'Meara. "Would you mind showing me around?"

"My pleasure. What would you like to see?"

"Let's start with Tom Jorgenson's floor."

* * *

As they walked, O'Meara explained that he worked the night shift because he was taking day classes toward a degree in law enforcement at Metropolitan State University. He had experience as an EMT and held a brown belt in tae kwon do. Hearing these things reassured Bo. O'Meara showed him all the possible routes to Jorgenson's floor. These included four public elevators, a freight elevator, and the stairs. The guard explained, as had Burke, that once the main doors were locked at ten-thirty, the only public entrance was through the E.R. Security personnel there barred unauthorized access to the rest of the hospital.

"Any other doors?" Bo asked.

"Four emergency exits. They're all secured against outside entry and have alarms. There's the loading dock. We lock those doors every afternoon at five. And then we go through the tunnel to the laundry and lock up there."

"Tunnel?"

"The laundry's in a separate building connected through a tunnel."

"Mind showing me?"

They descended to the basement and followed a corridor that brought them to an old, gated elevator. Laundry carts fitted with canvas bags were parked on either side of the elevator door. Bo and O'Meara took the elevator up a floor to the main laundry room, which was large and lined with industrial washers and dryers. Long tables were set in the middle for folding linen. Except for a man working on a pile of linen at one of the tables, the place was empty. The room felt stifling from the heat that had been generated during the day by the big machines. Classical music poured from a boom box on the table where the man folded linen. Bo spotted the exit door to the laundry, walked to it, and swung it open. The door led out to a small parking lot. Although the August afternoon was hot, the outside air felt cool compared to what lay trapped in the laundry.

"You say you lock up at five?"

"That's right," O'Meara confirmed.

"What happens if this door is opened after it's been locked?"

"An alarm goes off. Unless it's been disabled there." He pointed at the wall, to a metal plate and switch labeled ALARM.

Bo pulled the door closed. It was only four o'clock, and O'Meara made no move to lock up yet.

"The laundry staff has left for the day?"

"They're off at three. Only one here is that man, Max Ableman. He's the whole night shift."

"I'd like to talk to him."

"Hey, Max!" O'Meara called out.

The man seemed to notice them for the first time. He paused in his work and eyed them, but he made no move to come their way. Bo walked to him. O'Meara followed.

"Locking up already?" Max Ableman asked.

He was of average height and build, but Bo could see that his body was taut and muscular. He had thinning blond hair. His voice was gentle, feathery.

"No," O'Meara replied. "Just showing Agent Thorsen around. He's Secret Service."

Ableman nodded.

"Nice music," Bo said. "Debussy?"

Ableman shrugged. "It's quiet. That's all I care about."

"Mr. Ableman, after the doors are locked, do you ever step outside? For a smoke, say?"

"I don't smoke."

"Fresh air then? Maybe leave the door open for a while?"

"Never."

"You don't think it's hot in here?"

"You get used to it."

"I suppose," Bo allowed, although the man had rolled the sleeves of his T-shirt all the way up to his shoulders.

"Haven't seen you for a couple of days," O'Meara said in a friendly way.

"Flu," Ableman replied. He didn't seem interested in offering them anything further, but neither did he seem concerned that they'd disturbed his solitude.

"Thank you for your time," Bo said. He turned and headed away with O'Meara. "Those scars on his upper arms, any idea what they're about?"

"I don't know," O'Meara replied. "He's new, just started a few weeks ago, and he never talks much. Maybe he was in the military or something."

"And what's with the sunglasses?"

"He's ultrasensitive to sunlight, as I understand it. That's why he works the night shift."

chapter

ten

I t was an evening affair, the kind the president loved.

Before dinner, the Texas Panhandlers performed some fancy clogging for Clay Dixon and the guests assembled in the East Room of the White House. Then the president made a brief speech about preserving the heritage of the nation's folk traditions. The meal itself, served in the State Dining Room, paid homage to American cooking—fried chicken, mesquite barbecued ribs, corn on the cob, collard greens, corn bread, and watermelon. Afterward, the Dixie Maids played some lively bluegrass, and Clay Dixon asked if he could join them. He borrowed a banjo and sat next to a black-haired fiddle player. She worked her bow with a vengeance, and his own fingers danced. The guests of the White House enjoyed an old-fashioned hoedown, and they gave the president an exploding round of applause while the cameras of the press corps flashed like fireworks. D. C. Dixon was in his element and had the world by the balls.

When it was over, he approached the senior senator from Colorado, who sat at the banquet table with the president's daughter leaning against him. Stephanie's eyes were closed, and she appeared to be asleep. The senator said, "She's dead tired. Long past this young lady's bedtime. Be glad to give a hand, Clay."

"I'll take care of it," the president said.

"After that, I'd like a word with you."

Dixon nodded. "In my study." He eased his daughter upright. "Time for bed, kiddo." He lifted her and she laid her head on his shoulder. He carried her upstairs and helped her shrug off her dress and put on her pajamas. He pulled the covers over her.

"Read," she murmured, though she could barely keep her eyes open.

Dixon kissed her softly and said, "Tomorrow. Go to sleep, sweetheart."

He waited until her breathing was regular, then he tiptoed out and went to his study. The senator was waiting for him.

Senator William Dixon walked with a cane, a necessity due to injuries sustained during the Second World War. He'd been a hero. A bona fide hero with an array of medals to prove it. On his next birthday he would be seventy-eight and, God and the electorate willing, into his eighth term in the Senate. He was tall and lean and, with the help of his cane, stood straight. His linen suit, wrinkled from sitting at the banquet, smelled of cigar smoke.

Clay Dixon asked, "Care for a brandy, Dad?"

"Supposed to be on the wagon. Doctor's orders. Supposed to be off cigars, too."

"I never knew you to be a man who paid much attention to what someone else said you should do." The president handed his father a snifter and poured one for himself. "What's on your mind?"

"Same thing that's on everybody's mind. Kate." Dixon swirled his brandy and eyed his son sternly. "You and I haven't always seen eye to eye. Especially about that girl."

"Woman, Dad."

"Girl, woman. All trouble." He spoke with a broad accent that hinted at Oklahoma, where he'd been born and raised before he migrated to the cattle country of southern Colorado. His speech was slow and deliberate, a pacing that had nothing to do with his age. He drew a cigar from the inside pocket of his coat. "Mind?"

Clay Dixon handed his father a silver ashtray. The senator slowly unwrapped the cigar, snipped the tip, and lit up with a wooden match from a small box he pulled from the pocket of his pants.

"You've done a fine job as president. I've been mighty proud of you, son."

"But."

"But now you need to make sure you've got a bridle on that bride of yours."

"I can handle Kate."

"Can you? My impression is that she's on the verge of doing something drastic. She isn't considering leaving you, is she?"

"My marriage is my concern."

"If it stands to affect your election, and I'm beginning to think it may, then it becomes a concern for many of us. You need to handle your wife."

"Don't presume to dictate to me regarding my marriage. You of all people."

The senator pointed his cigar at his son. "As a presidential candidate, Wayne White continues to be very appealing. A war hero. A widower. That old allegation of spousal abuse will be forgotten quickly if your own wife were to abandon you at this juncture. And if she were to speak frankly about why."

"What are you suggesting?"

"It's a great deal stronger than a suggestion. I speak for the party, I assure you. Do whatever is necessary to make certain Kate stays at your side. If she asks you to get down on your hands and knees and lick the floor, then, by God, you will lick it. Because if you lose her, you may well lose this election. But frankly, if circumstances were different, it wouldn't break my heart if she left you."

"Dad—"

He waved off his son's objection. "We both know if I dropped dead tomorrow she'd do a little jig in celebration. I'm sure she believes I'm the devil himself, or at best one step away from him." He laughed, enjoyed a long draw on his cigar, then spoke through the haze he expelled. "Any man or woman who enters politics takes a few steps closer to the devil. Katie's a bright lady. I would have thought she understood that by now. In fact, considering that she *used* to share your bed, she should understand that occasionally one even has to sleep with the devil."

Although he tried not to show it, Clay Dixon was angry. Not so much at his father's barb as at the obvious fact that someone on the White House staff had been talking indiscreetly about the current sleeping arrangements in the Executive Residence. The telephone rang and he grabbed at it. "Yes?" He listened and said, "Send them up." He put the phone down. "John Llewellyn's on his way with McGill and Bobby Lee."

"They've got the most recent polls, I'd bet," William Dixon said. "By the way, how is Tom Jorgenson?"

"I spoke with Kate this afternoon. He's still unconscious."

"An unfortunate accident. Still, it will probably work to your advantage. Sympathy vote and all."

"What the hell kind of thing is that to say?"

"Nothing personal. You take your votes however you can get them." The elder Dixon rose, put his cigar in his left hand, took up his cane in his right, and walked to the door. He moved stiff as a man made of pipe cleaners. War had done much of that, time the rest. He put a hand on his son's shoulder. "Listen to me and to Llewellyn, Clay, and you'll be fine. You hear me?"

At the door to the Treaty Room, the senator encountered Llewellyn and the others.

"John," he said, extending his hand. "Good to see you."

"Senator."

"How's Doris?"

"Good. Waiting for an RSVP about Saturday night."

"RSVP? You know I'll be there."

"That's what I told her."

"I can see that you and the president have business. Good night, John. Gentlemen." He nodded to McGill and Lee, and he caned his way down the center hall toward the elevator.

"Was your father here on business or pleasure?" Llewellyn asked as he entered the study.

"The senator is never all about one thing. Brandy?" Dixon offered the others after they'd come in.

They declined, and the president decided that he'd had enough.

"How's Kate holding up?" his chief counsel asked.

"Fine, Bobby. I spoke with her this afternoon. She's hanging in there. Ed, I thought you'd gone home for the day."

"I was hoping to get an early report on the polls," McGill said.

"And did you?"

"Yes."

"Well?"

"Wayne White still has you by a margin that concerns us." He seemed to have more to say, but was reluctant.

"Go on."

"We believe it's because you didn't accompany the First Lady to Minnesota," McGill said.

"What?"

"It may have made you appear callous."

"It might help if you were to join her in Minnesota," Llewellyn said.

"Jesus Christ, John. This isn't a national disaster. I can't simply drop everything and go running to Kate. I leave for the Pan-American summit in less than two weeks. Before that I have a dozen campaign appearances. To say nothing of a government to run."

"This is different," Ed McGill argued cautiously. "He's your father-in-law, a man much in the hearts of Americans these days. Also, maintaining proximity to the First Lady would be helpful."

"It sounds like everybody's suggesting I ride into the White House on Kate's skirt."

"It will show your compassionate side," McGill said.

Clay Dixon exploded. "I showed my compassionate side by throwing my support behind the Basic Human Services Bill."

"This is different," Bobby Lee said quietly. "This is about family."

"You agree I should go?"

"I do."

"Tom Jorgenson doesn't like me."

"He's comatose. He won't even know you're there," Llewellyn said. "It would be very good for your image, sir."

Lee said, "You could easily join Kate for a day or two as a show of concern, of marital solidarity in this difficult time."

Dixon breathed out his anger. "When?"

"It will take a couple of days to set up," his chief of staff replied. "But Ed will have Patricia give a statement at the press briefing tomorrow morning."

"All right." Now Dixon felt ready for another brandy. "Is there something else?"

"No, sir," Llewellyn said. "I'll bid you good night."

"Bobby?" Dixon said as Lee turned to leave. "Could I have a word with you?"

The president closed the door behind the others, then walked to the window and stared through his own reflection into the night. "The economy's healthy. We're not at war. Crime is on the decline. But what do the American people care about? They care whether I scurry to the side of a man who doesn't particularly like me and a woman who, at the moment, treats me like a leper."

"If he dies and you didn't make a visit, you risk appearing heartless," Lee pointed out.

The president put out his hand and touched his image in the glass. "Before I married Kate, I asked him for his daughter's hand, did you know that, Bobby? I thought it was respectful. He said it didn't matter what he thought. The choice was Kate's. When I pressed him, he said, 'It's a rare man who doesn't become his father.' He never did give me his blessing. And when I ran for president, same thing.

Because of who my father is, he refused to give me his endorsement." He turned back to his chief counsel. "I'm not my father."

"No," Bobby said. "You're not. But almost everyone who advises you now speaks for the senator. The truth is he's casting a huge shadow over the White House, Clay."

"He'll get me reelected."

"Will he? The polls don't seem to be saying that. You know what I think? The American people want you to step away from your father so they can see clearly again just who you are. They'd love to see you leading the team."

"Do you have any numbers to back that up?"

"Gut feeling."

"Thanks, Bobby. I'll take that under advisement."

"Are you all right, Clay?"

"Just tired. I'll see you in the morning."

Dixon picked up the report Lorna Channing had delivered to him a couple of days earlier. So far, he'd had time only to glance at it. He took the document to his bedroom where he put on his pajamas, washed his face, brushed his teeth, and donned his reading glasses. He lay down on his bed, but found that he couldn't concentrate.

He was thinking about the things Bobby Lee had said. And he was thinking about Alan Carpathian, the man who'd been more a father to him than the senator had ever been.

When Carpathian died, something significant inside Clay Dixon had died with him. Certainty. That cocky assuredness that Carpathian had teased him about but loved. What replaced it was something very like terror. Without Carpathian's game plan, Carpathian's political savvy, Carpathian's unflagging optimism, Dixon felt paralyzed, absolutely afraid to move. It was like the nightmares he'd had while he was a quarterback, that he was on the field in the middle of an important game and he'd forgotten every play.

The senator had saved him, in a way. But you had to pay the devil sometime, and Dixon was feeling more and more that what was required of him was nothing less than his soul.

He put the report aside, took off his glasses, and thought about something more pleasant. Lorna Channing. Lately, a lot of his thinking eventually worked its way around to Lorna Channing. In the middle of briefings with her, he sometimes found himself amazed at the beautiful green of her eyes, the way she held her lips when she listened. He realized that whenever she walked away, he was already looking forward to the time when she would return. He didn't fool himself with the idea that it was love. But he knew that in its way, it was a force nearly as compelling.

He glanced at the heavy document that lay on the pillow where Kate's head used to rest. He'd requested the study to fulfill his promise to his wife and to please her, but she hadn't even bothered to look at it. The silence of its company was a bitter and lonely statement.

He closed his eyes, and when he fell asleep, it wasn't the voice of Kate he heard in his dreaming but the soft, chocolate laugh of the woman he'd known so well on the Purgatoire River.

chapter

eleven

W hen Nightmare was very young, his mother sometimes slept with him. He remembered the feel of her, warm through the flannel of her nightgown, her arms around him protectively. Her smell would stay on his thin pillow and unwashed sheets for a long time. When he was alone, he would bury himself there and breathe in the ghost of her presence.

Often he wouldn't see her for days. He would find plates of food on the basement stairs, left when he was sleeping, and after he put the empty plates back, they would eventually be gone. When she next appeared, her face would be pale, occasionally bruised, and her eyes would be distant. Her hair was long and dirty. Her clothes were drab. He would sit with her on the bed and they would be quiet together. Sometimes her lips moved as if she were talking to someone in the basement shadows, but if she spoke loud enough for him to hear, her words made little sense. Even these visits he cherished, for she was all he had.

When he was older, she would unlock the basement door after the old man had gone to sleep. She held a finger to her lips to keep him silent, and she led him outside, where they would walk together in the night. She couldn't see well, not like him for whom the dark was an old friend. He would take her hand and lead her. Away from the rotting old house. Away from the barn that was little more than a loose skeleton of weathered boards. Away from the monster sleeping in the second-floor bedroom. In the winter, nights were silent except for the crunch of their feet on the snow. In summer, the night air was alive with music, the song of tree frogs from the woods and bullfrogs in the marshy meadow and crickets everywhere. Mostly, she was sad, and he never tried to make her happy. He was sad, too, alone all day in the dark beneath the house. That's just the way people were. Sad. Or they were angry, like his grandfather. They were monsters, or they were the servants of monsters. Their souls were corrupt—born corrupt, beyond redemption—and they deserved to live in the dark, or they lived in the light, as his grandfather did. Above in the light. His mother lived there, too, but she would often visit Nocturne at night, in the basement where the old man seldom came.

Nocturne. That was how he thought of himself then, for that was what she called him. He'd never been given a real name. His existence had never been officially recorded. His grandfather sometimes called him "boy" or "spawn," but his mother called him Nocturne. It was the music of the night, she explained to him in one of her more lucid moments. Among the junk on the shelves in the basement, he'd found an old phonograph. It hadn't worked when he discovered it, but he tinkered, something he had a lot of time to do, and he coaxed the turntable into motion and began to listen to the old 78s he found boxed on the shelves. His mother told him they'd belonged to his grandmother and that when she died, the old man had put them in the basement, put away all reminders of her, and that he'd buried her in the fields somewhere. Some nights when Nocturne walked with his mother, she stopped and listened for a long time. She's crying, she would say. Do you hear her?

Yes, he would answer, although he heard only the frogs and the crickets.

They would walk in silence back to the house, to the basement, and Nocturne would put something gentle and sad on the phonograph, and they would sit on his old bed together in the dark while she wept.

At 10:30 P.M., in the laundry of the St. Croix Regional Medical Center, the man known to his coworkers as Max Ableman turned off his boom box. It had been a good evening. Except for the interruption by the Secret Service agent, everything had been quiet. Although Thorsen had surprised him, Nightmare wasn't greatly alarmed. In fact, there was one aspect of Thorsen's presence and questions that pleased him. If Thorsen was nosing around the hospital, it meant he was concerned about Jorgenson as well as Jorgenson's daughter. He was looking in two directions. His attention was divided. Nightmare knew the first rule of any successful operation was focus.

From his clothes locker, Nightmare took a roll of silver duct tape and a sealed glass cylinder fifteen inches long and five inches in diameter. He also lifted a small armload of dirty linen from a pile in front of one of the washers. He descended the stairs to the tunnel, selected a laundry cart, put the cylinder in the cart, and covered it with the soiled linen. Then he headed to the main hospital building. He rode the freight elevator to the fourth floor. The nurses in trauma ICU paid no attention to him as he went about his normal duty of collecting the laundry. He spent a few extra minutes in the room of a man who'd flatlined the night before, then he crossed to the room where Tom Jorgenson lay comatose. He had to wait less than thirty seconds before the alarm went off, signaling another cardiac arrest on the far side of the ICU. He heard the nurses call a Code Blue, and they directed their attention to the situation. He had a window of a few minutes.

He reached into the cart and drew out the glass cylinder and the duct tape. Inside the cylinder, cradled among Styrofoam pellets, was a length of one-and-a-quarter-inch PVC pipe. The pipe, capped and sealed to be airtight, contained C-4, a volatile plastic explosive. The

C-4 was fitted with a detonator that could be triggered remotely. A vacuum surrounded the pipe, a precaution that would prevent the scent of the C-4 from being detected by bomb dogs. The inner surface of the glass was coated with common airplane glue. There was enough air in the sealed PVC pipe itself to allow detonation of the C-4. In addition to the destruction caused by the explosion, the glue-coated fragments of glass would be like burning shrapnel, setting the room ablaze. Nightmare intended to attach the device to the underside of the bed with the duct tape and to detonate it the next time the First Lady visited.

He knelt beside the bed and leaned close to the man who lay there.

"Do you remember your *Iliad?* 'The day shall come, that great avenging day, which Troy's proud glories in the dust shall lay, when Priam's powers and Priam's self shall fall, and one prodigious ruin swallow all.' Old man, that great avenging day has come. You will die and the Troy you built on your lies will crumble." He glanced back through the door. The nurses were still occupied with the Code Blue. "But I wanted to give you something to take into the darkness with you. I wanted you to know *she's* going to die with you. That's why I didn't kill you in the orchard. I knew they would bring you here, and I knew she would come."

"Ableman, what are you doing?" The security guard filled the doorway.

Nightmare stood up and quickly tucked loose bedding into the mattress. "Straightening his bed."

"That's the nurses' job," Randy O'Meara said.

"They're busy trying to save a life." Nightmare dropped the bomb and tape back into the laundry cart.

"You were saying something to him," O'Meara pressed him.

"Praying for him."

"Didn't sound like a prayer to me."

Nightmare slipped past the guard and shoved his cart down the hallway. He made for the stairway.

The guard followed him. "Ableman, what did you put in that cart?"

Nightmare reached the stairway door and abandoned his cart. He hurried through the doorway into the concrete shaft of the stairwell, pressed himself against the wall, and waited.

Damn. He'd given in to weakness, to a desire to taunt his enemy, the mistake of a green recruit. And this was the result. This was always the result when you let yourself go, even for a moment. Now he would have to risk much.

When Randy O'Meara swept through in pursuit, Nightmare leaped at his back. He used the bigger man's momentum, pushed him forward, and hooked the guard's ankle with his foot. O'Meara didn't even have time to call out before he tumbled down the hard, concrete steps. He lay on the next landing, groaning. Nightmare sailed down the stairs, knelt, grasped the guard's head in the crook of his arm, and gave his neck a powerful twist. He could feel the satisfying snap of bone against his own muscle. Afterward, he quickly mounted the stairs and checked the hallway. The nurses were still working on the Code Blue patient. No one seemed to have noticed him or O'Meara. He glanced back down at the dead man. Something more had to be done to cover the deed, and Nightmare, who was no stranger to tense situations, knew exactly what that was.

chapter

twelve

Bo woke before dawn, as he sometimes did, from a dream of the days with his street family, Egg and Pearl and Otter and Freak. In the dream, they were all in the abandoned school bus, which floated on a river that was sweeping them away. Slowly, the bus was going under. Bo fought the steering wheel, but he could not make it turn toward shore. The dream was no mystery to him. He was still trying to save them. And still failing.

As a gray light crept over the orchards at Wildwood, Bo left his bed and checked in with Nick Pappas, the agent on duty in the Op Center. It had been a quiet night. Bo changed into his sweats and went for a run. He headed to the edge of the orchard along the river bluff and ran the perimeter of the Jorgenson land twice, a total distance of two miles. The grass was covered with dew, and his leather running shoes were soaked by the time he returned to the barn. He took a pair of four-ounce fingerless bag gloves and a black leather heavybag from where he kept them stored in a long bin. He hung the bag from a hook he'd installed long ago in one of the crossbeams.

Along with hay bales and orchard implements, he shared the barn with a plasma cutter, an angle grinder, a heating torch, and several half-formed iron sculptures taken from the studio of Roland Jorgenson when it was converted into the guesthouse. The dusty unfinished pieces and the equipment were among the few reminders left at Wildwood that once a famous artist had been at work there. The sculptures were wild things that gave the feel of monstrous forces barely contained. He didn't know much about Roland Jorgenson, but there was definitely something about the man's work that Bo found disturbing. In the bin where he kept his heavybag, Bo had come upon a portfolio containing early sketches for the sculpture *Goddess*. Accompanying the sketch on one of the pages was a note scribbled in what he guessed was the artist's hand: *For Kathleen*. Bo was no judge of art, but he thought the sculpture, if indeed it was supposed to represent Kate Dixon, did her no justice. He'd given the portfolio to Annie Jorgenson and had no idea what had become of it.

He donned the gloves and worked the bag for half an hour before Chris Manning appeared in the doorway, sunlight at his back.

"We just got a call from the sheriff's office. One of the security guards at the St. Croix Medical Center fell down some stairs last night and broke his neck. Fatal."

Bo pulled off the gloves and wiped the sweat from his face with his T-shirt, which was itself soaked with sweat. "Who?"

"Guy named Randy O'Meara."

Bo's gut twisted hard. "Give me the details."

Manning explained that at the change of shift, the security guard had not checked in. The other guards did a search and found O'Meara's body on the stairs.

"Which stairwell?"

"Does it matter?"

"It might. Did anybody see anything?"

"No, but it's pretty clear what happened. There were some marbles lying on the floor just inside the stairway door. O'Meara must have slipped on them and taken a fall. The marbles came from an aquarium in the ICU. There's an elderly patient—"

"Mr. Cooper," Bo interrupted.

"Right. The sheriff's people checked his room. The sleeve of his robe was soaked and there were some marbles in one of the pockets."

"Did he admit to anything?"

"According to the sheriff, he claims he doesn't remember taking the marbles."

"Have they scheduled an autopsy?"

"Medical examiner's doing it this morning."

"You think it's an accident?"

"Looks like."

"Just like Tom Jorgenson's," Bo said.

Manning looked at his watch. "We've got a briefing in twenty minutes. Get a shower. We'll talk more then."

Twenty minutes later, Bo sat down at the table in the library of the guesthouse. Manning and his people, Stu Coyote, and the agents on the duty roster for the Op Center that day were all there. Manning began the briefing by explaining the incident at the hospital. He nodded in Bo's direction, and his lips twitched in a way that was almost a smile. "Agent Thorsen, our own Oliver Stone, has scripted a conspiracy. He believes that the tractor accident wasn't, in fact, an accident. And I'm guessing he believes that what occurred last night is somehow related to—what is it, Thorsen? An assassination plot?"

"I believe, Chris, that more may be going on than is apparent to us at this time."

Any hint of a smile left Manning's face. "Let's assume for the moment what Agent Thorsen believes is true. This means that whenever the First Lady is in proximity to her father, we all need to be especially vigilant. Is that understood?"

"We should inform the First Lady," Bo said.

"Absolutely not. No one's going to mention a thing to her. She has enough to worry about."

"Additional security for Tom Jorgenson would be appropriate."

"Not our jurisdiction. Former vice presidents don't get our protection."

"Listen, Chris, if there's even a remote possibility that I might be right—"

"Is there anyone here who feels as Agent Thorsen does?" Manning looked around the table. Not even Stu Coyote rose to Bo's defense. Manning again addressed Bo. "I'm willing, for the sake of the First Lady's safety, to grant you some leeway here and to take precautions as far as she's concerned. But our responsibility ends there. *Your* responsibility ends there. If you lose your focus on the security here, I will have you removed from this detail. Do you understand? Now, you indicated you sometimes put agents in the orchard to patrol the perimeter."

"Yes."

"Do it," Manning said.

During the rest of the briefing, Bo spoke no more about his concern. Afterward, Stu Coyote pulled him aside. "Sorry, Bo. Manning's a jerkoff, but he's right."

"No," Bo said. "I may be wrong, but Manning's not right. Tom Jorgenson needs protection."

The First Lady and Annie headed to the hospital at 10:00 A.M. Shortly after that, Bo directed Jake Russell to take charge of the Op Center, then he went to see the Washington County sheriff. Doug Quinn-Gruber repeated what Manning had reported.

"Which stairwell was O'Meara found in?" Bo asked.

"South. Between the third and fourth floors."

"That means O'Meara fell down the stairs from the fourth floor. That's where Jorgenson's room is," Bo pointed out. "South wing."

"And geriatrics, where Mr. Cooper is a patient, is on the third floor, south wing. Look, Bo, it all fits. The marbles. Mr. Cooper. Nobody saw anything unusual. And I got a call from the medical examiner a little while ago. O'Meara's broken neck and other injuries are consistent with a fall down the stairs. Look, if someone were going to kill Tom Jorgenson, why not just kill him? Why kill the guard?"

"I don't know."

"Because this is Tom Jorgenson, I've been trying to keep an open mind. But there continues to be no concrete evidence of an assault, or even a motive for one. Still, I'll tell you what I'll do. I'll put a deputy outside his hospital room, at least until we're absolutely certain there's nothing funny going on. How's that?"

"Fair enough, Doug."

"Detective Timmons is checking a few other possibilities. If he comes up with anything, I'll let you know."

"Thanks."

Before leaving the sheriff's office, Bo got an address for Maria Rivera, the head nurse in ICU the night before. She lived in a town house in one of the new subdivisions of Stillwater. Although it was a little past noon when he rang her doorbell, Bo was concerned that, because of her late working hours, she might still be sleeping. He needn't have worried. When Maria Rivera opened the door, she looked as if she hadn't been able to sleep at all.

"You're Secret Service," she said, squinting at him in the sunlight. She wore a white terry cloth robe, no slippers. Her black hair, streaked with silver, was unbrushed.

"Yes, I spoke with you yesterday afternoon," Bo said.

"What do you want?"

"To ask a few questions, if you don't mind."

She stood aside and let him in.

It was a clean, well-kept home. White carpeting, vacuumed. Nice light-maple furniture. A new sofa, pastel floral design. A crucifix carved of dark wood hung prominently on one wall. Atop a bookcase sat framed photographs of what Bo imagined were children and grandchildren. In the center was a photo of a younger Maria Rivera with a handsome Hispanic man. They were smiling happily.

She saw Bo noticing. "My husband, Carlos. He passed away two years ago."

"I'm sorry."

"He is in God's hands now."

As Bo had noticed the previous afternoon, she spoke with a slight accent. "I'd like to ask about last night," he told her.

"I feel terrible. I should have insisted Mr. Cooper be restrained."

"Did you see Mr. Cooper last night?"

"No. But often we don't. He's so quiet, like a cat. For an old man, so quick."

"He denied taking the marbles?"

"No. He said he didn't remember. He often claims he doesn't remember."

"Claims?"

"Who can say?"

"As nearly as the sheriff's people can tell, the accident occurred sometime between ten and eleven-thirty P.M. After visiting hours. Did you, or anyone else, notice someone on the floor who shouldn't have been there?"

"No. I didn't anyway. And I don't recall anybody mentioning anything like that."

"But someone would have noticed?"

"Probably."

"How about regular staff? Would you have noticed regular hospital staff on the floor?"

"What do you mean?"

"A stranger you would have seen. But someone who should have been there, say for example Randy O'Meara, would you have noticed?"

"Not necessarily. Unless he stopped to talk."

"Who else?"

"I beg your pardon."

"Who else comes onto the floor that you might not notice if they were just doing their job? Particularly between ten and eleven-thirty P.M."

"Let's see." She thought a moment. "Orderlies. But usually we've requested their help. Housekeeping, although they're normally finished on the floor by ten. Central Service staff, but only if we've ordered supplies. The laundry man. Maintenance, sometimes. Sometimes a doctor. Why are you asking?"

"It's the nature of the job, Ms. Rivera. I ask a lot of questions, then I sort through answers."

"You're responsible for the First Lady's safety. What does the accident have to do with her?"

"Probably nothing, but we need to be certain, you understand."

"Yes."

"Thank you for your time." He turned back toward the door. As he stepped outside, he offered her his hand in parting and said, "I hope you're not taking the responsibility for what happened to Randy O'Meara on your shoulders. No one could have predicted it."

"Everyone says that. Why don't I believe it?"

She let go of his hand and closed the door.

Dee Johnson, assistant director of human resources for the St. Croix Regional Medical Center, greeted him cordially. "Come in, Agent Thorsen. Please sit down." She was a tall, handsome woman, a big-boned Scandinavian with a small-town demeanor, open and friendly. "Thorsen," she said, taking her seat at her desk. "There are lots of Thorsens out where I grew up."

"Where was that?" Bo asked.

"Blue Earth."

"No kidding. Ever hear of Harold and Nell Thorsen?"

"Oh, sure. They had that farm out north of town. Took in all those foster kids."

"I was one of those foster kids."

"Well, for goodness' sake. Can you beat that? Foster, you say? But you have the same last name."

"I changed it legally."

"Well, what do you know? Did you graduate from Blue Earth High?"

"I sure did."

"I don't remember you. But you look like you were probably a few years behind me. Go Cyclones," she said with a huge smile and a lift of her arms, reminiscent of the cheerleader she probably had been. "What can I do for you?"

"I'd like some information on the hospital staff. You do the hiring for most support services?"

"The initial screening anyway. Then I send the applicants to the department that's hiring."

"I'm interested in anyone who may have been hired recently for the shift that would cover the time between ten and eleven-thirty P.M."

Her face assumed a solemn cast. "The time of Randy O'Meara's accident."

"Yes."

"May I ask why?"

"The First Lady is visiting here on a daily basis. We want to be sure that anything unusual isn't somehow related to her safety. You understand."

"Of course." She accepted it without further question and spent a moment thinking. "We've hired two people for evening support service positions in the last six weeks. An orderly and a man for the laundry."

"Max Ableman."

"You know him?"

"I met him yesterday. What can you tell me about him?"

"Nothing really. I haven't had any contact with him since he was hired."

"Do you have a personnel file for him?"

"I'm sure it's thin at this point."

"Do you have his job application?"

"Of course."

"May I see it?"

"I'll have my secretary pull it."

Dee Johnson left the office for a moment. Bo's cell phone rang.

"Bo, it's Jake Russell. Manning and Dreamcatcher just returned from the hospital. He's mad as hell you're not here. He's on the phone to Diana Ishimaru right now."

"Thanks, Jake. I'll be back as soon as I can. Aside from Manning, is everything else quiet?"

"As a cemetery."

When he had Ableman's application, Bo looked it over carefully. Maxwell Frederick Ableman. Born in Duluth on April 1, 1960. Graduated from East High School there. Briefly attended a technical school in Bemidji. Worked for a landscaping firm in Milaca for ten years, then a couple of years as a short-order cook in Brainerd. His last job had been with E.L. Tool & Die in Sandstone, a job he'd left, according to his application, because the company closed.

"Did you check any of his job references?" Bo asked Dee Johnson.

She looked guilty. "The position he applied for is a hard one to fill. The hours are bad, the pay is low, and it requires handling unpleasantly soiled linen. I was just happy to get an applicant."

"You said you also hired an orderly. What can you tell me about him?"

"Tyrone Posely. He goes to school days at Metropolitan State University and works here nights. He's married, has one child."

"All this is verified?"

"Yes, I can vouch for Tyrone."

"May I have a copy of Max Ableman's application?"

"I'll have my secretary make one." As she stood, she asked, "Should we be concerned about Mr. Ableman?"

"I wouldn't say that, no. As I indicated, it's all routine. But I'd appreciate it if, for the time being, you didn't mention this to anyone."

When he left the hospital, Bo knew he should get back immediately to Wildwood. However, there was one stop he wanted very much to make.

The address on Ableman's application was a motor court outside Bayport, a river community just south of Stillwater. The motor court was old, white stucco, shaded by two big oak trees. A few decades earlier, it might have been a decent destination if you wanted to enjoy the river. Now it looked like the kind of place where you went to enjoy a different type of diversion. The sign on the Bayport Court indicated there was a ACANCY. Although it also indicated that rooms were available by the week and month, Bo figured the old place catered to a clientele mostly interested in rooms by the hour. In the office, he asked after Max Ableman and was directed to room number ten. Except for Bo's Contour, only two vehicles were parked in the potholed lot, a green Chevy pickup, a decade old and covered with dust, and a new, shiny, red Mustang. The pickup was in front of number ten, more or less. Bo noted the plate. The room curtains were drawn. Bo knocked on the door. No one answered. The sound of a television came through the window screen two rooms down, but from number ten, there wasn't a peep. He tried the knob. The door was locked. He checked his watch. Too early for Ableman to be at work. Bo knocked again, then decided he'd visit the laundry later on, provided Manning hadn't got him removed from protective detail in the meantime.

Bo turned and headed for his car. He didn't see behind him the slight parting of the curtains in number ten. He didn't feel at all the tiny red dot that settled on the back of his head. And he didn't hear the whisper that escaped Nightmare's lips as he watched Bo retreating.

"Bang!"

chapter

thirteen

Diana Ishimaru's silver Sable was parked near the guest-house. She was waiting inside. She and Manning were quiet when Bo walked in, but he had the feeling a good deal had already been said.

"Why don't we talk in the library?" Ishimaru suggested.

Bo went first, Manning after him, and finally Diana Ishimaru, who closed the door behind them.

"Thorsen," Manning began, "I thought we discussed this."

Ishimaru cut him off. "Just a moment, Agent Manning. Bo?" She looked to him for an explanation.

"Someone tried to kill Tom Jorgenson," Bo said.

"You have proof?"

"Nothing solid, but put everything together and it adds up."

"But you don't have any proof," she said.

"No."

"Any suspects?"

"Not at the moment. There's someone I'd like to check out a bit more."

"A motive?"

"I probably won't know why until I know who."

Diana Ishimaru gave her head a faint, unhappy shake. "I just got off the phone, talking with the Washington County sheriff. He appreciates your concern, but he doesn't share it. However, he has assured me that he'll keep a deputy posted outside Tom Jorgenson's room until further notice. And he has a detective assigned to the case. Bo," she said, almost regretfully, "this is no longer your concern."

"It should never have been," Manning threw in.

S.A.I.C. Ishimaru cast Agent Manning a cold look, then continued addressing Bo. "I need you to focus on Wildwood."

"Jake Russell's been in charge during any absence I've felt was necessary. He's as familiar with security here as I am."

"But Operations is your responsibility," she reminded him. "I know you would be the first to agree that a constant and consistent appraisal of the situation and environment is essential to effective security. I need you here, Bo. One hundred percent. The safety of the First Lady demands it." She stopped there and waited.

Bo knew that she was speaking carefully and dramatically because Manning's complaint was formal and much was at stake. "I'm here," he said.

"Good. Agent Thorsen, Agent Manning, I believe we've concluded our business."

Manning, who usually displayed his emotion as conspicuously as he did his underwear, was obviously upset. "That's it?"

She glared at Manning. "Did you want me to spank him, too?"

Bo walked her to her car. The sun was low in the sky. They stood in the long shadow of the maples, and Diana Ishimaru spoke quietly. "Are you okay, Bo?"

"Yes."

"We all care about him," she said. "But if he were able, he'd tell you to take care of his daughter first."

"I know."

"And Manning is just doing his job."

"I know that, too."

"I figured you did. Stay in touch." She got in her car and drove away.

Bo went into the Op Center and tried to call Detective Timmons at the Washington County Sheriff's Department. Timmons was unavailable. Bo asked to speak to the sheriff. He explained to Doug Quinn-Gruber his concern about Max Ableman and suggested the sheriff run a check of the man on the NCIC computer and also a check of the plate on the pickup parked at the Bayport Court.

"Thanks, Bo. We'll take it from here. But I'll let you know what we find out."

Bo sat down and looked over the log kept in the Op Center. Nothing indicated a need for concern. He checked the duty roster. It occurred to him that an electronic sweep of Wildwood still hadn't been completed. His own concern about Tom Jorgenson, coupled with Manning's objections, had kept him from seeing to it. The phone rang just as he'd begun to consider a good time for the sweep.

"Thorsen, here."

"This is Deputy Williams at the Washington County Sheriff's Office. The sheriff asked me to pass along some information."

"Go ahead."

"We didn't come up with anything on Ableman, Maxwell Frederick. The vehicle with the plate number you gave us is registered to Luther J. Gallagher, 352 Platte Street, St. Peter, Minnesota."

"Luther Gallagher," Bo repeated as he wrote it out on a notepad.

"Right."

"Deputy Williams, could I ask a favor?"

"Fire away."

"Would you check and see whether Gallagher has a criminal record, and if there's a photo available? And could you fax me that information?"

"I'd be happy to."

"Thanks."

The agents assigned to evening duty arrived. Bo briefed them all, and they relieved their day counterparts. He heated some of Sue Lynott's famous chicken and dumplings on the stove, then went into the Op Center.

He stood with his plate in his hand, eating as he scanned a screen that held an outline of the Wildwood perimeter. Two dots moved along the perimeter lines. These were the agents Manning had requested Bo detail to patrol the orchard. Each carried a transmitter that relayed the agent's location. If one of the dots stopped moving for too long, the Op Center would do a radio check to make sure there wasn't an agent down.

Before he could finish his dinner, he got a call from Chris Manning.

"The First Lady would like to see both of us right now."

Annie, the First Lady, and Chris Manning were in the kitchen of the main house. The room had a southern exposure and was full of early evening light. The windows were open, and a nice breeze came through the screens. Annie sat at the table with the First Lady. Manning stood leaning against the kitchen sink. A frosted pitcher was on the table, along with empty glasses.

"Tea, Bo?" Annie offered. She smiled, but Bo knew something else was behind her pleasant demeanor.

"Thank you, no. You wanted to see me, Mrs. Dixon?"

If earlier, Kathleen Jorgenson Dixon had appeared to be a simple country girl, she seemed anything but at the moment. She sat erect, assuming a solid, commanding aspect in the way she regarded both agents.

"I'm aware, have been aware for some time, of friction between the two of you. I'd like to know what's going on."

"It's of a personal nature," Bo said.

"If I feel that it affects my security, and I do, then it is no longer personal."

Manning said, "I assure you, whatever history exists between Agent Thorsen and me—"

The First Lady cut him off. "Chris, I want to know what's going on."

Manning's eyes flicked to Bo, and he said, "Agent Thorsen slept with the woman I was going to marry."

"She had no intention of marrying you," Bo said.

"We had an understanding."

"Maybe you did. She certainly didn't."

"Excuse me," the First Lady interjected. "How long ago was this?"

"Ten years," Manning said.

"Ten years?" The First Lady gave them a withering look. "My God, nations have waged major war and reconciled in less time."

The anger that had momentarily enlivened Manning's face seemed to disappear, and he said, "I assure you that whatever feelings Agent Thorsen and I may have toward each other, we're both quite able to put those aside and do our duty. Right, Bo?"

Manning had finally called him by his first name. Bo wasn't sure what that meant, but he agreed with the sentiment. "Yes. Absolutely."

"All right then," the First Lady said with a nod. "The next issue. When we left the hospital this afternoon, I noticed that a sheriff's deputy had been posted outside my father's room. What's that all about?"

Bo said, "I arranged for it."

"Why?"

"Considering the threats your father has received in the past, I thought it best. He's vulnerable right now."

"Right now? Agent Thorsen, if someone wanted to kill my father, they could easily shoot him when he's out alone in the orchard. Does this have anything to do with the questions you asked my aunt the other night about his accident?"

"Yes."

"What specifically?"

Bo looked at Manning, who gave no sign of his own feelings on the subject, then he proceeded to explain his concerns point by point.

The First Lady listened carefully. When Bo had finished, she asked, "You've pursued this investigation on your own authority?"

"Yes."

"I see. And what do you think of all this, Chris?"

"I don't want to make it seem as if I'm not giving any credence to Agent Thorsen's concerns. And I'm sure you would prefer that all precautions be taken in protecting your father. The reality is that any investigation related to your father's present condition is not our responsibility or jurisdiction. Your safety, not your father's, should be our only concern."

"I appreciate your position, Chris. How do you feel about this, Bo?

"My responsibility is here, protecting you at Wildwood."

"And if I prefer otherwise?"

Bo considered for a moment her stern, gray eyes. "With all due respect, your preference is not what governs my actions."

"I see." She folded her hands and regarded both men with an unflinching gaze. Finally she said, "Very well."

Agent Manning excused himself. "I have duties to attend to."

Bo started after him, and Annie rose. "Bo, let me see you out." She took his arm.

As they walked to the front door, Bo said, "I'm sorry about in there." He nodded back toward the kitchen. "But my hands are tied, Annie."

"You think that's the end of it?" She opened the door for him. As he stepped out she said, "You don't know Kate."

chapter

fourteen

The first time, he wasn't even fourteen years old.

The basement of the old farmhouse was home to Nocturne. In summer, the walls were cool and damp, home also to potato bugs, spiders, and centipedes. In winter, it was a cold, drafty place despite the ancient oil-burning furnace that heated water for the radiators upstairs. The basement was full of boxes stuffed with broken things and items that had belonged to Nocturne's grandmother and that the old man had put down there in order to forget. Nocturne's mother told him his grandmother had been a schoolteacher. Some boxes held books, some held magazines. Some were packed with clothing, others were full of small broken electrical appliances—a mixer, an iron, a table lamp, a heating pad, and the like. On her good, lucid days, his mother read to him. Although books and magazines were available, she always read from the Bible, always from the Old Testament. Sitting beside her, watching her finger move under the printed words, the boy had learned early to read on his own, and he loved it. In the long days by himself, he eventually went through all the printed material contained in the boxes, mostly elementary textbooks and stacks of *National Geographic*. He practically memorized every word of the books of the Bible. He devoured cover to cover a set of *Encyclopedia Britannica* with moldy pages. His favorite book was a sketchy biography of Harry Houdini. He also loved to fiddle with the old electric appliances so that he might understand their construction and make them run again. His mother was a reluctant conspirator. After he'd asked her many times, she sneaked him wire and tools. She cautioned him fearfully never to mention any of this to his grandfather, and Nocturne obeyed her absolutely.

There was an old RCA radio console in one corner that he worked on for weeks until he coaxed voices from the airwaves. From what he heard on the radio and read in his books, he formed ideas of the outside world. Although he loved the dark of his basement, he longed to see more. He sensed that his life was odd and that he must be odd to be living it. Yet, there were people in the world stranger even than he, people with lips like dinner plates and necks stretched like giraffes and green tattoos over every inch of their faces. In such a world, one more freak would hardly be noticed. Locked in the basement, Nocturne dreamed of those places and people. On the nights his mother released him and they walked outside in the dark, he imagined they were in Africa, and in the trees gorillas slept, and somewhere out of sight a village of big-lipped, long-necked, tattooed people were waiting to welcome him. He loved the night and the walks, and he hated waiting to be released. So he began to plan his escape.

There was a laundry chute, no longer used, that dropped from the second-floor bathroom to the basement. Although he'd often stared up into the black of the shaft, he was nine years old before he thought of it seriously as a way out. One night he piled crates and boxes high enough beneath the opening so that when he stood on the top box, his torso fit inside the chute. It was a square, fifteen inches on each side, lined with smooth tin. He tried to pull himself up, but there was nothing to grasp. He pressed against the tin sides and only felt himself slip. He realized his clothing allowed him no traction. He climbed down, stripped naked, then mounted once again. This time when he pressed against the sides of the chute, his body held. He inched upward, pushing with his palms, holding with the press of his legs. He made progress, but it was hard work, and he soon gave up, exhausted after moving only a few feet.

He began to exercise, to strengthen his body and keep it supple. The pipes that hung from the basement ceiling and that carried water to the sinks and radiators above him served as an obstacle course. He climbed over them and around them, slipping between the metal and the beams and the floorboards. He made a game of it, timing himself with a clock he'd found broken in one of the boxes and had repaired. At first, he was covered with splinters from the ragged beams, but as he progressed he could move swiftly and safely. Within a few weeks, he was strong enough to inch his way up the chute all the way to the second-floor bathroom. The first time he eased out of the opening upstairs, he wanted to shout in triumph. It was the middle of the night, however, and not far from where Nocturne stood, the old man was sleeping. He discovered immediately that with every step the old floorboards creaked, crying out his presence. That first night, all he did was stand at the bathroom window, staring out at the night and the stars, listening to the crickets and breathing the air of freedom. The next night, he made it through the window, across the roof, and down the porch supports to the ground. After that, any time he wanted, he could be free. Over the years, as his body grew, he practiced a discipline of concentration and patience and learned how to fold his body into that small chute and move upward by expanding and contracting the appropriate muscles, much like a snake.

He never told his mother. He understood that unlocking the basement door for him was the only gift she had to offer. Because he learned to move as silently as a breath of air, his grandfather never knew.

But his grandfather did discover eventually that Nocturne had other talents.

The old man seldom visited the basement except to check on the ancient furnace that sometimes faltered. Nocturne kept to the far corners whenever his grandfather came down. In addition to trying to hide himself, he tried to keep secret all the tinkering he did. To that end, he was careful never to turn the volume on the old radio console much above a whisper. One night as he was attempting an adjustment, his fingers slipped, and the sound of the Beatles belting out "Twist and Shout" seemed to shake the walls. It scared the hell out of Nocturne, and he panicked, fumbling desperately with the knob. It was too late. He heard the boom of his grandfather's boots across the floor above him. The padlock rattled, and the basement door flew open. The steps shook as the old man stomped down. He grabbed the string on the light and yanked. Nocturne stood exposed, quaking beside the old radio.

"What the hell, boy?" He glared at Nocturne and the console.

Nocturne expected his grandfather to hit him. Instead, the old man seemed to notice for the first time all the accomplishments hidden in the dark of Nocturne's world, all the electrical appliances pulled from the boxes and restored to life. He said nothing, no word of praise or encouragement for a boy who, from books and his own imagination, had unraveled the mystery of the old machines and much more. He simply grunted, turned, and returned to the world above. The next day, Nocturne received another visit. This time his grandfather brought with him a book. In the light of the basement's twenty-five-watt bulb, the old man opened the book to a page and stabbed a yellow fingernail at a picture. "Can you build this?" he asked.

Nocturne looked at the picture. It was a diagram, a blueprint labeled with words such as *detonator*, *fuse*, and *timer*. He recognized it immediately for what it was, a fairly simple device. He gave his grandfather a nod. The old man turned away without another word and left.

That night, the basement door opened and the old man called him up. He handed Nocturne a jacket, and he started outside. Nocturne's mother cowered in a chair in the kitchen, looking at her son as if she were terribly afraid for him, but she said nothing to stop the old man. Nocturne followed his grandfather across the yard to the barn. They went inside to a room that held a workbench and tools and the book lying open on a stool. The old man pulled a cord and the light came on—a hundred-watt bulb that made Nocturne blink.

"You got everything you need here," his grandfather said. "Let me know when you're done." The old man left him.

Nocturne constructed the device in little more than an hour. He left it in the room and stepped into the barn. He'd been there many times since he'd conquered the laundry chute. To a boy whose only physical recreation had been pipes in a basement, the barn was a great playground. Although it was a dilapidated structure with gaps between the wallboards and in the ceiling, it had beams and rafters and posts and great height, and Nocturne often spent hours climbing and swinging there throughout the night. He knew he was supposed to tell his grandfather he was done with the bomb, but the temptation of the barn was tremendous, and Nocturne gave in, telling himself he would climb once to the roof, then go see his grandfather.

He was on a beam twenty-five feet above the floor when the old man walked in. Nocturne froze. He watched his grandfather cross to the room, open the door, and step inside. The old man came out holding the bomb.

"Boy!" he hollered.

Nocturne didn't want to answer, but he knew the old man would find him eventually. "Here," he said in a small voice.

The old man's eyes rose upward and grew large when he saw the precarious perch his grandson straddled.

"How'd you get up there?"

"Climbed."

"Then climb back down. Now."

Nocturne quickly obeyed. He stood before the old man with his eyes downcast. His grandfather said, "Look at me."

Nocturne did. With his opened hand, the old man struck him hard across the face.

"You do what I tell you, understand? No more, no less." The old man's voice was cold, but didn't sound angry.

Nocturne fought tears, and he nodded.

The old man held the bomb. "Will it work?"

Nocturne hadn't considered the question before. He saw clearly his grandfather expected an answer, and he quickly assessed the device he'd constructed. "Yes," he said. Then he added in almost a whisper, "But I would have built it different."

The old man looked up at the rafter, then down at Nocturne. "Get plenty of sleep, boy, you hear? We got work tomorrow night." He shoved his grandson ahead of him toward the house.

Nocturne was waiting when the old man came down the next night. His grandfather had a big rolled sheet of paper. He turned on the light and spread the paper on the basement floor. It was a crude drawing of a building.

The old man said, "This is a bad place, and you and me are going to do something about it. That thing you built yesterday, we're going to put it right in here." He pointed to a window on the third floor of the building. "You're going to put it in front of a bunch of filing cabinets—metal cabinets with lots of drawers, understand?"

Nocturne nodded.

"Good. Let's go."

They got into the old man's truck. Nocturne had never ridden in a vehicle before and the sensation was wonderful. It was fall and the night was cool. The old man had the windows wide open, and the air blew through with a force that thrilled the boy. The fields flew by. The yard lights that were all so distant from his grandfather's isolated house rushed toward them, then past. His grandfather said nothing, didn't even look in Nocturne's direction, just kept his hands on the wheel and his eyes on the road lit in the headlights. The device was in a small backpack between them on the seat, but Nocturne hardly noticed. He was out in the world at last.

They came to a place with many houses set closely together. Every corner had a bright light like the yard light of a farm. His grandfather drove down an empty street between brick buildings with glass windows that had writing on them. Stores, Nocturne recognized. Shops and businesses. He realized they were in a real town. Although he'd wandered as far as he could in the nights when he escaped the basement, the farmhouse was so distant from everything that a tiny crossroads called Higgens consisting of a bar, a gas station, and half a dozen houses was the nearest he'd ever come to a community. He wanted to know what town this was but was afraid to ask. They drove past a building of gray stone blocks, standing by itself in the middle of a patch of lawn. Carved into the stone above the door were the words COUNTY COURTHOUSE. His grandfather backed into an alley and parked facing the stone building.

"That's it," the old man said.

Nocturne looked at the building. It was three stories, taller even than his grandfather's barn. The barn had wood supports to shinny up, but the stone building looked flat and solid. How did the old man expect him to climb to the third floor?

As if he'd read his grandson's mind, he said, "There's a drainpipe. See it?" He pointed to a black line that ran down the side of the building from the gutters along the roof. "That's your way up." He handed the backpack to Nocturne. "I put a steel pipe in there. Use it to break the window. Don't worry about alarms. Only the first-floor doors and windows have 'em. I'll wait here."

There was no moon. Where the streetlamps threw light, Nocturne ran quickly from shadow to shadow—a trash can, a bench, a maple tree—until he reached the side of the building. The bottom of the drainpipe was lost among bushes, and Nocturne merged with the dark there. His heart pounded wildly. He was so scared he thought he might wet his pants. He reached for the drainpipe. The metal was cold, but it was ridged and easy to grasp. Nocturne looked up. The third floor seemed impossibly far away.

Climbing proved easier than he'd imagined. Hand over hand, he pulled himself up the pipe, using the indentations between the stone blocks for toeholds. Concentrating on his task, he forgot his fear, and when he reached the place where the drainpipe ran beside the third-floor windowsill, he looked around him. He was higher than anything else in the town except the water tower. He felt as if he could reach out and grab a handful of stars.

The headlights on the truck flashed once, reminding Nocturne of his task. Holding to the drainpipe with his right arm, he reached back with his other and drew out the length of one-inch black steel pipe to break the window. The pane shattered with a crash that seemed to break the night itself. Nocturne pressed against the cold stone and waited for something terrible to happen. Nothing did. Sharp, jagged shards were left framing the window. He used the pipe to tap them out, then he eased himself through. Inside, he found the bank of filing cabinets, and he put the device in front of them. He set the timer, then left the way he'd come.

When he reached the truck, the old man asked, "It's done?"

Nocturne nodded.

The old man drove out of the alley, down the street between the closed shops, past the dark houses, out where the farmland began. He pulled into a lane between fields of harvested corn and turned off the engine. He drew a pocket watch from his overalls and checked the time.

Nocturne sat as silent as his grandfather, looking toward town. He wasn't worried. He knew the device he'd built would work. He'd done just as his grandfather asked. It was now only a matter of waiting, and that was something he was very good at.

After a few minutes, Nocturne felt the old man stiffen. "It should have gone off by now." His grandfather's fierce eyes settled on him with a look that froze the boy's heart.

"Your watch," Nocturne offered timidly. "I think it's fast."

At that moment, the sound of a muffled explosion rolled across the open field. The old man's head jerked around, and he watched as an orange glow slowly bloomed in the dark among the buildings and the trees of the town. Without a word, without a sign that he was pleased with the boy's accomplishment, he started the truck and drove home.

Nocturne's mother waited at the back door. He could see that she'd been crying, but she didn't speak as he entered with his grandfather. The old man hung his coat on a peg near the door. He looked at the boy.

"Tomorrow, we'll move you to a room upstairs."

"I like the basement," Nocturne said.

The old man shrugged and started from the kitchen. He turned back before he left and said to his daughter, "Don't lock the basement door no more."

For an hour, Nightmare watched the monitor and listened as Kathleen Jorgenson Dixon sat with her communications director, Nicole Greene, in the office of the main house and discussed the commitments that had to be rescheduled due to her extended stay at Wildwood. She outlined correspondences to be written on her behalf, giving the other woman specific instructions regarding content and tone. She spent an hour on the telephone—briefly with her husband, then for a longer time with her daughter, then with the White House chief of staff, with a reporter for the *Los Angeles Times*, with her lawyer, and finally with the president of Harvard University, who was obviously a good friend. Except for her daughter, to whom she spoke gently and lovingly, she communicated in a manner that conveyed power. Nightmare liked that. Bringing down powerful people had always made his work more satisfying. Before he himself had been betrayed and left for dead, he'd been assigned to kill for many reasons, and sometimes for no reason that he could see. He never wondered about a sanction he carried out against someone in a powerful position. Power was itself reason enough to draw a sanction. It was when he was told to kill someone who was no one that he wondered. Why end a life that was no life at all?

In South Africa once, he'd tracked a man for a month to learn the patterns and rhythms of his life. He did it to make a clean kill. In his surveillance, he found a lowly government clerk with a wife and three children, a man who liked bow ties, who drank Indonesian black tea under a kapok tree at lunch while he read the London *Times*, who visited his mistress every Wednesday afternoon, and who, in his position, wielded only the power of a rubber stamp. He also discovered that the wife was herself a mistress to an important political figure. He killed the clerk with poison, a few milligrams of aconitine in his black tea, and he was out of the country on an afternoon plane. The killing didn't bother him. By then, there'd been so many. It was the why of it, to remove a small man from the path of a greater man's desire, that ate at him. Murder as a political favor, granted as easily as an invitation to an embassy ball.

On the monitor, he watched the First Lady head upstairs. He switched to the camera he'd put in her room two weeks earlier, on a bookshelf, inside a hollowed-out copy of *Little Men*. He watched her undress, prepare to take a bath, and stand for a moment in front of the mirror on her vanity. She turned and studied her profile, drew in her stomach, lifted her breasts, shook her head in a disappointed way, and relaxed. She stepped toward the bathroom and out of range of the camera lens.

Nightmare sat back patiently. He was used to watching and waiting. However, he knew that on this kill, waiting could be a problem. The First Lady wouldn't stay at Wildwood indefinitely. And there was Thorsen. The man was a complication, one Nightmare would have to consider carefully. He would probably have to neutralize Thorsen. But later. Now he had to focus on his purpose, which was to sanction the lying abomination called Tom Jorgenson and his daughter Kate, whom Nightmare had once called his friend. It had been his intention to kill them both together at the hospital with the C-4 explosive. Because the security guard had caught him, the plan was ruined. At first, he'd been angry with himself. *Weakness*, he'd chided. After further reflection, he decided he'd unconsciously sabotaged his own strategy because he wanted the man and his daughter dead in a different way. Most of his life, he'd killed for reasons tied to politics, to economics, to the expediencies of closet diplomacy. This was different; this was personal. He wanted to confront the man and the daughter face-to-face before they died. Not to gloat, as he had at Jorgenson's bedside. That was a mistake. No, he wanted to be sure they went to their deaths with a full understanding of their guilt. This would probably mean killing them separately, and probably Thorsen somewhere along the way.

A knock on the van door startled him.

"Open up. Police."

Nightmare quickly turned off the monitor, shoved his Beretta into his belt at the small of his back, and opened the back doors of the van. Outside, it was twilight. The sheriff's deputy stood looking at Nightmare, his thumbs hooked over the leather of his gun belt. Behind him, at the side of the highway, stretched a line of parked vehicles, mostly media vans and cars.

"ID." The deputy held out his hand.

Nightmare gave the deputy his wallet.

"MCC," the deputy said. "Never heard of that one."

"Metro Cable Communications," Nightmare replied. "Usually we stick with city council and school board meetings, but this is too big to pass up."

"Parking here all night?"

"Unless the First Lady leaves."

"You know the rule. You let her motorcade pass, then you can follow at a reasonable distance."

"I know."

"All right, Mr."—he double-checked the ID—"Solomon. Good evening."

The deputy moved to the next vehicle in line, a white van that carried the call letters KSTP on the side. Like Nightmare's van, it had a small satellite dish mounted on top and a short broadcasting antenna.

Nightmare glanced across the road at the entrance to Wildwood. A Washington County Sheriff's Department cruiser was parked behind the stone arch, controlling access. Nightmare smiled at the futility of the effort.

fifteen

The fax came through a little before 9:00 P.M. Deputy Williams from the Washington County Sheriff's Department had moved quickly on Bo's request. Luther Gallagher had no criminal record. He was employed as an attendant at the Minnesota State Security Hospital in St. Peter, and the photograph on his hospital ID card was included. Bo only had to glance at the photo to see that it wasn't Max Ableman. Gallagher had a large square face and a bald head that reminded Bo of a professional wrestler. The presence of Gallagher's pickup truck at the motor court probably had nothing to do with Ableman.

Camera eight, mounted on the north side of the main house, went dead as Bo was studying the fax. He left the Op Center to check it out. A squirrel lay on the ground directly beneath the camera, stunned but not dead. It had happened before. For God knew what reason, the squirrels liked to chew on the camera cables. When they bit through the insulation, they shorted out the connection and zapped themselves in the process. He'd suggested to the Jorgensons that something be done to get rid of the squirrels, but they rejected the idea. The squirrels, Annie pointed out, were there long before the Jorgensons. Bo radioed to the Op Center and said he'd fix the cable himself. He spent half an hour installing new wire. In the meantime, the squirrel staggered to its feet and stumbled off into the orchard.

Bo had just finished and was folding up the ladder when Diana Ishimaru drove up and parked in front of the guesthouse. Jake Russell followed in his own car. Bo hung the ladder in the barn, then headed to the Op Center, where he found his boss, Manning, and Russell in conference.

"A change of plan, Bo," Ishimaru said when he joined them. "I'm pulling you off Wildwood. Agent Russell will be assuming responsibility for the Op Center."

"Why?" Bo asked.

"I'm reassigning you."

"To what?"

"Investigating Tom Jorgenson's accident."

Bo glanced at Manning, who gave no sign of how he felt about this turn of events. "I thought we'd agreed that wasn't our jurisdiction."

Ishimaru replied, "When the director of the United States Secret Service calls us personally and gives an order, we find a way to make it our jurisdiction."

Bo thought about Annie's final comment as he left the main house late that afternoon: *You don't know Kate.* It was true. He didn't know Kathleen Jorgenson Dixon. But he was beginning to.

"While the First Lady is at Wildwood, any concern regarding Tom Jorgenson's safety is to be viewed as a concern that involves the First Lady's safety as well."

"When do I start?" Bo asked.

"Immediately."

Russell offered his hand. "Good luck, Bo."

"Thanks." Bo flashed Manning a brief smile. "Looks like you got your wish, Chris. I'm out of here."

"Looks like you got yours, too," Manning said.

Bo gathered his things. Diana Ishimaru accompanied him to his car.

"Are you okay with this, Bo?"

"Yeah."

"You'll be working with Sheriff Quinn-Gruber. He's been notified. If any jurisdictional disputes arise, direct them to me."

"Yes, ma'am."

It was almost dark. The yard light was on. Ishimaru stood near Bo, and she shook her head. "I don't like this feeling that I'm authorizing a wild goose chase."

"Things don't add up, Diana. Somebody should be finding out why."

She took a deep breath of resignation. "Keep me posted," she said as she turned to her car.

Bo went directly from Wildwood to the St. Croix Regional Medical Center. It was 10:30 P.M., and a security guard was locking the front doors. Bo flashed his Secret Service ID and was allowed to enter. The guard relocked the doors behind him.

"The First Lady's not coming tonight, is she?" the guard asked. His name badge read: H. BLOCK.

"No. I'm checking on another matter. Mind if I head down to the laundry?"

"Be my guest. I'm closing up shop here and going down to the E.R. station. If you need me, that's where I'll be. My partner's finishing his rounds."

Bo took the elevator to the basement and followed the tunnel to the laundry building. The lights were on, but the laundry was deserted. Bo remembered that Ableman made a final trip to gather soiled linen near the end of the shift, so he waited. The laundry seemed a harsh place. The machines were huge, and the fluorescent lights glinted off the metal with a sterile gleam. The linen-folding tables were empty. They reminded Bo of rows of autopsy tables. The ceilings were high and full of pipes. The whole place had a cold industrial feel.

The laundry elevator began to climb from the basement. Bo waited. But it wasn't Ableman pushing the cart that emerged. This man was older and heavier. He stooped in his labor, and he eyed Bo with a sour look. "Who're you? What're you doing here?"

Bo offered his ID. "I'm looking for Max Ableman."

"Makes two of us." The man pushed the cart past Bo.

"I thought he worked evenings," Bo said, following.

"I thought so, too. Guess maybe he thinks different. Didn't show, didn't call. If I didn't need him so bad, I'd fire his ass." He positioned the cart between two big washers.

"Did you try calling him?"

"Hell, yes. No answer." He was wearing yellow rubber gloves, and he began to reach into the cart and sort out linen into different machines. Some of it was blue surgical linen heavily bloodstained and still wet. Some of it was bedding, badly soiled. The strong smell of blood and human waste rose from the cart, and Bo could understand why the job was a hard one to hire for and to keep filled.

"Has he pulled this kind of stunt before?" Bo asked.

"He was good for the first month. Lately, he's called in sick a lot. And tonight he didn't call at all." He looked with disgust at the linen in his hands. "Christ, I hate covering for these worthless jokers."

Bo left the hospital and headed to the Bayport Court. Several cars were parked in the lot, but the old Chevy pickup wasn't there. Room ten was dark. Bo knocked on the door and got no answer. He walked to the office. The hour was late, but the desk was still occupied. He was surprised by the desk clerk he found on duty. The kid looked to be no more than eighteen, and wore a white Stillwater High football jersey, number 7. There was innocence in his blue eyes and the natural blush of youth and health in his cheeks. He'd been watching a rerun of *Saturday Night Live* on Comedy Central, but he stood up as soon as Bo walked in, and he stepped attentively to the desk.

"You in charge?" Bo asked.

"Yes, sir. Need a room?"

"No thanks." Bo looked him over, then impressed the kid with his Secret Service ID. "You work here?"

"Not really. My uncle owns it. During the summer, he likes to spend time at his cabin up in Wisconsin, so I help out. I get a little extra money toward tuition, and a hell of an education." The kid smiled wide, white teeth in a face that could have done milk commercials.

"I'm interested in the man renting number ten. Have you seen him this evening?"

"No, sir."

"Have you ever seen him?"

"Sure. See him head off to work in the afternoon. Don't see him very often when he comes back. It's usually pretty late. Times I've seen him he's been covered with dirt. I figure he must work construction somewhere. Maybe roadwork they got going at night, you know."

"You haven't seen him today?"

"No, sir."

Bo glanced back at the lighted walkway that ran in front of the rooms the length of the court. "I'd like to see his room."

"I don't know—" the kid began.

"I can have a warrant in a couple of hours, but I'd prefer to see the room sooner. It may well be an issue of national security, son."

The kid caved easily. He reached into a drawer and drew out a key. "It'll open every door."

"Thanks." Bo started away but turned back and asked, "What does he drive?"

"An old pickup. Green, I think."

"Hang on a minute," Bo said. He went to his car, got the faxed photo of Luther Gallagher, and brought it back into the office. "Have you ever seen this man before?"

"No."

"Never in the company of the man in number ten?"

"No. But then, I'm not here that much."

Bo unlocked the door of Max Ableman's room, stepped in, and turned on the light. It looked as if no one had ever been there. The bed was neatly made. Through the opened doorway to the bathroom, Bo saw that the towels hung perfectly folded. He walked to the closet. Empty. He went to his car and punched in Diana Ishimaru's home phone number. She answered, sounding groggy from sleep.

"Diana, this is Bo. I need a fingerprint technician. Now."

chapter

sixteen

C lean," Rosie Mortenson said. "Not a print anywhere. Not even any residuals in the usual places. The bathroom fixtures, the lamp, the doorknobs, the jambs, the television. Christ, even the damn Gideon Bible. They're all absolutely clean. What does that tell you, Bo?"

"If this were the Hilton, I'd say excellent housekeeping." Bo shook his head. "He knew what he was doing."

"I did pull a few prints off the headboard, but they were in a place where someone might grab hold in the throes of passion, if you know what I mean. I'll run them, but don't get your hopes up."

"Thanks, Rosie."

"I wish I could have been more help."

"You came out at a god-awful hour, and what you found tells me a lot."

The fingerprint technician began to pack up her gear. Diana Ishimaru stood in the doorway to room ten, her hands stuffed in the pockets of her jeans, her eyes on the carpeting. "Who is Max Ableman?" she asked, more to herself than to Bo.

"I've been asking myself that for a while," Bo said.

"Do you have a photograph?"

"No. He probably had a picture taken for his hospital ID. I'll get it first thing in the morning."

"Let's contact the Washington County sheriff's office and have them put out an APB on the pickup."

Bo said, "I'd like to talk to Luther Gallagher."

Ishimaru glanced at her watch. "Not at this hour. Go on home and get some rest. You can check him out tomorrow." Rosie Mortenson slipped past them and went to her car. Ishimaru took one final look at the empty room. "I admit this is getting curiouser and curiouser, Bo. But we still have no evidence that connects Ableman to Tom Jorgenson's accident. For that matter, we still have no proof that a crime has been committed."

"I'll get the proof."

"Get it tomorrow, Bo. Tonight, get some sleep."

But Bo knew sleep was going to be impossible. There were too many unanswered questions, and he'd roll them over and over in his mind until the sun came up. So he took I-94 to the beltway, swung south of the Twin Cities, and picked up Minnesota 169 heading southwest toward St. Peter, where Luther Gallagher lived. As he drove out of the bubble of urban light, the country night closed in around him, and the number of stars in the sky seemed to multiply. Distant yard lights became beacons that indicated farmhouses set among broad fields. The moon lit the land, and the highway was a long white corridor between silvered stalks of corn and leafy soybeans. He was heading into the country that long ago had been the site of his salvation.

Bo's memories of his father were vague and shadowy. A huge shape looming over him, dark against the sunlit slats of venetian blinds. The smell of diesel fuel on big hands. A ride once atop broad shoulders to watch a parade. Only bits and pieces, as if he were always looking at fragments of torn-up photographs.

His father left when Bo was five years old. Ran off, according to Bo's mother, with some Frederick's of Hollywood whore who had all her brains between her legs. Bo never understood why his father would leave. Even Bo recognized how attractive his mother was. She was pretty enough to be in the movies. The men she brought home were always telling her that.

When Bo was fourteen, they lived in a run-down apartment building in an old section of St. Paul known as Frogtown, within sight of the golden horses that topped the capitol. His mother worked nights as a cocktail waitress; days, she slept off her weariness or slept off the booze. Bo was left pretty much on his own. Sometimes he went to school, but often he did not. He spent a lot of time on the streets. Although he was small for his age, he had an attitude that made kids much larger steer clear of him. He had a juvenile record, nothing serious, mostly truancy, a couple of incidents of shoplifting, one charge of criminal trespass that was eventually dropped. He'd done other things, just never been caught. Several social workers had threatened to put him in a foster home, but the truth was, and they all knew it, there were kids much worse than Bo, and much worse off. His mother kept a roof over his head and food in the cupboards. Bo knew how to wash his own clothes (and hers), and how to cook his own meals (and hers).

Bo loved his mother. He also sometimes hated her. It wasn't uncommon for him to leave the apartment in a rush of anger, aiming back over his shoulder a parting shot that usually went something like, *I wish you were dead.* They argued about everything. His truancy, her drinking. His friends, her boyfriends. His dreams, her realities. Sometimes as he headed out the door, she called him back suddenly and held his face between her hands. "You wouldn't ever leave me, would you?" she'd ask, as if she were seriously afraid. If it had been a good day, he'd answer *Don't be silly.* If they'd argued, he was likely to say *Don't bet on it.* Their fights could be verbally brutal, but until the last night he saw her alive she'd never laid a hand on him.

He was in a fight at school that day. He'd been talking to the girlfriend of a kid named Krakhauer, when Krakhauer gave him a hard shove from behind and slammed him headfirst into the lockers. Bo coldcocked the kid. It didn't matter that Bo hadn't started things. Krakhauer was the one bleeding all over the hallway floor when the vice principal showed up. Bo was suspended. No big deal. It always struck him as odd punishment, this banning him from school, because school was a place he'd just as soon avoid anyway.

His mother came home late that night, drunk, and not alone. Bo was awake, lying in his bed. He'd waited up, wanting to talk about the fight, the suspension. When he heard the other voice, he grew angry. Once things started on the other side of the thin wall that separated his bedroom from his mother's, he got up and got dressed. As he was heading toward the front door, his mother came from her room.

"It's one o'clock in the morning. Where the hell do you think you're going?" She'd thrown on an old robe that she held closed over her breasts with the clutch of one hand. In the other hand, she held an empty gin bottle.

"Why?" Bo asked. "You want me to pick up some booze for you?"

"Don't get smart with me." Her hair, long and blonde and disheveled from what had been going on in the bedroom, lay fallen over one eye. She brushed it away with the back of the hand that held the empty bottle.

"I'm going out." He gave a surly glance toward her closed bedroom door.

Her own eyes went there, too, and everything about her seemed to sag. She came close to him, and when she spoke again, she'd softened. "You wouldn't ever leave me, would you?"

Bo was sick to death of it. Sick to death of everything. And he said the cruelest thing he'd ever said to her. "He left you, you know, because you weren't pretty enough."

She drew back as if Bo had struck her. Then she let go her hold on the robe and slapped him. The robe fell open. Bo could see the stretch marks on her breasts and belly. "You will not speak to me that way," she said in a choked voice. "I'm your mother, goddamn it."

"That's not my fault, goddamn it," Bo threw back at her. He turned and stormed out the door.

It was a long way to the river, and Bo walked the whole distance in heated strides. The streets were empty. The season was autumn, the night cool and windy. All around him Bo heard the scrape of dead leaves on pavement. He made for a grove of cottonwood trees near the High Bridge where an old school bus sat wheel-less in tall grass. The bus smelled of urine and was full of litter, but it offered seclusion and a measure of protection, and kids often gathered there to get high and sometimes to crash. As he approached, he could see a glowing ember in the dark inside.

"Hey, man," a voice called to him in a laid-back greeting.

"Otter, that you?"

"Halloween in a couple of weeks, Spider-Man. I thought maybe you were a goblin." Otter laughed softly. He sat near the middle of the bus with his feet propped on the back of the seat in front of him. He was a tall kid, awkward-looking, but when he moved it was with a slow kind of grace that always put Bo in mind of a giraffe. "Late to be out, even for you."

"You, too," Bo said. He sat down across the aisle from Otter and accepted the joint his companion offered.

"The devil's in my old man tonight. Figure I'm better off here until he cools down."

Otter's old man was infamous. A huge railroad worker, he was a brute who laid into his son with frightening regularity. Bo had often sat in the bus with Otter while his friend smoked or drank away the pain of a beating.

"So what's up?" Otter asked.

They were hardly more than a stone's throw from downtown St. Paul, and the lights of the city drizzled a neon illumination over the grove of cottonwoods and the bus within it. Bo could see Otter's face, long and serene.

"Fight with my mom," Bo replied.

"I wouldn't mind fighting with your mom," Otter said. The attractiveness of Bo's mother was a constant subject of comment among Bo's friends.

"She hit me," Bo said. "She's never hit me."

"She hit you hard?"

"Doesn't matter. She hit me."

"It matters, believe me," Otter said.

They were quiet for a while. Bo saw something big moving on the river. The trees made it difficult to see exactly what, and the wind through the branches covered any sound.

"Hear that?" Otter said

Bo heard only the wind and the leaves.

"I think it's the dead getting restless."

"What are you talking about?" Bo asked.

"I've been hearing it a lot tonight. With Halloween coming on, I figure all those dead folks are getting anxious for a little action."

Otter was definitely stoned, probably drunk as well. The restless dead thing Bo decided to chalk up to altered consciousness.

Bo said, "I'm going to take a piss."

He left the bus and walked out of the trees to the riverbank. The Mississippi was like a strip torn from the night sky and laid against the earth. Bo could see the glow in the pilothouse of a towboat that was nearing Harriet Island. Maybe that was the sound Otter had heard, the deep thrum of the engine as the towboat had passed. Bo watched the light until it disappeared beyond a bend in the river, and he imagined what it would be like to escape on a barge bound for New Orleans. He relieved himself in the grass on the riverbank, zipped up, and returned to the bus.

Otter offered him a swig from a bottle of Mad Dog 20/20. Bo declined. "You going to spend the night?" he asked.

"Probably," Otter replied. "You?"

"Naw. Think I'll go back home." He headed to the front of the bus. "Later," he said.

"Later, Spider-Man," Otter called after him.

It was going toward morning by the time Bo returned to the

apartment in Frogtown. The walk had done him good. Probably the joint, too, and the mellow influence of Otter. When he stepped inside, the place was quiet. He could see that the door to his mother's bedroom was slightly ajar. An open door usually meant that the man who'd come with her had done his thing and left. Bo went to the doorway and peeked in. He saw the bedding in a jumble and saw the stains, black in the darkened bedroom. He hit the light switch, and he saw the rest—a bloodied broken bottle, and his mother's skin, once marred only by stretch marks, marred now, and forever in Bo's memory, by the deep cut of glass.

All his life, Bo would wonder if other people had a moment that clearly divided their lives. There was everything before, and everything after, and between, only one unforgettable heartbeat. Standing at the door to his mother's bedroom with his hand still on the light switch, Bo had his moment. It ended in a cry that brought the neighbors running.

They never found the man who murdered her. Bo hadn't seen him nor had anyone else, and there was little for the police to go on. Bo wanted desperately to move back in time. He wanted to protect his mother, wanted never to have said the things he said, wanted never to have deserted her. He also wanted to find her murderer and to kill the bastard with his own hands.

He kept all this to himself, kept it in his heart, which had become a fist. He refused to talk about it to anyone, not his social worker, not the psychologist social services provided, not the foster parents he was sent to live with and from whom he eventually ran away, not even Otter who joined Bo after he, too, split from home. All the time that he and Otter, and later Egg and Pearl and Freak, lived together in the bus in the cottonwoods, Bo never once spoke about what his mother's death meant to him. What would have been the point? They'd all been wounded. And Bo, like the others, believed that was just the way life was, harsh and unforgiving.

It was Annie Jorgenson who set him on the way to a different view of the world. He appeared before her in juvenile court after being arrested for petty theft. The cops had discovered the bus by the river and had taken Bo's street family into custody. Bo was prepared for the worst. What he received was something far different, something he would be grateful for all his life. A second chance at growing up.

He was brought into her office and left alone with her. She wore reading glasses and slowly scanned the documents in front of her. She looked up at Bo with her intelligent blue eyes.

"Thief," she said. "That's what it says here. You're a thief. Do you think that's true?"

Bo shrugged. Let her do what she wanted, he didn't care.

"I'm not asking if you stole things. We both know you did. I'm asking, do you think of yourself as a thief?"

The truth was that he didn't. He saw himself as a provider, a protector. Stealing was the means to that end. He was about to offer her another shrug, then changed his mind. He shook his head.

"No," she said, giving voice to his gesture. "As I understand it, you pretty much took care of—how many was it? four?—other runaways besides yourself." She glanced down again at the documents in front of her. She nodded to herself, then she took off her glasses. "I see a lot of runaways, Bo. Most of them end up here because they're being used in despicable ways by other people, usually adults. They're prostitutes. They're drug runners. They're thieves in a den of thieves. In my view, you've done your best to keep four other kids out of the hands of the people who would use them that way, and out of my courtroom. I think that's admirable."

Bo tried to remember the last time an adult had praised him in such a way. What was this judge up to?

"These other kids, were they your friends?" she asked.

"Family," Bo said.

"Family." She nodded. "Family is important." She folded her hands on her desk and leaned toward him. "Well, Bo, I have a couple of options. I can send you to the juvenile correctional facility at Red Wing. Your family there would be pushers, punks, bullies, some who go on to be murderers. Do you want that?"

No, he thought, but he gave no sign of it.

She locked him in her unwavering gaze. Her eyes were steady, not cold. Patient, not demanding. She seemed prepared to wait him out.

"No," he finally said.

She sat back. "There's a place I know that's a good place. People I know who are good people. I'd like you to spend some time with them."

"Why?" Bo asked.

"Because there are all kinds of families. I'd like you to experience a good one. If you give it a chance, you won't be sorry, I promise."

"Promises are easy," Bo pointed out.

She nodded, granting him that. "I imagine you've been lied to a lot. I imagine people have been a pretty big disappointment to you. I'm a judge. That gives me some power. The promises I make, I'm able to keep. All you have to do is give me a chance, Bo, give these people a chance. We won't fail you."

It had been a long time since he had believed an adult, but the woman judge seemed sincere. More than that, she seemed strong in a good way. And what the hell. If things didn't work out, he could always run.

"All right," he said.

"A good decision, Bo," she told him seriously. "I think you're going to like them. Their name is Thorsen."

Headlights dashing at him from behind yanked Bo from his memories. The vehicle rode his bumper awhile. Bo wondered why the damn thing didn't pass him. Then it dropped back and followed at a safe, legal distance. Bo kept glancing at the headlights reflected in his rearview mirror, and he began to imagine them as a pair of glaring eyes watching him.

Thorsen, you need some coffee, he told himself.

He pulled into an all-night gas/convenience store on the outskirts of St. Peter, and the vehicle that had been behind him flew past on its way down Minnesota 169. He didn't catch the make, but it certainly wasn't the creature with eyes his tired brain had imagined. After he'd filled the gas tank, he got some coffee and asked the clerk for directions to the street where Luther Gallagher lived.

The address was near an industrial park. Gallagher's house stood alone behind a wall of ragged lilac bushes. It was a two-story cadaver of a structure. Death by neglect, Bo thought. In the hard, brilliant moonlight, he could see peeling paint and window screens that carried long, open wounds. The yard was a mix of thin grass and hard bare dirt, reminding Bo of the coat of a distempered dog. He walked along a cracked and weedy sidewalk to the enclosed front porch. Five newspapers, still rolled in the cellophane bags in which they had been delivered, lay where they'd been tossed on the steps. Bo took out his penlight and checked the dates. Each was a Sunday edition of the *St. Paul Pioneer Press*. There was a mail slot beside the door. Bo mounted the steps and shined his penlight through the dirty porch window. Unopened mail lay in a jumble under the slot on the other side. He was tempted to resort to a little B and E but restrained himself. He returned to his car and headed back to St. Paul.

It was 4 A.M. when he parked in the garage of the duplex in Tangletown. He entered quietly, trying not to disturb his landlady, who lived below him. He stripped down, put on clean boxer shorts and a T-shirt, and made himself a cup of Sleepytime herbal tea. He had a lot of questions and no answers, but he needed sleep. He knew exactly what he wanted to do first thing in the morning, and he wanted to be clearheaded.

He sipped his tea and strolled to the living room window that overlooked the front yard and the street beyond. At that hour, he wasn't particularly concerned about being seen in his underwear. He caught sight of an old pickup, driving slowly out of the light of the streetlamp in front of his house. For a moment, he thought it might be the pickup truck he'd seen at the Bayport Court. Then he shook his head and drew the curtains.

You need some sleep, Thorsen, he told himself. You need it bad.

chapter
seventeen

The ringing of the telephone on the stand beside his bed pulled Bo from a deep slumber.

"Thorsen," he mumbled into the mouthpiece.

"You sound asleep," Stuart Coyote said.

Bo looked at the clock radio. 7:00 A.M. "I am. What's up?"

"Just checking in with my partner."

"Partner?"

"Diana took me off the Wildwood detail and assigned me to work with you on the Tom Jorgenson thing. Interesting developments last night, I hear. How about you fill me in completely over breakfast at the Broiler."

"When?"

"Is an hour enough time to make yourself gorgeous?"

"An hour," Bo said.

Coyote was already waiting at the St. Clair Broiler, drinking coffee, looking over notes he'd scribbled on a small pad. "You look like you didn't get any sleep at all."

"Not much," Bo admitted.

"Tom Jorgenson?"

Bo nodded. "The questions are piling up. The answers aren't."

Bo ordered black coffee and the Texas scramble. Stu Coyote asked for a Greek omelet.

"According to Diana, this is what we've got so far." Coyote glanced at his notes. "A laundry worker with access to Jorgenson's floor skips work the day after the apparent accident that killed the guard. The pickup he's driving is registered to one Luther Gallagher. He abandons his motel room wiping away all traces of himself before you can talk to him. Is that about it?"

"One more thing. Luther Gallagher hasn't been home in over a month."

"How do you know that?"

"I went to his house last night."

Coyote checked his notepad, then scowled at Bo. "You already went to St. Peter?"

Bo shrugged. "Couldn't sleep. Looks like he's a Sundays-only customer of the *Pioneer Press*. Five weeks' worth of newspapers are lying around his front steps, and a pile of unopened mail is sitting on his porch."

"What do you know about Ableman?"

"Not much."

"I can tell you the name's an alias," Coyote said. "Diana gave me the Social Security number you got off his job application and I ran it first thing this morning. It belongs to Max Ableman all right. But according to Social Security, Max Ableman is sixty-two years old and living in Florida. Looks like our guy plucked a name and Social Security number out of the air."

"Knowing it would be quite a while, if ever, before the error was discovered," Bo concluded.

Coyote referred again to his notes. "Gallagher works at the Minnesota State Security Hospital in St. Peter. Let's head down there this morning."

"You're reading my mind, partner," Bo said.

They drove in separate cars, giving them the flexibility to divide their time and energy if necessary. Bo led the way.

In daylight, St. Peter was a pretty little town set in the wooded valley of the Minnesota River. The Regional Treatment Center, of which the Minnesota State Security Hospital was a part, lay in the hills south of town. The facility was a mixture of imposing sandstone block buildings that looked several decades old and newer, more functional brick structures.

At the reception desk in the administration building, Bo and Coyote met briefly with the director of personnel, who arranged for them to talk to the program director in the Security Hospital where Luther Gallagher was employed as a security counselor.

The Minnesota State Security Hospital sat behind trees atop a hill a quarter mile west of the other buildings. It was a relatively new single-story facility, dull red brick, with barred windows, razor wire on the fencing, and a perimeter maintained with motion detectors and infrared cameras. Housed therein were the most dangerous of the patients remanded by the courts for treatment.

Helen Wardell, the program director, met them in her office, a gray, windowless room. She was a gaunt woman with dark circles under her eyes and a look on her face that seemed perpetually braced to deal with crises. The odor of cigarette smoke rolled off her clothing, and her voice was raspy in the way of someone long addicted to nicotine.

"Luther Gallagher," she said. It was clear the name was significant and not in a good way. "What's he up to now?"

"That's what we're here to find out," Bo replied. "We were hoping to speak with him, but apparently he hasn't been to work in quite a while."

"He went to Albuquerque. Christ, I could use a cigarette. You guys mind if we take this outside?"

They stepped out of the building into an internal courtyard reserved for staff. It consisted of two stone benches and a small patch of grass, separated from the sky above by a mesh screen.

Helen Wardell lit her cigarette and breathed smoke that drifted upward toward freedom.

"What's this about Albuquerque?" Coyote asked.

"Luther called one morning with some cock-and-bull story about his father having a heart attack in Albuquerque. He requested a leave of absence to drive down and spend a few weeks there while his father recovered."

Bo asked, "Why cock-and-bull?"

"Luther? Giving a good goddamn about his old man?" She started to laugh, but it turned into a hacking cough.

"He's not a particularly sensitive guy?" Coyote said, encouraging her.

"He's big, that's why he's here. Dealing with the kind of people we house, big is a definite plus. But sensitive? Yeah, like a rhino."

"Did he say when he'd return to work?"

"He was supposed to be back last week. We haven't heard from him."

Bo asked, "Does the name Max Ableman mean anything to you?"

She watched the smoke escaping through the mesh and thought a moment. "Should it?"

"I spotted a pickup truck registered to Luther Gallagher in a motor court in Bayport yesterday. According to the desk clerk, a man named Max Ableman was driving it. Ableman is an alias, but it's still possible Gallagher might have mentioned him."

"If he ever did, I don't remember it."

"Not that it will help, but why don't you describe Ableman," Coyote suggested to Bo.

"Probably in his late thirties, early forties, just under six feet tall, approximately one hundred eighty pounds, sandy hair, pale complexion, quiet. And scars." Bo made a couple of slashes across his upper arm.

Wardell paused with the cigarette just shy of her lips. "Sunglasses, even indoors?"

"That's him."

"Oh, my God." She dropped the cigarette on the sidewalk without bothering to crush it out. "Gentlemen, if you please." She signaled them to follow and returned to her office, where she asked them to wait. She left and came back in less than five minutes with a small, dark woman at her heels. "These are the agents. I'm sorry, I've forgotten your names."

Bo held out his hand and introduced himself and Coyote.

As she shook Coyote's hand, the woman said, "I'm Dr. Jordan Hart. I've asked Helen if we could go to my office and talk before we inform the local authorities. You seem to have information about Moses."

"Moses?" Coyote said.

"The man you call Max Ableman."

"Moses." Coyote grinned at Bo. "Brother, looks like we've found the Promised Land."

Dr. Hart was younger and less imposing than Bo imagined a psychologist who dealt with the criminally insane might be. He guessed her to be in her early thirties. She stood barely five feet tall, had a smooth, dark complexion, and intense brown eyes. She escorted them to her office. It was a neat little room, red brick walls decorated with tasteful Monet prints and lined with bookcases. The wide window overlooked another courtyard, one with a small flowerbed where a patient knelt, carefully pulling weeds and putting them in a plastic bucket.

"What's your interest in David Moses?" she asked. She poured water into a coffeemaker and flipped the switch.

Bo explained about Ableman, about his own suspicions concerning the death of the hospital security guard, and about his fear for the safety of Tom Jorgenson.

"What can you tell me about this Moses?" he asked.

"David escaped two months ago," the psychologist informed them. "We've had no word on him since."

"Escaped how?" Bo asked.

124

"He just walked away." Her words had a bitter edge.

Coyote looked surprised. "With all the razor wire you've got around this place?"

"David Moses is a unique individual." Dr. Hart offered them the coffee that had just finished drip brewing. "What do you know about him?" she asked.

"Almost nothing," Bo answered. "Except that he appears to be one step ahead of us."

"That doesn't surprise me."

She handed them their coffee in disposable cups, then sat down with a mug of her own, a big ceramic thing with printing on the side: SOMETIMES A CIGAR IS JUST A CIGAR.

"Before I can tell you anything, I need to see a court order allowing me to release information on David."

"I've told you what's happened," Bo said. "Do you think Moses could be responsible?"

She didn't say so, but her expression confirmed it. "Without a court order," she insisted, "my hands are tied."

Bo took out his cell phone and placed a call to Diana Ishimaru. He explained what he needed.

"It's in the works," he told the psychologist. "But if you wait until you have it in your hands, that might be too late. The more I know about this Moses, the more certain I am that he's already killed one man. And it may be only the beginning. You said he was a unique individual. Why?"

She spent a moment weighing her options. Finally she said, "When he was being evaluated for competency to stand trial, he was given the WAIS, Wechsler Adult Intelligence Scale, as part of the standard battery of assessments. Top score on the WAIS is a hundred fifty. David came in at a hundred forty-seven. I've never met anyone who scored so high, so when he was assigned to me I administered several additional tests to make sure his IQ score was accurate. It was."

"Competency to stand trial on what charge?"

"Manslaughter. Two years ago, he was arrested for the murder of a man in Minneapolis, a street person, homeless, as was David Moses. The killing took place outside a mission shelter. There were no witnesses to the actual murder, but apparently the noise of the brawl caused someone to call the police. When they arrived on the scene, they found David disoriented, hallucinating. He told them he was being followed. People were trying to kill him. The court ordered psychiatric evaluation. He was diagnosed as paranoid schizophrenic, judged not mentally competent to stand trial, and he was remanded here for treatment."

"He was put under your care?"

"At first, yes. This facility houses patients who have committed serious crimes. Usually sex offenders and murderers. Often, they're here for life. They've fallen into that dark area of the criminal justice system in which the constitutional rights of a citizen are abrogated. They'll never leave this place unless the doctors give them a clean bill of mental health, and that doesn't happen very often. At first, David was pretty hostile. In my initial sessions with him, he wasn't cooperative at all. After several months, he decided to toss me a few bones. I think he was testing me. It was obvious David wanted out, and he was trying to figure out how to do it. He tried to con me, but I wasn't fooled. So he got himself another doctor."

"How?" Bo asked.

"He accused me of sexual impropriety. It was a ridiculous allegation, but it got him what he wanted. Dr. Graves." She said the name with distaste. "Graves and I have never seen eye to eye. I tried to warn him about David, but he wouldn't listen. David worked him like clay on a potter's wheel. Two months ago, Graves recommended David be granted campus privileges."

Coyote looked up from his coffee cup. "What's that?"

"A patient with campus privileges has permission to walk the hospital grounds unsupervised. It's a transition step when we believe someone is almost ready for a return to society. Which I absolutely believed David was not. I said as much in the staff meeting when Graves put forward his proposal. I was overruled."

"So Moses just walked away and disappeared," Coyote concluded. "And you're the one talking to us because Graves was taken off the case."

"Yes." Her satisfaction was obvious.

"Just how dangerous is Moses?" Bo asked.

She didn't answer immediately. Instead she said, "Working with David is like stepping through a looking glass. With him, one never knows what's real and what isn't. Some patients try to manipulate me, but I can usually trip them up in their inconsistencies. David is far more clever. It's as if he allows you a true glimpse of his world, then slams the door so you're not certain exactly what you saw. Except that you know it was real and it was terrible."

"What can you tell us specifically?" Bo asked.

"What I know of the facts."

"Fine."

"David's an orphan. He spent some time in St. Jerome's Home for Children in the Twin Cities. He didn't graduate from high school but joined the military instead at seventeen. He was discharged eight years later. He appears to have no other criminal record."

Bo waited. When she didn't go on, he asked, "That's it?"

"In terms of facts."

"Nothing after his discharge?"

"Between the ages of twenty-five and thirty-five, his life is a blank. Or at least as far as any official records are concerned."

"He never gave you a clue about that time in his life?" Coyote asked.

"Yes. Only now we leave the realm of fact and we enter the Twilight Zone of David Moses." She hadn't touched her coffee, but now she took a sip. "Over the course of my treatment of David, I sifted through the notes and put bits and pieces together, and finally constructed the skeleton of a story. It's a chilling one if it's true. Do you have time?"

"As much as you need," Bo said.

Coyote held up his cup. "Got any cream for this coffee?"

chapter

eighteen

Sixty miles north of the State Security Hospital, in the small maze of St. Paul city streets known as Tangletown, Nightmare parked along the curb two houses away from the duplex where Bo Thorsen lived. The side of the white van he drove carried an antenna logo and below it the words METRO CABLE COMMUNICATIONS. He wore sunglasses, a gray uniform with the name *D. Solomon* sewn onto the shirt pocket, a gray cap that matched the uniform, and he carried a small toolbox. He whistled his way through the shafts of morning sunlight that slanted among the big American elms in the yard, and he climbed the front steps of the duplex. Through a curtained front window on the ground floor came the sound of a television tuned to *The Price Is Right*. He quietly turned the knob on the front door, but the door was locked. He set his toolbox down, glanced at the empty street, took a lock pick from his pocket, and in a few seconds was inside the house. To his right stood the door of the first-floor unit, to his left the stairway that led upward. Nightmare silently mounted the stairs. The door of the upstairs unit had only a knob lock and a dead bolt. Child's play. Less than two minutes from the time he'd left his van, Nightmare was inside Thorsen's apartment.

He paused and took in the feel of the place. The most imposing item in the living room was a massive bookcase that took up nearly all of one wall. The shelves were full. The other walls were sparsely decorated with small watercolors matted and delicately framed. The furniture was tasteful and spare, all light tones. The whole place felt clean and uncluttered.

Nightmare went to the bookcase and scrutinized Thorsen's taste in reading. The shelves were nearly equally divided between classic nonfiction texts that covered a lot of territory—Bronowski, Levi-Strauss, Chomsky, Jung, Heilbroner, Galbraith, Campbell—and fiction and poetry, almost entirely American—Mark Twain, Walt Whitman, William Carlos Williams, Faulkner, Steinbeck, Wharton, Dos Passos, Sandburg, Frost, Angelou, Mailer, Dove. Thorsen had a signed first edition in excellent condition of Tom Jorgenson's autobiography *The Testament of Time.* Years ago when the book had first been released, Nightmare had read it and thought that, except for hiding the fact that he was a liar and a betrayer, Jorgenson told a pretty good tale. The worn covers seemed to indicate that many of the books had been well read, although they may simply have come used from secondhand bookstores. Nightmare couldn't be certain yet. He was just getting to know Thorsen. The agent subscribed to several magazines. *Time, The New Yorker, Smithsonian,* and one of Nightmare's favorites since childhood, *National Geographic.* A television with a thirteen-inch screen sat like a forgotten child on a small table in one corner of the living room. There was also a sound system and a carousel of CDs that contained mostly jazz.

In the kitchen, the refrigerator was adequately stocked, though nothing in quantity. Fruit, yogurt, cheese, bagels, milk, juice. No leftovers. There were half a dozen chilled cans of beer, something called Pig's Eye. The cupboards contained a modest supply of dishware, the basics. The small dining room table had only two chairs.

In the bathroom, clean matching towels hung on the racks. The medicine cabinet held no prescription drugs.

The first bedroom that Nightmare checked contained only a computer desk, computer hardware, and a chair surrounded by shelves of books. Thorsen appeared to have an even more inquisitive nature than Nightmare had realized. In the second bedroom, the bed was neatly made. All of Thorsen's dirty clothing had been put in a wicker hamper. A paperback copy of *Lonesome Dove* lay on the nightstand. A makeshift bookmark, the ace of spades from a deck of playing cards, showed that Thorsen was nearly three-quarters finished, almost to the place where Gus bit the dust, a sad but truthful piece of storytelling. Thorsen had a large clothes closet. Half of it was used to hang suits, pants, and shirts. The other half was given over to a respectful housing of the uniform, armor, and sword of kendo, the Japanese art of fencing. Nightmare was intrigued that Thorsen was a man who apparently understood Bushido, the way of the warrior.

In the whole apartment, Thorsen had but two photographs on display, both framed and set on the bureau in the bedroom. The first was a black-and-white blowup of a beautiful woman in a party gown. From the cut of the gown and the style of the woman's blonde hair, Nightmare judged that the picture had probably been taken in the early 1970s. The picture was remarkable in one very particular way. In her face and in her Nordic build, the woman reminded him of Kathleen Jorgenson Dixon. Nightmare smiled and wondered if Thorsen even realized the similarities.

The second photograph was a shot of an elderly couple with their arms tenderly around each other. In the background stood a barn sporting a new coat of red paint. Nightmare was almost certain there were more pictures somewhere. Everyone had a history, and almost everyone had that history documented in photographs, in certificates and diplomas, in ribbons from high school track meets and medals from the Scouts. Some people kept everything, others very little. But almost everyone kept something. Nightmare discovered Thorsen's history in a big cardboard box under the bed.

Nightmare sat on the floor and removed the lid from the box. Thorsen at first appeared to have come from a large family. A lot of the photographs were of kids, adolescents mostly, and the same couple and the same red barn framed on Thorsen's bureau. The kids didn't look at all alike. Some were blond, some redheaded, some raven-haired. They were tall and short, and their skins were of different tones and colors. Deeper in the box, Nightmare found more photographs of the woman in the gown whose picture sat on the bureau. In one, she had her arm around a kid who looked like Thorsen. Below those photos was a collection of articles cut from newspapers. They were about the murder of a St. Paul woman named Helen Lingenfelter. Although not particularly flattering, the photos that ran with the articles were of the same woman who had her arm around Thorsen. The newspaper stories mentioned a son, Bo, fourteen years of age, but no husband. Also in the box lay a document officially granting Bo Joseph Lingenfelter a legal change of name to Bo Harold Thorsen. Nightmare now understood the large family of disparate appearance. Thorsen had probably been taken into some kind of foster home after his mother's death.

Beneath the change of name, Nightmare came across a certificate of valor awarded to Thorsen by the U.S. Secret Service. Near the bottom of the box was a packet of letters bound together with string. They were all sent by the same woman, someone named Robin, from a D.C. address. They chronicled a distant courtship dance that ended when, in her final communication, the woman claimed to agree with Thorsen that a relationship was impossible for two people dedicated to a career in the Secret Service. The postmarks were nearly a decade old.

The final item Nightmare drew out was an old sheet of lined, three-hole paper, the kind a kid might have had in a high school notebook. Carefully centered on the paper and written in capital block letters were three observations.

1. THE WORLD IS HARD. BE STRONG.
2. LOVE IS FOR ONLY A FEW. DON'T EXPECT IT.
3. LIFE ISN'T FAIR. BUT SOME PEOPLE ARE. BE ONE OF
   THEM.

Nightmare wasn't certain of the significance, but he appreciated the sentiments. He put everything back into the box in the way he'd found it and returned the box to its place under Thorsen's bed. Then he sat down to consider what he'd learned.

Thorsen was a loner. He had no bowling trophies, no pictures of a softball team. He had only two chairs for dining and kept only basic dishware. Thorsen didn't entertain much. Except for the letters from long ago, there was nothing to suggest romantic involvement. A man wedded to his job, Nightmare concluded. His small television and his large book collection indicated he preferred reading when he wanted to relax. His taste in books was eclectic, though not particularly original. Still, it suggested a thinking man, someone who might be willing to use an unorthodox approach in tackling a problem, and the fact that he read so widely in fiction suggested a fertile imagination. He had a tragic background, had suffered a painful loss at an impressionable age that left him without family. Although he'd managed to put together a life that had integrity and purpose at its heart, nothing about him seemed to trumpet happiness.

The similarities between his own life and Thorsen's were not lost on him. He felt a faint affection for the man, a rare thing for Nightmare. But that wouldn't keep him from killing Thorsen if he had to.

Nightmare had followed the agent to St. Peter the previous night and knew that Thorsen was now at the state hospital. Nightmare had taken the opportunity to better explore the nature of the man; the more he knew about an adversary, the less likely he was to be surprised. He'd come to Thorsen's home because he knew that a home held secrets. Uncovering those secrets took him a long way toward understanding the enemy. It was a lesson he'd learned very young and in a horrific way.

＊　＊　＊

It took Nocturne years to realize the monstrous secret of what lived above him in the old farmhouse.

By then, he had created, at his grandfather's direction, many more explosive devices. He liked the work. It was a game that tested both his mind and the steadiness of his hands. The devices had become increasingly complex and more powerful. Some the old man took and dealt with himself. Others, Nocturne was called upon to plant, usually at night, often after a long ride with his grandfather in the pickup truck. The old man said almost nothing on those drives, yet he seemed pleased with his grandson's labors, and Nocturne, sitting beside the silent, white-haired man, felt proud of himself. The bombs he built destroyed things, but his grandfather had explained that those things were worthy of destruction. He'd given Nocturne reams of paper to read, his own scribbled manifestos. Sometimes he visited the basement and vented his theories of conspiracy. Even though Nocturne could easily see that his grandfather's arguments were riddled with logical fallacies and fueled by hate, he held his tongue. The old man seemed to value Nocturne's work and his company. Sometimes his grandfather would fix him with a steely gaze and quote from Proverbs, "Iron sharpens iron, and one man sharpens another." The words made Nocturne feel connected to the old man, important in his eyes.

The basement door was almost never locked anymore. Those nights when Nocturne heard the padlock slipped into the hasp and snapped into place, he wondered: Had he done something wrong?

From his reading, he'd come to believe that the essential mechanism of the universe was cause and effect. Everything existed as the result of one thing that triggered another that triggered another that triggered another. He believed that if one were diligent enough, one could trace back to an ultimate source the reason for all things. Although he often indulged in rumination on the broader considerations of existence, just as often he applied his thinking to more specific matters. The locked door, for example.

He was sixteen when he set out one night to discover the reason the basement door was periodically (and randomly, it seemed) locked. Winter lay around the farmhouse deep and still. A storm had just passed, and snow was piled against the outside walls, drifted taller than a man, sealing in Nocturne and his mother and grandfather. For no reason that Nocturne could discern, the old man had slapped the lock in place before going to bed. When the house above was quiet, Nocturne stripped naked, rolled his clothing in a bundle that he tied to a rope looped about his ankle. He worked his way up the laundry chute, out the opening in the second-floor bathroom, and hauled up his clothes. When he was dressed, he stepped into the hallway. He'd walked the old house at night so often he knew exactly where to step to avoid the loose, noisy floorboards, and he slipped silently down the hallway. He stopped at the old man's room and listened. Inside, all was quiet. He carefully opened the door a crack. Although the curtains were drawn and the room lay in inky dark, Nocturne could see that the bed was empty. He closed the door, wondering. When he came abreast of the door to his mother's bedroom, he heard a familiar sound, the harsh suck and sigh of air from his grandfather when the old man was laboring hard. That the sound came from his mother's bedroom was bewildering to Nocturne. He reached for the knob. The metal was cold in his hand. He eased the door open. Although he knew he risked revealing his secret freedom, his curiosity was too great.

The storm had left in its wake a clear, brittle sky shattered by a glaring moon. The curtains were drawn back. Moonlight thrust through the window and slashed across his mother's bed. Nocturne stared, unable to comprehend what he saw.

She lay on the bed, naked. Above her waist, she was in darkness, but moonlight splashed over her narrow hips, making the damp skin of his grandfather, who'd wedged between her legs, glisten like melting ice. The old man was bent over her, his pelvis in rapid motion. Nocturne's mother lay rigid, staring at the ceiling above her, her eyes sightless as stones.

Nocturne had read about sex. He understood it as he did many things, in a distant, literal way. The gritty reality before him defied his comprehension, and he stood in the doorway, dumb with confusion. He must have made a noise, for his mother's eyes fell on him, and she caught her breath with an audible gasp.

The old man stopped his thrusting and looked where she looked. He considered a moment, then pulled back from the woman. He climbed off the bed and stepped toward Nocturne. His penis was erect, huge and wet. His eyes were black, sharp and penetrating. "I suppose you're old enough," he finally said. He looked back at his daughter. "You want her, after I'm done, you take her."

"No," she cried, weeping. "God, no."

The old man stepped back to the bed and slapped her across the face. "You'll do as I tell you."

Although he didn't fully understand the horror of incest, Nocturne understood his mother's pain. He exploded with a howl, and he charged his grandfather in a blind rage, driving him back against a bureau. The old man struggled to defend himself. Finally he grasped a heavy jar from the bureau and swung it against the side of Nocturne's head, shattering the thick glass. The boy dropped to the floor and entered into his beloved dark.

He woke on the cold, cement floor of the basement. How much time had passed, he couldn't say. His head hurt. He was thirsty. He stood up, dizzy, and made his way to the steps. Daylight seeped through the narrow gap between the bottom of the basement door and the kitchen floor. He tried to let himself out, but the padlock was still in place. He heard the floorboards of the kitchen creak. The padlock rattled and snapped free. The old man opened the door. Nocturne's grandfather stood in a blaze of light and held a shotgun aimed at the boy. Nocturne squinted painfully and turned his face from the glare. The old man grabbed him harshly by the arm and pulled him into the light. He shoved Nocturne ahead of him toward the stairway, up to the second floor, down the hallway to the bedroom where Nocturne's eyes had been truly opened. He forced his grandson inside.

135

The curtains were drawn against the sunlight. His mother lay in bed, covered by a dirty, wrinkled sheet. She stared up at the ceiling. Her arms were outside the sheet, slightly spread away from her body, each wrist bound in white gauze that was stained red. To Nocturne she seemed an angel fallen to earth, an angel who'd come to rest on that old bed, an angel with red-tipped wings. She blinked, but she didn't seem to be aware that her son was there.

"Like her mother," the old man spat. "Weak." He stepped between Nocturne and the woman on the bed. "Are you like her? Or are you like your father?"

Nocturne looked into the old man's eyes and understood everything.

He could feel a tearing inside, as if the flesh and the bone were splitting, as if he were giving birth to another self. From a place he'd never stood before, he looked back and saw the boy who'd walked with his mother in the beauty of the night, who'd held her while she wept at the sad music of the phonograph records, who'd learned a kind of happiness in the solitary dark with his books and his gadgets and his imagination and her as his sole companion. The new part of him looked at that child with deep contempt, for clearly the world was a different place, much simpler than he'd ever imagined. There were the powerful and there were the powerless. There were those who created nightmares and those who lived them. Nocturne had been one of the victims. But no more. In the world as he now understood it, there was no room for weakness.

He faced the old man and he heard his own cold voice answer, "Like you."

Nightmare had been born.

chapter

nineteen

I believe it was very soon after he discovered the incest that he killed his grandfather and his mother," Dr. Hart said.

"Whoa. He confessed to that?" During the story, Stuart Coyote hadn't touched his coffee. It no longer steamed in the cup in his hands.

"Another inference of mine."

"Killed them in anger? A sense of betrayal? What?" Coyote asked.

"Where his grandfather was concerned, I think David considered it justice, retribution. In his world, there was no law but the law of his grandfather, and death the only recourse."

"And his mother?"

"Anger at her betrayal is certainly a possibility. But I'm more inclined to think he believed he was setting her free."

"Anger's got my vote," Coyote insisted. "Christ, who wouldn't have been pissed?"

The patient who'd been working in the little garden in the courtyard stood up. Dirt circled the knees of his pants like brown patches, and he made a brief effort to brush himself clean. He looked down at the flowers he'd tended, then stared up at the sky that was fractured by wire mesh.

"Keep in mind that David's understanding of the world came largely from what he experienced in that dreadful house," she said. "His knowledge of what was beyond his basement he'd acquired largely from his reading and the radio. It would be as if you or I were trying to understand the cannibals of Borneo simply from reading textbooks. I think he was more outraged by his mother's suffering than by the incest. The killing ended her pain and his grandfather's tyranny. In his mind, the act was reasonable and justified."

"How did he kill them?" Bo asked.

"He blew up the house." Her brown eyes strolled between Bo and Coyote. "Swift and terrible."

Bo shook his head. "This all seems predicated on believing what he's told you. Do you have any facts that support his story?"

"Facts?" She smiled patiently. "He was placed in St. Jerome's Home for Children after he was discovered outside the burning remains of an isolated farmhouse in Isanti County. Investigators found explosives and other related materials in the barn. They determined David's grandfather was a man they'd been attempting to trace for some time, a man who called himself Short Fuse. In letters to the media, he'd taken responsibility for nearly a dozen bombings over a three-year period. All this was almost a quarter of a century ago, but I've checked the newspaper accounts. As far as I can tell, no suspicion ever fell on David. He was quite clever, even then."

"Is he criminally insane?" Bo asked.

"I would have expected his childhood experiences—neglect, abuse, exposure to incest—to contribute to psychosis. However, in David's case, I believe what resulted would better be characterized as an alternative reality. He is, in many ways, predictable because he lives according to an ethos. Not one many people would necessarily condone, but certainly understandable."

"Help us understand," Bo said.

"All right. You or I might consider killing someone in a fit of anger. We don't because we're conditioned to believe it's wrong to kill. In war, however, to kill becomes the moral imperative. For God, for country, for our comrades. And we hold in high esteem those who kill best. Think of David Moses as existing internally in a state of perpetual warfare. He kills not out of cruelty, but because it is in complete accord with the world as he understands it."

"If that's true, why hasn't he killed more?"

"He intimated that he has. Many times."

"A serial killer?" Stuart Coyote asked.

"Not if I've interpreted correctly what I've pieced together. A hired killer, Mr. Coyote. An assassin."

"A hit man?"

"Dr. Hart," Bo put in, "you said that before the killing in Minneapolis, Moses had no criminal record, is that right?"

"None that we're aware of."

"Men who do that kind of work are generally well known to law enforcement."

She didn't seem at all inclined to withdraw her conjecture.

"You believe all this?" Coyote asked incredulously. "Don't you think it's possible he fooled you? Or maybe that he was so deluded he made it all seem convincing?"

"With a man of David's intelligence, anything is possible. You indicated you'd seen the scars on his arms."

Bo nodded. "Self-mutilation?"

She shook her head. "Cicatrization. Ritual scarring. If I've put his story together correctly, he carries a scar for each killing. Those of least importance are on his appendages. The greater the import, the nearer he puts them to his heart. Another thing. He's very sensitive to sunlight. He prefers to wear sunglasses even indoors. He's been checked. There's no medical foundation for such a sensitivity. But to David, it's real."

"I asked you a question you never answered," Bo said. "Do you think he's dangerous?"

"Most patients are dreary repetitions of an unhappy theme. David Moses is different. I looked forward to our sessions. He's charming when he wants to be. When he deigns to be communicative, a conversation with him can be delightful and challenging."

"But is he dangerous?" Bo persisted.

"If he's truly delusional, he's fully capable of living out his delusion. If he's not, then he knows well how to kill." She paused and seemed to consider whether to say the rest of what was on her mind. "David doesn't belong out there. Out there, he *is* dangerous. But in here, he's a rare creature, and I would hate to see him destroyed."

They leaned against their cars in the visitor lot of the Security Hospital. It was late morning, already hot. They'd given the program director all the information they had on the man who was probably David Moses. Helen Wardell had called the Nicollet County sheriff's office, and two detectives were on their way to the Security Hospital.

Coyote said, "I was inclined to laugh when Dr. Hart said Moses might be a hired killer. But I've been thinking. A decade-long blank in his history, that's pretty suspicious."

"With this guy, I'm beginning to think anything is possible," Bo answered.

"Could someone have actually hired David Moses to kill Jorgenson?"

"I think it's more likely that he has his own agenda."

"He's driving Luther Gallagher's truck. We should take a look inside Gallagher's house."

"You mind handling that, Stu?"

"Fine by me. When the sheriff's men get here, I'll see if we can't get a warrant. While I'm at it, I'll check out activity on any credit cards Gallagher has. Might tell us where he, or Moses, have been lately and what they've been up to."

"My own instincts are telling me that Gallagher's dead. And if

David Moses is as clever as Dr. Hart believes, we're not going to find the body easily."

"Let's see where we stand after I've had a look at his place. What about you, Bo?"

"I'm going back to the office, see how quickly we can get hold of Moses's military service record. It might help in uncovering some of that missing history. I'd also like to find out about the fixation on Tom Jorgenson. What's the connection between Moses and him?"

"If he's whacked out, he could have seen Jorgenson on television and just fixated."

"You know where St. Jerome's Home for Children is, Stu? Less than ten miles from Wildwood. I don't think that's a coincidence. Dr. Hart said David Moses never completed high school. He dropped out and joined the service. I'm going to look into his time at St. Jerome's. I'd like to know who signed his enlistment papers and why."

chapter

twenty

I t took Bo an hour and a half to get to Minneapolis. He made one stop on the way at a market outside Shakopee to pick up an apple and some cheese for lunch, but he still felt hungry when he walked into the field office. The place seemed empty, as it usually did when someone important enough to warrant protection visited the Twin Cities.

He spoke with Rafael Ramos, the criminal research specialist for the field office, and gave him what information he had on David Moses. He asked Ramos to get a copy of the man's military record ASAP.

Diana Ishimaru was on her phone. She waved Bo in and pointed to a chair.

The office of the special agent-in-charge was a large and orderly room painted in light blue. On the wall behind her desk hung a photograph of a younger Agent Ishimaru shaking hands with President George Bush, the elder. She was an attractive woman, Bo's boss. Forty-seven years old, straight black hair that swept her shoulders, a well-maintained figure, dark Asian eyes. Like a lot of agents, she had a divorce somewhere in her past. Never remarried. Driven in a profession dominated by men, she'd advanced to her position through hard work, an astute understanding of the politics of the Secret Service, and an ability to engender fierce loyalty in those who worked with her.

Ishimaru hung up. "What do you have?"

"Care to step into the Twilight Zone with me?" He related what he and Coyote had discovered in St. Peter. She made notes as he talked. He finished with "I called the Washington County sheriff and let him know what we'd found out. He's putting additional security on Tom Jorgenson."

"How about Wildwood?"

"I talked with Jake Russell. He's going to relay the information to Manning. I figure it's Manning's decision whether to inform the First Lady and Annie."

"What are you going to do now?" she asked.

"Try to find answers to three questions. What's the connection, if any, between Tom Jorgenson and David Moses? Why would such a towering intellect choose to join the military at seventeen? And, because he was underage, who signed as his guardian on the enlistment papers?"

"Let me guess," she said, glancing at her notes. "You're going to St. Jerome's Home for Children, where you're hoping to find the answers to all three questions."

"You're scary," he said.

"Just good at this job. As you are. Well done, Bo."

He was heading for the elevator when Diana Ishimaru stepped quickly out the door of the field office and called to him. "Bo. I just got a phone call from the Washington County sheriff. Tom Jorgenson's regained consciousness."

Where I-94 snaked through downtown St. Paul, there was a rollover with injuries. Bo got caught in the snarl of traffic. He was delayed nearly an hour getting to the St. Croix Regional Medical Center. He observed immediately the intensified security. Additional hospital guards and sheriff's deputies made access to the fourth floor impossible for all but authorized visitors and staff. Consequently, the newspeople had set up camp in the main lobby. Media vans and cars that had been parked along the highway fronting Wildwood now sat in the hospital lot. Bo parked in a tow zone near the Emergency Room entrance and went in that way. He found the security desk manned by C. J. Burke, the guard who'd been on duty the night O'Meara died. Burke had the current issue of *Gamer's Magazine* open on the desk in front of him. He looked at Bo through eyes heavy with boredom.

"Sorry about your partner," Bo said.

"Partner?"

"O'Meara."

"He wasn't my partner. We just worked the same shift."

The guard wrote Bo's name in the log and went back to looking at his magazine.

Bo was angry that Burke didn't seem to give a shit about his fallen colleague, but he let it go. What good would it do to lash out? You cared or you didn't, it was that simple. He took the elevator to the fourth floor, where Tom Jorgenson now lay conscious. A sheriff's deputy stopped Bo the moment he stepped out, then allowed him to pass when he saw the Secret Service ID. Another deputy had been posted at the door to Jorgenson's room. Sheriff Doug Quinn-Gruber was using the phone at the nurses' station.

When the phone call ended, Bo approached. "Doug, have you had a chance to talk to Tom Jorgenson?"

Quinn-Gruber sipped vending machine coffee from a disposable cup. "He's pretty weak. The doctor's allowed only family in so far. The First Lady was here with Annie. They headed back to Wildwood just a few minutes ago. Ruth stayed. She's here somewhere." He glanced around. "Must've gone to the ladies' room."

"Any of the family know about Moses?"

The sheriff shook his head. "Manning didn't want to say anything until he knew more. We got a photo of David Moses over the wire from Minneapolis P.D. Everybody working security has a copy of it. Detective Timmons is at Hennepin County Courthouse checking the file they've got on Moses."

Bo glanced toward Jorgenson's room. "How's he doing?"

"Seems okay now. They had a scare when he first came to. He went ballistic. Disoriented, I guess. The nurses had to restrain him. The doctor asks him if he knows where he is. Jorgenson looks at him like the doc's the devil himself and says, 'Are you no man?' Doc tells him he's a physician and that this is a hospital. That settled him right down. He's been fine since." The sheriff shook his head. " 'Are you no man?' What kind of question is that?"

Bo went to the physician who was deeply engrossed in reading Jorgenson's chart, and he interrupted gently, "I'm Special Agent Bo Thorsen, Secret Service." The two men shook hands. "I know Tom Jorgenson's condition isn't good, but I'd like to talk with him."

"Can't it wait?"

"It's important or I wouldn't ask."

The doctor considered, then said, "All right. But keep it short."

Tom Jorgenson's eyes were closed. His face was sallow, his cheeks and sharp jaw grizzled with white stubble. A tube was attached to one arm, and another came out a nostril. He was hooked to electrodes connected to an EKG monitor. He reminded Bo of a puppet abandoned by whoever it was that usually pulled the strings. The shades over the windows were open to let in sunlight, but the glass was tinted, and what came through was subdued. The tint turned the blue of the river and the sky to deep gray. Bo drew up a chair next to the bed. Tom Jorgenson still wore a turban of gauze, and his eyes still looked as if he'd been pummeled in a prize-fight.

"Bo?" he whispered.

"Hello, Tom."

He spoke slowly. "What are you doing here?" He thought a moment, then answered his own question. "Oh, Kate."

"I'm only going to stay a moment, Tom. I need to ask you a couple of questions, okay?"

Jorgenson gave a faint nod.

"Does the name David Moses mean anything to you?"

Tom Jorgenson closed his eyes. Bo thought he might be drifting off, then his eyes opened again. "No," he replied.

"It might have been a long time ago."

"Sorry, Bo. Not so easy to think."

"That's okay. Tom, do you remember anything about your accident?"

"Getting on the tractor. Nothing else. Tree limb hit me, they say." A weak smile touched Tom Jorgenson's lips. "How's that for clumsy?"

Bo told him to rest, then he left the room. Outside Quinn-Gruber was waiting.

"You ask him about Moses?"

Bo nodded. "Nothing. But he's tired. I didn't want to push it."

He left the medical center and walked outside into the late afternoon sun. He stood beside his Contour and used his cell phone to contact Agent Russell in the Op Center at Wildwood.

"How are things there, Jake?"

"Quiet."

"Have you and Manning discussed informing the First Lady about David Moses?"

"We discussed it. He wants to know exactly what you have first."

"Is he there?"

"He's out looking at the equipment we've got along the bluff. He's not convinced the perimeter there is secure."

"Maybe he's right to be concerned. I've been thinking, Jake. If Moses did attack Tom Jorgenson in the orchard, it may indicate a good knowledge of Wildwood. I think we should put additional agents on the perimeter. Maybe call Diana and request—"

"Bo," Russell cut him off, but didn't go on. Bo understood the meaning. The security of Wildwood was no longer Bo's responsibility.

"Sorry, Jake."

"No problem, Bo. Just keep me informed."

"You've got it. Have Manning call me when he gets back to the Op Center. I'll fill him in on everything."

"Ten-four."

Bo stood blinking in the sun, wishing he could let go of the feeling that responsibility for so much rested on his shoulders. But it was a feeling as old as any for him, and if he lost it, who would he be then?

chapter

twenty-one

St. Jerome's Home for Children was a vast rectangular structure of red brick set at the edge of an alfalfa field. When Bo drove up, the playground beside the parking lot was full of laughing children. It was a fine setting, there in the country, but Bo knew firsthand that even in the finest of settings an institution was no substitute for a home and a family.

Sister Mary Jackson ushered him into her office. She wore a brilliant red skirt and matching jacket. Her dark hair was coifed short and stylish. There were lines at the corners of her eyes and mouth, smile lines deeply etched. Her eyes were warm brown and welcoming. Her office overlooked the playground, and as they spoke, the sound of children's voices floated in like music. Bo explained his situation. She turned to her computer terminal and entered the name of David Moses. The program searched for a moment, then reported it found no matches. No problem, she explained. While all recent files were in the system, anything older than fifteen years probably hadn't been entered yet. She led Bo downstairs into a cool basement room full of green filing cabinets and the musty smell of time. She turned on a dismal light, quickly found the cabinet she wanted, and pulled out a drawer. She began to flip through manila folders brittle with age.

Bo's cell phone broke the quiet of the basement. "Thorsen, here," Bo answered.

"This is Manning. You wanted to talk to me."

"Chris, can I call you back? I'm in the middle of something here."

"If you think it can wait."

"Hmmm," Sister Mary Jackson said.

"It can wait." Bo flipped the cell phone closed. "What is it?" he asked the nun.

"I can't find one for David Moses. It would have been approximately twenty years ago?"

"Approximately."

"And you're certain he was one of ours?"

"I'd pull up just short of certain."

"That's very odd. We should have a file somewhere." She accompanied Bo back upstairs and discussed the situation with a couple of the office staff. They looked in several places and came up empty-handed. "It's possible," she finally conceded apologetically, "that it's been misplaced. These things happen. If you'd like to talk to someone who may remember the boy, I'd suggest you speak with Father Don Cannon. He was the director here for nearly thirty years. He's retired now, but he's a wonderful resource."

She gave Bo a telephone number and an address in River Falls, a small town in Wisconsin, just the other side of the St. Croix River. As he was leaving the parking lot, his cell phone beeped. It was Stuart Coyote.

"I was beginning to think you'd gone on vacation," Bo said.

"It was a bastard finding a judge, or more precisely finding a judge who wasn't a bastard. First guy looked at me like he wondered how the hell I escaped from the reservation. We finally got the warrant this afternoon and went into Luther Gallagher's house."

"What did you find?"

"Nothing that relates in an obvious way to David Moses. But we stumbled onto some interesting appliances in the basement. Complicated wood and leather devices. The place looked like a dungeon. Luther Gallagher appears to have a fondness for rough fore-play of the medieval variety."

"What do you bet David Moses convinced Luther Gallagher he'd be his dungeon buddy if Gallagher helped him after his escape?"

"My guess, too. We found an address book, and the sheriff's people here are doing a rundown of the names to see if anyone knows Gallagher's whereabouts or has knowledge of any connection with David Moses. We found a telephone number for Gallagher's father in Arizona. The old guy says his ticker's never acted up, and he claims he hasn't seen his no-account son in almost a decade.

"Here's something else that's interesting. We found papers for a vehicle purchase made four weeks ago. Luther bought himself a new van. According to bank statements in the pile of mail, he cleaned out his savings and checking accounts. I'm going to run a check of his credit history, see what he's been up to lately in that department."

"Good work, Stu."

"One more thing, Bo. I went back to see Dr. Hart. I wanted to ask her a few more questions. I passed a couple guys in dark suits coming from her office. When I stepped in, she seemed surprised to see me, since she'd just finished talking at length with two of my colleagues."

"Colleagues?"

"The two dark suits. They told her they were Secret Service. Flashed IDs that Hart swore looked like ours. I went after them. They were gone. I didn't recognize them, Bo. I checked with the field office. Nobody but you and me on this case."

"What do you think?"

"I peg them for a couple of alphabet boys. CIA, NSA, DOD. Take your pick. I'm wondering if maybe Moses really is a hit man. Or was. For the government. And whoever he worked for doesn't want any-one to know it."

Bo considered the long, lost period in the history of David Moses after he left the military. He knew any of the agencies Coyote had mentioned were powerful enough to wipe a man's slate clean.

"Did you run this by Ishimaru?"

"Yeah," Coyote said. "She's working on it."

"Good."

"What's up on your end?"

Bo filled him in on his visit to St. Jerome's. "I'm heading to River Falls to talk to the old priest," he finished. "Maybe he can enlighten us about the adolescence of David Moses."

"We're closing in, Bo."

"Stay in touch."

River Falls was twenty miles southeast of Stillwater. Bo's watch read six o'clock straight up when he pulled onto Main Street. He was hungry. And tired. He needed food and coffee, but he wanted to talk to the priest first.

He found the home that matched the address Sister Mary Jackson had given him. It was a tidy little one-story frame on a street shaded by maples. Pansies lined the walk. He parked in the empty drive and went to the front door. No one answered the bell or his knock. He headed back to his car and stood a moment, considering his options. It was the dinner hour. The street was deserted. In a while, people would be out for their evening walks or watering their lawns or sitting in their porch swings. But at the moment, there was no one to be seen. Bo decided to eat and return later.

He found a homey-looking café called Ethel's. The place smelled wonderful, of meat loaf and gravy. Bo ordered the dinner special for the day, the meat loaf, and coffee. The café was nearly full, families, older folks talking quietly, a couple of farmers in clean, bib overalls and billed caps. Locals. It reminded Bo of Blue Earth and the rare dinners out with Harold and Nell Thorsen. Two or three foster kids were always along. They always ate at the Sleepy Eye Café, where the specials were pork roast or fried chicken or chicken fried steak with mounds of mashed potatoes and homemade gravy and green beans. Dinner always ended with fresh-baked pie. So little had been special in Bo's life before those days in Blue Earth that dinner at the Sleepy Eye Café became a landmark for him.

He finished eating, and as he sipped a final cup of coffee, he tried calling the priest. He got the message machine. "Hi. Don Cannon. Can't take your call, just leave a message and have a great day." Bo didn't leave a message. But so far, the day hadn't been too bad.

He returned to the house. No one answered his knock this time either. Next door, a bald man in a Hawaiian shirt and khaki shorts stood in the middle of his lawn. He had a garden hose in one hand and a beer can in the other. He was spraying a fine mist over the grass and eyeing Bo.

"Know Father Cannon?" Bo called to him.

"Sure."

"Know where he might be?"

"Thursday's his bowling night. Falls Lanes. West side of Main Street as you head north out of town."

"Thanks."

"You a cop?"

"Why do you ask?"

"I can tell. I used to be a cop, too." He lifted the beer in a friendly toast of goodwill.

The last of the day's sunlight fell across the town as Bo drove to the bowling alley. Trees cast long shadows down quiet streets. The air smelled faintly of fresh cut grass. If his concern had not been so pressing, Bo might have let himself linger awhile, enjoying the feel of the small town as evening settled in.

When he opened the door to the bowling alley, the country quiet was broken by the rumble of balls on oiled wood and the thunder of shattered pin sets.

The place was busy. A league night. Every lane was full. Bo had no idea what Father Don Cannon looked like. He didn't see anyone wearing a cleric's white collar. He made his way to the desk and took his place in a long line of people waiting to be served. As he stood there, he scanned the lighted displays above each lane that gave the names of the teams, the bowlers, and their scores. A team on lane eleven called themselves The Holy Rollers. The third bowler listed was Don. Bo stepped in that direction.

Father Cannon was a big man with bushy gray hair and a thick, unkempt beard. He wore glasses, a rumpled, blue knit shirt that barely covered his rotund belly, and tan slacks. He crouched low as he prepared to bowl, approached the foul line aggressively, and threw a powerful hook that sent the pins flying like demons fleeing the wrath of God.

Bo bided his time, waiting while The Holy Rollers and the team they opposed, The Wild Ducks, bowled two more lines. The Holy Rollers easily won. As the priest toweled off his ball and placed it in his ball bag, Bo approached him.

"Father Cannon?" he asked.

The priest looked up, smiling huge through the wild hairs of his beard. "Saw you watching. Wondered if you were a fan or just killing time."

"Bo Thorsen's my name. I'm with the U.S. Secret Service." Bo let him have a good look at his ID. "I'd like a word with you."

"About what?"

"David Moses."

The priest's face lost its smile, and a different look appeared there. As if Father Cannon had just heard something he'd been waiting a long time to hear. "You a drinking man?"

"On occasion," Bo replied.

"I think this is an occasion, Mr. Thorsen."

chapter

twenty-two

"D avid Moses," the priest said unhappily and shook his head. "It's been twenty years since I heard that name."

They sat at the bar in the lounge connected to the bowling alley. The television above the liquor bottles was tuned to a Twins' game, but the sound was turned down. Father Don Cannon fingered a shot glass of Dewar's that was backed up by a chaser of beer. Bo was nursing a bottle of Leinenkugel's. He'd already told the priest everything he knew about David Moses, and everything he suspected.

"You really think he tried to kill Tom Jorgenson?"

"I'm almost certain of it," Bo said. "I just don't know why."

The priest signaled the bartender. "We're going to a booth, Patrick. I'll let you know when we need another round." He motioned for Bo to follow, and he walked to a dimly lit booth well back in a corner. After they sat down, he slammed back his Dewar's and took a hard draw on his beer. "Did you know he chose his own name? David Solomon Moses."

"What do you mean, he chose it?" Bo asked.

"He didn't even have a name when he came to us. His existence had never been officially noted, and his mother had never given him a name. Or one that he would tell us. This was probably the least of the sadnesses in that boy's history."

"You know about his history?"

"Until he left us, anyway. David wasn't Catholic, wasn't anything really, and so what he shared, he shared with me only as his confidant, not his confessor. And more's the pity."

The thunder from the alleys almost drowned the priest's dour voice, and Bo leaned nearer.

"David came to us in unusual circumstances. He was sixteen, just orphaned. No other family that the authorities could identify. He wasn't a good candidate for adoption. Kids that age seldom are. The social worker assigned to his case believed that St. Jerome's was a better option than foster care. After I heard about David, so did I.

"He was the most remarkable young man with whom I've ever worked. Brilliant. He arrived at St. Jerome's with a limited understanding of the world and proceeded to read quite literally everything in our library. He soaked up knowledge. I remember many times sitting up with him in my study late at night deep in ecclesiastical arguments. He had a wonderfully analytic mind. I admit, at one point I entertained the hope he might even have a religious calling. But that was my own blindness.

"I knew there was great potential in David, both good and bad. And the bad wasn't his fault."

"His childhood?" Bo said.

Father Cannon finished his beer and wiped his mouth with the back of his hand. "That boy was raised in the basement of an old farmhouse by a man about as near to the devil as a man can get. By all rights, David should have been totally ruined, but he wasn't. There was a strength, a resilience in him that was remarkable. Do you believe we come already forged into this world, already created as the beings we will be?" He didn't wait for Bo to answer. "I do. David was born strong, and he resisted as well as he could the forces that sought to break him. He told me things about his childhood that made me weep, Mr. Thorsen." The priest paused a moment, and Bo thought his old eyes might yet be fighting back tears. "I believed we had David on the right track. He was in school. He'd made the gymnastics team. He'd joined the debating society. He seemed to have made friends. He was blossoming, and it was wonderful to see. In those days, I thought of him a little like Lazarus. He'd been dead, but he was alive again. Then the thing happened with Tom Jorgenson and his daughter, and we lost David forever."

The priest hesitated.

"You can't leave me hanging, Father. Tom Jorgenson's life is at stake."

"You're certain of that?"

"I'm just about to the place where I'd stake everything on it."

The priest thought it over. "We might need another round for this." He signaled the bartender. When the drinks came, he threw the Dewar's down his throat and followed it with a swallow of beer. Braced, he addressed Bo again.

"As I said, David was doing well. I knew some of what had gone on in his life, but I was aware there were things David kept inside. He was scarred in ways that didn't show immediately, and I was so full of myself, so pleased that I had this kid so quickly headed toward a normal life, that I ignored the warning signs."

"What signs?" Bo asked.

"We had an arrangement with Wildwood in those days. Kids from St. Jerome's were employed during the summer and on weekends in the fall to help with the work in the orchards. We bused them out, bused them back. I arranged to have David work there. His first day he met Kathleen Jorgenson.

"Girls were a topic David and I discussed occasionally. The only woman he'd ever really known was his mother, so the opposite sex was a mystery to him. The first thing I did was to assure him that this was normal. Actually, he was quite popular with girls at school. He was smart and athletic and the uniqueness of his circumstances, his being an orphan, made him attractive to girls his age. Although David was cordial enough, he kept them all at a distance, studying them, I think, so that he wouldn't be out of control. When he met Kathleen Jorgenson, all his precautions went poof, turned to dust. He fell head over heels in love with her. The problem was that she didn't feel the same way about him. Friends, that's all they were in her eyes. Good friends.

" 'How can I get her to love me?' he'd plead with me. He became a broken record, although he controlled himself admirably around her. Or so it appeared."

"Any idea what Tom Jorgenson thought of David?"

"From what I gathered, he liked the boy quite a lot. He invited David to stay to dinner on several occasions. I know what David thought of him. In many ways, he saw Tom Jorgenson as a father figure, admired his intelligence and his accomplishments.

"As summer drew to a close, David began coming back later and later from Wildwood. He didn't ride the bus with the other kids. He had this little motorbike he'd built himself from scrap parts he found in the equipment shed at St. Jerome's. He used it to get himself to and from the orchards. He'd come in late and refuse to talk about what he'd been up to. It was obvious he hadn't been drinking or using drugs. He was too independent to be involved in a gang. I was perplexed, but I let myself believe it wasn't serious. Then one night, I got a call from the sheriff's office. They had David in custody.

"I arrived at the county jail and found a young man I'd never seen before, a very different David. Cold. Eyes hard as steel. It wasn't anger or fear. It was something frightening, so void of compassion it hardly seemed human. He had a horrible bruise across his forehead and the side of his face. The sheriff told me Kate Jorgenson was claiming that David had attacked her, tried to sexually assault her. As if that wasn't bad enough, David was claiming it wasn't him who attacked Kate. It was Tom Jorgenson."

The priest stopped and lifted his glass to his lips. From the bowling alley came the crash of pins exploding out of their neat formations.

"Tom Jorgenson?" Bo asked incredulously.

"That's right."

"I don't remember hearing anything about that."

"That's because it was kept quiet. I arranged to speak with David alone. He told me that he'd been sneaking back to Wildwood in the evenings. He'd sit in the orchard in the dark and gaze up at Kate's bedroom window. The boy was love-struck. That night, he saw her leave the house and head toward the bluff overlooking the river. A few minutes later, Tom Jorgenson followed her. David followed them both. He claimed that when he reached the bluff, he found Tom trying to force himself on Kate, and he attempted to intervene. Tom vehemently denied it. He maintained he'd been working in the barn and had heard her screams. He hurried to the bluff and found David lying there unconscious. Kate's clothes were torn. She was hysterical. All of this was substantiated by Tom's brother, Roland, who'd heard the screams, too, and had come running.

"I didn't know what to do. I tried to reason with David, but he refused to back away from his story. Tom was beside himself. Who wouldn't be in the face of such circumstances? Any publicity, the slightest leak, and the whole thing could blow up into an ugly mess. An allegation like David's could do irreparable damage. Of course, neither the sheriff's office nor the county attorney had any intention of allowing such a statement made by a kid like David to become public, if they could help it. But no one was exactly certain what should be done.

"It was Annie who finally suggested the military. She pointed out that David was now seventeen, of age if he had the consent of his legal guardian. He was certainly bright enough and physically capable of handling the training. It was an option she occasionally offered in her courtroom to keep a kid out of jail. She suggested a compromise. If David agreed not to make his allegation public and join the service, no charges would be brought against him. If he refused, the county attorney was prepared to charge him as an adult with criminal sexual assault.

"I talked it over with David. I pointed out to him that it would probably come down to a question of his word against the Jorgensons'. In a trial, all the sordid details of his own past would become public knowledge. Did he really want that? He looked at me, and he asked, did I believe him?"

After a few moments of silence, Bo said, "Did you?"

The priest contemplated the last of his beer and thought awhile before he answered. "I've worked with troubled kids most of my life. Every once in a while they've fooled me, but not often. Yes, I believed him. Or believed, at least, whoever it was who attacked Kate Jorgenson, it wasn't David. But I also believed absolutely Tom Jorgenson wouldn't assault his own daughter. So there didn't seem to be a clear truth anywhere. This much I did know. Once a jury heard David's history, there was no way in hell they were going to believe him. In the end, I told him it didn't matter what I thought. But I did suggest that going away was an answer that would hurt no one. He looked at me as if I'd simply washed my hands of him, abandoned him completely. Shortly after that, I signed his enlistment papers." The priest finished his drink and shoved the empty glass away. "Now you tell me these things about David, and how can I not believe I had a hand in shaping him to this?"

The priest looked ready to slide under the table.

"Father Cannon, if David Moses has revenge on his mind, you may be in danger, too."

The priest waved off his concern. "I corresponded with him briefly after he left. I told him I prayed for his well-being. He wrote me back saying that he felt no animosity toward me. It was the Jorgensons who'd betrayed him." He sat back and rubbed his eyes. "Mr. Thorsen, I'm tired. Is there anything more I can do for you?"

"I don't think so. You've been helpful."

The priest picked up his ball bag and started out. He turned back. "What we are, we are forever. David may have done some horrible things, but inside him somewhere is still a remarkable human being. Please, whatever it is you ultimately have to do, try to keep that in mind."

The priest left through the lounge door and pushed out into the warm, dark night, leaving Bo to wonder what, ultimately, it was that he would have to do.

chapter

twenty-three

Nightmare checked his watch. Ten-forty. Sixteen minutes until the moon set. It was time.

He lay in the orchard grass, beyond the range of the motion detectors and the infrared cameras mounted on the stone wall. He wore midnight tiger camouflage fatigue pants and a T-shirt of the same design. The exposed skin of his face and arms was painted with a tiger stripe pattern of dark blue and black to match his clothing. Something fluttered among the trees behind him. Nightmare glanced back and watched an owl swoop and snatch up some small animal, then flap away, a black shape across the stars.

A dark figure walked along the edge of the orchard. Nightmare flattened himself against the ground. As soon as the patrolling agent had passed, Nightmare lifted the sod that covered the wood cap over the entrance to a tunnel just over two feet wide, and he reeled in his field pack. He'd crawled through the tunnel from the other side of the wall, dragging the pack that was tethered to his ankle by a short length of nylon rope. The weather in the two weeks since he'd completed the digging had been clear, and the passage under the wall was dry. The tunnel was exactly thirty-four feet long. He knew the capability of the motion detectors, and he'd placed the entrance and exit just beyond their range. Tom Jorgenson's lax concern about his personal safety had allowed Nightmare the freedom to construct the tunnel, which had taken him nearly three weeks, working nights after his shift at the hospital. He'd intended from the beginning to fall back on an assault against Wildwood if the hospital bombing plan had to be abandoned. From the pack, he drew out his Beretta 92F and the suppressor, a 7.4-inch M9-SD silencer. He fitted the suppressor into the muzzle of the Beretta and gave it a quarter turn to lock it in place. He slipped off his T-shirt and donned a dark blue Kevlar vest. It was uncomfortable against his bare skin, but it was essential. He pulled his T-shirt back on over the vest, hefted the pack onto his back, and began to track the agent who'd passed only a minute before. He knew the agent had night-vision goggles. Nightmare carried nothing of the kind, for to him the dark was an old friend.

The agent had no idea an intruder was at his back and made no sound when the silenced round entered the back of his skull. Nightmare knelt and from the belt of the fallen agent unclipped the transmitter that sent a location signal back to the Op Center. He pulled a battery-powered vehicle the size of a loaf of bread from his pack. It was a mechanism of his own construction, built from components he'd ordered from Radio Shack. It consisted of a powerful little motor and receiver on a chassis that would roll across the ground on small tank tracks. The receiver was set to follow the signal of a tiny homing device Nightmare had secured to an overhanging tree limb near the end of the orchard a few days earlier. He'd adjusted the tanklike mechanism so that it would travel at about the speed a careful agent might keep in making rounds. With a bit of duct tape, he affixed the agent's transmitter to the chassis and sent the device rolling forward under its own power along the same course the agent had been walking. For approximately eight minutes, the dot on the screen of the Op Center that monitored the agent's position would continue to move. Once the little tank passed under the tree limb where the homing device had been secured, it would stop. Three minutes later, the Op Center would try to make contact to ascertain the reason for the agent's pause. That gave Nightmare eleven minutes to complete his mission.

He sprinted across the orchard, ducking branches that bent low under the weight of ripening fruit. He knew that although the agents varied their rounds along the perimeter, they attempted to maintain their position relative to each other. Knowing the location of one, Nightmare could make a good assumption about the location of the other, and he moved to intercept.

He took the second agent down from the side with a single shot through the temple. As he'd done before, he snatched the location transmitter and taped it to a second motorized vehicle that he sent rolling through the orchard toward a homing device on the same heading the agent would have followed. Then he turned toward the main house.

He knew the range of the cameras mounted around the compound, and he'd already selected the best location for the next shot that night. He took up a position behind a gnarled old apple tree at the edge of the orchard behind the house. Sighting carefully on the camera mounted under the eaves that gave the Operations Center a view of the back door, he squeezed off a round and the camera jerked. He waited. Within a minute, the door of the guesthouse opened and an agent emerged. The agent went to the barn and came out with a ladder that he carried to the back corner of the house. He placed the ladder against the wall and shined a flashlight up at the camera. He unclipped a small walkie-talkie from his belt.

"Russell here. I can't tell what the problem is yet." He lifted his foot onto the first rung.

Nightmare put a round squarely between the man's shoulder blades. The agent went forward, as if shoved from behind, bounced off the aluminum ladder, and fell back in a heap. Nightmare ran to him and put another round between his eyes. He grabbed the walkie-talkie and spoke in a rough approximation of the agent's voice. "Squirrel damage."

"I copy that," the Op Center replied.

The locks on the back door took him only moments, and he was quickly inside the house, standing in the darkened kitchen. He knew that the agent on duty inside preferred the comfort of the living room, and he began to creep in that direction. He'd taken only a few steps when an old board beneath his foot sent a squeal into the quiet of the house. A moment later, a gray shadow touched the door frame. Nightmare knelt in a firing position. The agent stepped into the doorway and reached for the light switch. Nightmare fired twice at the silhouette, the silencer thumping as it spit out the rounds, the lead slugs thumping again as they slammed into flesh and bone. Nightmare put a new clip into the Beretta. He stepped over the downed agent and started up the stairs to the second floor. Slipping along the hallway, he passed the rooms he knew were occupied by Annie Jorgenson, Earl Jorgenson, and Nicole Greene, and he stood finally at the threshold of the First Lady's bedroom. Light from inside filtered under the door. On the monitor in the van parked on the highway, he'd watched her prepare for bed, slide under the covers, and lift a book from the nightstand. He figured she must still be reading. The knob turned easily and silently in his grip. He edged the door open.

She sat propped up against a pillow. The book lay open on her lap. Her eyes were closed. Her chin rested on her chest. The headboard that framed her was walnut, an antique. A beautifully carved angel with spread wings hovered above each of her shoulders. Nightmare smiled grimly. A fat lot of good they would do her now.

Her eyelids fluttered open at the touch of the silencer against her forehead.

"Waking you with a kiss seemed so cliché," he whispered.

She spoke not a word, but her eyes seemed to struggle for some kind of understanding as they stumbled between the barrel against her forehead and the face of her assailant. A small gasp escaped her lips. He put a finger to them, a warning against crying out.

"You don't remember me, do you?" he asked quietly.

She shook her head, barely more than a quiver against the silencer.

"You ruined my life and you don't remember."

"Who . . ." she began, but her voice failed her.

"David Moses," he answered.

It took a moment to register, but he saw that it did, and that pleased him.

"No," she pleaded softly. "Please, no."

"Oh, yes," he answered. "But not here. We're going for a walk, you and me. We're going to look at the moon together one last time."

Bo pulled out of River Falls, heading southwest toward the bridge at Prescott. The moon was just about to set. The night was dark, and the sky was full of stars. He drove with the windows down. The wink of fireflies filled the fields along the road, and from the marshes came the bellow of bullfrogs. It would have been a lovely night if Bo hadn't been so troubled by what he'd learned from the priest.

He'd been looking for a connection between Tom Jorgenson and David Moses, something powerful enough to be a motive for murder. He believed he'd found it—the confrontation long ago between the two that had brought an end to any hope Moses might have had for a normal life. Still, a lot of questions remained. If the motive was an old grudge held by a disturbed man, why act now? Why, after all these years, after a whole lifetime of opportunity, was Moses only just now making his move? And why all the complications—the hospital job, the charade of Max Ableman, the "accident" in the orchard? Why hadn't he just killed Jorgenson and been done with it?

His cell phone chirped. It was Coyote.

"Where are you, Bo?"

"Crossing the river into Minnesota. I'm heading back to Wildwood."

"I've got some interesting news."

"Shoot."

"Luther Gallagher's credit cards show a lot of unusual activity in the last month. Expensive purchases of sophisticated electronics. We're talking monitors, receivers, minidome cameras, pinhole cameras, audio transmitters, telephone transmitters."

"Surveillance," Bo said.

"Bingo."

"Of whom? Jorgenson?"

"Well, so far he's the only item on the menu."

Bo thought a moment. Things began to click. "Stu, I've got to go." Without waiting for an answer, he broke the connection and punched in the number of the Op Center at Wildwood.

"Agent Foster."

"Adam, this is Bo Thorsen."

"Evening, Bo. What's up?"

"Let me speak with Jake Russell."

"He's out fixing a camera. Damn squirrel chewed through the line again."

"Is Manning there?"

"Yeah. Want me to get him?"

"Thanks."

It seemed to take Chris Manning forever to come on the line. "What is it, Thorsen?"

"David Moses. He's got a possible motive for murder, and not just Tom Jorgenson. I think he may be after the First Lady as well."

"What have you got?"

"Moses worked at Wildwood a long time ago. Some pretty hard shit went down, things that could easily have made Moses bitter against the Jorgensons, Kathleen as well as Tom. I've been wondering why he didn't just kill Tom Jorgenson in the orchard. Maybe it's because he wanted to use the father as bait to lure the daughter here."

"Are you saying the First Lady has been his target all along?"

"He probably wants both of them dead. Look, Chris, he bought a lot of surveillance equipment in the last month. I think he may have bugged Wildwood."

On his end of the line, Manning was quiet for a moment. "We never ran a sweep."

"I recommend you put additional agents on the First Lady, and you do it now."

Bo heard Manning talking to Adam Foster. "Thorsen, I'm staring at the perimeter screen, following the dots that are your agents patrolling out there. Everybody's moving. We've had no indication of a breach. So we seem to be fine at the moment. I'm heading out to talk to Jake Russell right now. I'll have him put additional people in the orchard. Then I'll stand post in the main house myself."

"All right, Chris. I'm on my way."

Bo looked at his watch. Another five minutes and he'd be at Wildwood. He bore down on the accelerator.

Nightmare held the gun to her head as he guided the First Lady down the stairs. She hesitated and audibly caught her breath when she saw the agent lying on the floor inside the kitchen doorway.

"Step over the body." Nightmare pushed her forward. "Mind the blood."

He led her to the back door, opened it, and forced her outside.

"Oh, God," she said, catching sight of the agent on the ground at the foot of the ladder.

"Don't waste pity on the dead," he advised.

"He had a family," she shot back.

"Then he should have been an accountant. Into the orchard."

They hadn't taken a step when Nightmare heard the distant shutting of the door to the guesthouse. He shoved the First Lady against the wall, face first, muzzle of the silencer pressed hard against the back of her head. "Not a sound," he whispered.

He peered around the corner of the house and watched the agent walking in the glare of the yard light. The agent was headed for the front door of the main house but saw the ladder and changed direction, coming straight toward the shadows where Nightmare waited. As soon as the agent spotted the body and reached for his weapon,

Nightmare pulled the muzzle of the silencer away from its kiss of the First Lady. He dropped the agent with one shot in the chest.

"Please, God," the First Lady whispered, "this can't be happening."

"It takes a while to adjust to hell," he said, and he yanked her toward the orchard.

They moved rapidly. Nightmare saw clearly the sweep of the limbs that hung in their way, but the woman kept getting caught in the low branches, slowing them down. She tried to talk as they walked.

"Why?" she asked.

"I told you." He jerked her down to keep her from smacking another limb.

"I don't believe you. That was more than twenty years ago."

"There are no statutes of limitation on murder."

"Murder? What are you talking about?"

"You ended a boy's life."

"But you're alive."

He stopped and turned her harshly so that she had to look into his face. He moved near enough so that even in the dark she could see him clearly. "What I am is not alive. I am Death walking."

"I don't understand."

"Do you remember our last time here together?"

She hesitated, and he knew she was trying to read him. What kind of answer did he want?

"August twenty-eighth," he went on. "The moon rose at ten-o-nine, a day past full. You wore jean cutoffs, a sleeveless white blouse. Your feet were bare. You said you liked the way the orchard grass tickled your soles."

"David—"

"We talked about the year ahead. I tried to kiss you. My first kiss. You pulled away. Repulsed."

"No, David, not repulsed. I do remember. I was surprised, that was all. I hadn't expected it."

"Your father came then, interrupted us. He walked you back to the house. I told you I was going home."

168

"On your motorbike, the one you built," she said, with a little note of hope, as if remembering that small detail might save her.

"I parked it in the orchard on the way out, then came back and watched your room."

"I found out you'd often watched." It sounded like an accusation.

"I loved you," he said coldly. "Then I saw you leave the house, and he followed. When I reached the bluff, he had you in his arms. You were fighting him."

"He wasn't there, David. I swear to you."

"You tried to push him off you. That's when I yelled and rushed to stop him."

"It wasn't like that—"

"Three years ago, I was sitting in my own filth in a jungle prison. Open sores over most of my body, waiting to die. I realized my life had been nothing but one betrayal after another."

"Please, David, listen to me—"

"I decided I wasn't going to die there, forgotten, without purpose, in all that stink. I decided if I was going to die, it would be while trying to remove from this world as many of the liars and betrayers as I could. Know this: After I do you, I'll kill your father."

"We don't always see things the way they are." Her words tumbled fast, her voice desperately pitched. "We deceive ourselves. It's human. What you saw that night—"

"I know what I saw."

They left the trees and stood on the cliff overlooking the river. Behind them, the moon was slipping below the horizon. It looked like the last glimpse of a golden child being drawn back into the womb of the night itself.

Nightmare stepped between the woman and the moonlight.

"It's time," he said.

At the entrance to Wildwood, Bo swung his Contour off the highway. He stopped beside the county sheriff's car parked there.

"Everything okay?" he asked through his open window.

The deputy in the driver's seat said, "Sure, Bo." He sounded sleepy.

Farther down the drive, after the gates had swung open to let him pass, Bo checked in with Sumner, the agent on duty in the gatehouse. "Anything out of the ordinary tonight, Walt?"

"Heard we might get a display of the northern lights later. I wouldn't mind seeing that."

Bo pulled up to the guesthouse. Inside, everything was quiet. The main room was empty. The lights were out in the library. Someone had put a teakettle on in the kitchen, and it was just starting to whistle. Bo turned the burner off and stepped into the room that was the Op Center. Special Agent Adam Foster sat before the monitors. He glanced at Bo and lifted his hand in a greeting.

"Where's Jake?" Bo asked.

"Still out there working on the camera."

"Manning?"

"After he talked to you, he left right away. Didn't even bother to take the teakettle off the burner."

Good, Bo thought.

Then the perimeter alarm went off.

Bo's eyes followed Foster's to the monitor that picked up images from the tripod-mounted cameras that snapped on the instant the motion sensors were triggered. It was dark, but the infrared cameras easily captured the images.

"It's the First Lady and Moses." Bo noted the position of the perimeter breach. "They're heading to the cliffs. Contact the agents in the orchard and get them out there," he directed Foster. "Let Manning and Russell know what's up. I'm on my way now."

Bo hit the front door at a dead run, drawing his Sig from the holster clipped to his belt. He headed straight for the orchard, ran out of the spray of illumination from the yard light, and entered the silver and black of the apple trees in the late moonlight. The low branches made him run a crooked course, ducking and weaving. It was crucial to avoid the limbs not just because they would slow him down, but because the noise would alert David Moses to his coming. He approached the perimeter Moses and the First Lady had breached only a couple of minutes earlier, and he could see the black shape of the Kubota tractor, still parked where it had been left after the attack on Tom Jorgenson. Bo heard voices ahead, and he slowed. He crouched, came up behind the tractor, and pressed himself into its shadow. Shielded in this way, he crept along the body of the Kubota until he could see the edge of the cliff twenty yards ahead.

One silhouette stood against the backdrop of the Wisconsin hills across the river that were glazed with the last of the moonglow, but it was a silhouette with two heads. The First Lady and Moses were so close together Bo dared not risk a shot. The other agents would arrive at any moment and take up flanking positions. From a side vantage, Moses would be a clearer target. Bo could hear the First Lady speaking. Good, he thought. Keep him occupied.

"You made a mistake," she said. "You were always so smart, David. Be smart now. Consider that you might have made a mistake. I know about your life in that old farmhouse. Isn't it possible that what you saw you were predisposed to see, what your life up to that moment had conditioned you to see?"

"It's possible," Moses replied. His voice was cold and precise, not soft the way it had been when he spoke to Bo in the laundry. "But that's not what happened. He attacked you. You fought back. I tried to help. Then you both lied, and I was silenced in the only way I could have been. Although I'm sure your father would have been happier if my tongue had been cut off and my eyes plucked out."

"That's not what happened, David."

"Kneel down."

"Please, just listen to me. Let me explain."

"You have no more to say. Kneel down. It's time."

Jesus, where are they? Bo thought, wondering about the other agents. They should have a clear shot by now.

"Kneel down," Moses ordered again, angrily this time.

Yes, kneel down, Bo silently urged her. Get low, and I can take him out.

The First Lady said, "No, damn it."

Bo wanted to yell at her, but he knew that the moment he opened his mouth she was dead. He edged back along the tractor and stepped onto the running board. He felt over the instrument panel until his fingers touched the switch for the headlights.

"If you're going to kill me," the First Lady said, in a voice whose quiver seemed as much from anger as fear, "you'll have to look into my eyes while you do it. I won't get down on my knees for you or anyone."

For a long moment, nothing happened. Bo's eyes had adjusted to the moonlight. He could make out, just barely, the separation of the two bodies on the cliff, and he could see that Moses held a gun in his hand. Bo ached to shoot, but his own bullet might be as deadly to the First Lady as any fired by Moses.

"You've made up your mind to kill me. It doesn't matter what I say now or what the truth is."

Moses considered her. "If you get down on your knees and beg for your life," he said, "maybe I'll grant it."

The possibility of a way out seemed to break her anger. Bo saw her sway in her stance. Slowly she knelt and bowed her head. "Please, don't kill me."

"Admit that you lied. I want to hear you say it."

"I lied," she said in a voice gone suddenly soft.

Bo hit the lights. Moses blinked, blinded for a moment. Bo fired three times. Moses stumbled back. His weapon swung in Bo's direction. Although the silencer deadened any report, the gun kicked in his hand, and Bo knew he was attempting to return fire. The shots went high, harmlessly drilling into the night sky. Then Moses collapsed and lay still near where the First Lady knelt.

Bo walked forward cautiously, his Sig trained on the still form of David Moses. He saw Moses's handgun on the ground and kicked it away. The First Lady began to sob.

"Are you all right?" he asked.

"I . . . don't think I can move."

"Are you hit?"

"I don't know . . . I don't think so." Her body shook as she wept.

Bo shifted the Sig to his left hand and reached out to the First Lady. "It's all right now. It's all over," he said.

"Bo!" she cried.

Moses moved faster than Bo had ever seen a man move. From his prone position, he delivered a powerful kick, and Bo's leg buckled. Even as he went down, Bo tried to bring the Sig to bear on Moses, but the man rolled quickly away. Bo hit the ground on his knees. Moses executed a knife-hand blow that deadened Bo's arm, and the Sig dropped from his hand. In the same moment, Bo saw a flash of reflected light in Moses's right hand. Moses whirled, and Bo felt the thrust of the knife blade in his back. Instinctively, he rammed his arm backward like a piston, hammering his elbow into Moses's groin. He heard the man grunt in pain. Bo stumbled to his feet and turned to face the assailant. Moses lunged, leading with the knife. Bo parried with an arm bar. Although he deflected the blade from his body, he felt a deep slice across his forearm. He stepped left and delivered a kick that missed the knee joint that was its target, but nonetheless sent Moses stumbling backward. The man's momentum carried him to the edge of the bluff. Moses tried to catch himself before he went over, balancing for an instant, arms flailing like the wings of a night bird desperate to fly. Then he plummeted. Bo staggered to the cliff edge and looked over. All he saw was the dark, unbroken canopy of the trees below, and all he heard was the rasp of his own heavy breathing.

He was growing faint. He looked down at his arm. In the illumination from the tractor lights he saw a bright red spurting, and he realized, a little distantly, that Moses's knife had hit an artery. He was bleeding to death.

"Bo?"

The First Lady spoke behind him. He tried to answer, but all he could muster was a small grunt. He took a step away from the edge of the bluff, and his knees buckled. The First Lady knelt at his side.

"Oh, God," she whispered.

He fell against her, into her lap.

"Please," he heard her say toward the sound of voices in the orchard. "Agent Thorsen's badly hurt."

Bo lay in her lap with his head turned toward the tractor. The headlights had been bright, but they didn't seem so bright anymore. Whatever it was the First Lady was saying to him wasn't very clear. Not even the pain was distinct. What was most real to Bo was the desire to sleep. It had been so long since he'd slept well. But now it was time. He could finally let go. His job was done.

chapter

twenty-four

Bo dreamed of walking through falling white. Snow, maybe. Or ashes. Behind him, his footprints disappeared as quickly as he left them. Ahead of him, the white became a gauzy curtain muting everything beyond it to vague dark shapes. He sensed that something bad was out there beyond what he could see, something to be afraid of although he couldn't name it. *If this is snow*, he dreamed himself thinking, *then it's probably a wolf. If this is ashes . . .*

He woke before he dreamed the ending to that thought, woke to a touch on his arm, in a room full of white sunlight, in a bed with snow white sheets. Nurse Maria Rivera, in an impeccably white uniform, was taking his pulse. Bo lay on his stomach.

"I thought you worked nights," he said. He felt groggy, and his own voice sounded distant to him.

"I asked for days for a while." She noted his heart rate on his chart.

Bo watched her, and he remembered the afternoon they spoke in her home. "It wasn't your fault. Randy O'Meara, I mean. The man you knew as Max Ableman killed him."

"I know. Put this under your tongue." She stuck a digital thermometer in his mouth. When the thermometer beeped, she checked it and marked his chart.

"Do I have to be on my stomach?" Bo said.

"Not if you're careful." She helped him roll onto his side and propped him with a pillow placed so that it didn't touch the bandaged wound in his back. He'd been lucky, they told him. The blade had missed anything vital, and the wound had been easily closed. Gauze wrapped his forearm where the damage done to the artery and tendons had been repaired in surgery. "Someone is here to see you," she said.

Bo looked at the door. Stu Coyote stood in the threshold, a big, white-toothed grin on his broad Indian face. "Okay if I come in?"

"Sure. Thanks," Bo said to Nurse Rivera as she left.

Coyote stood at Bo's bedside. "For a national hero, you don't look so tough."

"National hero?"

"That's what the media's saying. But don't let it go to your head. They said the same thing about Custer for a while. How're you feeling?"

"I don't. They shot me full of painkiller."

Coyote drew a chair up and sat down. "You're looking pretty healthy for a man who almost bled to death."

"The First Lady's all right?"

"Yeah. You know she saved your life?" He smiled at Bo's look of surprise. "She put pressure on that wound and stopped the bleeding. Wouldn't let go until the paramedics got there."

"No kidding?"

"Damn straight."

"How about Annie? Is she okay?"

"Annie, Earl, and Nicole Greene are fine. Moses was so quiet, they didn't even wake up until they heard the shots in the orchard."

"What about the other agents."

Coyote's eyes slid away. "Jake, Dusty Owens, Jon Rude." He

shook his head. "Also Lucy Aguilera from Manning's team. She was on duty in the house."

"How about Manning?"

"He took a round in the chest, but he'll pull through."

"And Moses?"

Coyote's face turned hard. "He got away, Bo. Your shots didn't kill him because he was wearing body armor. We found a mashed slug from your Sig in the grass. When he went over the edge, he fell almost fifty feet. Went through branches that slowed him down, and he landed in some bushes that must've broken his fall. In the dark, our guys had a tough time climbing down. By the time they did, Moses was gone. He left a trail of blood leading down to the river, so it looks like he was hurt pretty bad. We found an inflatable kayak hidden in some brush. We figure he probably meant to use it in his escape, but he was disoriented or didn't have the strength to get to it and decided to try to swim. It's a big river with a fast current. His chances of making it were pretty slim."

"But they haven't found a body?"

"Not yet."

Bo closed his eyes. "I blew it, Stu."

"You didn't blow anything."

"Four agents dead, and Moses slipped away."

Coyote put a hand gently on Bo's shoulder. "Give yourself a break. If it hadn't been for you, the First Lady's name would have been added to the list."

"How'd he breach the perimeter at Wildwood?"

"Dug a tunnel. You know how lax security is out there when we're not around. He'd been watching everything all along. Remember the van bought in Luther Gallagher's name? We found it parked on the highway outside Wildwood, disguised as a media van. It was full of surveillance equipment. He'd been monitoring Wildwood since the First Lady's arrival."

Bo closed his eyes and shook his head. "The electronic sweep we never did."

"We also found plastic explosives in the van, along with detonators and timers. We're speculating right now that he intended to kill the First Lady and her father together when she visited the hospital. We figure he knew that any medical emergency at Wildwood would come to this hospital, so he arranged to have a job that would give him perfect access to Jorgenson's room. By the way, the guy who had the laundry job before Moses died from a fall down the stairs in his apartment. High level of alcohol in his blood. It was deemed an accidental death at the time. Washington County sheriff's taking a closer look at that now."

From the door, another voice spoke, "They're taking a closer look at a lot of things thanks to you, Bo." Diana Ishimaru came into the room. Her eyes were at the center of big, dark circles, but she'd pasted a small smile on her lips. "How do you feel?"

"Alive. I guess that's something."

"The First Lady and Annie Jorgenson are here now visiting Tom. They'd like to drop in, if that's all right."

Bo didn't reply.

"You did a good job out there. I'm putting you in for a citation."

"I don't want a citation."

Ishimaru moved closer, wedged herself between the bed and Coyote. She bent close to Bo, and her tired face loomed in his vision. "Listen to me, and listen good. We lost four of our people last night. Now that's a tragedy. I spent the whole morning with their families, and let me tell you I've had enough sorrow to last me a lifetime. We need to salvage something good from all this. And you're the ticket. You saved the life of the First Lady. The Secret Service did its job. You need to be a hero, do you understand? So lose the self-pity, Agent Thorsen. It's an indulgence we can't afford."

There was a small commotion outside the door. Ishimaru straightened and glanced back. The First Lady and Annie Jorgenson stood patiently, waiting to be asked to enter. "May we come in?" Annie finally ventured.

"Sure," Bo said.

Ishimaru gave him a stern look, then signaled to Stuart Coyote to accompany her outside. Annie went straight to the bed, bent, and kissed Bo's cheek. "You've always told me you believe I saved your life, Bo. I think you've repaid the debt."

"Whatever you say, Annie."

The First Lady stood in a flood of sunlight, looking almost shyly at Bo. She wore a black silk blouse and a black skirt. In mourning already for those who'd died doing their duty, Bo thought, and he appreciated it. They eyed each other for a long moment. Bo wondered if maybe there was something he should say, but he didn't know what. Finally she moved near him and sat down so that she could look into his face as he lay on the bed. She spoke quietly, so that no one but Bo and Annie could hear. "I thought I was going to die out there, Bo."

"I thought we both were. They tell me you saved my life. Thanks."

"You saved mine," she pointed out.

"I heard what you said to Moses on the cliff. It took a lot of courage. You spit right in the devil's eye."

"He wasn't the devil," she said. "But I can't help thinking of you as my guardian angel now."

Bo noticed a small white scar above the corner of her lip, noticed how when she smiled it swung to the right like a meter that gauged her happiness. It was such a tiny thing, and yet he found it enormously beautiful. He was afraid his eyes might give his thoughts away, and he closed them for a moment.

"You're tired, I'm sure," Annie said. "We should be going." She started toward the door.

The First Lady rose from her chair but hesitated before leaving. She leaned down carefully, and kissed Bo lightly above his left eye. "Thank you," she whispered.

He slept some more. In the afternoon, the Washington County sheriff dropped by with Detective Timmons. They asked Bo a lot of questions and took a formal statement. As they were leaving, Sheriff

Quinn-Gruber said, "I've put aside a couple of bottles of my best honey raspberry beer. We'll crack 'em open soon as you're out of here."

"Thanks, Doug." Bo managed a smile. "I'm looking forward to it."

Shortly after that, the two FBI agents who were formally in charge of investigating the murder of the federal agents at Wildwood paid him a visit. They spent a long time talking, and afterward Bo was exhausted. A bit later Maria Rivera came back in. "I'm going off my shift now. Tom Jorgenson sends his best wishes. Perhaps tomorrow you can see him. Now, I think you should lie on your stomach again."

She helped position him. He turned his head so that he could look out the window toward the east. The afternoon sky was a deep blue made almost inky by the tint on the window.

"It's not easy, is it?" she said.

"What?"

"Letting go of the feeling you are somehow responsible. Agent Thorsen—"

"Call me Bo."

"Bo, we cannot presume to know what is in God's mind. We live and we die according to his will. Blame?" The nurse shook her head, dismissing it. "Life is a blessing and death a deliverance. Both are gifts, and neither is in our hands." She patted his arm in a motherly way and stepped out of the room.

Bo lay awhile, thinking. He thought about the fact that in both interviews with law enforcement that day, he'd said nothing about the accusation David Moses had made twenty years before, an accusation Bo didn't believe for an instant. He knew that if it came to light, good people could still suffer, even after all these years. But agents were dead, and didn't death demand the truth? Wasn't that part of his duty? He thought about his duty, wondering what exactly that was now. He thought about those who'd died at Wildwood and whether he could have saved them if he'd only put everything together a little faster. He tried to tell himself that had Chris

Manning let him run the electronic sweep when he'd wanted to, maybe none of this would have happened. But Manning was lying in another room with a bullet hole in his chest. What good did blaming him do? It didn't change anything. Let go of the blame, Nurse Rivera had advised him. Lose the self-pity, Diana Ishimaru had ordered. Bo wished he could. He wished that all the confusion in his mind would pass. He felt sad and angry and deeply responsible. He didn't feel at all like a hero.

The sun went down. The sky grew dark. Bo buzzed the nurses' station. When a woman in white appeared, he said, "I'm going to try to sleep some more. Could you wake me at ten P.M.?"

"Why?" the nurse asked.

Bo laid his head down on the pillow. "I'd like to see the moon."

chapter

twenty-five

Air Force One touched down on Wold-Chamberlain Field and taxied to the north end of the runway system that the U.S. Air Force shared with the Minnesota Air National Guard and with Minneapolis–St. Paul International Airport. The president briefly addressed the gathered press, then proceeded to his hotel, the Riverfront Radisson in downtown St. Paul. John Llewellyn accompanied him. The rest of his staff were already at the hotel. Edward McGill was waiting in the president's suite.

"You look positively ecstatic, Ed. Did you just get laid?" Clay Dixon asked. He moved to the window to take in the view of the Mississippi River as it curved through the city.

"The numbers are very good. For the first time, you're up on Wayne White. By just two points, but that's a gain of four over the last poll."

"Because?"

"Well . . ."

"I'll tell you. I'm climbing toward office on the bodies of the dead. You know how slimy that makes me feel, Ed?"

John Llewellyn spoke. "It's not your fault, Mr. President. There's certainly no shame in the fact that the American people have reacted to the heroism at Wildwood in a way that benefits you."

"Will I visit Wildwood?"

"No, sir. The Secret Service is adamant."

He nodded. He'd never felt particularly welcome there anyway. "And the First Lady?"

"She'll join you at the hospital where you'll visit with the wounded agents and with Tom Jorgenson."

"And then we'll come back to the hotel?"

Llewellyn hesitated.

"What is it?"

"We haven't been able to get confirmation from the First Lady that she'll join you here."

Dixon waved off any concern. "She's stubborn, John, but she'll be here, you can bank on it. What about the memorial service for the agents who were killed?"

"That will be tomorrow morning. After that you fly to Baltimore for the fund-raiser there."

"Life as usual for us, while the families of those agents struggle with their losses. Christ, what a business." He shook his head. "When do we leave for the hospital?"

"As soon as you like, sir."

The drive to the medical center in Stillwater was brief. On the way, Clay Dixon thought about the last time he had been out that way, driving with Kate to Wildwood. It had been just before he announced his candidacy half a decade earlier. He'd come hoping in vain to secure her father's endorsement.

The state, local police, and Secret Service had created a wide corridor for the president through the media crowded in front of the hospital. The First Lady was waiting near the elevator. They embraced and kissed briefly as the cameras clicked away, then they stepped into the elevator, accompanied by two Secret Service agents. The president and First Lady stood at the back. The agents stood shoulder to shoulder controlling the elevator doorway.

"Kate," he said. Without the blunt eye of a camera on him, he took her in his arms and held her tightly, full of gratitude that she was safe and alive. "God, it's good to hold you."

Although she returned his embrace, he thought he detected a measure of reserve.

"What is it?" he asked.

"I'm just tired. It's been hard." She eased from his arms. "You didn't bring Stephanie?"

"I didn't want her out here. Secret Service wasn't exactly thrilled about my coming."

She nodded. "I suppose it's best for now."

"She's staying with Dad." He saw her tense. "I know how you feel about him, but Stephanie loves her grandfather."

The two agents kept their eyes straight ahead, as if absolutely deaf to what transpired behind them.

He studied her a moment. There was something different about her, about the way she wouldn't meet his gaze. It troubled him. "Are you all right?" he asked.

"Not really. It's a strange thing believing you're about to die. A lot becomes clear."

"Like what?"

She didn't have time to answer before the elevator doors opened onto the fourth floor, and the agents stepped out ahead of them. Ed McGill, who'd preceded the president to the hospital, was there to meet him.

"Who's first, Ed?"

"We thought Agent Thorsen, then Manning, then the First Lady's father. I've selected a few media people to observe. Believe me, Mr. President, this will play well in Peoria."

Clay Dixon stopped in midstride and turned angrily on his communications director. "I'm not interested in how this plays in Peoria, Ed. These men risked their lives in the line of duty."

"I'm sorry, Mr. President. I'll keep the press back and their presence discreet."

Dixon strode into the room where Agent Thorsen sat carefully propped in a sitting position on his bed. The president knew he'd sustained a knife wound in his back, but the hospital gown covered any sign of tape and gauze. However, his left arm was bandaged, and the effect of his ordeal showed in his face, which was pale and drawn.

"Agent Thorsen, this is a pleasure, indeed."

Thorsen shook the president's hand. "I apologize for not getting up, Mr. President."

"How are you feeling?"

"I've been better, sir."

"They tell me you'll recover fully."

"They tell me the same thing."

Smiling broadly, Clay Dixon glanced at his wife and caught the First Lady staring at the wounded agent. Her face held a look that the president had not seen on her in a long time. Admiration, respect.

"I owe you an enormous debt, Agent Thorsen. You saved my wife's life at the risk of your own. I can't tell you how much I appreciate your actions."

He waited, expecting the man to say something self-effacing—*Shucks, I was just doing my job*—but the agent replied simply, "Thank you."

The president could see that Thorsen was the kind of man he'd loved on the playing field, a man who knew who he was and what he was doing and didn't need to be told he was good at it.

"When you're better, I'd like to invite you for dinner at the White House, to thank you properly."

"I'll be there, sir."

"Good. If you'll excuse me, I'm on my way to visit Agent Manning."

"I'm honored that you stopped by, Mr. President."

"The honor is mine." He meant it.

Manning was in bad shape. He'd taken a bullet in the chest, very near his heart. He was hooked to tubes and wires, looked bloodless, and was barely able to respond. The press took no pictures.

The final stop was Tom Jorgenson's room. The old man appeared frail, but it was obvious he was on the mend. When the president offered, "God seems to have been watching over the Jorgensons," the former vice president replied, "I'm sure the Lord has more important things to see to. Like making sure the nation survives your foreign policy."

Both men laughed, although Jorgenson's laugh turned into a small cough. The press got photos of the president smiling down at Tom Jorgenson, offering his father-in-law his best wishes for a speedy recovery.

At the elevator, Clay Dixon said to the agents who shadowed him, "Gentlemen, the First Lady and I will ride down alone. We'll meet you in the lobby."

"Mr. President—" the agent named Dewey began to object.

"I said I'll meet you in the lobby."

The two Secret Service agents looked unhappy but accepted the president's dictum.

In the elevator, Clay Dixon said to his wife, "You said that things had become clear to you. What things?"

"Can we talk about this later?"

"What's wrong with now?"

"For one thing, the elevator doors are going to open any moment."

Dixon reached out and punched the Stop button. The elevator lurched to a halt.

"Secret Service will love that," Kate said.

"Forget Secret Service. What exactly has become clear?"

She closed her eyes a moment. "The things that are important, Clay."

"Important to whom? You?"

186

"Mr. President," a voice called from a few feet above. "Are you all right?"

"We're fine," he shouted.

"We'll have the elevator moving in a minute."

Dixon turned and faced his wife. "Tell me about these important things and what they have to do with us."

"In the two minutes we have before they get this car moving again?" She gave him an exasperated look. "Do you ever hear anything except what you want to hear?"

"You're answering a question with a question. You're trying to evade something. What?"

The elevator suddenly dropped an inch, then began a smooth descent. Dixon reached out and punched the Stop button furiously but to no avail. In a few moments, the elevator ceased moving and the doors glided open.

"We'll continue this at the hotel," Dixon said.

"I don't think so. I'm not coming back with you."

Dixon saw that in the lobby the throng of the press waited. He addressed his wife with quiet intensity, "Why?"

"I still need to think through a few things. When I'm ready to talk, we'll talk."

"Great," he said. "Just great. The press will have a field day speculating on this one."

"I'm sure Ed McGill can come up with a positive spin for you, something they'll love in Peoria."

"Fuck Peoria." He stepped out of the elevator, hauling up a smile for the media.

The President dined with his closest staff. Over a good Caesar salad and rare prime rib, the business of the government was carried on, especially discussion of Lorna Channing's report on national youth service. Although Clay Dixon's personal enthusiasm had waned, he gave it his full attention. Afterward, he asked Lorna to stay. He poured brandy for them both and lit a hand-rolled cigar, and they reminisced for a while about growing up on the Purgatoire River. She told him the smell of the cigar reminded her of sitting on the porch with her father after dinner and looking at the evening sky. It was a good memory, she said.

"Kate hates the smell of cigars," Dixon told her.

"Most women do, I think. You keep looking toward the door," Lorna finally noted.

"I thought Kate might come."

"Give her time, Clay. She's been through a lot."

"Time isn't the issue." He got up from the sofa and walked to the window. The sky outside was the color of blackberry jam and seeded with stars. The city lights were split by the dark curve of the river. "When did you know your marriages were over?"

"It can't be that serious," she said.

"When she looks at me, its like she's seeing me through a wall of ice. It's been like that for a long time now."

"I'm sorry."

He put the cigar in an ashtray and turned to look at her. "You have friends in D.C., Lorna?"

"Yes. Many."

"Me, I feel like I've got practically none. I have more acquaintances, more advisers, more hangers-on than I can keep track of. But friends?" He sighed heavily. "Bobby Lee, you, and Kate. And now I don't have Kate."

"You still have Bobby. And you still have me."

She left the sofa and walked toward him. Her feet made a soft *hush-hush* on the carpet as she came. He could smell her perfume when she drew near. The fragrance was a trigger for an explosive desire that had been building in him for some time. Impulsively, he took her in his arms and he kissed her. She didn't resist.

"That was nice," he whispered against her lips.

"Yes," she said. "Yes, it was." Very gently, she removed herself from his embrace. "And that's all there will be." She took a half-step back. "Clay, you're the president, and I'm your adviser for domestic affairs. I don't want that to be an ironic title. I know you're feeling alone right now, but this isn't the answer." She put her hand on his cheek. "I'm not saying it's not tempting. It's just not right, and you know it. Talk to Kate. Work things out. I know you can."

The phone rang and startled them both. Reluctantly, Dixon answered it. He listened a moment and then said, "Thank you." He looked at Lorna Channing. "Kate's here. She's on her way up."

"You see? Didn't I tell you?" She smiled. As she left the suite, she paused long enough to give the president a kiss on his cheek. "Good luck."

He didn't have much time to settle himself before Kate arrived. He was undoing his tie when she entered the room. She wore a lovely dress, black and sheer, and she looked wonderful in it.

"I was under the impression you wouldn't be here tonight," he said.

"I wanted to apologize for my behavior this afternoon. It's been a difficult time for me."

"I'm sure it has."

She lingered near the door, as if not entirely certain she should be there with him. "Clay, we all make mistakes. Horrible mistakes, sometimes. And there's nothing to be done about it except to hope we're forgiven."

"Is that why you're here? You're going to offer me forgiveness. Kate, I don't need—"

"I need to know that I can trust you."

"You can."

"I've watched you change, Clay. I'm not sure what you believe anymore. Sometimes I'm not even sure who you are."

"I am who I've always been. A not-at-all perfect man. But one who loves you."

She stared at her hands and seemed concerned that they held nothing. "We haven't been happy for a long time."

"We can find a way again."

"I wish I could believe that."

"Then do, Kate. Believe it. Believe me. Trust is a leap of faith, isn't it? Take that leap. Take it, and I swear I won't let you fall."

She considered him a long time. Finally he moved to her, crossed the room slowly, put his arms around her, and held her tightly. He could feel her soft and yielding in his embrace. Then she went rigid.

"Chanel," she said.

"What?"

"You reek of it." She pushed away from him.

"Kate—"

"I ran into Lorna Channing at the elevator. She bathes in Chanel."

"She was here, of course. She's one of my advisers," he explained calmly.

She looked closely at his face, and her own face frosted over. "And what exactly was she advising you on? There's lipstick smeared all over you."

"Kate, I swear nothing happened."

"Only because of my bad timing."

"Kate," he said, and he reached for her.

"Stay away, Clay. I don't want you near me."

The door of the suite shook as she slammed it behind her.

Clay Dixon's legs were shaky. He sat down. He felt as if he'd taken a long fall, and the wind had been knocked from him. He stared dumbly at the door, at the place where his wife had walked out on him. He understood quite well that at the moment, not only the fate of his marriage, but also of his reelection, perhaps even of his place in history, rested in her angry hands.

chapter

twenty-six

C lay Dixon sat at his desk in the Oval Office, scanning a State Department memo that dealt with the upcoming Pan American summit meeting. Beyond the window at his back lay a dripping sky. A storm front had moved through in the dark of early morning bringing with it a steady rain. Dixon's whole body ached. Whenever a front moved through, it was a curse, and the old football injuries rose up inside him, working some kind of painful voodoo on his joints and bones.

There was a knock at the open door. The president's chief of staff, John Llewellyn, stepped in. Senator William Dixon stood just behind him.

"Mr. President, may we have a few minutes of your time?" Llewellyn asked.

The president put aside the memo. "In five minutes, we have a meeting to discuss the Pan-American summit, but until then I'm all yours, John."

Leaning on his cane, Senator Dixon entered the Oval Office with Llewellyn and sat down.

The president sat back in his chair and crossed his arms. "You look like a delegation. What's up?"

"So she's left you." The senator's words were rife with both satisfaction and disapproval.

"I beg your pardon?"

"No use denying it. Kate's left you."

The president looked at his watch. "You have exactly three minutes, Dad."

"This won't take long." The senior senator from Colorado folded his hands atop his cane. They were huge hands. Although blemished by age spots, they still had a powerful, crushing look. "Was she worth it?"

A sick feeling began to knot his stomach, but Clay Dixon tried not to let his face show anything.

"Ms. Channing," the senator clarified. "Was she worth throwing away the presidency?"

"There's absolutely nothing between Lorna and me except friendship and the work of this administration."

"If you say so."

"And the presidency is secure."

"Is it? What do you imagine Wayne White would do if he knew your wife had left you? He'd gut you like a fish, Clayboy."

Llewellyn stood behind the senator's chair. He said, "Why didn't you tell me, Mr. President?"

"Because there's nothing to tell, John. It's a misunderstanding between Kate and me, and it's under control."

The senator said, "Is the First Lady coming back?"

"As soon as her father has recovered."

The senator smiled smugly. "My information is that she's through with you, had all she can stomach."

"Kate's angry right now, but she's not stupid. She'll calm down in a few days and we'll talk things through. We're handling it."

"We?" Llewellyn said. "You mean Bob Lee."

"Yes, John. I asked Bobby to help me on this one."

"I've got to tell you, Mr. President, I feel so far out of the loop I might as well be on the moon."

"This situation is personal not political."

Senator Dixon said, "In your position, there's no separation. Don't you understand that? What if she decides to tell the press the things she knows? Your presidency is hanging by a thread, son. And that wife of yours, she's a sharp pair of scissors poised to snip." He shook his head and offered his son a look dripping with sympathy. "You should have told me right away. Haven't I been there beside you all the way since Alan Carpathian died?" He spoke gently, in a tone probably meant to be fatherly but that struck Clay Dixon as foully patronizing.

"Maybe I don't need you there anymore," the president said.

"Don't need me?" For a moment, the senator appeared stung. But he composed himself and laughed. "You go right ahead and think that if you want to. In the meantime, we'll just go about the business of getting you reelected."

"How do you propose to do that? How much more slime do we all have to wade through?"

"You listen to me, Clayboy, and listen good. I'm not speaking as your father now. There's too much riding on this presidency for you to throw it away with your stupid sexual shenanigans or your little polished brass ideals."

"Take it easy, Senator," Llewellyn said.

"No, I won't take it easy." William Dixon sat back in disgust. "You want to know the truth? The best thing that could have happened was if that nut Moses had done what he set out to do."

The president went hot, fire in every cell of his body. "What did you say?"

"You heard me. Dead, her lips are sealed, and you're a widower. Huge sympathy vote factor."

"Bill," Llewellyn said. "That's enough."

The president stood. "Out of my office, Senator. I want you out now."

The elder Dixon cast his son a steely glare.

"Now," the president said.

William Dixon took his time rising from his chair. He drew his rigid frame to its full, impressive height. "You may be willing to stand there and let fate smack you between the eyes, Clayboy, but I'm not going to let that happen, by God. I didn't get you here just to have you turn the Dixon name into a national joke." With a show of great dignity, he walked to the door and left the office.

After the Senator had gone, Dixon turned angrily to Llewellyn. "How does he know about me and Kate? Where does he get his information?"

"I don't know. He just gets it. Mr. President, do you want my resignation?"

"Your resignation? What are you talking about?"

"It's obvious I don't have your confidence. Without that, I can't do my job. Do you want my resignation?"

"John, if I wanted someone else in your office, I'd let you know. I probably should have told you about Kate, but there are some things I want handled by Bob Lee, and that will never change. If you can't live with it, then do what you need to do."

"Do you trust me?"

"Right now, I don't know who in the hell to trust."

Llewellyn shook his head. "Then God help you, Mr. President, because you can't run this country alone."

As soon as his chief of staff was gone, Dixon went to the door of the Oval Office and spoke to his secretary. "Maryelizabeth, get Bobby in here now."

"He's waiting for you with the others in the Roosevelt Room," Maryelizabeth Hart said. "The meeting to discuss the summit."

"I didn't ask you where he is. I said get him."

"Yes, sir."

"And tell the others the meeting will be delayed awhile."

A long minute passed before Robert Lee stepped into the Oval Office.

194

"Close the door, Bobby."

Lee did as he'd been asked.

"Sit down."

Lee took a chair.

"Who did you talk to about Kate, Bobby?"

"No one other than those you asked me to speak with."

"One of them talked."

"What makes you think so?"

"My father was just in here, and he knows, Bobby. He knows."

"No one I spoke with would breach your confidence, Clay. They're our people, not the senator's."

"Well somebody sure as hell said something. My father's surprising in a lot of ways, but I assure you he isn't psychic."

"Clay, if you start distrusting those closest to you, you'll end up trusting no one. Is it possible Kate is the source?"

"She hasn't even told her father."

"You're positive?"

"She was definite."

Lee put an index finger to his lips and thought a moment. "You talked with Kate on the phone from the Residence."

"Yes."

"And we talked here."

"That's right."

"And I met with the others in my office. I know it sounds crazy, Clay, but maybe we've been bugged."

"The Secret Service is supposed to make sure all my communications are secure."

"Maybe we should have them do a full security sweep," Lee suggested.

"I agree," Dixon said.

He buzzed Maryelizabeth Hart. "Get Rich Thielman here and get him here now." He was speaking of the head of the Secret Service Presidential Protective Detail. He turned to the window behind him. The day was still weighted with the gloom that had settled after the morning storm. "Bobby, I have something I want you to take care of. My father made a comment that concerns me. It sounded like a threat, as if he intends to intervene somehow to save my presidential ass and the family name. I'd like to know exactly what he's up to."

"What do you want?"

"He's a man of amazing resources and little reserve when it comes to getting what he wants. And he doesn't want me to lose this election."

"More dirty tricks?"

"I don't know, but it would be good to keep tabs on him. I've had enough surprises already. Can you handle this?"

"I'll get someone on it."

"No, I want you on it personally. I know you're busy, but until we clear up the question of security around here I don't want this moving beyond you and me."

"All right," Lee said. "I'm on it."

"Be discreet when you're poking around, Bobby. The last thing I want is for the senator to know we're digging."

"When was I not the soul of discretion?" He smiled that charming smile the press loved.

chapter

twenty-seven

Ronnie Salone stepped into Bo's hospital room. He was a new agent, on temporary assignment from the Chicago office. In the wake of the incident at Wildwood, security measures had proliferated, requiring additional agents. Secret Service had assigned a detail to cover Tom Jorgenson and Bo while they were in the hospital, although officially neither man was eligible for such attention. Salone escorted a visitor.

"This him?" Salone asked.

"Yeah, Ronnie. Thanks," Bo said.

The agent left.

Otter shook his head. "Seeing you is like trying to get into Fort Knox. How're you doing, Spider-Man?"

"I've been better, Otter. Good to see you, man. Pull up a chair."

Otter sat down at Bo's bedside. He wore a green Hawaiian shirt, faded jeans, and old sneakers. He was clean-shaven, and he'd swept his long, graying hair back in a neat ponytail. There was nothing to be done about the beating his face had taken from alcohol and a tough life, but for Otter, he looked pretty good.

"I hope they didn't give you a hard time," Bo said.

"Made me sign in, give 'em an official address, show an ID. That was just the hospital security. Then your guys frisked me. The nurses, man, I think they wanted to disinfect me or something."

"You look good," Bo said.

"That job you told me about. The church janitor. I took it. It's working out. Got a nice room in the basement. And Greg, the pastor, he's in AA, too."

"I know."

"Thanks, Spider-Man."

"No problem."

Otter leaned his chair back and laced his hands behind his head. "First Lady. Man, you travel in some company these days. Who would've thought?" His gaze went distant for a moment. When it came back, he said, "Look, you need any plants watered at your place or anything taken care of while you're here?"

"They're artificial."

"I wish there was something I could do."

"In the drawer there." Bo pointed to the stand beside his bed. "There are some cards."

Otter reached in and pulled out a deck that Bo had been using for solitaire.

"Remember in the old bus, playing gin rummy for pennies?" Bo asked.

"Do I? You were terrible."

"That's because the cards had pictures of naked women on them."

Otter laughed. "Yeah, I used that deck because I knew it was a distraction for you."

"Deal 'em," Bo said. "I'm not distracted now."

They played a dozen hands before Stuart Coyote walked into the room.

"Sorry," Coyote said. "I didn't realize you had company, Bo. I'll come back."

"No, stay. Otter, this is Stu Coyote, my sometimes partner. Stu, this is Otter, my oldest friend."

"Bo's told me a lot of stories about you and him and an old bus," Coyote said, extending his hand. "It's a pleasure finally meeting you. Say, is he much of a cardplayer?"

"The worst," Otter replied. He looked from Coyote to Bo. "Looks like you've got business. I'll be on my way."

"How'd you get here?" Bo asked.

"Hitched."

"I'll get you a ride back."

Otter lifted his hands to decline. "You just worry about getting better. Nice meeting you, Coyote. Always good rubbing fur with another animal."

Otter left, grinning.

Coyote took the vacant chair. "You heard about Moses?"

"Heard what?"

"They found him last night. Washington County sheriff's office got a call at 0200 hours. Somebody reported a burglary in progress on an empty houseboat at a marina downriver, this side of Hastings. Cops show up. Shots fired. All of a sudden, the houseboat goes up in flames. When the fire's put out, they find a burned body. There's body armor, too, and a handgun. They got prints from the grip. They match Moses."

"Cops kill Moses? Or did the fire do that?"

"Neither. He ate a bullet."

"They're sure it's his body?"

"They're checking his files at the State Security Hospital for dental records to match. His military file, too. They're being careful about making any public statement until they're sure. But it's him, Bo."

Bo should have felt relief, but he was reluctant to let his guard down until he was absolutely certain the man was dead and buried.

"Ishimaru make a connection with Moses and those two alphabet guys who posed as Secret Service when they talked to Dr. Hart?"

"Not yet. She's had her hands full."

"How are things at the office?" he asked.

Coyote's face took on a sour look. "Investigators everywhere. The press is thick as locusts. It's understandable, but it's a grand pain in the butt."

"You don't have to tell me. I talk to a dozen different investigators from half a dozen jurisdictions every day. What about Diana? She holding up?"

"If she were food, she'd be hard tack. She's tough as they come."

"You look a little weary," Bo noted.

"Things feel pretty weird right now. Jake, Jon, the others, dead. Strange faces in the office. Everything we've done being questioned. The truth is, I asked for some time off. I've got vacation days, use or lose. Figured I'd take them."

Bo nodded. If he could hide for a while, he'd do it, too. "Going anywhere?"

"Home."

Meaning Oklahoma. Somewhere near the Wichita Mountains.

"When do you leave?"

"Tomorrow. I'll be gone by the time you hobble out of here. You'll be okay?"

"I won't be throwing any punches for a while, but I'll be fine." Bo held out his hand. "Take care of yourself. Rest up."

Coyote stood and clasped Bo's hand tightly. "You, too."

There was a moment of awkward silence, and a reluctance to release their grip on each other. Bo felt as if he were letting go of the last of all that was familiar to him and safe.

That afternoon, Nurse Rivera urged him out of bed and sent him walking. Bo's leg was sore from the kick Moses had delivered, his back ached from the knife wound, and his left arm throbbed. But he was glad to be up and moving. He walked from one end of the hallway to the other. Agent Salone was on duty, monitoring the activity on the floor. Other agents were posted downstairs. Although Bo's injuries weren't critical, the decision had been made to keep him in Trauma ICU along with Tom Jorgenson and Chris Manning so that security was easier. He was on his third round when Salone called to him, "Thorsen, Dreamcatcher's on her way up."

He never knew when Kate was coming. Secret Service varied her visits, the time of day, the length, to keep things unpredictable. Bo returned to his room as quickly as he could and checked himself in his bathroom mirror. It was ridiculous, he knew, but he found himself eager for her visits and always a little nervous. She came, of course, to see her father, but she always dropped in to talk with Bo awhile. Her visits had become the highlight of his days.

Through his door, he watched the First Lady step into her father's room. She glanced his way, and she waved and smiled just before she vanished.

A little while later Earl, all awkward motion and big grins, bounced into Bo's room.

"Hi, Bo."

"Hey, Earl. How you doing?"

"I'm real good. I'm real good." Earl had taken a deep interest in Bo's injuries and checked the scabbed wound on his forearm whenever he visited. "Does it still hurt?"

"They give me pills that keep it from hurting too much."

Earl seemed to think that sounded fine. "Can they give Katie some pills? She hurts an awful lot, Bo. She cries all the time, and I don't understand. Dad's better now."

"People hurt in lots of ways and for lots of reasons, Earl. Sometimes the wounds don't show."

Earl looked at him without fully comprehending. "I'm going home today." He was talking about returning to the group home in St. Paul.

"You like it there?" Bo asked.

"Oh yeah. My friends are there."

"Good, Earl. I'm happy for you."

"Bye," Earl said.

"Bye," Bo echoed.

In parting, Earl squeezed Bo's hand like he was crushing a rock.

Nearly an hour after she'd arrived at ICU, the First Lady stood in Bo's doorway. She was dressed for the summer heat, in a light cotton skirt, a sleeveless yellow blouse, sandals. Her gold hair was pulled back casually, held by some clasp he couldn't see. At the sight of her, Bo felt a little stumble of his heart.

"How's your father this morning?" he asked.

"Good. He slept well. He tells me you drop by now and again to say hello. He appreciates that, Bo. So do I."

"He's good company. I get bored easily around here."

"Maybe I can help with that." She offered him a gift that was wrapped in white tissue paper and tied with a blue bow. "I wasn't sure in what direction your tastes might run. I hope I guessed correctly."

He undid the tissue and found a book.

"I considered getting you crossword puzzles," she said.

"I'd rather read."

The book was *The Witness of Combines* by an author named Kent Meyers.

"It's about a young man on a farm who's forced to grow up too soon. Have you read it?" she asked.

"No."

"I thought about you and that farm you spent some time on when you were younger. I thought maybe you'd appreciate the story."

"Thank you." He put the book on the stand beside the bed. "I still spend time at the farm occasionally. Whenever I need to get away from everything for a while and just think. It's not that far."

"Blue Earth, right?"

"Right."

"And the Thorsens, are they still there?"

"Nell, yes. Harold passed away two years ago."

"I'm sorry."

Her eyes seemed suddenly grayer and her mood as well, as if talking about the dead had saddened her. She walked away from Bo and moved nearer the window. The sun hit her at a slant. Half her body glowed, while the other half lay in shadow. "They tell me David Moses is dead."

"They seem pretty certain."

"I suppose I should be relieved. But all I feel is sad."

"With something like this, it's best to put it behind you."

"I'm not sure I can." She turned back to Bo. Her right hand came up, as if she meant to offer him something. "I feel so sorry for him."

"Forgive me if I don't grieve for the man," Bo said.

He realized he'd spoken harshly and that he'd shattered a fragile moment between them. He wished immediately he could do something, say something that would bring back the feeling he'd had before either of them spoke about death.

"I should let you rest." She moved toward the door.

"I'm fine."

She smiled, but it was cordial, forced. "My daughter's arriving from D.C. this afternoon. I want to get a few things ready for her."

"Sure."

"Good-bye." She took his hand, then gave him a soft kiss on the cheek as well.

After she'd gone, he opened the book she'd given him, and he found the inscription she'd written by hand.

> *To Bo, my guardian angel.*
> *I will never say a prayer of thanksgiving without your*
> *name upon my lips.*
>
> > *Kate*

It was very nice, Bo thought. Full of gratitude. Then he chided himself for wishing it were full of something more.

chapter

twenty-eight

L ate that evening, the president sat in a stuffed chair in his residence, sipping a cup of decaf mocha and trying to concentrate on revising the address he was to deliver at the Pan-American summit. The speech was weak. But his mind kept drifting to another subject, one far more threatening to him than the idea of delivering a less than perfect address.

His father.

Dixon put down his papers and thought about the only man who could anger him without speaking a word. What had shaped William Dixon, in what hellish forge his character had been hammered, Clay Dixon could only guess.

His father had been another man once, or so Clay Dixon's mother claimed. When he was seventeen, he'd been a lean, long-boned young man with stiff, dusty hair and a cocky smile. He wore dirty jeans and scuffed boots and old western shirts. He'd been one of the hired hands on the Purgatoire River Ranch. And he'd been in love with the rancher's daughter. He didn't have a chance of marrying her in those days. The rancher was a tough, wealthy man, and he had no intention of giving his daughter's hand to a cowboy who had nothing to offer her but an appealing face and more self-assurance than his circumstances merited.

Pearl Harbor changed everything. Billy Dixon, along with thousands of other young men, enlisted in the marines. He trained at San Diego and was among the last of the armed forces to reach the Bataan Peninsula in the Philippines before the Japanese cut off the islands. He distinguished himself in the fighting that ensued over the next three months. When Bataan fell, he and seventy-five thousand other American and Filipino soldiers, most ill with malaria and weak from hunger and thirst, were marched along a sixty-five-mile stretch of jungle road on what would eventually be known as the Bataan Death March. He spent several months in the Cabanatuan prison camp before escaping with nine other men. They stole a small launch from a coastal town and, making their way by night, eventually reached Borneo and the Aussie forces there. But the war wasn't over for Billy Dixon. He saw action at Tarawa, Iwo Jima, and Okinawa, earning himself two Purple Hearts and a Silver Star in the process. When he was discharged in the late summer of 1945, he came home to Las Animas County, Colorado, a bona fide hero.

Whenever she spoke of the war, Clay Dixon's mother spoke of it sadly. Billy Dixon had gone away a cocky boy whom she couldn't help loving. But the man who returned to a hero's welcome and who was given her hand in marriage had become a stranger in many ways. Hard inside and distant. Although his mother never said as much, Clay Dixon believed that she'd married hoping she might somehow be able to resurrect the boy the war had killed. It never happened.

The ranch didn't interest William Dixon. It wasn't long before he ran for Congress and easily won. A few years later, he moved into a Senate seat.

Growing up, Clay Dixon seldom saw his father. He went to boarding school in Denver, St. Regis. Summers he spent on the Purgatoire River Ranch with his mother, who'd gone from being the quiet daughter of an overbearing father to the silent wife of an unattentive, powerful politician. She smiled little, drank much, and cried often, but always in the privacy of her home. Nothing was public then. She died young. Dixon never saw his father shed a tear of grief. He'd thought then that the senator had no soul. He believed something different now, that long ago in the body of a cocky cowboy his father had possessed a soul, but Senator William Dixon had readily exchanged it for the currency of power.

The president felt bile rising in his throat, and the anger that brought it up was not just at the senator but also at himself. Not long before, Kate had accused him of selling his own soul and that of the nation to the devil simply because he'd never made it to the Super Bowl. He was beginning to be afraid that maybe she'd been right.

The phone rang. It was Rich Thielman, head of the POTUS detail.

"Mr. President, the Technical Security Division has finished its sweep of the White House, as you requested."

"And?"

"Nothing, sir. They found absolutely nothing. I checked the roster for the White House Communications Agency last night myself. The personnel on duty are impeccable in their credentials. There's no evidence of a breach in the security of the communication line itself. I had Secret Service in Minnesota check the line at Wildwood. Nothing there either."

"I see," the president said.

"Sir, if you'd be willing to share the cause of your concern, I might be able to offer more assistance."

"Thanks, Rich. I'll think about it."

Dixon called Bobby Lee at his home on the Potomac outside Alexandria.

"Thielman just reported on the security sweep. No bugs, Bobby."

Lee hesitated before replying. "Which leaves us with the probability that someone talked."

"And that brings me back to my original question. Who knew, Bobby?"

"Only Sherm, Megan, and Ned Shackleford. Our people. We were sure we could trust them."

"Megan," Dixon said, speaking of his congressional affairs adviser. "She's good, but sometimes that Harvard mouth of hers moves way out ahead of her brain."

Lee said, "If I had to guess, Clay, my vote would be Ned. He's a little too ambitious for my taste."

Dixon hated this. Skewering the people he trusted, wondering about his own judgment. "What do you think, Bobby?"

"I think we need to know what the senator is up to."

"If we can figure that, maybe we'll have an idea how he's been getting his information."

"What would you like me to do?"

"Just keep an eye on him, Bobby. And make absolutely certain none of his people know you're watching." Dixon paused a moment, then said, "Jesus."

"What is it?"

"Our people, his people. My God, how did I let my presidency come to this?"

"You can still fix things, Clay. It may be late in the game and we may be deep in our own territory, but hey, you're Air Express. You've still got the arm."

For the first time in days, Dixon allowed himself to smile.

chapter

twenty-nine

Tom Jorgenson was built like a Viking, big and raw-looking. He'd lost most of his hair young. The thin, silver fringe that remained he kept bristle short. His eyes were Scandinavian blue and clear in the way of someone who'd come to terms with what he was and what he wasn't and had found a measure of peace.

On the morning Bo was scheduled to be released, he made his last visit to Tom Jorgenson's room. Kate's father was lying down, slightly propped by pillows. A tube came out the side of his chest, draining fluid that still collected in one of his lungs. He was clean-shaven, courtesy of the nursing staff, and he smelled faintly of lime aftershave, a nice contrast to the medicinal odor that permeated the room. He reached toward a glass of water on the stand beside his bed but in the end needed Bo's help.

"You and Kate seem to have become good friends," Jorgenson said after he'd sipped. "You like her?"

"What kind of question is that?"

"I'm her father. I'm allowed to ask all kinds of strange questions. It's a simple one. Do you like her?"

"Everybody likes the First Lady."

"I'm not asking about everyone."

"Yes," Bo said. "I like her. What are you getting at?"

Jorgenson said, "I think Kate's a little vulnerable right now. She's been through an ordeal. She's tired. She may not be thinking clearly about some things. That's all I'm saying." Bo waited for something more, an admonition perhaps, but apparently Jorgenson had said all he meant to. He reached out to shake Bo's hand in parting. "Thanks again for saving her life."

Ishimaru was waiting near the nurses' station. "Your discharge is official," she said.

"I thought you were going to have an agent drive me to Wildwood so I could get my car."

She said, "That would be me."

Before he left, Bo took a moment to drop by Chris Manning's room. Manning was fighting a severe infection that was the result of his wound, and no visitors were allowed. Bo stood at the door watching the agent's restless sleep. As nearly as he'd been able to tell, being near death hadn't changed Manning's perspective or personality, nor had it altered Bo's own disaffection for the agent. Still, he hoped sincerely that Manning would pull through.

He had one last stop. He found Nurse Rivera in the fourth-floor lounge, scanning the pages of *Better Homes and Gardens* while she took a break. At the sight of him, she got up, clasped his hands, stood on her toes, and kissed his cheek. "*Vaya con Dios*, Bo." He wondered if she said good-bye to all her patients in this way.

Ishimaru's Sable was in the parking lot. It was hot from sitting in the sun. Bo eased the window down to let in the breeze until the air conditioner could start cranking out something cooler.

"So what do you want to talk to me about?" he asked.

"What makes you think I want to talk?"

"Because you could have any agent do this."

Ishimaru pulled out of the lot and headed toward the highway along the river.

"Take a look at this," she said, tapping a folded newsprint publication that lay between them on the seat. "It's due to hit the stands tomorrow."

Bo picked it up. It was a tabloid, the *National Enquirer*. He was surprised to see on the cover a photograph of him and the First Lady standing together at his hospital window. Although sunlight reflected off the glass, Kate's image was quite clear, and she was quite clearly laughing. Bo's image was not so definite. It could have been almost anyone. The headline read "ROMANCE BLOOMS AT HOSPITAL BEDSIDE." Bo glanced through the text that chronicled the First Lady's daily visits to his room, quoted unidentified hospital staff about the intimacy of their relationship, and hinted that rumors of an as yet undisclosed indiscretion on the part of the president were sending his wife into another man's arms.

"Rumors? What rumors?" Bo asked.

"A rag like that doesn't need facts. It relies on innuendo and unfounded conjecture. So what about it?"

"You mean Kate and me?"

"Kate?" Ishimaru glanced at him, her eyes full of concern.

Outside Stillwater, they headed south toward Wildwood. They picked up the St. Croix Trail, which was less trafficked than it had been after Kathleen Jorgenson Dixon first arrived. Even considering the attack at Wildwood, she was already becoming yesterday's news. Bo knew the tabloid story would probably change that.

Ishimaru said, "The rag got the facts all screwy, but I'm thinking they may not have missed the target by much. She's beautiful, she's bright, and if there's any substance to those rumors about the president, she may be vulnerable right now."

"I'm nothing to her," Bo said. "Believe me."

"You underestimate your charm."

"Are you talking to me as my boss?"

"At the moment, as a friend. Think about what you're feeling and then think about what you're doing. And most of all, think about her."

Bo looked out at the wooded hills. For a while he rode in silence.

"You look tired," he said finally.

"Lots of people outside Secret Service are poking their noses into the incident at Wildwood. We're not getting a lot of support from above."

"You think someone's going to get hung out to dry?"

"I can't see it. I've reviewed everything, and we're clear on protocol."

He thought he noted some hesitation in her voice. He asked, "They want a scapegoat?"

"You just worry about getting yourself healthy," she replied. "And keeping your face off the front page of tabloids. I can handle the rest."

Just before they reached the turn to Wildwood, Ishimaru said, "By the way, military dental records for Moses arrived. Washington County ME says they're a match. The body on the houseboat was definitely him." She pulled into the drive, pausing a moment for the deputies there to ID her and Bo. At the gatehouse, an agent unfamiliar to Bo was standing post. After they'd passed through, he saw a newly dug trench running along the inside of the stone wall around the orchard.

"Underground, motion sensitive cable," Ishimaru explained.

Bo understood. Nobody wanted a repeat of the tunneling Moses had done. It was a measure Bo himself had suggested several times, but Tom Jorgenson always vetoed the proposal. "I live behind enough of a wall already," he'd complained. "And we both know that no matter how many security measures you put in place, someone bent badly enough on killing will find a way." Which, as it turned out, was undeniably true.

They passed a number of agents Bo didn't know. Ishimaru said, "The field office has been temporarily relieved of responsibility for security here. All our agents are back on normal duty."

"Punishment?"

"Not necessarily. We've been under a lot of strain."

"Diana, do you think I—"

She didn't let him finish. "You were the only thing that stood between Moses and the First Lady. In the end, you were all that kept her alive."

Not quite, Bo could have said. For Moses had offered the First Lady a chance at life. All she had to do was beg forgiveness for a sin he imagined she'd committed. Despite all his careful planning, Moses had hesitated. And that moment of hesitation was Bo's opportunity and the First Lady's salvation. Bo had written all this in his incident report, and he was sure Ishimaru knew it, so he said nothing.

She let him off at the guesthouse, where his car was parked. "Stay in touch," she said.

A couple of agents came out to greet him—Cole Dunning, with whom he'd worked briefly while on assignment with the Dignitary Protection Division during the years of George Bush Sr., and Mack McKenzie, who'd gone through training with him. They shook his hand, and laughed, and they called him a hero. They said it lightly, but they meant it.

He found the First Lady sitting under an apple tree, the last in the row. Before her, the orchard grass ran ten yards to the edge of the bluff. Far below lay the sweep of the river. It looked peaceful and unmoving from that distance, a blue snake sleeping in the sun. Kate stared at the water.

"Hello," Bo said.

She was startled, but she smiled when she saw him. "Bo. What are you doing here?"

"Came to get my car."

She stood up. He saw that her feet were bare.

"They finally let you exchange your hospital gown for civilian clothes," she said. "You look good."

He almost said, *So do you.* Instead he indicated an area far to her right where a pile of stone and sacks of dry mortar lay. "What's going on?"

"They're putting up a wall. Dad finally gave his okay. It'll ruin the

212

view." She stared again at the river. "They told me the body's been definitely identified. It was David Moses."

"Yes. It's over, Kate."

She gave her head a faint shake. "Once a thing happens, it's never really over. It's always there in your memory. In your nightmares."

Bo thought about his own nightmares and knew that what she said was true.

Another smile brightened her face. "By the way, you're invited to Sunday dinner. I hope you haven't already made other plans."

He decided she must not know about the tabloid story yet. He thought he should tell her, but he liked seeing her happy, and he liked feeling happy himself.

"I'll be there," he said.

He pulled into the garage behind the duplex in Tangletown. He climbed the stairs to his apartment and unlocked the door. Inside, he felt a little disoriented, as if he'd been gone on a long trip. He knew that in a way he had.

He put his things away, popped on a Miles Davis CD, and stood at the window in his living room. The street was quiet, full of sunlight and the shade of big trees. Down the block, a teenager ran a gas mower across a lawn. Nearer, a man in jean cutoffs hosed the suds off his car in the driveway. Bo could see kids on a swing set visible in one of the backyards. It all looked so normal, and it all felt so alien.

You're just tired, he told himself. He went to the bedroom to lie down. With him, he took the book she'd given him. He opened it and read again the inscription she'd written. ". . . *your name upon my lips.*"

He closed the book.

"Kate," he whispered.

It felt very good on his own lips.

chapter

thirty

The doctor had sent Bo home with pills. Penicillin to fight infection. Codeine to deal with residual pain. And Xanax to help him sleep. Bo sometimes had nightmares about Wildwood. The faces of the men and the woman who had died there haunted him. Often, in the nightmares, he relived the confrontation on the bluff with Moses. Sometimes in the nightmares, it was Bo who went over the cliff, and as he fell, he realized Kate was going to die, too. That nightmare always wrenched him from his sleep.

Awake in the dark one night, he got up to take some Xanax. He settled in front of the television and caught a late-night news program on cable. It was called "Profile of a Madman" and was subtitled "The David Solomon Moses Story." In the wake of the attack on Wildwood, most networks had thrown together reports, profiles, documentaries of one kind or another. In most respects, the one Bo watched seemed a rehashing of what he and everyone else already knew by now. Moses, the brilliant, troubled man with a horrendous history. The romantic obsession for Kathleen Jorgenson. The assault on Kate after she made it clear to him that she didn't return his affection. The choice between prison and military service. There were a couple of new twists. While in the army, David Moses had served with Special Forces. There were positive comments about him from superior officers who felt he'd distinguished himself during a number of assignments. His history after his discharge was vague but included rumors of psychiatric treatment in several VA facilities across the country prior to his arrest for manslaughter in Minneapolis. Bo thought about the alphabet boys. CIA, NSA, DOD. They had the resources to create a smoke screen past for Moses, a man whose association with them, if indeed there'd been one, they would certainly want to hide. Of course the documentary chronicled yet again all the bloody spectacle at Wildwood, which was explained (this was the popular theory) as an adolescent obsession finally finding an outlet in the adult fury of a deranged man.

The profile ended with footage of a simple burial in a cemetery in River Falls, Wisconsin. The final shot was a lingering image of Moses's gravestone. The marker was small. Chiseled there were his name, the date of his death, and a brief inscription: *Forgive us our trespasses*.

The only man Bo knew who'd befriended David Moses while he was alive had presided over his final rest in death. Father Don Cannon.

In the morning, Bo called the priest and arranged to meet with him.

"I made the request for disposition of the remains," Father Cannon said. "Nobody else wanted him."

They were having coffee in the priest's home in River Falls. They sat on a patio in the backyard. There was a feeder on a pole at one corner of the patio, and a hummingbird hovered there with its long beak thrust into the tiny tube from which it sucked colored sugar water.

"I would never have believed that the boy I knew could be capable of such brutality," the priest said.

"People change, Father. Or they fool us. Especially when we're inclined to want to believe the best." Bo sipped his coffee, a good dark French roast brewed from beans the priest had freshly ground. "It looked like you were alone at the service."

"There were no mourners, if that's what you mean. A lot of reporters unfortunately, stumbling over gravestones and one another. I'd hoped to keep it quiet, but newspeople . . ." He shook his head, and his wild beard brushed his chest.

"Did you pay for the plot and stone?"

"No."

"Who did?"

"An anonymous donor."

"Anonymous," Bo said. "Understandable. How were you contacted?"

"A card that contained the money."

"You still have the card?"

The priest gave Bo a wary look.

"Sorry, Father. Instinct." He waited a moment, then asked, "Do you?"

"Yes."

"Could I see it?"

"Why?"

"I'm not sure. Maybe I'm looking for some kind of closure. What would be the harm, if it's anonymous?"

The big priest considered, then stood up. The hummingbird shot away from the feeder, fast as a bullet. In a few minutes, Father Cannon was back, the card in his hand.

It was a simple note asking to be allowed to contribute to a resting place for David Moses. In return, the donor requested that, if possible, the gravestone contain an inscription. *Forgive us our trespasses.* Except for the inscription, which had been handwritten in a florid script, the text had been typed.

"You granted the request," Bo said.

"The contributor was more than generous. And the only one. And I quite liked the sentiment."

"Do you still have the envelope it came in?"

"If I did, Bo, I wouldn't let you see it. Anonymous, remember? I don't want you speculating from a postmark."

"The inscription is handwritten. Risky for someone who wants to remain anonymous, don't you think?"

"I'm sure it was never meant to be seen by anyone but me. Please don't make me regret I showed it to you."

"I'm sorry, Father." Bo watched the priest put the note away in his pocket. "By the way, is the cemetery plot hard to find?"

The middle of a hot August afternoon wasn't, apparently, a popular time to visit the dead. Except for a groundskeeper on a small tractor mower that moved lazily along the fence, Bo and Father Cannon were the only signs of life. The priest directed Bo to drive toward a far corner of the cemetery. As they approached, Bo saw a mounding of fresh earth under a lofty ash tree.

"Moses?" Bo asked.

The priest nodded.

Bo parked, and they walked together to the grave. Long before they reached it, the priest exclaimed, "Jesus, Mary, and Joseph."

Across the polished stone, someone had spray painted in black: MURDERER!

Standing beside the grave, Bo felt no sorrow for Moses. The memory of the agents killed at Wildwood and of the First Lady kneeling for execution, as well as the ache of Bo's own wounds, were all painful reminders that for Moses, dead was best.

After a while, the priest asked, "Enough?"

"I guess," Bo said. "I don't know what I was hoping for. Answers only he could give."

"The only answer you'll get is right there in front of you. And it's not a bad one."

Bo looked at the vandalized stone. The black paint nearly obscured the inscription.

Forgive us our trespasses.

chapter

thirty-one

A few days into his recovery, Tom Jorgenson suffered a stroke. Although not severe, it left him, according to Annie, weak and a little disoriented. Bo stayed away from Wildwood and spent his time reading and sleeping and thinking about Kate. The article in the *National Enquirer* had generated a lot of furor, and Bo's phone rang constantly. He monitored caller ID. One of the few calls he answered was from Stu Coyote, who told him if he wanted to escape the limelight for a while, he was welcome to come down to Oklahoma. "And feel free to bring your girlfriend," Coyote said. Bo didn't see the humor.

Finally, he knew he had to get away. One afternoon, he left the city behind and headed south through farmland thick with tasseled corn, squat milo, and fields of soybeans made silver-green by the bright sunlight. He could have driven the interstate a good deal of the way, but he stuck to back roads where he often found himself crawling behind a big farm implement lumbering between sections of land. He loved the smell of the country, especially in the late summer when the long hot days of August brought everything to ripeness. He passed acres of freshly mown alfalfa laid out in rows to dry in the sun, and the smell took him back instantly across two decades to the summers in Blue Earth when he worked with Harold Thorsen cutting, baling, and bucking hay, summers that were absolutely the best in all his memories.

It was nearing evening when he pulled onto the dirt lane that led to the Thorsen farmhouse. He bumped over a set of railroad tracks, then crossed a narrow bridge that spanned a creek lined with cottonwoods. Beyond the creek, tall corn walled the lane, blocking Bo's view of almost everything except the big red barn topped with a weather vane, the roof of the two-story white house surrounded by elms, and the blue sky that pressed gently against the land, holding all things in place like the hand of God.

Nell Thorsen was waiting on the porch. She was a small woman dressed in cornflower blue shorts, a white cotton shirt, and sneakers. Her legs were thin and tanned. Her hair had been recently done, short and silver. Although she looked out at the world through thick glasses, her eyes didn't miss a trick. She was seventy-nine and gave the impression she intended to live forever.

"Right on time," she said as she hugged him and kissed his cheek. She smelled of lilac bath powder. "I just finished setting the table."

Nell had grown up on a farm in South Dakota cooking big dinner meals served at noon for the hired hands and the threshing crews. Ham and beef and salt pork, three kinds of potatoes, beans, squash, corn bread and biscuits, everything drowned in gravy. Her father died of a heart attack at fifty-one. By the time Bo joined the Thorsen household, Nell was cooking with an eye toward health. Meats were lean, vegetables profuse and al dente, potatoes served with butter sparingly. What she'd prepared for supper with Bo was chicken salad on a bed of lettuce accompanied by a section of cantaloupe and a croissant. She offered him iced herbal tea from a big pitcher moist with condensation.

The mantel above the fireplace in the living room was crowded with photos of the Thorsen foster children. There'd been nearly thirty in all. Occasionally when Bo visited the farm, he bumped into one of the others who happened to drop by. He was happy only Nell was there that day because mostly he'd come to be alone.

Nell asked about Tom Jorgenson and Annie and the First Lady. She mentioned the awful incident at Wildwood only to say that she'd got on her knees and thanked God when she heard Bo would be all right.

"I got the flowers," he said. "They were lovely."

"I'd have come to visit but my damn sciatica was acting up so I could barely move."

Later, after he'd cleared the table and helped with the dishes, he took a walk alone along the creek. The summer had been dry, and the creek had narrowed to a thin trickle between flats of mud that had hardened and cracked. He'd spent a lot of time there when he was a teenager, wading in the water in search of crawdads and box turtles. Once he'd come out of the creek with a big black leech suckered to the skin between his toes. He was a kid fresh from the city then, and he had no idea what to do. He hobbled back to the farmhouse where Nell got the Morton's box, covered the leech with salt, and simply plucked it off. He'd been impressed with her practical knowledge and her nonchalance.

He went back to his car and took out the book he'd brought with him, the one Kate had given him, then he went to the barn and climbed into the loft that was filled with hay bales. From there he could see a good part of the farm and beyond. In the pasture to the northwest, cattle grazed. Three miles south rose the water tower in Blue Earth. All around were other farms nestled among their own fields, neighbors all deeply connected by more than just those distant property lines, connected by the land itself and the life it dictated. When he'd lived with Harold and Nell, he often sat in the loft after his work was done. Sometimes he had a book and he read. Sometimes he just sat and drank in the beauty of the place. Sometimes Harold joined him and they talked. He'd been a gorilla of a man, a blond gorilla, with a chest that had seemed to young Bo big as the grille of a Cadillac. Mostly he was quiet, but when he laughed it was a huge sound, like the earth rumbling, and it always filled Bo with happiness. He'd never known his own father. The fathers of the other kids he'd run with in St. Paul were men careless in their parenting. Or worse, brutal. If it hadn't been for Harold Thorsen, Bo would have grown up believing that being a man was a harsh and selfish thing.

"You up there?" Nell called from the bottom of the ladder.

"Yes."

"Figured. I've got some coffee made if you'd like some."

"I'll be right there."

Bo picked up his book and headed down.

Nell served the coffee on the porch where there was a small wicker table and two wicker chairs. It was a warm evening, early yet for mosquitoes.

"Were you reading in the loft?" she asked.

"Remembering mostly."

"Good memories?"

"I was thinking about the time I stormed up there and threatened to run."

"I remember that."

"Harold followed me up. I figured he was going to—I don't know—hit me or handcuff me or something. I told him he couldn't keep me here, working me like a slave."

"You weren't the first he'd heard that from."

"He sat down beside me. The sun was low in the sky, like it is now. I remember everything seemed very precise, either shadow or light. The fields were orange. The trees were black. But all I saw was red. Man, I was pissed.

"He didn't say anything at first. We sat for a while. Then he said, 'Give it a week. If you want to run after that, tell me where you want to go and I'll take you there myself.'" Bo held his coffee mug in both hands and laughed softly. "Bet he said that to everybody."

"Only the ones he was sure wouldn't take him up on it."

"I miss him."

"We all do." Nell lifted the book Bo had set on the table.

"A gift from a friend," Bo said.

"Good?"

"I don't know. She confuses me."

"I meant the book."

"Oh."

"But tell me about the friend."

"Nothing to tell." Bo looked away. The sun lay on top of the cornfield, a red ball bleeding onto the green stalks. "She's married."

Nell put cream in her coffee and stirred. In the still air of evening, the spoon made little clinking sounds against the cup. "A blossoming bedside romance?"

Bo gave her a dark look.

"I live in the country, not outer space. We have tabloids at the checkout counters in Blue Earth, too. You wouldn't believe the number of calls I've had from folks wondering if it's true."

"It's not."

Nell opened the book and read the inscription. "That's a lovely thing for her to say, Bo. I've always liked her."

She handed the book back, still opened to the page with the inscription. Bo looked down at the words, written in Kate's beautiful, florid script.

Nell said, "Harold and I always hoped you'd find a nice girl someday. We just imagined it might be someone not married to the president." She smiled.

In the elms around the house and in the cottonwoods along the creek, the cicadas began to sing. It was a one-note song, long and hypnotic. Just when it seemed the sound would go on forever, it suddenly died. Bo had been staring at the words written in the book, something almost coming to him for a long time. The moment the cicadas stopped singing, he had it.

"My God," he said in the quiet.

"What is it?"

"Nell, I'm sorry, I have to go." He stood up and wedged the book under his arm against his side. "Forgive me?"

"I could forgive you anything, Bo." She gave him a parting kiss and stood on the porch, waving as he turned his car in the yard and headed back down the lane.

It was well after dark by the time he reached Wildwood. He'd called ahead on his cell phone, so he was expected. After he passed through security at the gate and parked his car, he hurried to the main house and knocked on the door. Annie answered.

"She's upstairs with Nicole Green, working on First Lady business. She'll be with you in a minute. It must be important if it couldn't wait until tomorrow."

"How's Tom?" Bo asked.

"Tough. Alive. Thank God it was a mild stroke. It could have been worse."

Bo thought how Minnesotan that was. *It could have been worse.* How often had he seen tragedy dealt with in that way, a stoic comparison to a greater possible harm. He'd watched a news report earlier that summer after a tornado had ripped through central Minnesota. They'd interviewed an old Finn standing in front of the rubble that had once been his home. "I'm lucky," he'd said. "I got insurance." Then he'd glanced behind him toward the lake shore where a small structure still stood. "Heck, coulda been worse. Coulda lost the sauna, too."

Annie went to a bookcase near the fireplace. From where it had been folded and shoved into a dark nook, she took a newsprint publication, and held it up.

"Bo?"

It was a copy of the *National Enquirer.*

"That's garbage, Annie."

"I know. I'd just like you to be careful. There's so much at stake."

"Am I still invited to Sunday dinner?"

"You're always welcome here." At the sound of feet on the stairs,

Annie folded the tabloid and put it back into the dark place from which it had come.

The First Lady appeared, looking a little tired. She smiled when she saw Bo.

"I wondered if you'd like to take a walk with me," Bo said.

"Now?"

"We need to talk."

Kate glanced at Annie, who offered her only a brief shrug. "Of course," she said.

They walked out onto the dark porch and down the stairs. The moon was almost directly overhead, a quarter moon dimmed by a high haze. However, the yard light mounted on the barn was bright, and in its glare, the asphalt of the drive shone like black opal and the grass blazed with a false flame. Bo headed toward the dark nearer the orchard.

"To the bluff?" Kate asked.

"No," Bo said. "Secret Service will follow us there. I'd rather we talked alone."

He paused at the rail fence that separated the compound from the apple trees. The door of the guesthouse opened and an agent appeared against the light inside.

"It's okay," Bo called. "We're not going any farther."

The First Lady waved. "Thank you."

The figure held a moment longer, then closed the door.

In front of the guesthouse, the sculpture by Roland Jorgenson, the curled sheets of polished metal called *Goddess*, caught the harsh glare of the yard lamp and glowed as if white-hot. A long flow of reflected light spilled from it across the ground toward the place where Bo and the First Lady stood.

"All this sounds so serious, Bo. What is it?" Her face was a blur of pale skin and shadow.

"Forgive us our trespasses," Bo said.

Only a moment before, there had been the suggestion of a smile on her lips, but it vanished in an instant.

"I don't understand," she said.

"Forgive us our trespasses. It's on his grave."

She opened her mouth, a dark hollow in all that hard, artificial light, but she didn't speak.

"I talked with Father Cannon," Bo said. "He took me to the grave of David Moses. He showed me the note from the anonymous donor. The handwriting on the note matches the handwriting of the inscription in the book you gave me. You paid for the plot and the stone and the burial of the man who tried to kill you. Why?"

She folded her hands and put them to her lips.

Bo said, "I'll tell you what I think, then. I think you lied all those years ago about what happened on the bluff that night. I remember something I read in your father's autobiography, *The Testament of Time*. He wrote that he went through a dark period after Myrna died, after he came back to Wildwood, and he turned to drinking as a way of forgetting. Was he drunk that night? Did he attack you while he was drunk? Did David Moses tell the truth? Did you frame an innocent man?"

Her fingers spread now, like the pickets of a fence across her mouth, preventing any words from escaping. But something crept out at last, a whisper. "Yes . . . and no."

Bo stepped back and waited.

"Yes, I lied," she said slowly. "David didn't attack me. He was trying to help. It was just that he saw everything wrong." She turned from him and walked away a bit, wading into the light that spilled off the sculpture. "It wasn't my father with me."

"Who was it?" Bo asked.

"I'm not sure there's any way to explain it. I can tell you how things were. Maybe that will help you understand.

"When we came back to Wildwood, my father was devastated. He was lost to us in a lot of ways. He'd begun drinking, yes. We were all a little lost, Ruth and Earl and me. I was afraid. It felt like our whole world had collapsed. Annie did her best to hold us together, but she had her own judicial career, and we needed something more than she could give, the kind of strength my father used to have. We found it. Or for a while thought we did. It came from Roland.

"He was ten years younger than my father, different in so many ways. Not reserved or cautious. He was bold, exciting. He and Dad had never been close. We seldom saw him before we came back to live at Wildwood. But we all fell in love with him. He was like this wonderful, blazing sun. Wildwood was his studio, so he was here for us all the time. We loved his energy, his enthusiasm, his attention to us. He seemed so strong, in so many ways. Those great hands of his. His laugh. He could be very gentle. You should have seen how he was with Earl."

She stared at the glowing metal sculpture.

"You and your uncle?" Bo said. "An affair?"

She still wouldn't look at him, but she nodded. "I knew it was wrong, but I didn't care. I was so in love, so . . . in need, really. After a while I began to see the flaws, the faults. He could be selfish, manipulative, possessive. Then I began to consider the consequences, the dangers, and I knew it had to end. That's what I was trying to do on the bluff that night, the night David discovered us. I'd told Roland it was over. He was furious. We argued. David blundered in. They struggled. It was terrible. I was so scared. David was lying there unconscious. I begged Roland to go. If the truth were ever known, I mean, incest, my God. On top of what Dad was already dealing with. Roland went back to the house, I tore my clothes and, God forgive me, I accused David. And he accused my father. It was a nightmare. I've told myself over the years that if they'd prosecuted David, I would have told the truth. But I don't know. He just . . . went away, and it was fixed. Roland and I were over. It all became the past. The terrible past."

"Your father never knew the truth?"

"He figured it out later and confronted Roland. It's the only physical fight I know of that my father was ever in. He was no match for Roland, with all those muscles from his metal work. But Roland wouldn't fight back. He just let my father hit him. Then he got himself drunk and he drove his car into a tree.

"It sounds so sordid, I know." She finally looked at him, turning her back to the sculpture, her face fully shadowed. "What do you think of me now? Hardly heroine material, huh?"

"I think it was a mistake," Bo said. "And I think it was a long time ago, and far behind you."

"I thought so, too. Until David . . ." Even in the shadow, her tears somehow managed to glisten as they rolled down her cheeks. "All those people, Bo. He killed them because of me."

"No, he killed them because of who he was, not you."

"It feels like it's my fault." She bent her head, and her shoulders shook as she wept.

Bo went to her, took her in his arms, and held her. He laid his cheek against her hair and closed his eyes. He felt an ache himself, as if her pain were his own. He wished he could make her hurt go away, that somehow he had the power to absolve her. And he knew that he loved her. He knew it beyond all doubt.

She drew away. Her nose was running, and she wiped at it with the back of her hand. "What do you do with a confession like this, Bo?"

"I'm trained to keep secrets."

She reached up and touched his cheek. "Whenever you're with me, I feel safe." She stood on her toes and gently kissed his lips. "Thank you."

The door of the guesthouse opened again, and this time the dark form of the agent there came forward.

"It's late," Bo said.

"I'll see you tomorrow. Dinner."

"I'll be here."

She left him. Bo watched her disappear into the shade of the porch. He saw her once more briefly in the light as she opened the door and stepped inside.

"Thorsen." It was Stan Calloway who, in the absence of Chris

Manning, now headed the FLOTUS detail. "What the hell do you think you're doing? My God, that's the president's wife. We've got that kiss on tape."

Bo knew Calloway from his days in D.C. A good agent. A little humorless, but solid in the right ways.

"The kiss wasn't my idea, Stan."

Calloway put a hand to his forehead. "Jesus, what am I supposed to do with this?"

Bo reached into his pocket and pulled out his car keys. "Do whatever you feel you have to do with it. I'm going home."

Calloway took his arm and held him back a moment. "A lot of people are looking up to you right now, Thorsen. Don't blow it."

Bo glared at Calloway's hand until the grip was released. He said, "Good night, Stan."

He got in his car, drove home to Tangletown, and readied himself for bed. Then he sat at the window in the dark, trying to find a place inside himself to lock away what he felt. It was too big, this affection. It was way out of hand. What not long before had been only a pleasant conceit was suddenly something with substance, real enough to cause him trouble. What was the point? He had Kate's confidence, but he could never have her love. And even if by some miracle she were to feel the same way, what could she do? She was not just a married woman. She was the First Lady.

"Christ, Bo, you've done it this time," he whispered.

chapter

thirty-two

It was well after dark by the time Clay Dixon returned to the White House. In the last forty-eight hours, he'd been to Atlanta, Miami, New Orleans, Houston, Dallas, and Oklahoma City, trying to drum up votes and campaign contributions for himself and the party candidates in those constituencies. He was tired, but he felt energized, as he usually did after working crowds. He loved that part of his job. He went directly to the Residence on the second floor of the White House. Although it was late, he decided to call Wildwood. He missed his daughter. And he missed his wife. He longed to have Kate back, to be able to talk with her about the campaign swing and how good he felt. Love was more about quiet things than about bedroom noise. It was something he'd always known, but he was feeling it deep down now where the real truths resided.

Annie told him that Kate wasn't there. She was out looking at the moon. She'd have Kate call him back when she returned.

Dixon hung up feeling unaccountably anxious. He was tired, and knew he should go to bed. But he wanted to wait for Kate's call. If it came. She was still angry with him. She'd made that clear in the few conversations they'd had recently. He thought about the report Lorna Channing had prepared, and that got him to thinking about one of its chief proponents, Bobby Lee. And thinking about Bobby got him to wondering what his friend had been able to scrape together on whatever it was that Senator William Dixon might be up to.

The phone rang. Kate, he thought happily.

"Mr. President, John Llewellyn is on the line for you."

"Put him on."

"Mr. President, I apologize for disturbing you at such a late hour," Llewellyn said.

"No problem, John. Where are you?"

"In the West Wing, in my office."

"Working late."

"Mr. President, FBI Assistant Director Arthur Lugar is with me."

Dixon heard the tension in John Llewellyn's voice. "What is it?"

"It's about Bob Lee, sir."

His first thought was *scandal.* But he knew Bobby Lee, and he'd never known a more decent man. "What about him?"

"Sir, he's dead."

Robert Lee had loved to sail. For twenty years, every Saturday that he could slip away, he'd taken his sailboat out onto Chesapeake Bay and spent the day cutting across salt water. Often his sons went with him, but that summer they were both gone, counselors at a camp in the Blue Ridge. Maggie, his wife, was prone to seasickness. So lately, Robert Lee had been sailing alone.

According to the only eyewitness, Lee had been in a small, isolated inlet on the sound of the Choptank River. It was early evening. The wind had shifted. The boom, as it swung around, caught Lee squarely on the side of his head, and he went overboard. The eyewitness sailed immediately to that location, but Bobby Lee had already gone under.

Divers from the Talbot County Sheriff's Department had been called out. They arrived near twilight and began a search for the body, which they quickly found. It took them a bit more time to make the ID, to be certain that Robert Lee, to whom the sailboat was registered, was also the drowned man. The FBI had been notified immediately.

"Is the eyewitness reliable?" Clay Dixon asked. He sat in John Llewellyn's office with Llewellyn and the assistant director of the FBI.

"Former ATF agent, sir," Arthur Lugar replied. "Received a citation as a result of Waco. A longtime sailor. Totally reliable."

"Does Bobby's family know?"

"Not yet, Mr. President."

"How about the media?"

"We haven't released any information."

"Can you wait until morning?"

"Certainly, sir."

"Thank you," he said to the assistant director in a tone that indicated they were finished for the moment. "I want to be kept apprised of your investigation."

"Of course," Lugar said, and he rose to leave.

When they were alone, Dixon said to Llewellyn, "I'll need new counsel."

"Why don't you go with Ned Shackleford? He's always been Bobby's right hand."

Dixon knew he was shoving his feelings down, pushing the grief to the back while he dealt with the business of keeping things under control, making sure his administration moved forward whatever the circumstances. Nonetheless, he felt a deep emptiness in his heart and a profound absence at his side. As soon as he was certain everything was in order, he would allow himself to grieve long and hard for his friend Bobby Lee.

"Did you tell my father?"

"I've told no one but you, sir."

"Good. I'd like to be alone for a while, John."

"Certainly, Mr. President."

Dixon rubbed his eyes, feeling more tired than he'd ever been.

"Don't say anything to the press. I'd like to make the call to Bobby's wife myself. And one more thing. Let me tell the senator in my own way."

"Whatever you prefer."

When Llewellyn had gone, the president lifted his phone and spoke to the White House operator. "Get me Lorna Channing. If she's not in her office, try her cell phone."

"Oh, Clay. I'm so sorry."

Lorna Channing put her arms around Dixon and held him for a moment. They were alone in the president's study in the Executive Residence. She'd come immediately after she'd received his call.

"It's such a terrible thing. Such a tragic accident."

He spoke against her cheek. "It wasn't an accident, Lorna."

She leaned away from him and looked into his face.

"I'd asked Bobby to keep an eye on my father. The old bastard's up to something. Next thing I know, Bobby's dead. It's no coincidence."

"You're saying your father is responsible?"

"I'm not sure what I'm saying." He went to the phone. "Get me Senator Dixon." A moment later he said, "Thank you." He put the call on speakerphone so Lorna could hear.

"Mr. President, it's late." It was the tone of a tired, grumpy father.

"I know, Dad. I just got some terrible news. Bobby's dead."

There was a pause at the other end.

"Lee? How?"

"An accident."

"I'm sorry, son. I know how close you two were." There was the squeak of bedsprings, the rustle of linen. "Have you thought who'll replace him?"

"That's what I wanted to talk to you about."

"The choice seems obvious to me. Shackleford."

"John thought the same thing."

"Good. Then we're on the same page. Does Lee's family know?"

"Not yet."

"Tragic business," the senator said. There was the sound of scratching, the flare of a match, the old man's huffed breath as he lit a cigar. "Shackleford will do just fine."

"Thanks, Dad."

" 'Night, Clayboy. Get some rest. I reckon you'll need it."

When the call was ended, the President looked at Lorna Channing.

"Ned Shackleford," he said. "There's our leak. Jesus, when did he go over to their side?"

"Your father already knew about Bobby," she said. "Even I could hear it in his voice."

Dixon nodded. "How do you suppose that came to be?"

"He heard it on the news?"

"The press hasn't been informed yet."

"Llewellyn?"

"He promised to say nothing."

"Maybe he broke his promise."

"Or never intended to keep it in the first place." All the possibilities seemed dark in his thinking. "Could it be they both knew about it, knew even before it happened?"

Lorna put her hand on his cheek. "Clay, I can understand mistrusting your father and Llewellyn, but I'd caution against looking for conspiracy. I guarantee that if you look for it, you're going to see it. Everywhere."

Dixon took a deep breath and sat down. "If I don't trust someone, Lorna, I'll go crazy."

"You have me," she said.

"Standing by me could be dangerous."

"I'll take the risk."

"We need someone else to take up where Bobby left off, someone who knows how to find out things and how to watch his back." The president closed his eyes and tried to think. Everything seemed black and hopeless. "Christ," he said, "isn't there anybody in this city we can trust?"

chapter

thirty-three

Bo got the call Sunday morning. He was trying to read, but he wasn't able to concentrate. All he could think about was Kate.

The phone startled him, and he answered it quickly.

"Thorsen here."

A woman at the other end of the line informed him that the president of the United States was calling.

"Agent Thorsen, how are you?"

Although surprised, Bo replied casually, "I'm fine, thank you, Mr. President."

"Glad to hear it. I'll come right to the point. I never had the opportunity to thank you properly for your valiant actions at Wildwood. I'm hoping you'll accept an invitation to be my guest for lunch here at the White House."

"Of course, sir. It would be an honor."

"How about tomorrow?"

"Tomorrow?"

"Short notice, I understand. But I have this Pan-American summit coming up next week, and I'll be gone for several days. I'll have my staff arrange your flight and hotel accommodations."

"It would be my pleasure."

"Great. One more thing, Agent Thorsen. I understand you're on medical leave."

"Yes."

"Does that mean you don't have to be back in the office for a while?"

"Another ten days."

"But you still get around pretty good?"

"Just fine, sir."

"Excellent. I'll have my staff contact you with the details."

After the president had hung up, Bo sat for a moment, considering the president's invitation. Surely Dixon's staff had made the president aware of the article in the *National Enquirer*. Was that what this was about?

When Bo arrived at Wildwood for the Sunday meal, he found Kate, her seven-year-old daughter, Stephanie, and her brother, Earl, tossing a football on the lawn.

"You're the one who saved my mother," Stephanie said as she shook Bo's hand. She crooked a finger, brought him down to her level, and gave him a kiss on the cheek. "Thank you," she said seriously.

She had her mother's long blonde hair and gray-blue eyes. She was tall, like her father, and seemed to possess a self-confidence beyond her years. He liked her immediately. The kiss on the cheek helped a lot, too.

"Goody," Stephanie said. "Now we can play a game."

"Mr. Thorsen's recovering from serious injury, Steph," Kate said. "I'm sure he'd rather relax."

"I'll play," Bo said. "As long as I don't have to run much or get tackled, I'll be fine."

"You're sure?"

"I'm sure. In fact, doctor's orders. I'm supposed to stay active. Helps promote healing."

"We won't play long. Dinner's in half an hour."

"You can be on my team," Stephanie said. "All you have to do is just throw me the ball."

Earl grinned and pointed a finger at Bo. "We're gonna cream you."

Kate gave him a marvelous smile. "Thanks, Bo. Steph's been begging for a game since she got here."

Bo had dressed casually, a blue shirt with a white T-shirt beneath, and khakis. He took off his blue shirt and he faked a few warm-ups.

"Who kicks off?" he asked.

"I do," Stephanie said.

Bo was skeptical until he saw the football, a small thing of orange and black foam, grooved for easy spirals. They played on the grassy side yard, between the main house and guesthouse. The dirt lane that led from the barn into the orchards was the equivalent of the fifty-yard line. It was warm and sunny and the sky was a flawless blue. A perfect afternoon for football.

Even at seven, Stephanie was quite a player. "My daddy used to be quarterback for the Broncos. They called him Air Express because he was so good at passing. I think it was more fun than being president."

"I'm sure it was," Bo agreed.

She called her own patterns—hooks, fade-outs, posts. She caught everything that came near her. Her task was made easier by Earl, who defended against her. Mostly, he ran around waving his arms and laughing.

Kate quarterbacked for the other team. She was better at it than Bo, but she got very little help from her brother, who couldn't have caught a football even if his hands had been soaked in glue. He had a lot of fun whenever he somehow managed to get hold of the ball and Stephanie chased him, trying to make the tag. Kate was careful around Bo, obviously concerned about his injuries. When she tagged him, she did it gently. Even so, for a long time after, he could still feel the touch of her hands on him.

Some of the agents on detail in the Op Center or on FLOTUS detail gathered along the sidelines and cheered them on.

Twenty minutes into the game, Kate called, "Halftime!" and she fell in a heap onto the grass. Bo sat down with her while Stephanie and Earl went into the house to get something cold to drink.

"Are you doing okay?" she asked.

"A little sore, but nothing a couple of aspirin won't cure." He waited a moment, then told her, "I got a call this morning from the president." He was conscious that he'd refrained from saying *your husband.*

"Oh?"

"He invited me to the White House. He says he wants to thank me properly for saving you."

"When are you going?"

"Tomorrow."

"So soon?"

"You saw the article in the *National Enquirer?*"

She nodded.

"I wondered if maybe he saw it, too, and is planning on having me shot."

"Not Clay. Something like that, he'd want to do himself. He'd invite you to step outside and put up your dukes." She looked Bo over appreciatively. "It would be a good match."

"You're not angry? About the article?"

She'd begun to pluck at leaves of clover growing among the blades of grass. "That kind of thing goes with the territory. How about you?"

"I took some heat."

"I'm sorry."

"Nothing I can't handle." Bo swept his own hand idly over the grass. "I can't imagine anyone believing what they read in those rags."

"I can't imagine," she said. She smiled at him and held out her hand. "Here. For you. A four-leaf clover."

"For good luck?"

"You're going to need it in the second half."

Earl and Stephanie came out the front door and joined them.

"Come on, you guys," Stephanie said. "Let's play."

They got up, but before they could separate to their own ends for the kickoff, Annie shoved open the screen door and came out quickly.

"Kate, I just heard it on the news." Her face was pinched with concern.

"What is it?"

"Bobby Lee. He's dead."

"No. Not Bobby."

"The radio report said it was a boating accident. He drowned."

Kate put a hand to her forehead. "Oh no, no. Poor Maggie."

She was speaking, Bo knew, of Robert Lee's wife.

"And Clay," she said, looking stricken. "When did it happen?"

"Yesterday."

"Oh, Annie, I didn't call him back last night. He must have known then." She turned to Bo, and the pain she felt was obvious. "He and Bobby were like brothers. I've got to call him. Excuse me, will you?"

"Of course."

"Uncle Bobby?" Stephanie said. She looked toward Annie.

"Come here, sweetheart." Annie put her arms around the girl.

"I'd best go," Bo said. "You've got a lot to deal with."

"I'm sorry."

"That's okay, Annie. I'll be in touch." He reached out and shook Earl's hand. "It was a pleasure playing against you."

"Bye, Bo," Earl said, looking confused.

That afternoon he received a call from the White House with his itinerary, and after that he packed. As the sun dropped behind the trees and the shadows crept up and overtook his windows, he stood looking out at his neighborhood. Tangletown. It was an area of old homes, big trees, green lawns. Most of the houses belonged to families. The backyards had swing sets. In the evening people sat on their porches, husbands and wives, talking quietly of the things that married people shared.

He'd never known his father. He'd mostly seen his mother use or be used. Harold and Nell Thorsen had given him a glimpse of what was possible between a man and a woman, but when he joined the Secret Service, he made a decision about his life. To live that life, he'd willingly isolated himself. Not all agents chose that course. Some, like two of the dead at Wildwood, had married, created families. In the end, they'd left behind them more grief than Bo could imagine.

Not for him, that responsibility. Better, he told himself, to be alone.

The phone rang.

"Bo, it's Kate." Her voice on the other end was feathery and sad.

"Hi."

"I'm sorry about this afternoon. I know I rushed away."

"That's okay. Understandable. Are you going out to D.C.?"

"Just for the funeral. I'm coming back the same day. I want to stay here until I'm sure my father's out of the woods." She breathed a heavy sigh. "Know what Dad wants to do first thing when he comes home, Bo? He wants us to watch the moon rise over the St. Croix, all of us together. Isn't that just like him? You're welcome to be there, you know."

"Thanks. I'll think about it."

The line fell silent. Bo desperately grabbed at something to say.

"Maybe I'll see you in D.C."

"Honestly, I doubt it, Bo."

He'd said all the inane things he could think of. It was time to say good-bye, but he couldn't bring himself to let go of the sound of her voice, couldn't stop hoping that he could make himself say something that was true.

"I'd better go," she said.

"Take care," he said.

"You, too."

She hung up and left Bo still searching for words that never seemed to come to him when he needed them most.

chapter

thirty-four

Just after 10:00 A.M., Bo checked into his hotel room in Washington, D.C. As he hung his slacks and blazer in the closet, someone knocked on his door. He opened up to find a tall, attractive woman with long chestnut hair. She stood in the hallway outside his room holding a brown, leather briefcase. It took him a moment to place the face.

"Ms. Channing," he said, unable to hide completely his surprise.

"Good morning, Agent Thorsen. May I come in?"

Bo stood away from the door and allowed her to enter. They shook hands, and she glanced around the room. Her gaze settled on one of the two chairs bathed in the sunlight pouring through the window.

"May I sit down?"

"Please do."

Channing sat, then indicated with a look and a nod that Bo should take the other chair.

"I'm surprised you knew who I am," she said.

"Good memory for faces. Something I work at. Yours isn't hard to remember."

She leaned forward. "Bo Harold Thorsen. You've been with Secret Service fourteen years. Postings in New York, D.C., London, San Francisco, Miami, and Minneapolis. One citation for merit and another in the works. Expectations that you would go places. Four years ago you put in for a transfer to a small field office in the Midwest, a move most observers of your career considered a dead end."

She paused here expectantly, as if awaiting an explanation.

Bo said, "I didn't see it as an end. I still don't. I just wanted to come home."

Channing reached down to the briefcase she'd settled at his feet and took from it a rolled newspaper that she dropped on the floor between them. Bo saw that it was the *National Enquirer* with the photograph of him and the First Lady on the front.

"When you saved Kate Dixon's life, was it duty?"

"Does it matter?"

"It may."

"It was my job, but I'd have done it even if it weren't."

Channing studied him. "You impressed the president when he met you at the hospital after the incident."

"We spoke only a few minutes."

"Sometimes the measure of a man takes only a handshake. Or so the president believes." Channing picked up the tabloid and put it back in her briefcase. "You're going to have lunch with him in a couple of hours. But lunch isn't the reason you're here, Agent Thorsen. The president is going to ask a favor of you. A rather large favor. He'd like you to know what it is in advance so that you have time to consider before giving him an answer. Before I go any further, however, I need your word that whatever we discuss here, regardless of your decision, will remain between us. You must say nothing to anyone."

"You have my word."

To Bo, what he'd just given was the most important measure of who he was and, with the exception of his heart, was as near to sacred as anything he could offer. Nonetheless, Lorna Channing spent a long moment considering him before she went on.

"The president believes that Robert Lee's death wasn't an accident. He'd like you to look into it."

"That's the FBI's jurisdiction."

"Normally, yes. But the president feels there's reason to believe his own security may be at risk."

"Rich Thielman is in charge of the president's security."

"Technically, this investigation falls outside Agent Thielman's purview. In fact, the president wants no one to know about his suspicions except you."

"With all the media coverage since the Wildwood incident, I'm not exactly an ideal candidate for undercover work right now."

"Don't take this the wrong way, but you do have a forgettable face." Channing paused a moment to see if Bo might object. When he made no comment, she went on. "The president's less concerned with the public nature of your profile than he is with your integrity and ability. He wants very much for you to accept this assignment."

"Assignment? This isn't exactly occurring through official channels."

"You're on medical leave. Your time is your own, is it not?"

"I know D.C.," Bo said. "It won't be long after I've asked a few questions that anyone who cares will be on to me."

"Then you'll have to come up with answers quickly."

"I'd like to think it over."

"Of course. That's why the President sent me." Channing stood, took up her briefcase, and went to the door. "I hardly need to remind you, Agent Thorsen, that if the President is correct, one man has already been killed in his service. Think about it carefully. We'll see you at lunch."

This was not Bo's first visit to the White House. He'd been there many times when he was assigned to the Dignitary Protective

Division during his years in Washington. Nor was Clay Dixon the first president to shake his hand. However, dining with the president was a first.

He was ushered into the Oval Office. As Bo came in, the president stood up, stepped from behind his desk, and extended his hand.

"Thank you for coming, Agent Thorsen. Is it all right if I call you Bo?"

"That would be fine, sir."

Dixon's hand was huge and strong. Bo could easily imagine a football nestled firmly in that grasp.

"How are you feeling? Recovered from your wounds?"

"A little sore now and then."

The president smiled and nodded his head. "Every morning when I get out of bed I have to pop things back into place that got knocked out playing ball. I know about sore." He indicated a door to Bo's left. "Lunch is ready. Shall we eat?"

They were served by a navy steward in the president's private dining room just off the Oval Office.

"I hope you like fish," Clay Dixon said. "It's Chilean sea bass."

"I understand the White House kitchen staff works miracles with everything."

The president laughed. "So you don't like fish. Honest but diplomatic. An admirable combination for D.C. I wish there were more of it here, especially the honest part."

"I lived and worked in the capital for a lot of years. I know men and women here honest to a fault. On the other hand, not one of them is a politician. The sea bass is excellent, by the way."

The president sipped from a glass of mineral water. "I understand the First Lady and my daughter had a wonderful time playing football with you yesterday."

"You have a fine family, sir."

"Thank you. I think so, too. If I recall correctly, you were adopted, yes?"

"Not legally. But official papers don't always tell the whole story."

"They don't, do they," Dixon said.

After they'd eaten, the president suggested a walk in the rose garden, which was odd, for it was a muggy day out. After a bit, Clay Dixon removed his suit coat and slung it over his shoulder as they strolled. In a few minutes, they were joined by Lorna Channing.

"Bo," the president said, "you came close to being killed saving my wife. How do you feel about that?"

"About protecting her, pretty good. Not so good about some of the rest of the incident."

"The agents who were killed, were they friends of yours?"

"Some, yes."

The president paused and stared across the bright green lawn, beyond the Ellipse, toward the Washington Monument, jutting like a bony finger above the trees.

"I asked you here because I believe you're a man of great integrity, and I need your help. I was supposed to leave for the Pan-American summit first thing tomorrow morning. I've delayed departure so that I can attend Robert Lee's funeral."

"I was sorry to hear about his death."

"I know Lorna explained to you already that I don't think Bobby's death was an accident."

"I thought the FBI determined it was."

"As you said, official papers don't always tell the whole story. At the risk of sounding paranoid, I think there's something going on that may have compromised the integrity of the FBI investigation." He glanced at the White House. "And the integrity of my own security as well."

For the next dozen minutes, Dixon related the events that had brought him to that startling conclusion.

"What is it you want from me?" Bo said.

"To find out what Bobby knew or was about to learn that made it incumbent on someone to have him killed."

"Someone? Mr. President, from what you've told me it sounds as if you think your father is involved."

"I do. I'm concerned about the integrity of the White House staff as well."

"Why me?"

"You're a trained investigator. You risked your life in the line of duty. And you're outside the network here."

"There's no one here you trust?"

"Someone I trust may already have betrayed me."

Bo looked behind him. Under the pillared colonnade, two Secret Service agents stood post near the French doors that opened into the Oval Office. He didn't know them. They looked grim and focused. He wondered what they thought of Dixon, the man whose life might someday require the sacrifice of their own.

Dixon said, "I don't know what you think of me personally, but this situation transcends any personal consideration. It's a matter of national security, with implications far beyond who I am as a man or as a president. Your country needs your help, Bo. Will you give it?"

Bo said, "Yes."

"Thank you." The president warmly shook his hand.

Bo glanced at Channing. "I've given this some thought. I'll need a way to communicate with the White House that doesn't raise suspicions."

"You can communicate with me directly," Channing said.

"I should use a code name," Bo suggested.

"All right."

"How about Peter Parker?"

Channing cast him a questioning look.

"Are you familiar with the comic book hero Spider-Man?" Bo said. She shook her head.

The president smiled. "Peter Parker is Spider-Man's real name, Lorna."

Channing said, "Peter Parker it is."

Bo left the White House carrying a large manila envelope, and he went straight to his hotel. He took off his blazer, loosened his tie, and undid the top button of his white shirt. He bent to the small refrigerator and took a bottle of Heineken from the refreshments supplied by the hotel. He popped the cap off and carried the cold beer to the desk near the window. He picked up the envelope, dumped out the contents, and sat down to work.

The president had supplied him with a copy of all the documents related to Robert Lee's death and the preliminary investigation. Although a number of jurisdictions had been involved, the paperwork wasn't overwhelming, a sign that thus far in the thinking of the investigators, there was nothing unusual about the case.

The initial radio transmission had been picked up by the Coast Guard at 1902 hours and relayed to the sheriff's office in Easton, Maryland. A boat had been dispatched, arriving on the scene at Bone Creek Cove at 1927 hours. The eyewitness who'd reported the accident directed divers in their effort to locate the victim. The body was pulled from the water at 2010 hours.

The sheriff's people made a tentative ID from both the boat registration and a driver's license found among the personal belongings aboard the victim's sailboat. When they discovered that they had the president's legal counsel under a blanket, they called the FBI, who took over the investigation from there.

The autopsy showed a depressed skull fracture and acute subdural hematoma beneath the right temporal bone, consistent with a blow to the head. No other wound or unusual marks had been noted. The lungs were filled with brackish salt water. (An accompanying lab report indicated the water in the lungs was chemically and biologically similar to samples taken from Bone Creek Cove.) The cause of death had officially been listed as drowning.

According to the statement given by the only eyewitness, a woman named Jonetta Jackson, Lee had been sailing across the inlet, north-by-northwest with the wind. She happened to be following him, a hundred yards back and slightly east, also running with the wind. They were the only boats in the area.

There'd been a lull in the breeze. Both sailboats had come to a stop, sitting dead in the water. Then the wind picked up again, only it had shifted, coming now from almost due north. As she prepared to come about, her attention was focused on her own boat. When she glanced again at Lee's sailboat, she saw him begin to stand, his attention apparently grabbed by something on the shore. At that moment, the boom swung around and caught him in the head. She saw him go overboard.

Ms. Jackson had sailed as quickly as she could to his location. By the time she reached his boat, he had gone under. She immediately radioed the Coast Guard. In her statement to the FBI, she indicated she was a very good swimmer, and she had entered the water, hoping to locate Lee. Unfortunately, the murky water of the inlet prevented her from seeing anything below the surface. She'd held her position until the sheriff's boat arrived, and she'd directed the divers in their efforts. According to the notes of the agent who'd interviewed her, she seemed quite shaken by the whole experience.

The Bureau had done a routine background check on Jonetta Jackson. The eyewitness was a consultant with a firm called Hammerkill, Inc. that specialized in high-tech security issues. Prior to that she'd been a special agent of the Bureau of Alcohol, Tobacco and Firearms, a veteran of twenty years, who'd been cited for meritorious action at Waco. Her love of sailing was well known. Her credentials as a witness were impeccable.

Given all the evidence, the FBI was comfortable with a determination that Robert Lee's death had been the result of a tragic accident and nothing more.

Looking at the evidence himself, Bo thought the same thing.

However, the president was convinced otherwise.

Bo walked to the window. He had a good view of the nation's capital, a city that quivered in the heat of the August afternoon in a way that reminded Bo of a mirage in a movie. It was a city built on promise, on compromise, on inspiration and empty rhetoric both, on history poorly remembered and easily bent, and once in a while, on good people with the best of intentions who battled against the distrust, misdirection, and deceit that was politics as usual.

He thought about his meeting with Dixon. What had he sensed from the man? Decisiveness. Sincerity. Calm in the face of a difficult situation. All these character traits bumped against something in Bo, something that had to do with how he felt about Kate. He knew it would be easier to feel for her what he did if he believed the man who was her husband was terribly flawed and badly tarnished.

But he liked Dixon.

So, assuming that the president was correct and Robert Lee was onto something, what could it be?

Jonetta Jackson agreed to meet Bo at a Starbucks on Dupont Circle. She was a tall woman, muscular, with sharp dark eyes. As she spoke of her experience on the inlet of Chesapeake Bay, it was obvious the tragedy still affected her.

"I didn't know who it was. Sometimes I wonder if I had, would I have tried harder, reached him sooner."

"How far away were you?"

"Less than a hundred yards. I kicked on the engine and motored over as quickly as I could." She shook her head. "Even so, when I reached his boat, he'd already gone under. I dove. Jesus, I went down a dozen times, but that water was so murky."

She was dressed in a dark blue skirt and blazer, with a cream-colored blouse. She looked like an athlete, like a woman who could have pulled Robert Lee to safety if she'd been able to find him. She sipped from the cappuccino Bo had bought for her, and she nibbled on a croissant.

"You radioed for help right away?"

"Before I went into the water. I knew I'd need medical backup at the very least."

"You said in your statement that he was alone. You're certain?"

"I was close enough that I could see his boat pretty well. He was alone."

"You also said something seemed to have caught his attention. Any idea what?"

"Like I said, the wind came up suddenly and shifted. I was busy with my own boat, preparing to come about. When I looked back at him, he was just beginning to stand, looking toward shore. I saw that big boom swinging, and I knew what was going to happen. I even opened my mouth to yell, but it was too late." She let out a deep breath, as if she'd just gone through the experience again. "So, no. I didn't see what he was seeing. I was watching him."

Bo took a sip of his iced coffee. "When you were ATF, you were cited for valor at Waco."

"Yes."

"What happened? If you don't mind me asking."

"We got the order to go. Then all hell broke loose. They fired on us from the compound. One of my fellow agents went down. I just pulled him out of there."

"I understand you were wounded yourself at the time."

"I didn't realize it then. I was pretty intent on getting Alex out."

"Alex?"

"The other agent. We partnered on occasion."

"Alex. Did he make it?"

"No."

"I'm sorry." Bo listened to the ice crack in his coffee. "Somebody tipped them off, right?"

"Yeah. But hell, we knew that going in. It was a mistake. A criminal decision." She sounded bitter. Bo wondered if that had anything to do with her choice to move into the private sector.

He wanted to bring the discussion back to the issue at hand, Robert Lee. "On the map, Bone Creek Cove appears small and out of the way. What were you doing there?"

"Probably the same thing as Lee. The bald eagles. Because the inlet's isolated, there are a number of bald eagles that nest there.

They're quite beautiful." She lifted her coffee cup, but before she drank she said, "Not a lot of people know that. I'd just as soon you keep it to yourself. I'd hate to see that lovely place overrun."

"Maybe that's what caught Robert Lee's attention. He saw the eagles."

"Maybe."

"Did you see any eagles that day?"

"No. That day all I saw was a man die." She pushed her croissant away, barely touched. "Mind if I ask you a question?"

"Go right ahead."

"You're Secret Service. The investigation was FBI. What's your interest?"

"His proximity to the president. We just want to be on the safe side."

"A good idea," she agreed.

After they'd separated, Bo thought about Jonetta Jackson. He figured if she hadn't been able to save Robert Lee, probably no one could.

chapter

thirty-five

Bo pulled up to the northwest gate of the White House at 6:00 P.M. The Uniformed Division officer on duty checked him through. Bo drove to the West Wing, where Lorna Channing awaited him.

They'd agreed that it might be best for Bo to conduct whatever investigation he felt was necessary within the White House in the evening when many of the staff had gone home for the day. Even so, there seemed to be an enormous amount of activity in the West Wing.

Bo knew the White House employed more than 1,600 personnel. He'd heard it described as a small kingdom made up of innumerable fiefdoms, each with its own rules and ruler. Within such a setting, he could easily imagine intrigues. As he and Channing proceeded to the second floor, Bo caught glances directed his way. Eyes latched onto him and held in a way that made him feel exposed. How secret was his mission, he wondered.

Upstairs, Channing paused at a modest outer office. "Working late, Dorothy," she said to the secretary there.

The nameplate on the desk said D. DELVITTO. She was a small

woman, and when she glanced up from her computer screen, she looked tired. "There's so much to do these days." She gave Bo a quick once-over.

"I'm picking up some items from Bob's office," Channing said.

Dorothy Delvitto nodded somberly. "The president left word you'd be dropping by."

Channing led the way inside and Bo followed, closing the door behind them.

He stood in the middle of the room. He didn't know where to begin, so for a moment he simply tried to take in the place, hoping to get a feel for how Robert Lee might have worked, how he might have organized himself, where he might have put certain things. All of which would have been easier if Bo had the slightest idea what he was looking for.

Lee was a neat man. The office was clean and orderly. There were shelves of books dealing with law and with congressional issues, several filing cabinets, and near the window, a hutch with a computer, monitor, and printer. In one corner sat a large safe. A big desk was central and, except for a couple of neat stacks of papers, was free of clutter. To the left on the desktop, set in a gold frame, was a photograph of Lee standing proudly beside his docked sailboat. Another photograph, in a much larger frame, occupied a place to the right. This one was a family portrait, Lee and his wife flanked by two sons who very much resembled their father. They all looked happy with life and with one another.

"Where do we begin?" Lorna Channing asked.

"Let's see what he's got on his desk."

Bo began by checking the stacks of papers. Memoranda, mostly, composed but lacking Lee's signature initials. Not sent? Nothing of their content leaped out at Bo as significant to his purpose. Channing shook her head as well.

They went carefully through the desk drawers and drew a blank there.

"The computer?" Lorna Channing said.

Bo went to the hutch and turned on the PC. It booted and asked for a password. Bo looked at Channing, who just shrugged her shoulders.

"Ask Ms. Delvitto if she knows," he said.

When she came back, she said, *"Maggie."*

Lee's wife. It made sense. Bo typed in the name, but was denied access.

"He must have changed it without telling his secretary."

"I wonder when," Channing said. "And why."

Bo sat back a moment. "What are his sons' names?"

"Nick and Cal."

Bo tried them both, then Nicholas and Calvin. No luck.

"Any pets?"

"Not that I know of."

"All right," Bo said. "Let's check the file cabinets."

He abandoned the computer and, with Channing, went through the cabinets, drawer after drawer. He didn't hope to stumble across anything marked as obviously as *Senator Dixon's Conspiracy*, but he hoped something might click. Nothing did.

He turned his attention to the big safe, which occupied a whole corner of the room. It was a Wilson, bolted securely to the floor, and locked. "Do you know the combination?"

"No," Channing said. "Maybe Dorothy does."

She stepped outside and returned a minute later.

"Aside from Lee, only Ned Shackleford and John Llewellyn know the combination. I'd rather not alert them to what's going on."

Bo sat in the chair at Lee's big desk, made a steeple of his fingers, and thought for a while. He looked at the family portrait and considered how Lee's death hadn't just robbed a man of his life. It had destroyed the lives of those who loved him as well.

He looked at the photo of Lee with his beloved sailboat and recalled the documents and reports he'd gone through that dealt with the investigation of what had happened on the inlet of Choptank River. He nodded to the computer.

"Try *Gryphon,*" he said, and spelled it out.

"Gryphon?"

"It's a mythical animal. Body and hind legs of a lion, head and wings of an eagle."

Lorna Channing stepped to the keyboard and typed. "We're in," she said. "How did you know?"

"It's the name of his boat."

First Channing did a search for files whose label names contained the words *William Dixon.* There were none. Next she searched for files that contained *William Dixon* in the text. There were several dozen.

"This could take a while," she said.

"Try files created since the president put Lee on the senator's tail."

There was only one, a file labeled *W. D. Schedule.*

"Let's see what it is," Bo said.

A document several pages in length came up. The upper right-hand corner of each page contained the notation *William Dixon.*

Bo said, "What do you make of it?"

Channing looked the pages over. "I'd say they're Senator Dixon's daily schedules. Meeting agendas, appointments. They don't look like much."

"Sometimes important things don't. Let's print it out."

When the printer had finished, Bo gathered the pages. "I'll take these and see if I can make anything of them. Are you sure you don't want to contact Shackleford or Llewellyn about the safe?"

Channing shook her head. "The fewer eyebrows we raise around here, the better."

It was nearing seven-thirty when he returned to his hotel. He hadn't eaten since he'd lunched with the president, and he was hungry. He ordered a chicken Caesar from room service, and while he waited for his food, he took a careful look at the documents he'd taken.

On the surface, the information provided seemed pretty mundane. As Lorna Channing had surmised, they were simply the daily schedules for Senator William Dixon over a period of three days. They began the day after the president had asked Lee to look into the activities of his father, and they ended Friday, the day before Lee was killed. They didn't appear to be formal schedules, the kind Dixon's office might prepare, but had been created, perhaps, from the information such schedules might provide. Bo scanned the list of appointments and meetings. The senator seemed to be very conscientious in greeting his visiting constituents. A substantial portion of each morning was dedicated to this. The senator also met with several lobbyists every day. He attended committee hearings. He had physical therapy sessions, and an appointment with his dentist. There was one meeting Bo couldn't quite decipher. It was simply noted as "NOMan. 3:00 P.M.–5:00 P.M." Apparently Robert Lee had had trouble with this one as well. Parenthetically, to the side, he'd queried, "(National Operations Management?)." For some reason, the name rang a bell with Bo, but he couldn't quite place it. He made a note to check what the hell NOMan was.

By the time he finished his dinner, he'd gone over the pages of scheduling several times. Nothing of particular importance leaped out at him. Still, he hoped there was something he was missing.

Bo knew what his next move should be, but he was reluctant to do it. He should check Robert Lee's home for anything he might have left there. However, Lee was to be buried the next day, and Bo didn't want to intrude on the family's preparations, nor did he particularly relish the thought of wading into all that grief. On the other hand, if the family knew the concern, they'd probably want him to pursue his investigation with all due speed and thoroughness. Or that's what he told himself, anyway.

He called the White House and was connected with Lorna Channing. Because of the uncertainty about the integrity of White House phone communications, she and Bo had agreed to exchange information only when they met in person. Bo didn't explain what he'd found on the computer, but he was clear about what he now needed. Channing agreed to help.

* * *

Robert Lee's home was outside Alexandria, along the south bank of the Potomac, in an area where the houses were big, mostly brick, with yards the size of football fields, and surrounded by stately trees that had probably been around when the British still ran things. Several cars sat parked in the drive when Bo pulled up. He walked a long sidewalk to the house. The door had a black wreath hung on it. Night had come. The wide porch was lit by a fixture styled like an old gas lantern. Moths bumped against the glass. Bo rang the bell.

A white-haired man answered the door. He wore a black knit shirt and black slacks. His face wore a black expression.

"Yes?"

"I'm Special Agent Bo Thorsen. Secret Service." He held open his ID.

The man looked at him blankly. "What do you want, Agent Thorsen?"

"I understood the White House would call about my visit."

"I don't know anything about that."

"Grandpa." A kid, maybe seventeen, stepped up beside the older man. He had brown hair and brown eyes, like Robert Lee. Under other circumstances, he might have had Bobby Lee's famous smile as well. Bo recognized him from the family portrait on Lee's desk in the West Wing. "Mom got a call. She knows someone's supposed to be coming to get some things from Dad's office. She said to let them in."

"Oh." The man stepped back and allowed Bo to enter. "Can we handle this without disturbing my daughter? She's upset. Understandably so."

"Of course," Bo said.

"Nick, will you show this gentleman to your father's office."

The young man nodded. "Follow me."

Bo went with him down a hallway that led past the living room, where several people sat talking quietly. They glanced up at Bo as he passed. Their expressions seemed to ask what he was doing intruding in this stricken home. He followed the kid named Nick to a large room at the back of the house. Nick stepped inside, and Bo came in after him.

"This is Dad's office," Nick said. He looked down. "Was."

It appeared to be a combination study and den. A desk, a computer, two file cabinets, a few shelves of books. There was also a twenty-seven-inch television, a compact refrigerator, a small bar, and a gas fireplace. The wormwood paneling was hung with lots of photographs. Bo saw that several of them were of Robert Lee, sailing. In some, he was alone, but most included his sons, and in a few, his wife was with him.

"You all sail?" Bo asked.

"Mostly Dad, Cal, and me. Mom sometimes gets seasick," Nick said.

"But you didn't sail Saturday."

"No." Nick shook his head. He gazed out one of the windows. "I got a job working in a summer camp in the Blue Ridge. Cal works there, too." He nodded toward a picture that included a kid slightly younger than Nick, and a little stockier. "This summer, Dad sailed alone most of the time."

Bo could tell it ate at Nick. He'd probably been telling himself if only he'd stayed back, gone sailing with his father, this never would have happened. Kids took a lot of useless blame on their shoulders. Bo knew that.

"The boat your father was sailing. Is it a big boat?"

"A twenty-six-foot Seaward. It's not exactly a yacht but it's a handful."

"Is it hard to sail alone?" Bo asked.

"For me, yeah. But not Dad."

"I don't know about sailing, Nick. Your father's accident, does that kind of thing happen a lot?"

"Not to sailors like him."

Bo glanced around the room again. "Look, Nick, I wonder if I could be alone here for a while."

Nick thought about it and nodded. "I'll be down the hall."

Bo checked the desk. It was neat, no stacks of paper, only a few letters that looked like they were awaiting Robert Lee's reply. He opened the drawers, then checked the file cabinet. He considered the computer, wondering about files Lee might have created. Going there would be time-consuming and intrusive. He went to the door. Nick stood down the hallway. When he saw Bo, he returned.

"Find what you were looking for?" Nick asked.

"Not yet. I may have to get into the computer. Do you know the password?"

"Yes."

Bo didn't want to go there if he didn't have to. "Nick, is this where your father did all his office work when he was home?"

"His paperwork. If he was thinking about something, usually he'd go out to the greenhouse and goof around. He's got a board out there that he writes stuff on."

Bo thought about it. It would be easier than scanning computer files. "Could I see the greenhouse?"

"Sure. This way."

They went out a sliding door in the study. The back lawn was large. Bo could feel the sweep of the Potomac somewhere in the dark beyond it. There was a swimming pool, a garden, and the greenhouse. Inside the greenhouse, the heat and the humidity of the night became oppressive. There were rows of long planter boxes that held flowers, exotic-looking things.

"Dad loved raising orchids and tropical flowers," Nick said. "It seemed boring to me, but I guess he found it relaxing." Nick touched one of the boxes. "Safer than sailing anyway."

On a wall near the door was a large chalkboard, full of scribbling. Nick pointed toward it.

"That was Dad's notebook. If he thought of something out here, he'd chalk it up there. If he couldn't find a place, he'd just erase enough other stuff to fit it in."

It was a mix of information. Telephone numbers, some with identifying names, some just floating. Snippets of thought. *Get clear on Snyder-Brookins bill.* Cryptic things. A quote Bo recognized from John Donne. *No man is an island.* There was a drawing of a horse. Or maybe it was a dog. Lee was no artist. Written small, down in one corner, was the name Dixon. It was not identified as Clay or William. Just Dixon. Bo wondered if there was something somewhere on the board that connected with the name.

He was sweating in the humid heat, and he took off his blazer. He pulled out a pen and a notepad from the inside pocket and began to write everything down that was on the chalkboard, noting where in relation to everything else it was. He wrote quickly, but carefully, while Nick stood quietly and watched him.

As Bo began to write the Donne quote, he realized he'd made a mistake when he first read it. It didn't say, *No man is an island.* It said, *NOMan is an island.*

NOMan. National Operations Management. Bo felt as if he'd finally found something he could hold on to. He finished recording everything from the chalkboard, then he put his pen and notepad away.

"Thanks, Nick. I think I have what I need."

Nick saw him to the front yard, skirting a trip through the house. Bo appreciated that. On the front walk, Bo asked, "The inlet where the accident happened, do you know it?"

"Sure. It was one of Dad's favorite places. He usually ended his day's sail there so he could watch the bald eagles. He liked it because there's almost never any other boats around. He liked having the water and the eagles to himself."

An isolated place Robert Lee was known to frequent. It violated the most basic rules of protection.

"I'm sorry about your father," Bo said.

"Thank you."

He shook the young man's hand. Because there was nothing more he could offer, and nothing more he needed, he turned away and headed to his car.

chapter

thirty-six

Bo had breakfast at Afterwords, the café in Kramerbooks on Connecticut Avenue, a place he'd often eaten during the years he was assigned to duty in D.C. At nine o'clock, he walked through the door of the Old Post Office Building on Pennsylvania Avenue and took the elevator up. When he got off, he proceeded down a long, quiet hallway. At the end he came to a set of double, glass doors with NATIONAL OPERATIONS MANAGEMENT painted in white block letters across the panes.

The reception area was small and reminded him of the waiting room in a dentist's office. There were a few magazines on a low table next to a love seat. Near the window was a fish tank with a lot of lazy-looking fish. Outside the window was a sunny view of Western Plaza with its crisscross of white lines that was a depiction of L'Enfant's original plan for the capital city.

The receptionist was on the phone. She glanced up when Bo came in and flashed him a nice smile. She made a notation on her desk calendar, finished her conversation, and hung up.

"May I help you?"

"I'm sure you can," Bo said. "I need some information."

"What kind?"

"Pretty general, really. For starters, I'd like to know what National Operations Management does exactly."

She laughed gently. "We don't make the front page very often, do we?" She reached into a drawer of her desk and pulled out a brochure that she handed to Bo. "I think this pamphlet will give you a very nice overview of NOMan."

"Thank you. Mind if I sit down and read it here?"

"Be our guest."

Bo sat and read.

NOMan, as the text kept referring to the organization, was a division of the General Accounting Office. It had been created by an act of Congress on March 10, 1963. Its purpose, according to the pamphlet, was to "standardize, facilitate, and oversee the security of communications and procedures within and among the various branches of the federal government." Headquartered in Washington, D.C., NOMan had regional offices in several cities across the country.

"Standardize, facilitate, and oversee the security of communications and procedures," Bo read aloud. "In layman's terms, what does that mean?"

The receptionist, a Ms. Hoeffel, according to her name tag, looked up from the computer on which she was working. She gave him another of her nice smiles. "We do forms mostly. Make sure all departments use the same, or at least similar, documentation. We design documents for interdepartmental exchanges of all kinds. Procurement, travel, you name it. Not the most exciting office in the government, but we like to believe we help things run more smoothly."

"What about this security aspect?"

Although still friendly, she seemed to be growing a bit tired of Bo's interruptions and questions. "We're responsible for the design and maintenance of the security system that keeps secret documentation and communication, well, secret."

"Sounds like pretty important stuff to me," Bo said.

"I'm glad you think so. We certainly do."

"Can I get a tour?"

"We're not one of the more popular stops for tourists in the capital. We don't really give tours."

"How about a public relations person?"

"That would be Laura Hansen."

"Could I speak with her?"

"Not without an appointment. She's very busy."

"I'd like to make an appointment, then."

"Certainly. Just a moment."

She punched in a number on her phone. "Dan, it's Mary Jude. I have a gentleman here who'd like to make an appointment to see Laura." She listened. "General interest," she said. "Uh-huh. Hang on a sec." She glanced up at Bo. "Your name, sir?"

"Bo Lingenfelter."

She repeated the name over the phone, then she smiled again at Bo and asked, "Is now a good time for you?"

"Now? Really?"

"Really."

"All right."

"Fine, Dan. And thanks." She hung up. "You're in luck. Laura will be right out."

While he waited, Bo watched the fish in the tank. They didn't seem in any hurry, which was good because they didn't have anywhere to go.

The door behind the receptionist opened, and a woman in a light gray skirt and matching jacket came out. She was a small woman, but a lot of energy seemed to be contained in that slight frame. She smiled broadly at Bo.

"I'm Laura Hansen." She extended her hand.

"Bo Lingenfelter. From Pueblo, Colorado."

"Really? You sound more midwestern."

"Transplant," Bo said.

"What can I do for you, Mr. Lingenfelter?"

"Truth is, I'm county chair for our party's local committee. I'm trying to understand all the duties and responsibilities of our senators so that we can translate it for the voters back home. Now, it's my understanding that among the other responsibilities he has, Senator Dixon also attends NOMan meetings. I'd like to know what that's about."

"Of course. Why don't you come back to my office and we can talk a bit."

She led the way. Behind the door, the office widened into a large area partitioned into dozens of cubicles where staff seemed diligently at work. The noise in the area consisted mostly of the click of keyboards, the ringing of phones, and the hum of voices. Laura Hansen guided Bo through the maze and into a real office with a real door, which she closed.

"Senator Dixon," she said as she sat behind her desk. Bo took the chair opposite her. "He's played a very important role in NOMan. In fact, he cosponsored the legislation that created our office. Over the years, he's functioned in many capacities. Currently he serves as an adviser to several committees. Around here, he's known as Senator Bill."

"What does he do as an adviser?"

"Offers opinions, his expertise. He no longer has a voting role in committee decisions, but he often sits in on meetings of particular interest."

"Are the minutes public?"

"Some. Not all. Sometimes the meetings deal with security issues, and for obvious reasons those minutes aren't available to the public."

"He was in a meeting here last week. Wednesday. Was that a secret meeting?"

"Last week?" She thought a moment. "I don't think so. But then I'm not privy to everything here."

"Would it be possible to get a copy of the minutes? If they're a matter of public record."

"I'll see what I can do."

She made two calls, and within five minutes, a man stepped into her office with a folder. "Thanks, Hank," she said. She glanced at the contents, then handed the folder to Bo. "It's not very exciting, I'm afraid. Mind-numbing, in fact. Discussion of revising a document that's used when departments purchase from one another. But you're welcome to it."

"Any chance I could get a tour of things here?"

"That would have to be arranged, cleared at a higher level."

Bo stood. "Thank you, Ms. Hansen. You've been very helpful. I'll mention you to Senator Dixon when I see him and to the folks back home."

She escorted him to the reception area, shook his hand, and Bo left.

He got a cup of coffee at the Old Ebbitt Grill and took a look at the minutes of the meeting Dixon had attended the day after Robert Lee began his investigation of the senator. It was, as Ms. Hansen had characterized it, a mind-numbing subject. Reading through the minutes, Bo had two big questions. First, why would a busy man like Dixon waste his time with a meeting that discussed a cross-payment document? And second, why had Dixon made no comments whatsoever during the meeting?

When Bo looked up, he saw that the television behind the bar was tuned to news coverage of the funeral of Robert Lee. The scene was graveside in Richmond, Robert Lee's hometown. The president was there with Kate, both of them standing next to Lee's widow. Flanking the woman on the other side were her sons. Everyone appeared to be weeping. Even President Andrew Clay Dixon wiped at tears. Bo could understand why. Everything he knew about Bobby Lee told him a good man had died. And that probably he had died unjustly.

In the minutes of the NOMan committee meeting, the name Donna Plante was among those listed as attendees. Bo tracked her down at the Department of Agriculture in the Whitten Federal Building. He caught her at her desk just as she was preparing to leave for lunch. When she saw his Secret Service ID, she agreed to delay her meal.

"I just want to ask a couple of questions about NOMan," Bo said.

"Sure."

Donna Plante set a small brown sack on her desk. Bo could smell the tuna sandwich inside.

"You sit on a NOMan committee."

"Yes. Lots of employees from various departments do. It's part of our assignment."

"You were in a meeting last Wednesday with Senator Dixon, yes?"

"I was there."

"I've looked at the minutes, and I find it odd that the senator offered no comments during the meeting."

"Not odd. He wasn't there."

"In the minutes, he's listed as an attendee."

"He showed up, was noted, then he left. He sometimes does that."

"Where does he go?"

"I don't know. I just know that I envy the fact that he gets to skip out. Those meetings." She gave an exaggerated yawn.

"Do you ever participate in meetings that discuss security issues?"

"Right. They're going to let a clerk in USDA listen in about security issues." She looked at her watch.

"Thanks," Bo said. "You've been very helpful."

"What does all this have to do with Secret Service."

"You know those meetings you don't get to sit in on because they're about security?"

"Yeah."

"So's this."

In the Secret Service Memorial Building on H Street, Bo checked through security and received a temporary access ID. As he made his way to the Technical Security Division, he bumped into several agents he knew from previous assignments. All congratulated him on his work at Wildwood.

Robin Agnew was at her desk, deep in the reading of a thick report. She was so engrossed that she didn't notice Bo. He was glad, because it allowed him, for a moment, to watch her without worrying about what his face might betray.

Her hair was a premature but absolutely beautiful silver. She'd shortened it since he last saw her. She worked her jaw as she read, an old habit. When she looked up, her eyes showed her surprise. Then she laughed.

"Bo. Jesus, you scared me."

"Hello, Robin."

She got up and hugged him. "What a nice surprise. I hadn't heard you were coming."

"I didn't know myself until a couple of days ago."

"Business?"

"Sort of."

"I thought you were on medical leave after the Wildwood incident."

"I was. Am."

"Good work, by the way. I always knew you were hero material. I understand Chris is doing fine, too. I'm glad."

Manning. A lot of years ago they'd gone through some strange permutations, the three of them. Manning and Bo had stayed single afterward. Robin wore a wedding ring.

"Did you have any trouble with him?" she asked.

"Nothing either of us couldn't handle. You ever run into him out here?"

"Not often. It's awkward whenever we do. I think he still has issues, even after all these years."

"How about you?" Bo said. "You doing okay?"

"I married the right man. Not Secret Service." She smiled. "So what's up?"

"I came to beg a favor."

"Anything."

"Could I use your computer?"

"That's it?"

"That's it."

"All the way from Minnesota just to use my computer?"

"All right, how about your computer and you let me buy you dinner?"

"Oh, Bo, I'd love to. But I have to pick up little Gus at day care. And then Jamie and I have an early meeting at church tonight. You wouldn't care to baby-sit, would you?"

"No thanks. I did enough of that on Dignitary Duty. Sounds like a good life, Robin."

"The best." She glanced at her watch. "Oh, shoot. I'm late for my workout. Let me log off." She sat down at her computer and ended her connection with the system. "I'll be back in an hour or so. Will that be enough time?"

"Should be." Bo smiled. "You look good, Robin."

"So do you, Bo. So do you." She kissed his cheek. *"Ciao."* And she left.

Bo logged on and accessed the Internet. He did a search for NOMan and came up with 427 hits. He scrolled until he found the home page for National Operations Management. He went there, then clicked on a side bar notation that read "History."

The precursor to NOMan, he learned, was an agency within the Department of Defense called the Office of Branch Communications. Created following World War II, it was responsible for coordinating communications among all the branches of the military. Headed by Marine Colonel Woodrow (Woody) Gass, the office proved so effective that it came to the notice of Congress. On March 10, 1963, it was made a part of the General Accounting Office, its name was changed to National Operations Management, and the scope of its authority was broadened to include all areas of government service. Every division of every department was required to have an employee whose responsibility, in part, was as a liaison with NOMan.

Although the agency was officially under the aegis of GAO, the director of NOMan didn't report to GAO's comptroller general but was responsible instead to Congress directly. The term of appointment was the same as that for the comptroller general, fifteen years, which made the position less vulnerable to shifting political whims. Woody Gass was the first director of National Operations Management. He served in that capacity for thirty years, or two terms. When he stepped down, he was replaced by the current director, a NOMan veteran named Arlo Grieg.

In its capacity as watchdog for effective, interdepartmental communications, NOMan had been credited with saving the government billions of dollars through consistent monitoring and upgrading of communication channels. It had effected a network that, within one of the largest and most complex bureaucracies in the world, had become a model of efficiency.

This was the official line, anyway.

Bo clicked around some more, looking for anything that might shed a more unofficial light. On a Web site that called itself Big Brother Buster, he found a discussion of the budgets for several government offices, NOMan among them. According to the information presented there, NOMan didn't operate in exactly the way its official budget indicated. Much of the operating expense of NOMan was picked up by the offices it served. Not only did each office pay a fee for service (that indispensable help with efficient communication that Bo, as an agent of the federal government for nearly two decades, had yet to see), but it also picked up the entire salary cost for the mandatory employee who served as a liaison with NOMan, employees like Donna Plante of the USDA. Therefore, any dollar amount appearing officially in the federal budget as allocated to NOMan to cover operating costs in fact represented only a small percentage of the actual money NOMan had available for its use.

It wasn't a new idea. Bo knew the CIA had been operating that way for most of its history.

He found a government Web site that gave a long list of individuals whose service to the nation included sitting on NOMan committees. Among them were representatives of the FBI, CIA, NSA, IRS, WHCA, as well as a number of well-known congressional leaders.

He stumbled across a discussion of Woodrow Gass, former director of NOMan. Woody Gass appeared to be a feisty son of a gun. A marine commander in the Philippines during World War II, he'd been taken prisoner on Bataan, been on the infamous Death March, survived a year of prison camp at a place called Cabanatuan, escaped with several other prisoners, and had made his way to the Australian forces on Borneo in a stolen boat. He'd continued to serve in a distinguished manner for the rest of the war. Afterward, he was outspoken about the blundering in the Philippines. To quiet him (the discussion implied), he was put in charge of an insignificant new division that dealt with communications.

The information was interesting, but what was more interesting to Bo was the name of one of the men who'd escaped from the Philippines with Gass. Private William Dixon.

"Still at it?"

Bo looked up from the screen. Robin was back. She had her blazer slung over her arm, and there was a slight gloss to her skin.

"Good workout?" he asked.

"Great. But I wilted walking back through that damn humidity." She eyed her desk and the chair in which Bo sat. "Get what you needed?"

"I'm not sure what I got."

"Anything I can help with?"

"No. I'll figure it out." He allowed himself one final, approving look. "You're gorgeous, you know that?"

"I do. Jamie's a lucky guy, and he knows it."

Bo laughed. "I've got to go, Robin. Take care of yourself."

"You, too. And if you see Chris, tell him I wish him well."

"Will do."

They hugged briefly, then Bo headed off.

Robin was right. It was hot and humid outside the building. Bo was dripping by the time he reached the cool sanctuary of his hotel. He went to his room and laid out everything he had so far.

He had a suspicion that Senator William Dixon was involved in something darker than mere back room politics. He'd found a strong connection between Dixon and NOMan, a very low profile organization with a finger in every branch of the government. He'd discovered a wartime link between Dixon and the man who'd organized and headed up NOMan for several decades. But how this information fit into the death of Robert Lee, if it fit at all, was still unclear.

Bo checked his watch. It was still early enough that he could make one more visit.

The receptionist gave him an odd look when he stepped in.

"Mr. . . ." She thought a moment. ". . . Lingenfelter."

"You're good," Bo said.

"We don't get many visitors. And almost no one who comes twice in one day."

"I'd like to see Ms. Hansen again. And no, I still don't have an appointment."

"I'll see if she's available." She punched in a number on her phone. "Dan, Mr. Lingenfelter is here again. He'd like to see Laura. Again." She flashed him a playful smile. "Uh-huh. All right. Thanks." She hung up. "Someone will be right up."

Bo checked the fish again. They were darting around now, as if looking for something in that empty water. Bo figured it must be close to feeding time.

The door behind the receptionist opened. Ms. Laura Hansen was not who appeared. But the man who did come out was someone Bo had seen before. Although they'd passed only briefly in the Stillwater hospital after Tom Jorgenson was attacked, the man's damaged face, the bubble of burn scars that welted his right cheek, his reconstructed right ear, all made him impossible to forget.

Bo hoped his own face was really as forgettable as Lorna Channing seemed to think.

"I'm Hamilton Gaines, Mr. Lingenfelter. An assistant director here at NOMan. I understand you have quite an interest in our office."

"It's an interesting office," Bo said.

"Not many people share your view. Ms. Hansen is unavailable at the moment. I wonder if there's something I could help you with."

"I hope so," Bo said. "As I explained earlier to Ms. Hansen, I'm on a little fact-finding mission for the party folks back in Pueblo. She was kind enough to give me some minutes of a meeting that our Senator Dixon attended last week. But it's my understanding that the senator had to leave that meeting very early. In fact, I understand that he often leaves early. I was just wondering what might pull him away while he's here at NOMan."

"I'm afraid I can't answer that," Gaines replied.

"You don't know the answer?"

"It's more a security issue, Mr. Lingenfelter. Senator Dixon has been associated with this office for a very long time. We rely on his expertise significantly, particularly in areas that deal with sensitive information and security. If we know he's here, we often ask him to sit in on a meeting when such issues are being considered."

"Ms. Hansen seemed to be under the impression that there weren't any meetings like that last week."

"Ms. Hansen is responsible for public relations. She's not necessarily aware of everything that occurs here at NOMan."

"Of course. I wonder if it might be possible to get minutes from some of the other nonsensitive meetings that Senator Dixon was scheduled to attend recently."

"I'd be happy to have them sent to you."

"That's okay. I'll pass on it. But I'm sure the folks back home would be interested in knowing why Senator Dixon's presence is consistently recorded at these meetings if, as I've been told, he often slips away."

"That's not an issue I can address."

"I see. Would you mind if I asked you a personal question?"

"About my face," Gaines said, as if that was always the question. "Vietnam. Napalm burns."

"I thought it was our side who dropped napalm."

"Friendly fire, as they say. A mistake that wiped out most of my platoon. Is there anything else, Mr. Lingenfelter?"

"That wasn't actually what I was going to ask about."

"No? I'm sorry. What would you like to know?"

"What do you think of our senator?"

"In my opinion, a great man."

"The folks back home will certainly be glad to hear that."

"Please give my best to those folks. In Pueblo, wasn't it?"

"That's right."

"Right." Gaines smiled broadly but unconvincingly. "Good day, Mr. Lingenfelter."

Outside, Bo stood on the sidewalk pondering questions that lay on him even more oppressively than did the heat of the afternoon sun. What was Hamilton Gaines doing at the hospital in Stillwater? And was there a connection between Tom Jorgenson and NOMan?

He looked back at the Old Post Office. *NOMan is an island*, Robert Lee had noted on his chalkboard. Lee had purposely distorted the quote to fit the truth. NOMan had done its best to secure a place in the vast, bureaucratic ocean, a place isolated from general knowledge and public scrutiny. Bo sensed something dark and creepy beneath the organization's mundane exterior. Whatever that darkness was, it spread out far beyond the agency's office, beyond even the capital itself. In a hospital room a thousand miles away was a man Bo had always admired greatly. Now he wondered if Tom Jorgenson lay in the shadow of that darkness, too.

He had to hit three used bookstores before he found what he wanted, a copy of Jorgenson's autobiography, *The Testament of Time*. Several years had passed since he'd read it. This time around he'd be looking at it with a different eye.

Bo knew of a cyber café near Dupont Circle. He grabbed a taxi and in fifteen minutes was on the Internet again, calling up the Web sites he'd found earlier using Robin's computer. He printed out the information he felt might be useful, then did a search with the terms *Thomas Jorgenson* and *NOMan*. He got no hits. He tried various combinations but came up with nothing pertinent. Next he searched using *William Dixon* and *Philippines*. He got the whole story. Bataan. The Death March. Cabanatuan. The escape and sea journey in a stolen boat. He got something else, too. The names of all the men who'd escaped with Dixon and Gass. One by one he searched them on the computer.

Four of them had served very long terms in Congress. Two of them were still there. One of the men had been an assistant director of the CIA before establishing a consulting firm. One had been an assistant for national security to a previous president. One had died in the war. The final man was someone named Herbert Constable. He'd been a cryptographer for the army, stationed in Manila at the outbreak of the war. He claimed to have broken the Japanese code prior to Pearl Harbor and to have notified his superiors of the impending attack. He died in a mental institution in 1950.

Bo printed out all this information as well, gathered up everything, and left. Back in his hotel room, he grabbed a Heineken from the room refrigerator, lay all the material out on the table, and looked things over carefully. It was on his third pass that he caught two small, but important, details he'd missed earlier.

One: The man who'd been an assistant director for the CIA was named James J. Hammerkill. The company he'd established after leaving the government was Hammerkill, Inc., a security consulting firm that now employed Jonetta Jackson, the only eyewitness to Robert Lee's death. Bo thought about Jackson, a strong woman, trained to be capable of killing. It wasn't a huge leap of logic to speculate that she might have been more involved in Robert Lee's death than as a mere witness. On that isolated inlet, a small army could have been involved, and no one would have been the wiser.

Two: Senator William Dixon had been one of the two sponsors of the bill that created NOMan. His cosponsor had been the then freshman senator from Minnesota, the Honorable Thomas Jorgenson.

Bo lay down on his bed and stared up at the ceiling. Jonetta Jackson. Hamilton Gaines. William Dixon. These were people who, in the service of their country, had placed their lives in jeopardy. They deserved to be honored. Yet they were involved in an organization that was not at all what it seemed and that may have been responsible for the murder of Robert Lee. To what end did they betray their honor, if indeed betrayal it was?

That was a question Bo couldn't answer, but he was pretty certain he knew who could. He used the hotel phone, called Northwest Airlines, and made a reservation on a flight the next morning that would take him back to Minnesota. Then he picked up *The Testament of Time* and began to read.

chapter

thirty-seven

As the 747 dropped low over the Minnesota River valley and Bo saw the wetlands gliding beneath him, he was, as always, happy to be home. He took a shuttle to the remote lot where he'd parked his car and from there drove directly to the St. Croix Regional Medical Center in Stillwater. It was late morning when he arrived. Tom Jorgenson was awake. The stroke had left him weakened, particularly on the right side of his body, but no permanent damage had been done. He greeted Bo with a smile, albeit a lopsided one. The black around his eyes that the E.R. doctor had called battle signs had faded to the point where the shadows simply made him look exhausted.

"Invitation to the White House," Jorgenson said. He spoke slowly.

Bo sat down beside the bed. "I've been there a lot of times, but never as a guest."

"How's Clay?"

"I'd say he's having a tough time right now."

Jorgenson nodded gravely.

Bo held up the copy of Jorgenson's autobiography that he'd purchased in D.C. "A fine book, Tom. Just finished rereading most of it."

"Nothing better to do?"

"I was especially intrigued with the section in which you discuss your experience on the U.S.S. *Indianapolis* during World War Two. When it was torpedoed and sank, nearly a thousand men went into the ocean, is that correct?"

"Nine hundred."

"Without lifeboats, food, or water. After four days, after countless shark attacks, after the effects of exposure, only what, three hundred survived? It must have been a nightmare."

"It was hell."

"In the book, you blame the military command. A Japanese submarine was in the area, but that information was never communicated to the ship's captain. After the torpedoes hit, the ship's distress signal was ignored. And nobody seemed to notice or to care that the *Indianapolis* was long overdue for docking."

Jorgenson shook his head. "Criminal neglect."

"You were bitter."

"A waste of fine men."

"Still bitter?"

Jorgenson seemed surprised by the question. "What are you getting at?"

"Do you know a man named Hamilton Gaines?"

Jorgenson's eyes, only tired before, grew wary.

"Now there's a man with plenty of reason to be bitter," Bo said. "Senator William Dixon, too. What do you suppose men like that do to deal with all that bitterness? Do they maybe find ways to get even?"

Jorgenson waited. "Some of them," he finally replied.

"Not all?"

Jorgenson shook his head. "Not all."

Bo leaned over the edge of the bed. "Tell me about NOMan."

Jorgenson didn't reply.

"Did you know that while you were in a coma, Hamilton Gaines was here, asking questions about you?"

Jorgenson's face, already the color of biscuit dough, went even whiter.

"That's right," Bo said. "What do you suppose that was about? Could it be NOMan was afraid that in your weakened state you might give away secrets?"

Bo moved even closer, so that as he spoke his breath rippled the casing of the pillow.

"Don't play dumb, Tom. You cosponsored the legislation that created NOMan. You and I both know that what NOMan appears to be and what it is are two very different things. NOMan scares me. And looking at you right now, I'm guessing it scares you, too. Talk to me."

Jorgenson closed his eyes. "I don't know anything."

"NOMan assassinated Robert Lee."

The blue eyes opened a crack.

"I'm certain of it, Tom. I just don't know why. I think more people are going to die, but unless I can figure NOMan's motive, I don't know who those people are or how to help them. I need answers and I need them now."

Jorgenson spoke in a voice quieter than could be accounted for by his weakness alone. "I can't help. NOMan and I parted ways a long time ago."

"Tell me about that."

Jorgenson stared at the ceiling.

"Please," Bo said.

Jorgenson finally gave an almost imperceptible nod. "NOMan. Woody Gass loved that name. You know your Greek mythology, Bo? The Cyclops Polyphemus demands to know the name of the man who outwitted him. Odysseus replies, 'No man.' Gass loved the idea of a normal man defeating a giant."

"For Gass, what giant?"

"The monster that is the federal government. The horrendous bureaucracy." He rolled his head and spoke toward Bo. "What do you think is the most powerful weapon in the modern world? Some nuclear device?" He shook his head. "Information. A man who knows the right things has leverage that can move the world. Gass understood that. NOMan was designed to know everything."

"To what end? The assassination of its enemies?"

"To make sure information that might prevent global blunders reached those who needed it. A noble motive." He paused, as if gathering his strength. Bo could tell this was difficult for him, physically and emotionally. "But there was always division, always those who were eaten up inside by the desire for revenge or for power—"

"Like William Dixon?"

Jorgenson nodded. "That kept him out of the White House, you know. NOMan wanted one of its own in that office. Dixon and I were the contenders. NOMan chose me. They positioned me for ascendance. Then Myrna died, and I lost my heart for it. Came home to Wildwood. They were understandably disappointed in me. Until I established the Institute for Global Understanding. That proved to be quite useful to NOMan, and NOMan was useful to me."

"They fed you information?"

"On occasion. To negotiate successfully between men or countries or regions divided by hatred takes logic, cajoling, bribery, sometimes a little blackmail. Information is essential. Six or seven years ago, things began to change. The old guard of NOMan began to die off or step back, disappearing from the picture. New blood came in, with selfish motives. Dixon stayed in the thick of things, gathering more power for himself personally. Eventually, I was frozen out. NOMan and I have been strangers since. I've sometimes wondered, given what I know, if my days on this earth are numbered."

"Maybe that's what Gaines's visit was all about." Bo sat back. "If you're concerned for your safety, why haven't you told this to anybody before?"

"I decided long ago that my safety takes a backseat to the good that I might do, and NOMan helped me accomplish a lot of good things. I've hoped the organization would come to its senses."

Jorgenson breathed a weary sigh, but not for himself. "Robert Lee. What a tragedy. Does Clay know?"

"He suspects. We need proof."

"What you need is an army. NOMan is everywhere." He reached out and took Bo's arm. Bo could feel the weakness of the man's grip, the quiver of the tired muscles. "What are you going to do?"

"I'm not sure, Tom. Would you be willing to go on record with what you know?"

"That's a pretty big Rubicon to cross. NOMan would be a formidable enemy. Let me think about it." He let go, and his hand fluttered back to the bed.

"Sure." Bo stood up. "I'll be back. You get some rest."

"Have you seen Kate yet?"

"I'm on my way to Wildwood now. Just to say hello."

"You won't say anything about Lee and NOMan?"

"Of course not."

"Good." Jorgenson closed his eyes as if preparing to sleep. "Keep her safe."

The orchards of Wildwood lay green under the sun, the fruit turning red like hearts hung from the branches. The deputy in the cruiser at the entrance to the drive waved him on through, but when Bo came to the gatehouse, he was forced to stop.

Special Agent Fred Turner bent to talk through the car window.

"Sorry, Bo. I can't let you pass."

"Why not?"

"Got a directive this morning."

"Whose directive?"

"S.A.I.C. Ishimaru."

"Diana? What's going on, Fred?"

The agent shrugged. "You need to see Ishimaru, Bo."

Beyond the gate, through the cut in the orchard where the drive ran, Bo could see the main house and the yard. He saw the pool and, sitting in the shade of a table umbrella, Kate. The sight of her seemed to suck out his soul. He wanted to grab Fred Turner and throw him aside. Instead he turned the car around.

On the fourth floor of the Federal Court Building in Minneapolis, he punched in the security code for the lock on the main door of the field office. The door would not open. He tried again. Nothing. He stepped back to the bulletproof window that opened onto the reception area just inside, and he pushed the buzzer. A moment later, the receptionist, Linda Armstrong, appeared. She was a woman in her late forties, smart and trim. She'd grown up on a farm in Nebraska, and she and Bo had often swapped farm tales. When she saw who it was, her face took on a pained expression.

"I need the new code, Linda." He spoke louder than was necessary.

"Just a minute, Bo." She vanished again.

Diana Ishimaru accompanied her when she returned. Ishimaru opened the door.

"What the hell's going on, Diana?" Bo said.

"In my office, Agent Thorsen." She turned, and he followed.

Her office was not empty. Another man sat in a chair near her desk. He stood up as Ishimaru and Bo entered.

Ishimaru said, "Agent Thorsen, this is Assistant Director Bill Malone."

Malone. Bo had never met him, but he knew him by reputation. He was reputed to possess, as a result of his long and varied career with the Secret Service, an excellent understanding of the exigencies of the job. Malone shook his hand, then indicated another chair.

"Have a seat, Agent Thorsen."

"I'd like to know what's going on," Bo said.

"The assistant director asked you to sit down," Ishimaru said.

Bo sat.

"I'll cut to the chase, Agent Thorsen. Special Agent Chris Manning has made certain allegations concerning the appropriateness of your actions prior to and during the incident at Wildwood."

"What allegations?"

"You'll be receiving a full statement shortly. I'm here to convene an internal board of inquiry. I've directed S.A.I.C. Ishimaru to suspend you with pay pending a finding by that board."

"What?"

"Take it easy, Bo," Ishimaru said.

He gave her an angry look. "My ass is about to be nailed to the wall, Diana. Are you okay with all this?"

"This is standard procedure, Bo, and you know it." Then she added, "In this, my hands are tied."

"Bullshit. Is this why I've been denied access to Wildwood?"

Malone said, "Until the board of inquiry has reached a finding, we don't want you to communicate with any of the principals involved."

"Right. And it just happens to keep me conveniently away from the First Lady."

"That's another issue, Agent Thorsen," Malone said. "One we need to discuss."

"I'm through discussing," Bo said. He stood up.

"Agent Thorsen," Ishimaru said. "Sit down. We're not finished."

"I am." Bo walked out the door.

He was halfway down the hall when Ishimaru caught up with him. "Agent Thorsen, at the moment my patience is dangerously thin and your actions are very close to insubordination. We need to talk."

"Talk about what? You know everything that happened at Wildwood. What more is there to say? From now on, Diana, if you want to talk to me, you go through my lawyer."

"Bo—"

He didn't stay to hear what else she had to say. If he'd remained a moment longer, he'd have put his fist through the wall.

chapter

thirty-eight

B o drove to his apartment in Tangletown, the whole way bat- tling against rage. Losing control of himself now was the last thing he needed. When he mounted the stairs to his apart- ment and discovered his door was unlocked, his mood didn't brighten any.

Fortunately, it was Otter he found inside.

"Used the key you hide in the garage," Otter said. He saw Bo's dark look and added without apology, "You told me anytime."

"Yeah," Bo said, relenting. "I did."

Otter was at the kitchen table with some playing cards spread out before him.

"How was the trip?"

"It was fine."

"You sure? You look like you just drank spoiled milk."

"Bad day," Bo said.

He went to the phone and dialed Wildwood, the direct number for the main house. The call was intercepted by Secret Service. When Bo identified himself, he was told politely that he couldn't be connected.

"Shit," he said as he hung up.

Otter looked up from his cards. "What's the problem?"

"Everywhere I turn, somebody's dropping a wall in front of me." Bo sat down at the table. "What are you doing here?"

"I thought you could use something to keep you busy during your convalescence. So I brought you a little gift."

Otter got up and went to the living room. He lifted a plant in a terra-cotta pot and held it up for Bo to see.

"It's a dieffenbachia," Otter said. "A real one. I know you like the artificial things because they don't require your attention, but they don't give you anything either. Now this dieffenbachia, you take care of it, water it, talk to it, it'll give you something in return, Spider-Man. It'll grow for you."

Otter put the plant back in the sunlight.

Bo went into the bedroom, set his overnight case down, and laid his garment bag on the bed. He walked to the closet, cleared his shoes from the floor, and pulled back a flap of carpet. There was a safe built into the floor underneath. Bo worked the combination, lifted the door, and pulled out his Sig Sauer. He took the holster from where it lay on the closet shelf, snugged the weapon into place, and clipped it to his belt. When Bo returned to the living room, Otter took a look at the weapon on his hip and whistled.

"Big gun, Spider-Man."

"I'm beginning to think not big enough. Look, Otter, I've got to run."

"That's okay."

"You sticking around for a while?"

"Just long enough to water your plant."

"Lock up when you leave."

It was late afternoon when Bo headed to the St. Croix Regional Medical Center for his second visit with Tom Jorgenson. He never made it to Jorgenson's room. A Secret Service agent, one of the new ones, stopped him as soon as he stepped off the elevator.

"Sorry, Thorsen. You're not allowed up here now. Orders."

"Ishimaru?"

"These came from Assistant Director Malone himself."

Bo was only yards from the room, but he knew he'd get no closer now. It was useless to argue. He went down to the lobby and used a pay phone.

"St. Croix Regional Medical Center."

"Would you connect me with room four-twenty-two B, please?"

"Just one moment."

More than a moment passed. Bo didn't recognize the voice that came on the line.

"Yes?"

"I'm trying to reach Tom Jorgenson."

"Your name?"

"How about yours first?"

"This is Special Agent Pederman, Secret Service."

"My name's Gaines," Bo said, figuring it was a name Jorgenson would respond to. "Hamilton Gaines."

"Just a moment, Mr. Gaines." Bo waited another moment that wasn't. "I'm sorry, you're not on the list of authorized callers."

Bo hung up without the courtesy of a good-bye.

He stood at the pay phone, trying to get a handle on the situation. Was this really about the incident at Wildwood? Or was the ubiquitous hand of NOMan behind the stone wall he'd encountered? His head ached, and he realized he hadn't eaten all day and he was hungry. He decided he could think better with a little food in his stomach. He left the hospital and headed for St. Paul.

The sun was setting as Bo parked in the lot of O'Gara's, a popular Irish bar on Snelling Avenue. The place was crowded, but he found an empty booth in the back and sat down. He had to wait a few minutes before a waitress spotted him, then he ordered a Leinie's and a Reuben. The beer came, and he settled back. While he waited for his sandwich, he tried to put together in a coherent way the pieces of information that he had.

It was clear his worst suspicions about NOMan were correct. Tom Jorgenson had confirmed the dark turn the organization had taken, but Bo had no solid proof of its current nature, nor of a conspiracy to murder Robert Lee. The testimony of a man like Tom Jorgenson might be enough to generate a full, formal investigation, but who knew how deep the darkness of NOMan ran or how broad the shadow it cast?

He needed a way to get back to Jorgenson. Every avenue so far had been blocked. But what if the contact came from someone else, someone of higher authority than Bo, from the White House itself? It was time to call Lorna Channing and brief her. He'd had no contact with her since before he left D.C. She didn't even know he was in Minnesota. He took out his cell phone and from his wallet pulled out the slip of paper on which she'd written her number.

"Excuse me."

Bo folded the paper and slid it into his shirt pocket, then he looked up.

Two men stood at his table. They wore jeans and sleeveless T-shirts, a little dirty, and work boots. They both held beer mugs in their hands. They looked like construction workers drinking after a day on the job.

"Me and my buddy here have a bet," one of the men said. His hair was long and sandy colored, and he had a scraggly mustache of the same color. "I say you're that Secret Service guy who saved the First Lady's ass. My buddy bets I'm wrong."

"Your buddy wins," Bo said. He put the cell phone in the inside pocket of his sport coat.

"Told you," the other man said. "Come on, Lester."

"Now wait a minute. I seen your face on the cover of the *National Enquirer*, and I never forget a face. It's . . . Thorsen, right?"

"Leave him be, Lester."

"That must've been something out there. I mean, taking a bullet for the First Lady."

"It was a knife," Bo said.

"There, see. See, I told you it was him. Your glass is almost empty, man. Let me buy you a drink."

The other guy offered Bo a look of sympathy. "Better do it. He'll pester you till you do."

"What'll it be?" Lester asked.

"Leinie's."

"Leinie's it is. Curtis, get this man a beer."

Curtis headed off toward the bar. Lester sat down in the booth across from Bo.

"So. What was it like?"

"Look, Lester, your drink I'll take. Your company I'd rather forgo at the moment."

"Drinking alone? Bet it's the pressure of the job does that. Seems to me I heard the rate of alcoholism and suicide is pretty high with you guys."

"That's dentists," Bo said.

Curtis returned. "Here you go," he said. He set the beer in front of Bo.

"To a real hero," Lester said and lifted his glass in a toast.

Bo drank with them, from the beer they'd bought him.

"Come on, Lester," Curtis said.

Lester slid a napkin toward Bo. "Say, could I get your autograph?"

Curtis grabbed his buddy by the shirtsleeve and pulled him away. "Sorry to have bothered you," he said to Bo.

Bo was grateful to be alone again. His Reuben arrived immediately, and the smell brought home to him just how hungry he was. He still had to make the call to Channing. He got his cell phone out again, but before punched in the number, he realized that the noise in the bar would make a coherent conversation almost impossible. He decided to wait until he was in the quiet outside O'Gara's.

He hadn't eaten all day, still hadn't touched his sandwich, and the beer was beginning to affect him. He was feeling light-headed. He took a bite of the Reuben. The food didn't seem to help. He was dizzy and getting sick to his stomach. He pulled out his wallet, dropped a few bills on the table. Hoping the fresh air might help, he made his way outside.

As he leaned against the side of the building, the sky above him flashed and thunder followed almost immediately. Bo felt the first drops of rain from a summer storm. The rain was cold and sharp, but it didn't seem to be any help in clearing his head.

He was having trouble standing up now. He tried to remember where he'd parked his car. He pushed away from the building, and the world seemed to come at him in a slant.

"Whoa, buddy. You okay?"

The voice was familiar to Bo. Lester, who'd bought him a beer.

"Sick . . ." Bo managed to say.

"Come on, we'll help you to your car." It was another familiar voice, but more distant than the first.

Bo felt support slip under each of his arms. He tried to help them, tried to walk, but he couldn't seem to make his legs move. He felt himself slipping, going under. But before he was gone completely, he had one lucid thought.

How did they know which car was his?

He felt the vehicle moving and he smelled exhaust. And then he was driving again. Driving the old bus. He sat behind the wheel, as he always did in his dreaming. The bus was on the river, caught in the sweep of a strong current, and he was trying desperately to turn toward the safety of the riverbank. The wheel spun uselessly in his hand. He felt himself and the others who rode with him, all those who relied on him, sweeping toward a blind curve of the river, beyond which something terrible awaited them.

A big bump threw him upward and he hit his head. He half-woke and opened his eyes. There was dark all around him, and the smell of exhaust and water on hot metal, and the rattle of the undercarriage as it negotiated old pavement, and the hiss of tires on wet asphalt. He wondered dreamily, *Where am I?*

* * *

He woke again to the feel of hands and the sound of voices.

"That's right, Thorsen. Time to go night-night."

They lifted his legs and turned him so that he was sitting up, more or less. Bo saw a line of lights like a string of bright pearls against the black throat of the night and the rain.

"Come on, buddy. Just a few steps and you're there."

They helped him up. He stood unsteadily. He looked back. At first he saw a huge, gaping mouth. Then he understood that it was a car trunk. They'd lifted him out of a car trunk. That seemed odd. But they were helpful.

"You can do it, Thorsen. That's right. A step at a time."

Rain fell against his face, cooling and refreshing. The fresh air felt good after the stuffy car trunk. The air carried on it a familiar scent. The dank, muddy smell of the Mississippi River.

"There we go."

They leaned him against a metal railing. Bo looked down. In the flash of lightning, he saw the river far below him, black and shiny for a moment, then lost in the dark again, and the rain.

He knew where he was. His old stomping grounds. The High Bridge over the river. In the shadow of that bridge, he'd lived with his family of runaways in the old bus.

"Damn it, Curtis, hold on to him."

"It's the goddamn rain. He's slippery as an eel."

Bo felt them grasp him low around his hips. He knew he was about to travel again on the black river he'd driven so often in his nightmares.

But this was no nightmare.

Bo gathered himself around that small, hard realization and acted without thinking. His body moved in the way he'd trained it for nearly two decades. He yanked his arm loose and delivered a hard kick to the knee joint of the man to his right, who went down howling. The other man Bo struck with a forearm blow to the middle of his face, and a fountain of blood squirted into the rain. Bo lurched away from the railing toward the car that sat idling on the bridge.

"Christ, don't shoot him," one of the men hollered.

Bo tumbled into the car parked at the curb, and he slumped over the wheel. As he jammed the stick into gear, the front door on the passenger's side popped open. He hit the gas, and the car shot forward. Behind him, someone screamed a curse.

Bo sped across the bridge into St. Paul. He was sleepy, barely able to keep his eyes open or his foot on the pedal. The car swerved across lanes. He mounted the bluff to Summit Avenue and headed west along the rain-swept street between rows of big, fine houses.

Where? he tried to think.

Not to Tangletown. They would look for him there.

Then he thought of Diana Ishimaru. She lived on East River Road, less than a mile from Tangletown. All he had to do was stay awake for a few more minutes and he would be there.

He drifted, heedless of stoplights. Dimly, he understood that it must be very late because there was almost no traffic. On East River Road, he tried to remember which house was hers. In the dark and the rain, it was hard to tell. He pulled to the side of the street, and the front right wheel jumped the curb. He jerked the door handle and tumbled out onto the pavement. He stumbled up the walk to the front door, leaned against the clean white wood, and pounded.

The porch light came on. The locked clicked, the door opened, and Bo fell forward. A man caught him and stood him up.

"Diana?" Bo said.

"Ishimaru? Diana Ishimaru? She lives next door." The man swung his hand in that direction. He wore a white robe and an angry look.

Bo took a couple of steps back into the rain and almost toppled over.

The man said, "Drunken asshole," and slammed the door.

Bo crossed the wide lawn, tramped through a flower bed, reached the porch of the next house, and hit his fist against the door.

Diana Ishimaru answered immediately. Despite the hour and being dressed in a red chenille bathrobe, she looked wide awake.

"Bo? Jesus, come in out of that rain." She reached out and took his arm.

Bo stumbled into the hallway. "Tried to kill me . . ." he mumbled.

"What?"

"Coffee," he said. He leaned against the wall. He felt so tired.

"Out of those clothes, first. You're dripping all over my rug."

She led him to the bathroom. By the time she came back with dry clothes, he'd curled up on the tile floor and was drifting off.

"Bo." She shook him. "Here, let me help."

She worked him out of his shirt and then his pants. That left him in boxers. "I've done all the helping I'm going to. Get out of those wet Skivvies and into these things." She dropped a set of gray sweats into his lap. "I'm going to make some coffee."

Slowly, Bo finished what Ishimaru had started. She knocked on the door, came in, helped him stand up, then walked him into her living room, where she settled him on the couch.

"I'll get the coffee and be right back."

Bo laid himself down. The couch cushions felt so good, so soft, so welcoming.

Diana Ishimaru was an enigma in many ways. Although Bo knew where she lived, had driven past her house many times, he'd never been invited inside. So far as he knew, none of the agents in the field office had. In this way, and others, she'd kept her personal distance. As he took in the interior of her home, Bo was treated to a side of Ishimaru he'd never seen. A pair of gold-flaked screens decorated with cranes separated the living room and dining room. In the middle of the table near the front window sat a zen rock garden, six stones in raked white sand. On top of her bookcase were two clay pots containing tiny bonsai trees. On the wall behind the sofa hung a mirror in a blond wooden frame into which had been carved the delicate image of birds perched on branches. Bo was surprised by all this, for in her office, Ishimaru kept little evidence of her ancestry. He was just closing his eyes, ready to dream of the Orient, when Ishimaru shook him vigorously.

"Wake up, Bo."

She pulled him upright and shoved the coffee cup into his hand. As he sipped, she drew an armchair near him and sat down.

"All right, what's going on?"

In a stumbling patchwork of narrative, Bo told her everything. About the president's request. About his own investigation into NOMan. About the men who'd drugged him and tried to throw him from the High Bridge. Although he got all the information out, he wasn't certain how coherent it was. At the end, he felt better, but only a little less tired than before.

Ishimaru looked thoughtful. "I haven't been able to sleep, thinking about everything that's going down now. I've had a bad feeling about a lot of this, but I couldn't put my finger on what exactly it was that felt hinky."

"Sorry about blowing up this afternoon," Bo said.

"Forget it. We've got more important things to worry about." Ishimaru stood up, stuffed her hands into the pockets of her robe, and began to pace. For a little while, she said nothing, then she looked at Bo, who was tilting to one side. "That coffee hasn't done you much good. Go ahead and lie down. Get some sleep. You deserve it."

Bo followed her suggestion. "What about you?" he asked as he let his eyelids close.

"I've got some heavy thinking to do. Considering the cloud you're currently under, you're not going to be viewed as the most reliable source. But rest, Bo. Let me worry about that now. You've done a good job."

Bo appreciated that. Coming from Ishimaru, it meant a lot. He finally gave himself over to the sleep that had been calling to him for what seemed like forever.

In his sleep, he heard the sound of thunder, but it was a different kind of thunder. Fragile. More like the shattering of glass.

He struggled to come up from his good, pleasant dreaming. As he opened his eyes, his head exploded. A stunning blow sent him right back into the dark from which he'd just climbed. Deep enough to dream again, this time a nightmare full of blood, but only for a moment before he tried once more to pull himself back to consciousness. As he did so, his body was yanked upright.

"Good," he heard a voice that was all too familiar say. "Now put the Sig in his hand."

He felt the press of a gun butt against his right palm, and a hand molded his own hand around the grip. He felt the trigger slip under his index finger.

"Where?" the voice asked. "I think between the eyes."

"No. Stick it in his mouth. An agent like him would eat the bullet."

Bo felt his hand rising under the power of another hand. An alien finger wormed its way into his mouth, prying his jaws apart. The finger tasted of leather.

Bo bit down hard.

"Jesus, God," the voice screamed. "He tried to bite my finger off."

Bo dimly aimed the gun in the direction of the voice and he fired. The sound of confusion followed, the clatter of upended furniture.

"Move, goddamn it," someone shouted.

Two figures, vague in Bo's vision, merged with the dark near the back of the house. A door slammed shut. Everything fell quiet.

Slowly, Bo stood, wavering in his stance, trying to pull his senses together. His head hurt and his eyes still felt heavy. He took a step forward, and he stumbled, but not from his own weakness. He looked back at what he'd tripped over. His heart nearly broke.

Diana Ishimaru lay at his feet, her eyes half open. Had it not been for the small, bloody hole in her forehead, Bo might have thought she was simply staring at the ceiling. Although he knew it was useless, he reached out and felt at her neck for the pulse that was not there. From beneath her head, from the exit wound Bo knew would be large and ugly, blood leaked, spreading across her clean beige carpet, staining it steadily fiber by fiber.

"No," Bo cried. "God, no."

He stood up and gripped the gun tightly in his hand. He wanted to kill the men who'd done this. He wanted to blow their fucking hearts right out of their fucking chests.

He stumbled toward the dark at the rear of the house where the men had fled. As his thinking cleared, he realized the uselessness of pursuing them. They were well gone by now. He looked back and saw that he'd tracked blood across the room. Her blood.

He stared down at the gun in his hand. It was a Sig Sauer. He checked the registration number. His Sig. And he was pretty sure that the only prints on it were his as well.

Slicing through the sound of the storm outside came the whine of a siren approaching. Someone had called the police.

chapter

thirty-nine

Otter opened the side door of the church and stared as if Bo were an apparition straight from a nightmare.

"Christ, Spider-Man, you look like shit. You're soaked to the bone."

Bo stepped in out of the night and the rain. Barefoot and dripping wet, he stood before his friend.

"What happened to your shoes?"

"I was in a hurry."

Otter looked past him at the wet, empty street. "Where's your car?"

"I walked."

"From your place? Barefoot? In this rain?"

"I need to sit down," Bo said.

Otter shut and locked the door. "Come on downstairs. We'll get you into something dry."

It was a big, stone church, quiet and deserted at that hour. They walked past vacant pews dimly illuminated by a single light above the altar. Otter opened a door to a stairway and they descended to the basement. They crossed through a large gathering room with a kitchen off to one side, then they snaked down a couple of hallways, past the boiler room, and through an open door that let them into Otter's quarters.

The room, whitewashed cinder block, reminded Bo of a monk's cell. A narrow bed, a table and two chairs, a chest of drawers straight from the Salvation Army, a small kitchen area with a compact refrigerator, a sink, and a short counter on which sat a microwave and an ancient-looking electric coffee percolator. Through a door at the other end, Bo spied a tiny shower stall and a toilet. Plants hung in every corner, Otter's own touch that mitigated the austerity of the place. Despite what Bo knew must be a lack of direct sunlight, the plants seemed to be thriving.

"Get out of those wet things," Otter said. "I'll be right back."

He left the room and Bo stripped off the sweats Ishimaru had given him. Otter came back in a few minutes with an armload of folded things that included pants, shirts, socks, tennis shoes, and even a clean pair of boxer shorts.

"You prayed up a miracle?" Bo asked.

"Donations. We're collecting for a mission in Africa." He took Bo's wet clothes and hung them in the bathroom. "You look like you could use a cup of java." Otter went to the cupboard above the sink and brought out a can of Folgers. He started coffee percolating.

"The police will be looking for me," Bo said.

"You do something criminal, Spider-Man? Thought you'd outgrown that behavior."

Over his second cup of coffee that night and dressed in his second ensemble of borrowed clothing, Bo laid out for Otter what had happened.

At the end, Otter shook his head. "And I thought I was the one who saw spooks everywhere."

"I know it sounds crazy, Otter. I can imagine what the police would say."

"You got to tell 'em, Spider-Man, no matter how crazy it sounds. You got to let somebody know."

"Nobody's going to listen to me. I'd end up in a locked cell, and right now I don't want to be anyplace NOMan could find me."

"What do you think they're up to?"

Despite the coffee, Bo wanted to lie down. He felt weary in every muscle, his feet were bruised, and he knew his thinking was fuzzy and desperate.

"Otter, you mind if I sleep here for a while? Then I'll figure things out."

Otter waved toward the only bed. *"Mi casa* is *su casa."*

"I owe you," Bo said.

"It never worked that way, and it never will. Sleep, Spider-Man. I'll stand watch."

Bo laid himself out on the rumpled sheets of Otter's bed and was asleep almost immediately.

Bo came out of his dreaming as if he'd been yanked. He grabbed the hand that had been laid on his arm.

"Take it easy, Spider-Man. It's just me."

Bo stared into Otter's face.

"You were having a nightmare," Otter said.

Bo released his grip and relaxed back down onto the mattress.

"You okay?" Otter asked.

"What time is it?"

"Almost four."

"I didn't sleep long."

"Four in the afternoon."

Bo realized that sunlight lit the opaque basement windows. Otter had put a fan on a chair, and it blew damp, basement-smelling air across the bed. The current also carried the aroma of coffee.

Otter sat down at the table and lit a cigarette. He studied Bo for a minute, then he said, "They're looking for you. It's all over the news."

Bo sat up. "Have they been here?"

"Relax. You're safe."

"What are they saying?"

" 'Famous Secret Service agent wanted for questioning in the shooting death of his boss.' There are reports of a fight yesterday in your field office."

"Fight? I barely raised my voice."

"I'm just telling you what they're saying on the news."

A knock at the door made them both fall silent. Otter motioned Bo toward the small bathroom. Bo slipped in and closed the door. He listened, but all he could hear was the low murmur of voices.

Otter tapped at the bathroom door. "You can come out now, Spider-Man. The coast is clear." When Bo stepped out, Otter said, "That was Sandie Herron from the church office. She asked me to help her with a computer problem."

"Do you know anything about computers?" Bo asked.

"Not much." Otter smiled shyly. "I think she likes me."

Bo came back with a grin of his own. "Well, good for you, Otter. Sandie, huh? Nice name."

After Otter had gone, Bo put some toothpaste from the bathroom cabinet on his finger and did a quick rub of his teeth. He poured himself coffee from the electric percolator, opened one of the windows a crack, and peeked out at the sunlight. The wet smell of the earth near the window was the only evidence of the heavy rain the night before. He couldn't see much. An old Victorian home across the empty parking lot. Patches of blue sky between big elms. Probably a lot like the small square of the world a prisoner would see from the window of his cell.

Bo turned on Otter's radio alarm clock and tuned in KSTP, a Twin Cities all-news station. He sipped his coffee and didn't have to wait long before a report about Ishimaru came on. It didn't sound good. Nor did it look good, him dropping off the face of the earth while he was being sought "for questioning."

He wondered if he should try to contact Lorna Channing. The slip of paper with her number on it was in the clothing he'd left at Ishimaru's place. Any attempt to go through White House communications would end up with Secret Service involved. And maybe

NOMan. As well informed as NOMan seemed to be, he couldn't even be certain that using the code name Peter Parker would be safe.

He had to think, to sort everything out.

Someone had tried to kill him, probably because of his investigation into Robert Lee's death. He was pretty sure that the someone was NOMan. But what was the broader picture? What specifically had Lee's probing, and now Bo's, threatened? Uncovering the connection between NOMan and Senator Dixon was too simple a reason in itself, and too simply explained if brought to light. There was something darker in the works, something that questions, any questions at this point, might jeopardize. But what was that something?

In half an hour, Otter was back. He knocked and announced himself. When he came into the room, he said, "I've been thinking, Spider-Man. These NOMan people, they seem to know what you're up to. That means that they probably know who you've talked to, right?" Otter poured himself some coffee. "I'm wondering about Tom Jorgenson. I mean, if he knows things and talked to you, wouldn't they want to shut him up?" Otter sipped from his cup. "He's got Secret Service and all, but they don't know about NOMan."

"Jesus," Bo said. "Why didn't I think of that?"

"The last few hours haven't been exactly normal for you."

"I need to call the field office."

"If you call from here, won't they trace it?"

"I need wheels."

Otter hesitated. "Well, the church has a van. And I know where they keep the keys."

He called from a phone booth outside a liquor store at the intersection of two busy streets, Snelling and University. When Linda Armstrong, the receptionist, answered, Bo said, "Who's in charge there, Linda?"

"Bo?"

"Who's in charge?"

She hesitated a long time, as if she were debating answering at all. "Assistant Director Malone, for the moment."

"Any of our people around?"

Another long pause. Then a different voice came on the line, a voice unfamiliar to Bo and attached to a name he didn't know.

"This is Special Agent Greer."

"You'll have to do. You listen to me and listen good, Greer. Tom Jorgenson is the target for a hit. An attempt will be made on his life very soon. You should get him out of the hospital and back to Wildwood, where security is tighter."

"Who's going to make this attempt?"

"I don't know. I just know that it will happen."

"Come in, Thorsen, and we'll talk about it."

"No."

"How do you know this information?"

"It's too complicated to go into over the phone."

"Then come in."

"I can't."

"Where are you?"

"Do it, Greer. His life is in your hands."

"Thorsen—"

"Just do it." Bo hung up.

Otter was waiting in the van with the engine running.

"They buy it?"

"I don't know. But I don't want to take any chances. We're going to Stillwater, Otter. Step on it."

They took I-94 east, then I-694 north, and finally shot east again on Highway 36 ten more miles to Stillwater. Otter pushed the van as fast as it would go, but it was in need of an alignment. Much over fifty and the chassis shook so badly Bo's teeth rattled. Just outside the river town, they turned north again and scooted along the crest of the hills that fronted the St. Croix until the tall concrete tower that was the Medical Center burst into view.

"Park there," Bo said, indicating a curb at the corner.

He checked his Sig Sauer. The clip still held six rounds. He shoved it under the waistband at the back of his trousers and let his shirttail hang over the butt of the firearm.

"What do you have in mind?" Otter asked.

"You stay with the van."

"What about you?"

"I'm heading in. Play it by ear."

"That's your plan?"

"You got a better one?"

"You're the professional. I just thought—"

"Wish me luck."

"You got it."

The sun was low in the west. It bathed the hospital tower in a tangerine hue and all the western windows had a glaring orange glint that made Bo think of a many-eyed beast watching him. The parking lot was full. He wove among the vehicles, working his way toward the entrance. The fire lane was lined with police cruisers, county and state. Uniformed officers were posted at the doors. Keeping to the cover of the lot, Bo headed toward the Emergency Room entrance on the south side. A police cruiser was parked there, too. He thought about the outside door of the laundry room in the building that adjoined the hospital on the northeast side. It was possible that door hadn't been locked yet. He headed that way.

Even if he gained access to the hospital, he had no idea what he would do once he was inside. After his call to the field office, every law enforcement officer would be looking for him. But he was responsible for putting Tom Jorgenson's life in danger, and he couldn't simply sit and wait to see what move NOMan made. He followed a lilac hedge that bordered the hospital grounds, then trotted across the empty parking area behind the laundry building. He mounted the stairs to the loading dock and tried the door. It was locked.

As he stood considering what next, a chopper swung over the hill, hovered above the roof of the hospital tower, and descended toward the pad there until it was out of Bo's sight. He could hear the thump of the blades slowing after it landed.

Down the hill overlooking the town, Bo saw a SuperAmerica gas station/convenience store at the next intersection, and he had an idea. He bounded off the loading dock, raced across the laundry parking area, and jogged down the sidewalk to the store. He found a pay phone near the pumps, but where the phone directory should have been there was only the dangling end of the chain that had once held it in place. He pushed through the door of the store and leaned on the counter, breathing hard.

"I need a phone book. It's an emergency."

The clerk, a kid with gold wire-rims and the look of a failed poet, said, "Be with you in a minute." He reached to the cigarette bins above his head and pulled down a pack of Winston Lights for the customer ahead of Bo.

"I need that phone book now."

"I said just a minute." The kid gave him a stern glare weighted with all the authority of a clerk in charge.

Bo drew his Sig. "Give me the damn phone book."

The customer, a balding man with eyes that had bloomed huge as two chrysanthemums, stepped out of Bo's way.

The clerk kept his gaze on the barrel of the Sig, reached to the phone book that was on a stool near the register, and handed it to Bo.

"I'll need fifty cents for the phone, too."

The clerk rang open the register, fingered out two quarters, and handed them over.

"Thank you," Bo said. He pushed out the door and ran to the phone.

As he looked up the number of the St. Croix Regional Medical Center, he heard the chopper lift off from the pad on the hospital roof. He glanced up and saw it zip away over the hills to the south. He dialed the hospital operator, gave his name as Doctor Lingenfelter, and asked to be connected to the nurses' station in

Trauma ICU. When he was connected, he asked if Maria Rivera was on duty. She was. He asked to speak with her.

"Hello, this is Nurse Rivera."

He pictured her clean, white uniform, her kind eyes.

"Maria, it's Bo Thorsen."

She was quiet.

"I need a favor, Maria."

"What?" she asked carefully.

"Just tell me if they've put additional security on Tom Jorgenson."

She didn't answer.

"It's important, Maria. His life may be in danger."

"He's not here," she finally answered. "A helicopter just picked him up and took him to Wildwood."

"Thank God," Bo whispered into the receiver.

"Bo, what can I do to help you?"

"You've done it, Maria. Thank you."

"Be careful, Bo."

He hung up. He looked back through the glass of the convenience store and saw the clerk on the phone. Calling the police, no doubt. Bo beat a hasty retreat.

Otter was still in the van, the engine idling.

"Let's get out of here," Bo said. "But slowly and carefully." He crouched on the floor of the van so that he couldn't be seen.

"How'd it go?" Otter said, signaling to pull away from the curb.

"If they thought I was crazy before, they'll be damn sure of it now."

By the time they returned to St. Paul, a gray evening light hung over the quiet neighborhood and the church. Otter pulled up to the back entrance and gave Bo a key.

"All the doors are locked. Nobody will disturb you. Go on in and wait for me. I'm going to gas up the van. Then there's a good Greek place a mile or so up Snelling. How about I grab us a couple of gyros. I don't know about you, but this spy stuff makes me hungry."

"I'm starved. Thanks."

Bo shut the van door, and Otter headed away.

Inside, the church was dark and deserted. Instead of heading to Otter's room in the basement, Bo went to the sanctuary. He was still tingling from the adrenaline rush of his dash to Stillwater. He wanted to relax for a few minutes. The church sanctuary seemed as good a place as any.

It was a vast room with great stone arches that reminded Bo of a cathedral. There were a dozen stained glass windows set high in the walls along the sides and behind the altar. Probably when morning light streamed through them, they were dazzling. As it was, with the dark of night closing in behind them, they seemed lifeless. Aside from the red glow of the exit signs, there was only one light in the sanctuary, directly above the cross on the altar. Beyond the chancel rail, the light faded quickly so that the sides of the great room and the far back corners lay in a charcoal gloom. Bo walked to a pew near the rear of the church and sat down next to the center aisle. He removed the Sig Sauer that had been stuffed in the waist of his pants and laid it beside him on the pew. For a long time, he stared at the gold cross on the altar.

Until he went to live with Harold and Nell Thorsen, he'd never gone to church. They insisted that every Sunday he accompany them to Valley Lutheran. He went mostly because he grew to like the people who made up the congregation, people like Harold and Nell, farm families. But he never got the God part of things. In all his growing up, he'd never felt safe, protected, watched over, cared for in any but the most careless way. Although he knew she loved him, his mother had failed miserably in giving him any sense of security. Whenever Harold or Nell suggested to him that God's hand had guided his way to their farm, he was clear in pointing out that it was the hand of the Minnesota justice system that had brought him there, and the judicial shoving of Annie Jorgenson in particular. As grateful as he was to Annie, he'd never been inclined to think of her as an angel of God. What he'd wanted in all those Sundays, demanded silently in church, was something on the order of a miracle. He challenged God, "Give me a sign, something I can't miss, and I'll believe." The miracle never came. For Bo, church remained an experience based on community rather than religion. Eventually, in place of a religious doctrine, he established for himself a credo of his own, three simple dictates that he tried to live by.

> 1. *The world is hard. Be strong.*
> 2. *Love is for only a few. Don't expect it.*
> 3. *Life isn't fair. But some people are. Be one of them.*

Over the years, he'd considered adding others—*Laugh when you can; the opportunities are few;* and *Women are easy; compliment their shoes*—but he'd always kept it limited to the three he formulated in that small country church outside Blue Earth. He had no complaints. He suffered only when he broke one of his commandments.

With his eyes on the dull reflection off the cross he whispered, "The world is hard. Be strong."

From directly behind his right ear came the click from the hammer of a pistol being cocked. Bo felt the cold kiss of a gun barrel against the bone at the back of his head.

"Two: Love is for only a few. Don't expect it. Three: Life isn't fair. But some people are. Be one of them." A small laugh accompanied the recitation. "Briefer than the Ten Commandments and the Bill of Rights," David Moses said, "but not a bad way to live, Thorsen. Not bad at all."

chapter

forty

"S urprised that I'm alive?" David Moses said. "But why would that be? Isn't this a place that celebrates resurrection?"

Bo glanced at the Sig beside him on the pew.

"Uh-uh. Eyes on the cross." The muzzle of the gun barrel pushed Bo's head gently toward the altar. An arm reached alongside Bo and sent the Sig sliding to the far end of the pew.

"What now?" Bo said.

"Now? We talk."

"About what?"

"I read about you in the papers, that they suspect you killed your boss. Anybody who has any idea of who you are wouldn't believe that bullshit for a moment. You were framed. I'm wondering by whom."

"How did you find me?"

Bo was trying to come up with a plan, a move that would give him some advantage. But at the moment, he could think of nothing. Moses was in complete control. Keep him talking, Bo thought.

"The real question is, how did I find you when the authorities couldn't. They look in all the obvious places. They've staked out your apartment. They're watching that farm you grew up on in Blue Earth. They've even got a detail posted at your partner's place. What's his name? Coyote? But I know you, Thorsen. And I know how you think.

"Specifically, I asked myself when a man's got no place to run, where does he turn? To family? Too obvious. Maybe to a close coworker. But your boss is dead, and Coyote is out of town. How about a friend? I'm sure the authorities thought about that, but anyone looking at you on the surface would think you didn't have any friends. So the question for me was, if you turned to a friend, how would I identify him?"

There was a moment of silence in which, apparently, Moses waited for a response. Bo heard the creak of the old wooden pew as Moses leaned forward and spoke into his ear.

"Simplicity itself. I secured a copy of the visitor's log kept by the security guards at the hospital during your convalescence. Lots of cops dropped by to see you. But only one who decidedly wasn't."

"Otter."

"Who gave this address to the guard."

The quiet of the sanctuary was broken by the rise of a siren wail. It grew in volume, passed, diminished, was swallowed by distance and the night.

Moses said, "You know, I've been inside lots of churches all over the world trying to figure out this Christianity thing. Get this. 'Christian soldiers are to wage the war of Christ their master without fearing that they sin in killing their enemies or of being lost if they are themselves killed. . . . If they kill, it is to the profit of Christ; if they die, it is to their own.' A good Catholic saint said that. Pretty bloodthirsty, don't you think?"

"I never argue religion."

"Gets you nowhere, right? You know what Mark Twain said? 'If Christ were here now, there is one thing he would not be—a Christian.'" Moses laughed softly. "What do you think of this whole God thing?"

"Does it matter?"

"It does or I wouldn't have asked. I did a little checking on you. You had a tough time of it growing up. Orphaned. In trouble with the law."

"You had a pretty shitty childhood yourself."

"You think so? I never thought of it that way, actually. A little lonely, maybe, but what kid isn't? My mother was available to me probably no more or less than yours was for you. She read to me, held me sometimes, relied on me. And my other companionship was with books. You like books, too."

"I didn't kill my mother."

It was almost a full minute before Moses spoke again. Whether he was thinking or fuming, Bo didn't know, but his words, when they finally came, were oddly gentle.

"Have you ever put an animal out of its misery?"

"Don't tell me you did it out of pity."

"No. What I knew of love. I would do things differently now, but at the time, it seemed reasonable."

The pew behind Bo gave another creak, more pronounced this time as Moses leaned nearer.

"Am I any worse than the God whose house this is?" Moses asked. "The God who sends plague and conflagration and misery and suffering to whole populations who piss him off. The Old Testament, now there's a chronicle of brutality."

"That's how you deal with your guilt? Pointing a finger at a greater guilt?"

"Who said I had any guilt?"

"What I'm wondering is why you're still alive."

"Why, I can't say. But if you're interested I'll tell you how."

"I'm interested."

"Buckle your seat belt, Thorsen," Moses said. "You're in for a bumpy ride."

chapter

forty-one

A t first there'd been almost nothing. No day. No night. Only darkness, perpetual and full of pain.

Death? David Moses had wondered. If so, then why the voices and the press of hands? Why the visitations and the dreams? Was death a long remembering and a longer regret?

Should I give him more? A voice like the crackle of dry brush.

A touch. Then another voice, *No. Vitals are too erratic.*

He screams sometimes.

Not from the pain. Dreams. His dreams, I'll bet, are terrible.

They were worse than terrible. They were the loneliness multiplied by the longing, the betrayal multiplied by a desperate trust.

He was not dead, he thought in one lucid moment, for hell would have been easier.

Moses dreamed.

He was in the cell they called *el Cuarto del Diablo*. The Devil's Room. He was naked, strapped to a wooden apparatus they called the Devil's Bed. His nose was filled with the odor of vomit and blood and excrement that had soaked into the wood.

The filthy guard the prisoners had nicknamed La Cucaracha stood near the barred window. The sky beyond was full of gray clouds. The guard held a long black stick. A Paralyzer shock baton. Eighty thousand volts in his hand. La Cucaracha turned from the window and began to walk toward Moses on the Devil's Bed. His dark eyes traveled the length of Moses's naked body, looking for the right spot. He grinned as he gazed at the shriveled testicles. His mouth was like a dark cemetery, his gapped teeth like gravestones. Moses felt his jaw go rigid as the baton descended toward his genitals. He squeezed his eyes shut, trying in the dark of this awful dream to will himself awake.

He's screaming again. What if someone hears?
There's no one to hear. Keep him sedated. Keep him restrained.
Christ, I hate his screams.
Just be glad you don't have his nightmares.

When he finally awoke, it was with a sudden tensing of his whole body. Moses lurched from unconsciousness and snapped instantly alert. In seconds, he'd assessed his surroundings.

He was in a small room. No windows. One door. The room was lit by a low-watt bulb in a brass standing lamp a few feet away. He lay on a hard cot with a mattress so thin he could feel the iron webbing beneath it. His hands and his ankles were shackled to the cot frame. A tube fed into his left arm. The tube ran down from a nearly empty fluid bag hung on a mobile IV unit. Near the cot was a metal table on which lay a syringe and several capped vials. The dim lamplight illuminated stained green walls and a cracked plaster ceiling. In the corner where two walls and the ceiling met, a spider had spun a web. The spider must have successfully captured all the flies, for there was not a sound in the room. The smell of mildew came off the walls, but the scent of the sheet that covered him was clean and fresh.

He made an inventory of his body, moving first his legs. His left thigh throbbed. His left hip was sore. His lower back ached. There was a sharp pain in his chest when he breathed deeply. His hands and arms seemed all right, but when he moved his right shoulder, he nearly cried out in agony. His right eye was swollen almost shut.

Good, he thought. Feeling in all my limbs. I'm not dead and I'm not paralyzed.

From beyond the only door crept the sound of music, very faint. The Beatles. "Penny Lane."

He began to consider his situation. The last thing he remembered was the struggle on top of the bluff at Wildwood. He remembered teetering at the edge, and he realized he must have fallen. That would account for all the damage to his body. In fact, as he considered it, he figured it was a miracle he'd lived.

So, where was he? Obviously not in a hospital. The mildewed walls and cracked ceiling suggested someplace less officially sanctioned. Someplace isolated, he assumed. Someplace hidden from prying eyes.

Who was hiding him? Not the police. In America, the police operated in a glare of public light. But there were other agencies in the States whose standard MO was covert operation. And one in particular with which he was well acquainted.

He tested the cuffs that shackled him hand and foot to the cot. No give. He scanned the room. It was empty except for the lamp, the IV unit, and the table with the syringe and vials. The single door, undoubtedly guarded, presented another challenge. He began to contemplate a weapon. The syringe and vials were a possibility. The iron webbing of the cot might provide the metal for a shiv. He could always use the standing lamp, swinging it like Davy Crockett did Ol' Betsy at the Alamo. Contemplating the image of his own last stand, going down wielding a floor lamp, gave him a moment of amusement.

The door opened and let in a slice of daylight. The music was louder then. The air that came in smelled of honeysuckle. Two figures stood in the doorway, silhouetted against the daylight. The door closed. One of the figures slowly crossed the room and entered the drizzle of light near the cot. It was a man. He was smiling. Moses recognized him immediately.

"Hello, David," Kingman said. "It's been a long time."

Kingman carried a tray of food. The man behind him brought a gun. Kingman set the tray on Moses's lap and unlocked the cuffs. He left Moses's legs shackled to the cot. Kingman stepped back and said, "I'll take it from here."

The other man nodded and left the room.

Moses looked at the food. Dry, burned toast. Scrambled eggs that could have used another two minutes over the fire. Mandarin orange slices from a can.

"You never learned to cook," he said.

"Another talent you had that I could only envy," Kingman said.

Moses began to eat, carefully. Almost any movement hurt him.

"I'll give you more Demerol if you'd like," Kingman offered.

Moses declined with a shake of his head. The pain was better than the fog of the Demerol. The pain kept him focused.

"Breakfast," Moses noted of the food. "Must be—what?—around seven A.M."

Kingman returned to the door and leaned against it. He crossed his arms and scanned the windowless room for what might have given Moses a clue to the time. "What makes you think so?"

"You used to get up every day at five-thirty to work out for an hour. You're in good shape, so I'd bet that's still your routine. You've shaved. I can smell that damn Old Spice you use. And your hair's still wet from the shower. What time is it?"

"Seven-ten." Kingman smiled. "You're some piece of work, David."

"You had your moments, too, Walter. Still do, apparently. I'm impressed that I'm here. Wherever here is. They're not looking for me?"

"We've taken care of that. What do you remember?"

"The hand-to-hand with that Secret Service agent."

"Thorsen."

"The next thing I know, I'm here."

"You took a pretty nasty tumble. Fell at least fifty feet. You were lucky you didn't die."

Moses looked up from his eating. "How long's my luck going to hold?"

Kingman didn't answer.

"Was it luck you found me?"

"A little luck, a little careful planning."

Kingman left the darkness near the door and stepped into the dim light of the lamp. He wore a white linen sport coat over a black T-shirt. Gray had replaced most of the brown in his hair. He looked a lot older than when Moses had seen him last.

"When you skipped out of that mental hospital," Kingman said, "I asked to lead the team the Company sent to track you down. Picked my own people. We couldn't find a trace. Then this Thorsen shows up, asking a lot of questions. When I realized the Secret Service was interested, and that the First Lady was in town, I put two and two together. I didn't know what your interest in the First Lady was or even if Thorsen was on the right track, but it was all we had to go on. I put a man out front of Wildwood. I got myself a launch and watched from the river. That was the planning part. The luck was that I was there when the shooting started. When you fell off that cliff, I figured you for dead. Next thing I know, you're crawling into the river, trying to swim away. You're one tough bastard. You always were."

"Wasn't that why you recruited me?"

Kingman smiled. "I was surprised when I heard you were killed at Agua Negra."

"The report of my death was greatly exaggerated."

"Coates filed the report," Kingman said.

"Coates." Moses nodded.

"Maybe he was simply mistaken."

With the back of his hand, Moses wiped a few toast crumbs from the corner of his mouth. "Didn't you ever wonder why Coates would assign someone in my line to a place like Agua Negra? Some god-forsaken jungle camp manned by a bunch of bush-league drug agents."

Kingman shrugged. "Your expertise?"

"My expertise was political sanction. Quiet, solitary work. Those guys were noisy, ill-trained, and brutal. It didn't surprise me at all when we were attacked. Everybody died, cut in half with machine gun fire, or hacked up with machetes. Everybody except me. Me, they took alive. They locked me up in a hellhole and took their time trying to kill me with a daily dose of humiliation and torture. They almost succeeded."

"Why didn't they?"

"Because Coates made a mistake. The son of a bitch couldn't help gloating." He put his fork down and shoved his tray aside. "The captain of the guards was a guy we all referred to as La Cucaracha. A piece of shit on two legs. I had one of my weekly sessions with him on an apparatus the prisoners called *la Cama del Diablo*."

"The Devil's Bed."

"I wasn't particularly lucid. I never was after a session. La Cucaracha grabbed my hair and lifted my head up so I could see. And there was Coates, standing beside that filthy guard like they were *compadres*. They were both grinning. And do you know what Coates said to me? He said, 'When you die, David, you'll think hell is a vacation.'"

In that hellhole of a prison, when he understood that Coates had betrayed him, he'd entered a period of despair. He obsessed on the past and realized that his life had been nothing but one betrayal after another. First his mother and his grandfather. Then there were the lies told by two other people he'd once loved and trusted. Tom Jorgenson and his daughter Kate. And finally there was Coates.

Hate had festered inside him, swelled huge and hard, barely contained by his intelligence. Patience, he told himself. Wait. Plan. Execute.

Execute, he did.

He'd observed that there were only two ways of leaving the prison compound. Most men left dead. They were executed on their knees in the yard or killed by disease or a beating or died on the Devil's Bed. The others left because they were no longer dangerous. They were the broken men, the empty ones, the ones with hollow eyes. The other prisoners called them los espectros. *Ghosts. They wandered the yard freely, drifting inside the razor wire, until one day the gate opened for them. They left for brief periods on work detail, chained together on the back of a flatbed, accompanied by several guards. Usually they cut back the brush that threatened to engulf the perimeter fence, or they repaired the jungle road.*

One day the gate opened for Moses.

Over a period of six months, he'd allowed himself to dissolve, to become one of los espectros. *In the end, he whimpered when he was taken to the Devil's Bed. He'd wet his pants before he got there. He no longer cursed La Cucaracha after the violations. He never looked another man in the eye. He lost weight because the other prisoners stole his food. Then they, too, began to abuse and to beat him.*

Eventually, he was gathered up with several los espectros, *chained on the flatbed, and driven out the gate. A jeep containing four guards armed with old Soviet SKS semiautomatic rifles accompanied them. They drove five miles until they came to a stream where the road had been washed away. Big mounds of rock and gravel for repair had been dumped beside the road. Each man was given a shovel.*

As soon as the shovel was in his hand, Moses sank the sharp metal edge into the face of the guard nearest him, and he grabbed the man's SKS. He dropped another guard with a heart shot before anyone had a chance to react. The third guard got off a hurried round that sizzled past Moses's head, then Moses clustered three shots dead center in his chest. The last guard made for the jungle. Moses dropped him before he was forty yards out.

The driver of the truck had plopped himself down on the running board. He held a pack of cigarettes in one hand, and he sat paralyzed in the middle of pulling out a smoke. He eyed Moses from under the brim of a ratty cap with YANKEES *sewn in silver across the crown.*

Moses put the barrel of the rifle against the driver's forehead.

He considered letting the driver go. The man was a local who worked for the prison. He wasn't one of the policia. *He looked like the kind of man who might have a wife and children. But to spare him would have required compassion, an emotion that had become even more rare to Moses than fear.*

The bullet made only a small entry wound between the man's eyes, but it splattered the back of his head across the side of the truck. Moses dug the keys out of the dead man's khakis, shoved the body aside, and climbed into the cab. The other prisoners had watched the whole scene placidly, and none made a move to join him.

Within a day, he'd reached the embassy in Bogotá and the Company had been notified.

Returning to the United States, Moses had three missions. To kill Coates. To kill Tom Jorgenson. And to kill Kathleen Jorgenson Dixon. Attempting any one of those assassinations was probably suicide, but David Moses was a man with nothing left to lose. His life had already been taken from him. What remained was little more than vengeance breathing.

The Company had given him a hero's welcome. Even Coates shook his hand warmly. Two days later, Coates was found dead in his home. He was naked and bound to his kitchen table. A car battery had been set on the kitchen counter. Two wires ran from the battery terminals and were connected to the man's genitals, which, when he was found, were charred to a black the color of cockroaches.

* * *

Kingman said, "A lot of us knew what kind of man Coates was. We all figured it was only a matter of time before you moved ahead of him and were the one giving the orders. Coates must have figured it, too. I was with him when he got the news that you were alive and on your way home. I'm not sure I've ever seen a man quite as frightened. But when you returned to the Company, you didn't say a word."

"I came back to kill him. You think I should have announced that?"

"You might have saved yourself a lot of trouble if you'd just gone through channels."

"Channels." He nearly spit.

"After you killed Coates, why did you come back to Minnesota?"

"Business," Moses said.

"You killed a homeless man here, David. What kind of business was that?"

"An accident. I thought he was Company. One of you, undercover. I was, I admit, a little delusional by then. He'd been eyeing me. Later, I realized he probably just wanted to steal my watch." Moses shifted, and Kingman's right hand shot under his coat, to the shoulder holster there. "Let me ask you a question, Walter. Why didn't the Company sanction me while I was in the Minnesota Security Hospital? It would have been easy."

"My doing. I wanted you alive."

"Why?"

Kingman knocked on the door. The other came in, gun drawn. Kingman approached Moses. "Your hands," he said. He cuffed Moses to the bed and took the tray. As he turned to the door, he said, "You're not the only one who's ever been betrayed by the people he trusted."

The next day Kingman opened the door and came in. He carried a rifle in one hand, a small cardboard box in the other. On his hands, he wore black leather gloves. Another man hung back at the door. Kingman set the rifle and the cardboard box on the metal table. He unlocked the cuffs that shackled Moses's hands to the frame of the cot. He turned to the table, picked up the rifle in his gloved hands, and held it toward Moses.

"Take it, David," he said.

The man at the door had what looked like a P-series Ruger, probably a nine millimeter, trained on Moses's heart. Moses took the rifle. It was an M40A1, a sniper rifle, forty-four inches in length with a twenty-four-inch barrel. Weight 14.5 pounds. Muzzle velocity 2,550 feet per second. Maximum effective range 1,000 yards.

"Not the latest technology, but it was always your favorite," Kingman said. "Grip it hard."

Moses tightened his fingers around the stock.

"Now pull the trigger."

Moses did. Kingman reached out and took the rifle. He laid it back on the table, opened the cardboard box, pulled out a rifle scope, and handed it to Moses. It was a Trijicon ACOG military scope, excellent for night shots over a long distance.

"Good," Kingman said after Moses had put his prints on it.

He took the scope from Moses and set it back in the box. Next he extracted five cartridges and held them out for Moses to take. They were .308 Winchester loads, a good precision caliber. Moses handled each round and gave them back to Kingman. Kingman cuffed him to the cot frame again, then nodded to the man at the door. The man, who also wore gloves, holstered his Ruger, picked up the rifle and the cardboard box, and left the room.

As Kingman slowly shed his gloves, Moses was thinking. He'd believed it was the Company who'd tracked him down and taken him after Wildwood. He figured their stake in him was the embarrassment factor. If it became known that a former operative of the United States government had attempted to assassinate the First Lady and her father, the Company would suffer tremendous public embarrassment, one more in a long line. Taking him quietly and disposing of him in secret was a much preferable scenario.

But he hadn't been disposed of. Not yet. The reprieve was

Kingman's doing. Moses was beginning to wonder how much the Company really knew about what Kingman was up to. "This isn't Company business," Moses said. "Who are you working for?"

Kingman sat down beside the cot. He smiled. "Remember Budapest?"

"I remember everything."

"I'll bet you do. A long and troubled recollection. But Budapest is a good memory. For me, anyway. A time when I still trusted the Company."

Moses just stared at him.

"We believe in our country," Kingman began. "We believe in the ideals it was founded on. But the ideal and the reality are worlds apart. You know it, too. Look at you. Consider all you risked and all you gave up, and in the end, those you trusted betrayed you. We've all been betrayed, all of us who are now brothers and sisters."

"You? Betrayed?"

"I had a daughter."

"Lucy."

"Lucy." Kingman nodded. "For her high school graduation I gave her a trip to Europe. Her and her best friend, three weeks on the Continent. She was so excited. I saw her off at Dulles. It was the last time I saw her alive. She was in a café in Marseilles ten days later. A car bomb went off in the street outside. The flying glass tore her apart."

Kingman looked toward the dim lamplight. There was a gloss to his eyes.

"The bomb was planted by a man who called himself Abu al-Afghani, working on behalf of the Group Islamic Army. It was meant to kill an Algerian diplomat who was also dining in the café. The Company knew beforehand about the bombing, but they did nothing to stop it. You see, sometimes al-Afghani worked for the Company." He shook his head. "They could have told me, David. They could have warned me to keep Lucy away from Marseilles."

"You used the past tense with al-Afghani."

"We got him."

"There's that 'we' again. Are you a mole now or what?"

"Not in the way you think of it. However, my loyalty has shifted."

"What do you want from me?"

"It's simple enough. You tried to kill the First Lady, right?"

"Yeah."

Kingman looked him hard in the eye. "You still want to?"

chapter

forty-two

In the quiet of the church, Bo heard the blower kick on, and a cool draft touched the back of his neck. It was not as cold as the muzzle of the gun Moses held there.

"You declined their offer?" Bo asked.

"If offer it was. They didn't need me. They had my prints all over the weaponry. If in fact they wanted me to pull the trigger and put the round into her, it would have been the last thing I ever did. So I took my leave."

"Just like that?"

"When I was stronger, they exchanged my handcuffs for a strait-jacket. A mistake. It was a Posey," he said. "Posey makes four kinds. The one they chose is the simplest to escape. The weakness is the buckles. You work them against any sharp, hard edge, the frame of a cot for example, and you can knock them loose pretty quickly. Took me three minutes. Houdini could do it in less time and while he was hanging upside down. Now there was a genius."

Moses resettled himself in the pew behind Bo. The kiss of the gun barrel ended, but Bo knew the weapon was still trained on him.

"You continue to have resources," Bo noted.

"An elementary piece of any stratagem. Always have a backup cache somewhere," Moses said. "What I've been wondering since I read about your crime spree in the papers is what's the connection. I'd guess the people who framed you are the same ones who nabbed me."

"What difference does it make?"

"I hate a puzzle with missing pieces. Who are these people, Thorsen? Why do they want the First Lady dead?"

"Why do you want the First Lady dead?"

"I have a pretty good reason. And I think you know it."

"You're wrong."

"About you knowing?"

"About the good reason. About what really happened that night on the bluff at Wildwood twenty years ago. What you think went down didn't. It wasn't Tom Jorgenson with Kate. It was his brother, Roland. All this time you've hated the wrong man."

"Of course you're lying. Your job is to save her."

"Think about it for a minute. Two brothers very similar in build and appearance. One, a man committed to peace. The other, an artist with an unconventional lifestyle. One, a father. The other, an uncle who'd been generally distant. Think about the strength of the man you fought. A politician or a worker in iron? Ask yourself who was more likely to have been with Kate that night."

The blower shut off and the church lapsed again into a deep silence. Moses didn't speak. The figures in the stained glass windows were dark images now, barely discernible as human.

Bo said, "It was incest no matter how you cut it, but Tom Jorgenson wasn't guilty. The guilty one is dead."

"Why didn't she tell me this herself?"

"You never gave her a chance. I was there. Every time she tried to explain, you cut her off. You didn't want to hear. But you know what? I also think you didn't really want her dead."

"Didn't want her dead? I should have killed her years ago, and her father."

"Why didn't you?"

"I thought I'd found a family in the Company. I thought I'd found a place I belonged. Until I spent time on the Devil's Bed. That pretty well cleared my thinking. I knew what I had to do."

"What was that? Kill everyone who ever lied to you? If you're like most of us, it would be a long list."

"I didn't care about everyone."

"Only those you'd hoped would be family? I talked with Father Cannon. I know about Wildwood."

Moses didn't argue, but neither did he agree.

"But when you had the chance to kill Kate," Bo said, "you offered her her life. After all your careful planning, why did you even hesitate? You know what I think? I think in that moment when you had her on her knees, you understood that she wasn't the real monster, that all those years ago she was just a scared kid involved in something way over her head. It was her father who needed killing. Except that it wasn't. The man you really wanted dead killed himself a long time ago."

"How is it you know her personal history?" Moses asked.

"She told me."

"She could have lied."

"When you had the gun barrel to her forehead and looked into her eyes on the bluff, were they the eyes of a woman who was lying?"

For a long time, Moses said nothing. Bo could hear the man breathing at his back, could feel the warm breath breaking against his neck.

"Why did they frame you?" Moses asked.

"Because they tried to kill me and couldn't. They want me dead because I know who they are," Bo said.

"And that would be?"

"NOMan."

"NOMan?"

"National Operations Management. It's a federal government

agency, established as an information conduit. Ostensibly. I'm pretty sure that all along it was meant for something else."

Bo explained what he knew about the organization. When he'd finished, Moses laughed quietly.

"Ever read the *Odyssey*, Thorsen?"

Bo heard a door open in the far recesses of the church. The pew behind Bo creaked.

"It's just Otter," Bo said quickly.

"Bo?" It was Otter's voice preceding him.

Bo spoke quietly over his shoulder. "Look, Moses, we can work this out together. We both have a stake in what happens."

Moses didn't reply. Otter stepped into the dim illumination from the light above the altar, and he looked around. A few moments passed before he saw Bo.

"Sorry that took so long. What are you doing there all alone? Praying?"

Bo slowly turned and looked behind him. Moses was gone.

Otter came down the aisle, carrying a white bag that smelled of the hot gyros inside it.

"I've got to go, Otter."

"Why?"

"Moses was here."

"The dead guy?"

"He's not dead."

Otter's eyes jumped around the darkened church. "How'd he find you?"

"Because he's a goddamn genius. He may get it in his head to call the police. Until I figure all this out, I can't take a chance on getting picked up."

"Where will you go?"

"I don't know, but it's not like I haven't been on the streets before."

"This sucks, Spider-Man. What can I do to help?"

"You've already done enough."

Otter handed him the bag of food. "Wait here." He was gone a few minutes. When he came back he carried a rolled blanket tied with a rope that was looped in such a way that it created a sling to make the bedroll easier to carry over his shoulder.

"It's a good blanket," Otter said. "Kept me warm a lot of nights when I didn't have a roof over my head. And here." Otter shoved a handful of money at him. "Only forty-seven dollars. It won't get you to Mexico, but it'll keep you fed for a few days."

"I can't—"

"Take it, Spider-Man. I've got food, and a paycheck's on the way. You've got to keep yourself together until things get cleared up. God knows when that'll be."

Bo had always been the one offering help. It had been a long time since he'd needed any himself. He found it hard being on the other side of charity, having something as simple as an old blanket and spare change mean so much.

"Thanks."

"No thanks necessary. Just be careful, okay?"

Bo retrieved his Sig from the church pew and stuffed it into the bedroll. Otter's final offering was a strong hug, then Bo took his leave.

He walked the streets as the dark of night hardened around him. Clouds rolled in from the west and blotted out the stars. He stopped once, at a convenience store to buy toothpaste and a toothbrush, and to use the phone. Directory assistance was unable to help him. Lorna Channing's telephone number was unlisted. Bo tried the White House using the code name Peter Parker, but he got nowhere.

When he reached the river, he followed the east bank of the Mississippi, walking along a jogging path that finally ended in the broken concrete of old docks and landings no longer used and fallen into disrepair. Behind him, the towers of the downtown district spiked toward a sky domed with an overcast that reflected the glitter and glare of the city. Ahead of him, high above the river, a row of lit globes slanted down from Cherokee Heights like a broken string of pearls. The High Bridge. Bo passed under the girders and made his way to the place where once, long ago, the old bus had sat on blocks and sheltered his street family. The bus was gone, but the site was still a deserted stretch of riverbank guarded by cottonwoods and cushioned by tall grass. Bo rolled out the blanket and sat down. A muddy smell flowed up from the river, thick as the water itself. He was in a place where eons before, glacial flooding had carved a deep chasm in the layers of sandstone. The houses atop the Heights were set back too far to be seen from the river, and the bluff beneath them was invisible in the dark. The great bridge seemed to connect with nothing at all. Bo recalled that only a couple of days before he'd been on top of the bridge, poised to plunge to his death, to ride into eternity on the current of the black water below.

His body hurt. His feet ached because the shoes Otter had given him were too small. His head was packed with facts and conjectures that whirled round and round and sucked all his thinking into a confusing maelstrom. He tried to sort a few things out.

He was certain now what NOMan's goal was.

The assassination of the First Lady.

The murder of Kate.

It was possible that with Moses now truly at large and with Bo complicating things, they may have decided to call off the operation, but he knew that these were people accustomed to manipulating events on an enormous scale. The network of NOMan was so tightly woven into the mundane fabric of the legitimate system that it was almost invisible. They'd been operating so long and so effectively that by now they may have considered themselves invulnerable and were still determined to proceed with the killing.

But how? And where? And when?

He contemplated the wisdom of calling the field office in Minneapolis and telling them everything he knew and everything he suspected. Several considerations held him back. In the first place, there was the time a call like that would take. They'd have him located in a matter of moments, and they'd descend on him with extreme prejudice. If they took him into custody, NOMan would know exactly where he was. Bo wasn't eager to become a stationary target for an organization that may well have infiltrated the Secret Service in the way it had other agencies. He could easily be killed before he had a chance to state his case. He'd end up just one more incident discussed by conspiracy theorists on the Internet.

He considered spilling the whole story to the newspapers. Again, no guarantee his allegations would make it into print. He had no proof of anything. If Tom Jorgenson didn't offer supporting testimony and if NOMan called off the hit and nothing happened, he'd be labeled loonier than ever.

The most hopeful strategy would be to anticipate their move and intercept them. This ran contrary to all his training and to the protective doctrine of the Secret Service, which was to cover the protectee and evacuate. But evacuate where? Under assault by an organization as ubiquitous, invisible, and determined as NOMan, was any place safe?

Bo was exhausted. He lay back on the blanket, looked up at the empty night sky, and thought about Kate. He wondered what she must think of him now. Probably, she was thinking he was insane and she was lucky that he hadn't gone berserk when they'd been alone together.

The sound of thunder came from far away, but Bo didn't see any lightning. A few drops hit him in the face. Great. On top of everything else, it was going to rain.

chapter

forty-three

President Daniel Clay Dixon was somewhere over North Carolina. Sitting alone in his private compartment aboard Air Force One, he took a moment to look up from the White House news summary and appreciate the color of the evening sky. It looked like a great fire was burning somewhere beyond the Blue Ridge. Then he took another moment to sit back and close his eyes.

He was feeling good. The Pan-American summit had gone well, ended with a signing of a good-faith agreement by all the heads of state in attendance. The president had been accorded the honor of giving the closing address, and his words had been received with a standing ovation. He felt that something significant had been accomplished. In his presidency thus far, that had been a rare feeling.

He was about to return to reading the news summary, a document prepared for him four times daily, when his phone rang.

"Mr. President, Lorna Channing is on the line."

"Go ahead," Dixon said. "Lorna, what's up?"

"Have you read your news summary?"

"I'm just doing it now. Something I should know?"

"Page three."

Dixon thumbed the summary and saw what concerned Lorna.

A brief article reported that Special Agent-in-Charge Diana Ishimaru, head of the Minneapolis field office of the Secret Service, had been found shot to death in her St. Paul home. Authorities were searching for Special Agent Bo Thorsen, who was wanted for questioning in the shooting death. Thorsen's car was found at the victim's home, and neighbors reported that a man matching Thorsen's description had been observed in the area just prior to the time of death. Earlier in the day, Thorsen reportedly instigated an altercation involving Ishimaru. Thorsen was currently under suspension from his duties pending a formal inquiry into the events surrounding the attempted assassination of the First Lady at her family home in Minnesota.

"Christ, what's going on?" Dixon said.

"If you believe the reports, our man's gone postal."

"Has he contacted you?

"Not a word. I didn't even know he'd left D.C. I've talked with Stanton. He'll be here when you arrive. I thought it would be best if we were briefed together." She was talking about Gerald Stanton, director of the Secret Service.

"Good." The president glanced out the window again, at the sky that seemed to reflect a distant fire.

"John Llewellyn's got a burr under his saddle," Lorna said. "He's talking resignation."

"Maybe that won't be necessary."

"No?"

"Maybe I'll just fire him."

Stanton was a big, strong-looking man with a wide face, gray hair, and a glare that he wielded like a stone ax. A veteran of more than a quarter century with the Secret Service, he had, among other assignments, headed the POTUS detail for two presidents. While he was always respectful of the office of the chief executive, he'd seen too much of the human side of the presidency to be intimidated by the man who occupied the Oval Office.

Stanton sat in a wing chair and Channing in another. The president sat on the sofa opposite them.

"What have you got?" Dixon asked.

"From the beginning," Stanton said. "One. Wednesday afternoon, Agent Thorsen tried to get into Wildwood. When he was denied access—"

"Denied?"

"His actions at Wildwood before and during the recent attack on the First Lady are the subject of a formal investigation. In addition to certain procedural irregularities, there have been accusations of dereliction of duty lodged by Special Agent Christopher Manning. It's all spelled out in this memo I've prepared."

Stanton handed the president a folder.

"Because the First Lady and several of the family members will be called as witnesses in the inquiry, any contact with Thorsen at this point is out of the question.

"Two. Thorsen entered the field office Wednesday afternoon and engaged in a verbal altercation with his superior, Special Agent-in-Charge Diana Ishimaru. According to eyewitnesses, Thorsen left in an agitated state. Later that evening, he was seen leaving a bar in St. Paul, reportedly so drunk he could barely stand. According to Ishimaru's neighbors, a man fitting Thorsen's description pounded on their door at one A.M. looking for Ishimaru. He appeared to be quite inebriated. The neighbor directed him to Ishimaru's home. At one-thirty-seven, this same neighbor heard shots fired next door and called the police. The officers who responded discovered Ishimaru dead from a gunshot wound to the head. Thorsen's clothing was found in the home. His car was parked—badly—on the street in front of the house.

"Three. Agent Thorsen has disappeared."

"And that's where things stand now?"

"No. There's more. Thorsen contacted the Minneapolis field

office this evening, claiming that Tom Jorgenson was the target of another assassination plot. The agent who spoke with him said he sounded like a man gone over the edge. A short time later, Thorsen showed up at a gas station next to the hospital where Jorgenson was recuperating. He threatened the clerk and a customer with a gun. As much as I hate to say this, it appears more and more likely that Agent Thorsen is under severe emotional strain. At this point, we consider him extremely dangerous."

Dixon nodded and sat back.

Stanton said, "Sir, it's my understanding that Thorsen was involved in an investigation here in Washington just a few days ago. At your request."

"I asked Thorsen to do me an unofficial favor."

"A favor? I have reason to believe the investigation was of a very serious nature."

"I asked him to look into a few matters concerning Robert Lee's death."

"Were you worried about your own safety?"

"When I'm ready to share my concerns with you, Director Stanton, I will."

Stanton's face grew perceptibly stonier. "Sir, I would like nothing more than to be able to clear Agent Thorsen and to remove this dark cloud that's hanging over the Secret Service. Can you tell me anything that might help me do that?"

"No." He and the director locked eyes a moment. It was Stanton who finally broke. The president said, "I expect to be updated on everything that occurs in your investigation of Thorsen. Thank you for coming, Director Stanton. We'll remain in touch."

After the director left, Dixon turned to Lorna Channing. "What do you think? Has Thorsen gone over the edge?"

"It certainly appears so."

"I'm thinking that nothing anymore is the way it appears."

"It's hard to imagine this has all been orchestrated. And to what end?"

"I don't know, Lorna. But I'm sure my father's hand is behind all this. I don't know how he's done it, but it's him all right. I can feel it."

He walked to the middle of the room where presidents before him had stood and had faced the crises that made them great or marked them to be all but forgotten. He felt the weight of history on his shoulders. The burden was his. Not Carpathian's or Llewellyn's or William Dixon's. It was his call, the way everything would go from that moment forward. It was a daunting realization, but he wasn't afraid. In fact, he felt the tremble of an old excitement flowing through him, the kind that had been so familiar on the playing field.

"Lorna, get our people together, all of them, here. We have work to do. And get my father here first thing in the morning."

"What do I tell him?"

Dixon thought for a moment. "Tell him it's fourth and long. And his son has decided to go for it."

chapter

forty-four

Bo had breakfast at a small greasy spoon on West Seventh called Oscar's, not far from the river. It was full of people who shopped the Salvation Army regularly, guys who'd hustled enough change to cover the $1.99 two eggs, hash browns, toast, and coffee special. Bo fit right in. He could have used a shower, a shave, and a clean change of clothes. However, all things considered, he was in good spirits because beyond a few drops, it hadn't actually rained the night before, and he was still a free man. The coffee tasted as if it had been made from mud scooped off the bottom of the Mississippi, and the egg yolks were like clay. Bo ate every last bite and sat for a while at the counter, bent over his coffee mug, trying to figure out what to do next.

In his possession was the weapon that had killed Diana Ishimaru. He'd argued with her at the field office in front of witnesses. And there'd been witnesses, too, who had placed him at the murder scene, apparently drunk. That was plenty for a good prosecuting attorney. Probably even a bad one. What did he have for a defense? A pathetically paranoid-sounding tale of conspiracy for which he had not a single shred of solid evidence.

He was pretty well screwed.

NOMan's desire to assassinate Kate was a greater concern to him, but he was stumped. Wildwood was so tight now a snake couldn't crawl in without being detected. Moses had told him about the sniper rifle. If that was the way they'd go, where would they try the hit? The buildings at Wildwood were protected by orchards. The wooded hills along the highway to Wildwood offered a number of good opportunities, but the First Lady's car was armored and nothing short of a direct missile hit could penetrate it.

Bo noticed a sudden rippling and exodus among the clientele of Oscar's. Several hard-looking customers dropped money on the counter or their tables and left. Within a couple of minutes, the place was half empty.

"What's up?" Bo asked the man at the grill behind the counter.

The guy wore a shirt that may have been white once. His belly hung over his belt, obscuring his buckle. If he wasn't careful, he'd fry his own fat along with the bacon. He was in worse need of a shave than Bo. "Cops," he said, scraping a layer of grease off the griddle. "Come in here every morning at eight-twenty-five. Like clockwork. The cockroaches take a hike, come back around nine when the boys in blue are gone."

Bo dropped three bucks on the counter, picked up his bedroll, and slid off the stool. The guy at the grill gave a short laugh and shook his head.

The cruiser pulled up as Bo stepped outside. He turned and walked away from Oscar's at an easy pace.

Like clockwork.

He took the corner and hunkered in the shadow cast by a video store advertising "the finest erotic collection in the Twin Cities." An old woman passed him by, pushing a grocery cart full of discarded aluminum cans. Bo stared at the big smokestacks of the Minnesota Brewing Company a few blocks down West Seventh.

Like clockwork.

He thought about the sniper rifle and the nightscope. He mulled over the question of opportunity, and he considered the tenet that anybody involved in protective services knew: Routine was the deadliest enemy of all.

Like clockwork.

Bo had a pretty damn good idea of how NOMan would make the hit.

He used fifteen bucks of the money Otter had given him, and he took a taxi. He got out a block away from the church and stood at a safe distance, looking for any sign of police presence. On that sunny Friday morning, with doves cooing on the gutters along the eaves, everything seemed fine and peaceful. Bo didn't trust appearances anymore, so he circled awhile, casing the building. Finally, he knew he had to take a chance. He went in the front door and walked through the sanctuary. He passed the suite of offices that were used for administration, and he heard a copy machine running. Quickly, he made for the stairs to the basement and headed down to Otter's room. The door was locked. He knocked lightly. No answer.

Damn. He hadn't counted on Otter being gone. He spent a moment considering, then climbed the stairs and walked quietly toward the door that opened onto the suite of administrative offices. The sound of the copier had stopped. The desk in the reception area was unoccupied at the moment. A hallway behind the desk ran to the end of the wing, and several doors along it on either side were open. From one of them came the sound of voices deep in conversation. Bo crept toward the desk. He opened the bottom left-hand drawer and drew out a small metal box. Inside, he found the van keys he'd seen Otter borrow the day before. He took the keys and dropped them in his pocket. He put the box back, closed the drawer, and began to back out of the room. He didn't make it.

A woman stepped into the hallway. Seeing Bo, she smiled and came quickly forward. "Hello," she said brightly, as if the presence of an unkempt man in her office were an everyday occurrence. "May I help you?"

She was dressed casually in jeans and a yellow sweatshirt, and she wore tortoiseshell glasses that complemented her eyes and her hair. In her hands, she held what looked to be half a ream of copied paper. She saw him eyeing the copies.

"The bulletin for Sunday services," she said.

"Ah," Bo replied. He nodded a few times, stalling. Then something occurred to him. "Sandie Herron?"

"Why yes? Do I know you?"

"I'm a friend of—" He hesitated, wondering whether people here called Otter by his real name.

"Otter," she finished, as if to say *of course*. She set the papers on her desk and shook Bo's hand.

"I'm . . . Spider-Man," he said. "I'm looking for Otter."

"He's not here at the moment."

"Do you know when he'll be back?"

"Not for a while. At least that's what he said when he left."

"Did he leave alone?"

"I don't know. I was busy in the copy room. Was he expecting you?"

Bo shook his head.

"Would you like to wait?"

"I can't, thank you."

"May I give him a message?"

"Yes. When you see him, tell him I hope I haven't gotten him in too much trouble. Tell him I'm sorry."

"Well," she said, puzzling this. "Sure."

Bo turned to leave but paused a moment. "You don't happen to know what time the moon rises tonight?"

"No, I'm sorry." Sandie Herron looked at him, and added with sincerity, "It was nice meeting you, Spider-Man. God bless you."

Bo could see in her the same goodness that Otter obviously saw, and he was happy for them both. He said good-bye. Then he went out to the parking lot and stole the van.

* * *

In the last fifty miles of its flow, before it delivered itself into the sweep of the Mississippi, the St. Croix River cut among heavily wooded hills. Along many of the steep slopes, the topsoil had eroded away, exposing the underlying sandstone in long wall out-croppings or in solitary pinnacles. Ten miles south of the interstate bridge at Hudson, a little river called the Kinnickinnic cut its own way through the rock strata. It was a clear, fast flow favored by anglers because of the trout that swam in its shaded pools. In order to protect and preserve the beauty of the waterways and the unique landscape surrounding them, the state of Wisconsin had set aside the area at the confluence of the Kinnickinnic River and the St. Croix River as a state park.

Bo didn't need to read the brochure the ranger had handed him after she'd taken his entrance fee. He pretty well knew these things already. Or the important part anyway. The sandstone formations. The brochure did tell him something he didn't know. That the park closed at 10:00 P.M. And the ranger herself had told him something else. That the moon would rise at 10:06. A moon nearly full. A shame, she'd said, that no one would be in the park to enjoy it.

He drove the van along a narrow road that threaded its way among meadows of tall prairie grass and stands of white-barked poplars. There were parking areas that afforded access to hiking trails among the hills. Finally he entered a forest that was a mix of oak and evergreen. A half mile beyond that, the road ended at a pic-nic area perched on a hill overlooking the place where the Kinnickinnic spilled into the St. Croix. A dozen cars sat in the lot, gleaming under the hot August sun. Bo pulled into a slot away from the other vehicles. He took his bedroll with the Sig stuffed inside, and he left the van. A few families were gathered at the shaded pic-nic tables. Bo could hear the squeals and laughter of children some-where out of sight toward the river. He walked a path that took him beyond the picnic area to a wooden observation platform con-structed at the precipitous lip of the hill. The orientation of the plat-form was to the south. Far below, he could see the little blue-white thread of the Kinnickinnic snaking toward the grand sweep of the St. Croix. Over thousands of years, a curving delta of sand had formed at the confluence of the two rivers and a stand of tall cottonwoods had taken root. Several pleasure boats lay anchored along the shore of the delta, and Bo saw people strolling the beach. Beyond the delta, the river made a slow curl southeast. A few miles beyond, far out of sight, the St. Croix finally fed itself to the Father of Waters.

What lay to the south didn't interest Bo. It was what crowned the bluffs directly across the river that had drawn him there. The orchards of Wildwood.

Two tall spruce trees blocked any clear view a visitor might have of Wildwood from the platform itself. Bo left the observation area and scouted along the crest of the hill, peering among the trees, carefully eyeing the slope. He stumbled upon a trail that cut down to the St. Croix, and he followed it, arriving quickly at a protected inlet with a beach and a swimming area full of children. This was the source of the laughter he'd heard from the hill above. As he approached the beach, the parents who lounged on blankets there gave him a wary look. He realized how out of place he appeared in his long, borrowed pants and shirt, his too-small shoes, his bedroll, with his hair uncombed, and his face unwashed and unshaven. They probably thought he was a vagrant, maybe a predator. He hurried on, lest they alert the park authorities to his presence.

He made his way along the bank of the river, studying the broad hillside as he went. It didn't take him long to spot what he'd been looking for. A beige outcropping, three-quarters of the way up the hill, almost directly below the observation platform. Wedge-shaped, maybe fifteen feet from side to side, it thrust out a dozen feet or more from the hillside. Because trees walled the outcropping on three sides, it was invisible from the picnic area on the hilltop, but it had a perfect, unobstructed view of Wildwood.

Bo took a good ten minutes to make his way up the slope, fighting through a tangle of undergrowth. As he drew nearer, he saw that the freeze and thaw of a lot of winters had created deep fractures in the outcropping. The ground around the base was littered with talus, great chunks of stone that had broken away from the main body of the rock. By the time he stood on the flat top of the outcropping, he was sweating heavily and breathing hard. He stood looking across the river at Wildwood, and he allowed himself a moment of triumph. He was certain this was the place.

Many pieces had to come together in his thinking. There was what he believed about NOMan, that for whatever reason the organization was intent on assassinating the First Lady and that Tom Jorgenson was probably a target as well. There was the information given by Moses about the weaponry he'd been forced to handle, the sniper rifle, the .308 Winchester rounds, and the Trijicon scope. With .308 loads, the M40A1 would be effective to a range of a thousand yards. Although he didn't have a range finder with him, Bo calculated the bluffs at Wildwood to be no more than six hundred yards away. The Trijicon ACOG—Advanced Combat Optical Gunsight— was a night-vision scope with high magnification capability. It would not be difficult to sight a target on the bluffs across the river, especially in the light of a full moon. Kate had told Bo that the first thing Tom Jorgenson wanted to do when he came home to Wildwood was gather with his family on the bluff overlooking the St. Croix and watch the moon rise. For two nights, the sky had been rainy or overcast. But it was cloudless now and promised to stay that way. If someone wanted to kill Kate and her father, tonight when the moon rose would be the perfect time.

The question that lay before him now was what to do next. His instinct was to alert Calloway at Wildwood. If he was right, the Jorgensons had to be kept away from the bluffs. If he was wrong— and considering the amount of speculation involved, there was every possibility that he was—he'd just be giving them more evidence to use against him at a mental competency hearing.

What he also knew, and what was extremely troubling, was that NOMan had infiltrated most, if not all, government agencies, and the

Secret Service had probably not been spared. Alerting the FLOTUS detail might also result in alerting NOMan. Bo had no idea anymore whom to trust.

It was sunny and quiet on the rock. A gentle breeze blew over the hillside from downriver, smelling vaguely of evergreen and dry prairie grass. Near the delta, a motor launch revved its engine, pulled away from where it had been anchored, and headed south with the current. Bo could hear the murmur of the Kinnickinnic as it tumbled over the last smooth boulders before it joined the St. Croix. He also was aware of voices coming from the observation platform thirty yards above him and hidden by the two spruce trees. As soon as he focused on the voices, a jolt of recognition hit him. They were male, two of them, and he'd heard them before. In O'Gara's, offering to buy him a drink. And then on the High Bridge, coaxing him to the railing. And finally in Diana Ishimaru's home after she'd been murdered. Between the limbs of the spruce trees, Bo could see a bit of movement on the platform. He shuffled to his right in an attempt to get a clearer view. He was perilously near the lip of the sandstone, and he could see the chunks of talus scattered below over the slope of the hillside. On the platform above him, something metal flashed in the sun. Bo edged farther to the right, desperate to see. The moment he did, he heard the sharp crack of stone. He glanced down and saw another piece of rock break away from the outcropping and plunge to join the talus below. Unfortunately, it was the piece of rock on which he stood.

chapter

forty-five

The senator caned his way to a chair in the Oval Office and sat down. He wore an expensive gray suit, and he smelled of talc. He smiled like a man who'd walked into a parlor for an afternoon bourbon and a pleasant smoke.

"Glorious day, Clayboy. Makes me feel almost young again."

Lorna Channing closed the door and positioned herself to the left of the senator. She folded her hands and waited for the president to speak.

Dixon rose from his desk and approached his father. He stood above the old man, looking down at that maddening smile.

"A few minutes ago, I spoke with John Llewellyn. I asked for his resignation."

The senator's smile collapsed. "You what?"

"It's been clear to me for some time that we have many ideological differences."

"Ideological? Ideology is for high school debates, Clayboy. This is the White House. This is the Super Bowl of politics. Here, you play to win, and winning is all that matters. Screw ideology. John Llewellyn knows politics."

"His kind of politics. Not mine. Not anymore."

The senator pursed his lips, and wrinkles spread out like a newly spun web. "All right. We can deal with this. Who's your new chief of staff?"

The president looked toward Lorna Channing.

The senator snorted. "I'm sure there's never been a woman in that position."

"Then it's time there was."

William Dixon craned his neck and looked askance at the new chief of staff. "I remember you on your first horse down on the Purgatoire. You fell off a lot."

"I ride well now, Senator. I never fall off."

The senator nodded slowly. "All right then. We can do this. We can still win this election."

"Not we, Senator," the president said.

The elder Dixon lifted his head, his nose high, as if sniffing something in the air. "Cutting the old man loose, too?"

"Since Alan Carpathian died, this presidency has had no heart. No soul. For all intents and purposes, this room has been empty." He crossed the Oval Office and took his seat at his desk. "It's not empty anymore."

"Carpathian. The man was a fool."

"I'd rather follow a hopeful fool than a man on the road toward hell." He spread his hands flat on the desktop. "I've scheduled a press conference for this afternoon. I'll announce the change of the White House staff, and I'll also announce a new legislative initiative based on the report Lorna delivered to me."

"Based on Kate's foolish notion, you mean."

"I don't think it's foolish. I'm taking back the presidency, Senator. I'm going to do all I can to help this nation find its heart again."

"They'll slaughter you."

"Then I'll go down fighting for something worthwhile. I'm through fighting just to win."

The senator drew himself up slowly and turned away from his

son. The rubber tip of his cane made a small squeak on the nap of the rug at every step. At the door, he paused.

"You don't realize it, but you need me now more than ever. I'll still be there for you when you come to your senses."

"Senator, good day."

The old man shook his head, turned, and his huge hand enveloped the knob.

That evening after the cameras had ceased their click and whir and the press corps had rushed to file their stories, Clay Dixon stood near the window in his private study on the second floor of the White House. In his hands he held the cup he'd received as the MVP when he played in the Rose Bowl with Bobby Lee. The sun had set and the sky held a golden afterglow. The longer he stood, the more the light through the window, reflected in the long curve of the trophy, faded. It seemed to Dixon like an eye closing on the glory of a time long before.

He looked up and found Lorna Channing standing in the doorway.

"I'm sorry," she said. "I didn't mean to disturb you."

"That's all right. Come on in."

Channing stepped into the room. "A shining moment."

Dixon nodded, gazing down at the trophy. "It was."

"I was talking about the press conference."

"Shining moment? I may have sealed the coffin on my presidency."

"For what it's worth, you've never been more a president in my eyes than you are at this moment."

Dixon smiled. "Thank you, Lorna. That means a lot to me." He looked out the window. Above the trees on the White House lawn, he could see the Washington Monument reflecting the last light of evening. "I never realized until now how much I love this country."

"You proved that this evening." She was quiet for a few moments. "Are you all right?"

Dixon turned to her. "Better than I've been in quite a while. For the first time in my life, I'm not concerned about losing."

"You haven't lost yet. Americans are an unpredictable bunch. Forget the pollsters and the pundits. God alone knows what the future holds."

"I like your optimism."

"I'm just saying what Alan would have said, and Bobby."

"Thanks, Lorna. Thank you for standing with me."

"I'll be down in my office if you need me. I've got a lot of work to do."

"And I can't think of anyone who'd do it better."

"Thank you, Mr. President."

Alone again, Dixon sat down. He hadn't turned on a lamp. Along with the world outside, the study was sliding toward night. He looked around him at the plaques and trophies and other darkening mementos of a time when he'd believed he was golden in a way, when the future was bright and full of promise, when he'd known that greatness awaited him. He was a different man now. Older. Tired. But still hopeful. Except the greatness he wanted was not for himself but for the people he served, for the nation he deeply loved.

As he stood up to leave, the phone rang. He answered it.

"Yes?"

"Mr. President, the First Lady is on the line."

"Thank you. Hello, Kate."

Her voice came to him across a thousand miles, sweet as the first breeze of the first dawn.

"Clay, I love you."

He smiled and closed his eyes. And he whispered, "I love you, too."

chapter

forty-six

Pain brought Bo to consciousness. Pain, and the knowledge that he had an absolute duty left undone. That understanding had never deserted him, not even in the confusion of his fevered nightmares. His first thought when he came to, even before he groaned in agony, was that Kate was in terrible danger.

Ropes of fire twisted down his leg. He gritted his teeth, and a soft moan escaped his lips.

"What was that?"

The voice came from high above him. He opened his eyes to the dim gunmetal gray and stark black hues that were the colors of early night. The trunks of the trees were obsidian pillars. The slope of the hillside on which he lay was solid charcoal.

"I didn't hear anything," the other voice, which Bo recognized as Lester's, said. "Must be your nerves."

"Christ, I hate this waiting."

"You won't have to wait much longer."

Bo lay on soft ground, hard up against one of the chunks of sandstone that had long ago fallen from the outcropping. He felt through the material of his pants, felt the swelling at his knee. Bruised, torn cartilage maybe, maybe even broken. His eyes were shut against the pain, and for a few moments all he saw were fireworks. When he looked again, he saw the river below him, flat and slate-colored, reflecting a sky lightly salted with stars. He gazed upslope. The fall from the rock had been maybe twenty feet, and he must have rolled after he hit the ground, for he now lay a dozen yards below the base of the outcropping. Lucky even to be alive, he thought. He took inventory of the rest of his body. His right eye was swollen half shut, and above it he felt a crusty mass of dried blood. The knife wound across his left forearm had not reopened, but the wound on his back ached, and when he touched his shirt there, he could feel that the fabric was wet. Bleeding, but not dead. Not yet. His right shoulder was sore. Although most of his body ached, his leg seemed to be the worst of his injuries. He was surprised to find that the rope that held the bedroll was still slung over his shoulder. He checked the blanket. The Sig was still tucked safely inside.

For a little while, he lay perfectly still. Night was falling, with moonrise not far behind it. On the cliff above him, the two men who'd hunted him in the city were poised for an assassination. If they knew their business, and probably they did, they'd been there for hours, citing landmarks on the bluffs at Wildwood that would give them range guidance when the moon was up and it was time for the shot. They'd be dressed in Ghillie Suits, uniforms onto which had been sewn clusters of burlap strips that broke the outline of their bodies to help them blend into the hillside. If the agents at Wildwood scanned this side of the river, the snipers would be all but invisible. There was no time, no way to get word to Calloway. If someone were going to intercede, Bo was it. Fire raged through his right leg every time he moved, but there was nothing to be done except endure. He clenched his teeth, dug his left heel into the ground, and with his good leg, began to shove himself upslope toward the rock.

He moved in inches. The hillside was thick with undergrowth and alive with mosquitoes that buzzed incessantly around Bo's head.

Probably, they were lighting and feeding, but he hurt too much to care. He crawled among the chunks of talus and realized how fortunate he'd been not to have hit one in his fall.

Although he took less than five minutes to reach the base of the outcropping, he felt the time as an eternity. When he finally leaned his back against the sandstone to rest, he was soaked with sweat.

Far below and to the south, he could see fires on the beach of the Kinnickinnic delta where boats had anchored for the night. He heard distant laughter, and even an occasional word he could almost discern. He thought of those people, blissfully unaware of the tragedy that was about to unfold above them. He envied their ignorance and their lack of involvement.

He inched along the ragged juncture where the sandstone met the hillside, hugging the rock. His bum leg was nothing but dead weight. Worse, it was fiery dead weight that sent constant, wrenching spasms through him. Bo fought a constant battle against his urge to cry out.

He made it three-quarters of the way before he paused, nearly exhausted. Every muscle burned with fatigue, and his brain was getting fuzzy. The last of the faint evening light was gone, and night was solidly on the land. He tried to figure out what to do when he reached his goal, how to play his position, but he couldn't get beyond focusing on making the last few yards up the hill to the top of the rock.

"How long?" one of the voices asked. Curtis.

"Couple minutes."

"See anything?"

"Not yet."

"I'll be glad when this is over."

"It's never over."

They were quiet after that.

Then Lester said, "Wait a minute. I see someone."

"Her?"

"Can't tell yet. It'll be easier once the moon's up. Keep your eye on that scope."

Bo eased the bedroll off his back and brought it to where he could reach for his Sig. His fingers touched the grip.

"Someone else now," Lester said.

"Who?"

Bo inched upward as they talked, and he worked at pulling the weapon free.

"A guy. Secret Service, I'd guess."

"Is *she* anywhere?"

"Not yet."

The rock above Bo dripped with bright light. He glanced at the hilltop and saw the rising moon fragmented through the trees. He looked across the river where the highest branches of the orchard at Wildwood were now gilded in silver. There was no time left. He prepared for a hopeless rush toward the top, bum leg and all.

Before he could move, he heard the muffled report of a silenced gunshot. It came not from the outcropping but from the hillside above. In the next instant came another muffled shot. Bo hesitated, hunkering in the shadow of the ledge. Lester and Curtis were quiet. After a moment, he eased himself up and peered over the lip of the rock.

Because the moonlight was scattered in its passage through the trees, the flat sandstone was a patchwork of shadow and light. Bo could see two prone, unmoving human forms near the far edge. Their outlines were fuzzy, the effect of the Ghillie Suits. Between them was a squat mound Bo supposed was the sniper rifle on its bipod, camouflaged with burlap. Each man lay in a small dark pool that glistened in the moonlight. Bo heard a shiver among the bushes up the hill, and he slid down, hidden behind the outcropping.

The figure came forward, a black shape that had separated itself from the larger black of a tree trunk. It made its way carefully to where the dead men lay. Like the sandstone, the figure had become, in the tattered moonlight, a crazy quilt of shadow and light.

Bo swung his Sig over the top of the rock and used the glowing dots of the tritium sight to level the barrel on the figure's heart.

"Police," he shouted. "Drop your weapon."

The figure made no move to comply, simply turned its head in Bo's direction.

"Thorsen," David Moses said, sounding not at all surprised.

"Drop your weapon."

Moses nodded toward the men at his feet. "NOMan."

"Drop your weapon now or I'll shoot."

Moses looked at him, his face glowing in a shaft of light. He seemed a little bewildered. "Do you think I came to kill her? Then why did I take these two out? Why not just let them go about their business?"

"Because this is your kill."

"You're right there. If I still wanted her dead."

"How'd you know they'd be here?"

"The same way you did, I imagine. Putting two and two and two together. It didn't take a genius."

"I'll say it only once more. Put the weapon down."

Moses moved very slowly, turning so that all he presented to Bo was a profile, a slender target.

Bo said, "I'm betting you don't have armor this time. This time you thought you had all the advantage."

"There's no reason to shoot me," Moses said.

"Putting the First Lady aside, there are the four agents you killed at Wildwood."

"They were soldiers in a war. Their choice."

"I'm a soldier in the same war. I'll take you out without a second thought."

"The world is hard. Be strong. Is that it?"

"Don't test me."

For the briefest instant, a smile touched his lips. "How could I not? You're the best I've ever come across."

Moses stood stiff as a soldier doll. The moon glinted off his face as if his skin were white porcelain. His eyes, too, were like glass, dark and unblinking. His mouth was a fine, thin line that seemed merely painted on.

Yet when he moved, he moved with a speed that was almost more than human.

But this Bo had anticipated, because he'd seen Moses react before, on the bluff at Wildwood. The logical tactic was for Moses to lurch toward the cover of the trees uphill. However, the moment Moses broke from his stance, Bo swung his Sig in the other direction, toward the dark emptiness beyond the edge of the rock. Moses did exactly as Bo had expected. He took a running leap off the sandstone toward the river. As Moses's airborne body crossed his gun sight, Bo pulled off a round. He followed with two more as Moses arced down toward the slope below, but he had little hope either slug would hit its mark. He heard the heavy thump as the man hit ground, and then the crackle of the underbrush as he rolled toward the river. Or ran. Bo couldn't be sure which. He dragged himself across the outcropping to the lip and shoved the barrel of his Sig over the edge. The sounds below had stopped. He peered at the patches of moonlight littered among the trees. He scanned the river, but the water remained a broad silver-gray sheet with not even a ripple to warp the surface.

A slice of rock leapt out an inch from his cheek. Bo realized that the moon at his back made him a perfect, silhouetted target for Moses. He slithered back a foot to safety and listened. If Moses were moving among the bushes below him, he did it quiet as an ant.

In sliding back, Bo had bumped into the camouflaged sniper rifle, and he remembered the weapon had a night sight. He stuffed his Sig into the waist of his pants, pulled away the burlap covering, and hefted the rifle. He drew the bolt back and found a chambered round. Scooting away from the edge of the sandstone, he crawled quietly toward the cover of the trees upslope. He veered south, keeping low, until he reached a place several yards to the left of the outcropping where a fallen tree gave him some cover. He brought up the rifle and directed the scope toward the area below the cliff.

At first, he saw nothing but underbrush and tree trunks and the pieces of fallen rock that littered the hillside. Then he saw the edge of one of those rocks move. He refocused the sight. There was Moses, with his back pressed hard against a big chunk of talus. Less than fifty yards separated them, and Bo had a clear shot. He knew the round in the rifle was unjacketed, that it would tear a hole in Moses a truck could drive through. But he hesitated. Moses should have been moving, trying for a different angle, changing his location. Instead, he was just sitting there. Bo saw him put a hand to his chest, then study his palm.

"I have the sniper rifle," Bo hollered. "Night sight, remember? I've got a bead on you right now."

Moses turned his head in the direction of Bo's voice. A grin played across his lips. He lifted his hand and gave Bo the finger. After a moment, his other hand came up high. Bo could see the gun he held. With a weak toss, Moses threw the weapon away.

Bo pulled himself up and began to make his way down the hill-side slowly, painfully. The moon, as it cleared the trees behind him, lit the slope, and he could see Moses clearly, even without the night sight. Moses watched him coming. Bo stopped a few feet away and stood with the barrel of the rifle leveled at Moses's chest.

"If you try anything, I'll open you up like a window," Bo said.

Close now, he could see the blood soaking through Moses's shirt.

"You were right." Moses's words were a slur. "I thought I didn't need the armor. Didn't expect you."

"Did you come to kill her?"

Moses looked up at him, and an understanding came into his eyes. "For you, there's more to this than duty. Should have guessed." He shook his head. "Love is for only a few, Thorsen. Don't expect it." His lids fluttered closed, and just when Bo thought he was gone, he opened his eyes again, no more than a slit. His voice was a whisper.

"You and me, we'll always be alone. The difference is that in a few minutes, I won't care anymore." He smiled faintly.

Bo took a half step back.

Just in time.

Moses swung his foot in a powerful kick that, had Bo not anticipated it, would have connected with his already pained and swollen knee. Missing its mark, the kick sent Moses rolling over where he lay facedown, panting.

"You burned me once with that possum routine," Bo said.

"Not much left to work with."

Moses tried to roll over, to get his face out of the dirt, but he didn't appear to have the strength. Bo could see a ragged hole in the back of the man's shirt and a dark soaking that spread huge around it like a continent on a map of the world. The exit wound with a river of blood coursing from it. Moses wasn't lying about one thing; in a few minutes, he would undoubtedly be dead.

Bo limped to a nearby rock and sat down to await the end. Moses's breathing was shallow and labored, and there was nothing Bo could do to help, even if he'd wanted to. He didn't know what dead was, but he believed it couldn't be any worse than what life had offered David Moses.

"Stars," Moses, grunted. "Like to see the stars."

Bo understood. If he were the one lying there with his life leaking out, he'd rather look at the stars at the end. But that would mean getting close again. Even now, with the man leaning into a long fall toward forever, Bo had nothing but respect for David Moses's ability to surprise.

"Life's not fair," Moses whispered. "But some people are. Be one of them."

Bo set the rifle down and pulled the Sig Sauer from the waist of his pants. "I'm going to turn you," he said. He limped to Moses, put the barrel of the weapon against his temple, and rolled him over.

"Thanks," Moses said.

Bo moved back to the rock where he'd been sitting. They were both quiet after that. Moses fought to breathe. His eyes grew glassy staring at the sky. Bo had seen dying only once before, the long vigil he'd kept at Freak's bedside. This wasn't any easier.

"Night," Moses said in a soft voice as if he were dreaming.

Bo wasn't sure what that meant.

Above them, from the direction of the picnic area parking lot, came the sound of car doors slamming, muffled pops that reminded Bo of the silenced rounds that had taken out the assassins.

"Dark," Moses said a few moments later. "Blessed dark."

Bo glanced up where fingers of light poked through the trees on the hilltop.

Moses took three short breaths, air grasped desperately from the night, then he uttered the final word of his life. "Home."

Bo saw him yield, saw his body go slack and relax into the earth. He waited and watched, looking for a twitch that would give away Moses's charade, if charade it were. He heard crickets now, felt the kiss of a breeze, saw how lovely the river was, strewn with diamonds of light thrown down by the moon.

The pain of his knee gradually drew all his attention. He slid to the ground and sat propped with his back against the rock. He was sitting this way when the men with drawn weapons swept down the hill and gathered atop the sandstone outcropping.

"Down here," Bo called.

Several powerful flashlight beams played across him.

"Police! Freeze!"

Bo didn't move.

"It's Thorsen, for God's sake."

Bo recognized the voice of Stu Coyote. A minute later, Coyote was at his side.

"You hurt, Bo?"

"S'okay," Bo said. "I'm getting pretty used to it. What're you doing here?"

"I located Otter," Coyote said. He gently took the gun from Bo's hand and sat on the ground beside him.

Special Agent Stan Calloway joined them and directed the beam of his flashlight toward the body. "Who's this?"

"Moses," Bo said.

"David Moses?" Calloway threw the beam up to the outcropping. "How about up there?"

"The enemy," Bo said.

Calloway looked him over and said, "Don't go anywhere."

"Wasn't planning on it," Bo said.

Calloway headed back up the hill.

"Otter sent you?" Bo said to Coyote.

"In a way. I came back as soon as I heard about Diana. I figured you'd turn to a friend, and the only friend of yours I ever met was Otter. I got his address from the visitor's log security kept during your stay at the hospital."

Bo smiled grimly. "You and Moses."

"What?"

"Never mind. So you put two and two and two together?"

"That's pretty much it. I talked to Calloway at Wildwood. We kept the First Lady off the bluff tonight."

"And then you came over here because you thought he'd try the hit from here."

"Not exactly. We got a call from the St. Croix County Sheriff's Department. A farmer a mile north of here found a pickup truck parked on his land. Truck was full of ordnance. Had a Minnesota plate."

"Let me guess," Bo said. "Registered to Luther Gallagher."

Coyote nodded. "We were up there investigating when we got the call on shots fired here."

"Agent Coyote, I have to ask you to step away." A man in a dark suit stood looking down at them. "This man is still wanted for questioning in the death of Diana Ishimaru."

"FBI," Coyote said to Bo. Before he stood up, he said, "Need anything?"

"A doctor would be nice. My knee's pretty screwed up."

Coyote glanced up at the federal agent. "Get paramedics down here."

"We'll take care of everything."

Bo looked across the river. The bluffs at Wildwood were so bright in the flood of moonlight that even from this distance he could make out details. But it was not what he saw that made him smile even in his pain. It was what he did not see.

forty-seven

Bo lay on the hospital bed, staring up at the ceiling light in his room. A casing of wire mesh protected the bulb. Tendrils of cobweb fuzzy with dust hung from the mesh like unraveled threads. Although there was no breeze that Bo could feel, the tendrils gently waved in some high current of air.

They'd transported him to the nearest medical facility, the St. Croix Regional Medical Center. They'd done a CAT scan to make sure there was no internal damage from his fall. They'd x-rayed his knee, had found bone chips, and had immobilized the joint pending surgery. They'd cleaned and dressed the wound on his head. Then they'd isolated him in the Psychiatric Unit. No one had come to see him since he'd been taken into custody and had told his story. He hadn't been read his rights, nor had they given him an opportunity to make a phone call. He was not under arrest, they said. Since they'd locked him in the room hours before, he hadn't seen a living soul.

He didn't mind the isolation. It gave him time to think. And what he thought about was David Solomon Moses.

Moses had done terrible things. Killed many times over. Murdered agents Bo knew and respected. That he'd lived, according to Dr. Jordan Hart, in a world that he perceived to be in a constant state of war, much of it directed against him, didn't alter greatly Bo's impression of the man. He'd hunted Moses as he would an animal, a sick, dangerous animal. He'd thought of him as hate stuffed into a thin sheath of flesh. Yet on the cliff, with Kate on her knees, Moses had offered her a chance at life. Why? And later he'd killed the men whose assignment it was to assassinate her. Had that been for his own dark reasons? Or had Bo, in that St. Paul church, actually convinced him to let go of vengeance? Father Don Cannon claimed people came into the world with much of their spirit already formed. If that was true, then maybe something had been in David Moses when he was born, some possibility of goodness that all the cruelty and betrayal in his life hadn't managed to destroy completely. Bo would never know for sure. Moses had taken all the answers with him.

Like the ceiling light, the windows in the room were covered with heavy wire mesh. Above the door a security camera was mounted to the wall. Bo guessed he was being watched. By whom was a concern, for he knew all too well that NOMan was everywhere. They could shoot him in that room and make it look like anything they wanted to. He had refused the pain medication the medical staff offered. If he was going to die, he wanted to be awake for the event.

They came for him after many hours. There were three of them, men in dark blue suits, accompanied by an attendant in a white uniform. It was the attendant who unlocked the door, and who brought a wheelchair.

"Let's go, Thorsen," one of the suits said.

"Where?" Bo asked.

"Shut up," another suit said.

Bo didn't want to give them any reason to kill him if that's what they were looking for. He went without protest.

They didn't go far. He was wheeled into an adjacent room, this one with a table and three chairs and no window. Most of one wall was reflecting glass, a two-way mirror. Two of the chairs were already occupied by other men in suits. One suit was light gray, the other a charcoal pinstripe. Bo was positioned across the table from the two men. The gray suit nodded to the blue suits, who left the room.

"Do you know who I am?" the gray suit asked.

"No."

"I'm Assistant Director James Norton, Secret Service."

Bo knew the name, although not the man.

Norton nodded toward the pinstripe. "This is FBI Assistant Director Hector Lopez."

Lopez said, "We've been looking into the story you told. Your allegations concerning National Operations Management are, quite frankly, pretty crazy. We've done some preliminary investigating, and we can find nothing to indicate that NOMan is anything other than what it purports to be."

Norton said, "You contend that NOMan wanted the First Lady assassinated, and you've alleged that Senator William Dixon is involved. Yet you have no evidence of this. Nor can you give us any reason why any of these people would instigate such an action."

"I've been thinking about that," Bo said. "My guess is that it has something to do with the president's reelection. Newly widowed, Dixon would be hard to beat. And NOMan could lay the blame on Moses."

"I've got to tell you, Agent Thorsen," Lopez said, "this conspiracy theory of yours sounds like paranoid raving. The raving of a man already wanted in connection with a murder in St. Paul. As a matter of fact, we believe there is sufficient evidence at this point to seek an indictment against you, should we choose to advise the federal attorney to do so."

"An indictment would never hold up in court," Bo said.

"Wouldn't it?"

"Is this a threat?"

"It's a potential, Agent Thorsen," Norton said.

"Funny, it sounds just like a threat."

Norton put on a pair of half glasses and lifted a cordovan attaché case from the floor beside his chair. He snapped it open and pulled out several pages of typed documents that he slid across the table to Bo.

"This is your statement of the events leading up to the death of David Moses." Norton cast a look at Bo over the flat rim of his half glasses. "The most recent death."

Bo scanned the document. "This isn't my story. This makes no mention of NOMan. It says Moses acted alone."

"This is the statement we want you to sign."

"This is bullshit."

"Agent Thorsen," Norton said, "consider the impact of your accusations. If the American people believe your story, imagine the erosion of public confidence, the chaos."

Lopez said, "The Bureau is already at work very quietly assessing the true threat of NOMan. If this organization is anything that you contend it is, don't you think we want to combat it as much as you? I'm an assistant director of a federal agency, but I'm an American citizen first and foremost. I love this country. I have every intention of preserving its laws and the integrity of the system that governs it."

"If there is any truth at all in what you say, we have to consider how to address this situation," Norton said. "At the moment, we feel that silence on your part is the best way."

"And if I don't agree?"

Lopez said, "Charges will be brought against you, and the federal government will do its best to prove, in the case of the *People v. Bo Thorsen*, that you did willfully murder Special Agent-in-Charge Diana Ishimaru."

"No jury would convict."

"Do you want to take that chance? And in the meantime, drag your name through the dirt?"

"And alert NOMan and contribute in no small way to that organization's ability to cover its tracks."

Bo stared at the pages on the table. "It says here that I believe David Moses killed Diana. That's not true."

"It may have to be true. For now."

"There's a greater good that needs to be considered, Thorsen."

Bo read the final page of the documents. "This is a letter of resignation."

Norton said, "We feel it's best if you step out of the picture entirely."

Bo studied the men. Things began to blur, not just his thinking but his vision. He felt a little faint. He couldn't remember the last time he'd had a decent night's sleep. Or a good meal. Or felt as if the weight of an enormous responsibility didn't rest on his shoulders alone. He glanced at the mirror, wondering who would be there if he stepped through the looking glass. There seemed nothing real to hold to anymore. No one to trust. Were these men connected to NOMan? Or were they really trying to control the damage that might be wrought if the public knew that such an organization had so effectively infiltrated the entire federal government?

He looked down at the pen that Norton held out to him, and he took it. He poised to sign. Before he did, he leveled his eyes once more on the faces of the men across the table.

"You both were field agents once?" he asked.

His question seemed to puzzle them.

"We were," Norton said.

"If you were in my place, if you'd seen Diana Ishimaru, a good agent and a good friend, murdered, would you sign this document?"

A moment passed, then Norton said, "Yes."

But what he said didn't matter. Because between the question and the answer, Bo had seen the truth in the eyes of both men.

Bo put down the pen. "Gentlemen, we remain at odds."

"You're making a mistake, Agent Thorsen," Norton said, but it sounded more like words than belief.

"If so, it's a mistake of my own choosing. And I'll take my chances."

* * *

They finally fed him. He'd grown accustomed to the pain, to the constant throb deep in his knee. He was tired, but he fought sleep. Whenever he started to drift off, he jerked his leg to the side and gave himself an eye-opening jolt of agony. Even so, his thinking was beginning to get as fuzzy as the wire mesh over the light fixture.

He had no idea how long he'd been isolated like this when the door of his room opened and Lorna Channing stepped in, alone.

"You should have called me," she said.

"When I needed you, I didn't have the number," Bo replied.

"For want of a nail, the shoe was lost."

"We won the battle," Bo pointed out.

"And we're going to win the war, Agent Thorsen."

Channing walked to the window and touched the heavy mesh with her hand. It was day outside, late afternoon Bo judged from the position of the sun in the sky. Channing's shadow fell across the floor behind her, stretching all the way to where Bo lay.

"Before she was killed, Diana Ishimaru made a telephone call," Channing said. "She called the hotel room of Secret Service Assistant Director Bill Malone who, I'm sure you're aware, was in the Twin Cities ostensibly to oversee the investigation into your actions at Wildwood. Malone immediately placed a call to a cell phone number. The number's been traced to one of the men shot dead last night, one of the men you claim was preparing to assassinate the First Lady. I'm guessing it wouldn't surprise you to learn that years ago Assistant Director Malone was the Secret Service liaison to NOMan. Although he's unaware of it at the moment, we now have him under constant surveillance." Channing turned back to Bo. "I've just come from Wildwood. I had a long visit with the First Lady and her father. I gave them a copy of your statement. *Your* statement, not that crap Norton and Lopez tried to ram down your throat. We've spoken with Tom Jorgenson and he's told us quite a lot. Pretty incredible things. According to him, NOMan was established to help mitigate the influence of incompetent leadership and to nudge the world away from aggression. Kate told him she didn't consider her assassination a milestone on the road to peace."

Channing allowed herself a brief smile.

"Information is power," she continued. "Any organization with power and that operates under a cloak of secrecy and darkness becomes a breeding ground for monstrous abuse, no matter how good-intentioned the goals are initially. In the isolated beauty of his orchards, away from the microphones and the cameras, Tom Jorgenson accomplished miracles. William Dixon used NOMan in a different, brutal way. I think we'll find as we dig deeper that NOMan has been used to advance all kinds of agendas, personal and political.

"The roots run deep, Agent Thorsen. The tendrils are widespread. We have a long, hard struggle ahead of us, but thanks to you, I'm confident we'll be able to deliver a good old-fashioned butt-kicking." She crossed the room and stood beside Bo's bed. "The president sends his greetings, and has asked me personally to express to you his profound gratitude." She offered Bo her hand. "As for me, I'm just glad you're on our side."

chapter
forty-eight

L orna Channing opened the door to the Oval Office. "He'll see you now, Senator."

William Dixon came in, grinning as if he'd just arrived at a barbecue in his honor. "Well, well," he said, seeing the president and the First Lady standing together. "Now there's a lovely family portrait. Good to have you back, Katie. Brought Stephanie home, I hope. I've missed that little girl."

"Sit down," the president said.

"Thank you, I believe I will. The leg's been acting up a bit lately. Keeps me awake at night sometimes." The senator eased himself onto the couch and settled his cane beside him. "Know what I do at night when I can't sleep, Clayboy? I lie there remembering. Couldn't tell you what I had for dinner last night, but I can tell you the color of your mother's dress the first time we met. Blue, just like a Colorado sky." He stared at the rug a moment, as if he were seeing woven among the threads an image from nearly sixty years before. Then he lifted his dark eyes toward his son. "I remember a lot of strange old things at night. I remember the first man I ever saw die.

A kid named Jorge Rodriguez. From Spanish Harlem. A Jap sniper put a bullet right there." He touched a spot below his left eye. "That was on my first day in the Philippines. I saw a lot more kids die after that. Too many to remember them all."

"That's war, Senator," the president said.

"Know what I would like, Clay? I would like it if you called me Dad."

"This isn't—" the president began.

"I know what this isn't."

William Dixon looked steadily at his son, then at his daughter-in-law. Behind him, in that long moment of silence that fell over the room, Channing very quietly opened the door to the Oval Office.

"I'd like to tell you a story," the First Lady said.

"I'm all ears, Katie." William Dixon looked up at her with an indulgent smile.

"In Minnesota, the Ojibwe used to tell of a monster that sometimes came out of the woods to prey on villages. It was called the Windigo, a terrible beast with a heart of ice who fed on the flesh of the Ojibwe people. Because it was so large and so fierce, it terrified even the bravest warrior. There was only one way you could fight the Windigo. You had to become a Windigo yourself, submit to whatever dark magic was necessary to turn you into an ogre, too. But there was an awful risk. You had to be sure that someone who loved you was waiting with hot tallow for you to drink after you killed the monster. The hot tallow would melt your icy heart and bring you back down to the size of other people. If there was no one to help you in that way, you ended up staying a Windigo. You became forever the thing you set out to destroy."

"Interesting story, Katie, but I'm afraid the point missed me."

"I want you to know I forgive you, Bill. It's my way of offering hot tallow."

He stared up at her with an uncomprehending look. "That's wonderful, really. But I still don't understand."

"NOMan," Clay Dixon said.

The senator's eyes swung toward his son, and for an instant, his face seemed to soften. "That's a pretty chilly tone. You sound like a man whose heart is ice."

The president said, "I've ordered a suspension of all functions performed by National Operations Management, and mandatory administrative leave for NOMan personnel."

"That's quite a layoff. It could alienate a lot of voters."

"Even as we speak, evidence is being gathered by federal law enforcement agencies. I anticipate a number of indictments against key government officials, both inside and outside NOMan."

"Evidence of what? Indictments on what charges?"

"We both know what I'm talking about. National Operations Management, or NOMan as you seem to prefer it be called, operates from a much different agenda than its mandate calls for. From what we're uncovering, it's evident that NOMan has worked for decades in a covert manner to influence events of national scope and importance. Let me be clear. By covert, I'm speaking of nothing less than murder.

"Most recently, NOMan was responsible for the murder of Robert Lee, for the murder of a Secret Service agent named Diana Ishimaru, and for a plot to assassinate the First Lady and her father. I've asked for further investigation into the death of Alan Carpathian, whom, I'm now convinced, you had killed in the hope of opening the door of the White House to NOMan.

"These actions, and others that are coming to light, go far beyond murder. They're clearly treasonous in their effect of subverting the authority of the federal government. They strike at the heart of the legal and constitutional processes that underlie this nation."

The senator clapped his hands. "That's quite a speech. Where are the cameras?" He shook his head. "You know, Clayboy, to the average American voter you'll sound like a lunatic. If I were you, I wouldn't rely too heavily on the things Tom Jorgenson has said. After what that poor man's been through, that awful head injury and then his stroke, I'm betting it won't be hard to convince the

American people that he's just a little confused. You go public with your accusations and you'll throw the election away."

"My first responsibility is to this nation, Senator, to do my best to see that it's secure from enemies outside our borders and within."

"Enemies?" A deep, angry flush colored the senator's usual white pallor, and his knuckles humped tight over the head of his cane. "I remember the first time I laid eyes on you. You weren't much bigger than my hand. I promised myself that my son would never go through the kind of hell I'd gone through. I promised myself that if I had anything to do with it, no man's son ever would.

"I'm going to speculate here for just a minute. If NOMan actually functioned in the way you seem to believe, it could be that this country never had a better friend. Do you have any idea of the number of international blunders, partisan follies, and just plain crazy decisions made by the men in this office that have resulted in tragedies of catastrophic proportions?" He pointed a finger at his son. "You presidents. You come here with a dream, at best. At worst, you've got a laundry list of ill-conceived notions. You're here for a few years, and then you're a footnote in history. In war, it would be like letting green recruits play general. You have no idea of the havoc you wreak.

"But maybe there are those who do, men and women who know firsthand the pain caused by the bunglings and betrayals of this office and others. And if they've committed their lives and their fortunes to doing their best to help this country avoid disaster whenever possible, then I'd certainly be tempted to applaud them.

"Enemies? Clayboy, you're so concerned about keeping all those trophies of yours polished that you wouldn't know a friend if he bit you on the ass.

"I'll tell you something, *Mister President*. You can shut down the agency. You can draw up a mountain of indictments. But an organization like that can't be stopped. Its people are everywhere. You go forward with all this, and I swear you'll be nothing but history's whipping boy."

"Are you finished?"

"Not by a long shot."

"I think you are."

"We'll see," Dixon said. "We'll just see." He stood and turned toward the door, but found his way blocked by a man in a wheelchair whom Lorna Channing had quietly brought into the room.

The president said, "Senator, I'd like you to meet Bo Thorsen. In my estimation, a great patriot. This man risked everything, his reputation and his life, for his country. I wanted you to see him and him to see you. In war, you should look into the face of your enemy and understand that it's human. Bo, I'd like you to meet Senator William Dixon. One of the fathers of NOMan, and my father as well."

The senator fixed Bo with a stony glare. "When I look at you, it's not a patriot I see."

Bo replied with a pleasant smile, "You know, you're much smaller than I imagined."

chapter

forty-nine

K ate wheeled him through the Rose Garden. She wore a yellow dress that made her look, among all those flowers, like
a flower herself, the loveliest of them all, Bo thought.

It was a mild afternoon, a beautiful day, early September. In a few
weeks, the green would drain from the trees and the leaves would
turn to fire. A wonderful chill would slip into the morning air. Winter
would follow, probably too soon, but Bo knew that for a brief while
the world would seem perfect.

As if she'd read his mind, Kate said, "We're heading into my
favorite time of year."

"Election?"

"Funny." She laughed lightly. "I love the fall. Full of sweet nos-
talgia."

Her hand, warm as the sunshine, lit on his shoulder. She wheeled
him to a stone bench in the shade of a hedge, turned him toward the
White House, then she sat down.

"Mind if I ask you something?" Bo said.

"Go ahead."

"Have you really forgiven the senator?"

"If he'd succeeded in having me killed, believe me, I'd have no compassion." She smiled briefly. "The courts will judge him, I'm sure. As for me, how could I not forgive him? I think about David Moses and all he forgave me."

"You're being generous. I was with Moses in his last moments, and I'm still not sure what drove him, what was in his heart at the end."

She looked away, and her gray-blue eyes reminded Bo of a November sky, hinting at winter. "I think the human heart's a mystery only God knows the answer to."

Bo followed her gaze, which had settled on the colonnades outside the Oval Office. "It's a big place," he said.

"The human heart?"

"I was talking about the White House."

"Oh." She laughed again, and her mood brightened. "You get used to it. By the way, I have a gift for you."

Earlier, she'd hung a canvas bag over one of the handles on Bo's wheelchair. She pulled from it a package wrapped in white tissue paper tied with a red bow. Bo took the gift and carefully removed the wrapping. It was a picture frame, scuffed gold metal. Bo grinned when he saw that it framed the photograph that had appeared on the cover of the tabloid not long before, the photo showing him and Kate together at the hospital in what was rumored to be a burgeoning romance.

"It was Clay's idea," she said.

"He never took me seriously as a threat, huh?"

Kate put her hand out and cupped Bo's cheek. "You're a very special man, Bo Thorsen. The best guardian angel anyone could ask for."

Looking into her eyes, he said, "I have a confession."

"What?"

"I didn't vote for him."

"No? Why not?"

"I thought he was just a jock."

"For a while, I thought so, too."

"I'll vote for him this time."

"I'll let him know. I'm sure it will please him."

A White House aide appeared at the end of the hedge and motioned.

"My car's here," Bo said.

Kate got up and wheeled him forward. As she neared the end of the hedge, she slowed, as if they were coming to the end of a road she was reluctant to abandon.

"I plan to visit Wildwood as soon as the election is over," she said.

"If I'm not in jail, I'll stop by."

"You know they won't bring charges, Bo. Not after everything that's come to light."

"Then I'll see you for sure."

"I'm already looking forward to it." She bent and kissed his cheek. "Good-bye."

The aide took her place behind the wheelchair, and she headed away. A moment before the shadow of the White House swallowed her, she turned and waved to Bo one last time.

He caught a late flight out of Dulles, and as the plane climbed to a cruising altitude of thirty thousand feet, Bo caught a glimpse of the setting sun. At first, the country below him was on fire, but the nearer he came to Minnesota, the more the land settled into the deep, peaceful blue of evening. By the time he landed, it was solid night and a moon was rising, nearly full.

"You heard the news?" Coyote said when he met Bo at the airport. "Chris Manning's had a change of heart. Dropped all his allegations about your handling of Wildwood."

"They told me."

"There's talk they're going to put you in charge of the field office," he said as he slung Bo's bag and crutches into the backseat.

"I'm not doing anything until I've had a long rest. It's almost harvesttime. I'm thinking of heading down to Blue Earth, maybe give a hand on the farm for a while."

"With that leg?"

"I'll find some way to help."

"But you'll come back," Coyote said.

"I don't know. Worrying about something as simple as drought and hail and tornadoes sounds pretty appealing right now."

Coyote hit Highway 5 heading into St. Paul. "You'll never give up the Secret Service."

"Why's that?"

Even in the dark, Bo could see Coyote's big grin. "You'd miss me too much."

Coyote helped him out of the car in front of the duplex in Tangletown. "Let me give you a hand with that bag."

"I can handle it. But thanks anyway."

"Get some rest, okay? And stay in touch."

"Thanks, Stu." Bo leaned on his crutches and watched until the taillights of Coyote's car were lost around a wide curve.

The night was clear, the moon butter yellow. It washed the stars from the sky and cast hard shadows across the ground. As Bo started up the walk, a dark shape separated itself from the deep shade under the porch awning and came at him, startling him so that he instinctively raised a crutch to defend himself.

"Take it easy, Spider-Man. It's only me."

Otter stepped into the moonlight. "Coyote told me he'd be dropping you off. I thought you might want a little company. Hoped you would, anyway."

"A little company would suit me just fine, Otter."

Otter looked up at the sky. "Nice night. Okay if we sit for a bit while I have a smoke."

"Sounds like a plan."

They settled themselves on the front steps. Otter lit an unfiltered Camel. "You know, I haven't seen Freak for a long time now."

"Maybe the dead have finally gone to rest."

"They never do, Bo."

He thought about the dead who were with him now and who always would be, and he knew Otter was right.

Otter put an arm around his shoulder. "Good to have you back, Spider-Man."

"Good to be home," Bo said.

They sat a long time while the moon climbed toward the middle of the sky, and the shadows shrank to puddles, and Otter smoked his cigarette, and Bo, who reminded himself that he was not alone, for a little while let himself be happy.